Welcome To Dorley Hall

Welcome To Dorley Hall

Alyson Greaves

First published in 2024 by Neem Tree Press
This edition published in 2026 by Wilton Square Books

Wilton Square Books
29 Wilton Square,
London N1 3DW

www.wiltonsquarebooks.com

A CIP record for this book is available from the British Library

ISBN 978-1-80677-093-9 (paperback)
ISBN 978- 1- 80677-102-8 (ebook)

Printed in Great Britain by CPI Group UK Ltd, Croydon CR0 4YY

1 3 5 7 9 8 6 4 2

Our authorised representative in the EU for product safety is:
Logos Europe, 9 rue Nicolas Poussin, 17000, La Rochelle, France
contact@logoseurope.eu

Content warning: this story engages with some dark topics, including but not limited to torture, manipulation, dysphoria, self-injury, nonconsensual surgery, and kidnapping. While this isn't intended to be a dark or dystopian story, characters are carrying a lot of baggage, and the exploration of the premise might be triggering for trans readers.

Royal College of Saint Almsworth
Houses of Residence: Dorley Hall

I

Welcome To Dorley Hall

16 OCTOBER 2012 — TUESDAY

"I'm telling you, I'm worried about your brother."

"He's fine! It's just teenager stuff. That's what Dad says."

"*We're* teenagers, and we're not like that."

"Older teenager stuff, then. Something happens in your brain when you turn eighteen that turns you into a massive prick. It's the hormones. They go into overdrive."

"Russ, I'm serious. He didn't come to my birthday this year—fine—and he *barely* had one of his own—okay—but now he won't even reply to my texts!"

"Stef, seriously, it's nothing. He's at uni now; I bet he's decided it's uncool to keep texting his little brother's best friend. It also probably is, dude."

"If you talk to Mark, can you please just tell him to text me back?"

"Fine, if it'll make you feel better, but I've barely talked to him in ages. *You've* talked to him more than I have this year."

"*Barely.* Russell—"

"*Stefan!* It's fine. He's fine. He's probably just depressed about his acne. Now shut up; teacher's coming."

Stefan obliges and stops glaring at Russell. He glares at his World History textbook instead, in the unlikely event that he can intimidate it into making sense. Next year he can finally drop this stupid subject and never look back, but for now he really needs to commit whatever a *castellan* is to memory, and decide from the evidence supplied whether they were in servitude to the counts or ruled over them with an iron fist. Assuming castellans even *had* fists. Or iron. They could have been giant cats for all Stefan knows.

He's too distracted. Too worried about Mark.

It's not normal to be close with your best friend's older brother, especially when he's four years older than you. But not only do the

Rileys and the Vogels live on the same road, very nearly opposite each other—with the cardboard telescope from Stefan's subscription to Junior Science Magazine (plastic lenses free with first issue!) you can watch TV in the Vogels' house from Stefan's bedroom window—but Stefan very nearly shares a birthday with Russell's older brother.

Every year on September 2nd, Russell, Mark and their dad trek over the road to Stefan's house to celebrate his birthday, and every year on September 3rd, Stefan, his mum, his dad and his baby sister return the favour, visiting Russell and Mark's extended family for fun, festivities, and rather more expensive cake and presents than Stefan's parents can afford.

But this year, on Stefan's fourteenth birthday and Mark's eighteenth, it didn't happen, and no-one saw it coming. Yes, Mark's had a hard year, though no-one seems to know exactly why—Stefan's asked and Mark's refused to answer—but their shared birthday has always been important to Stefan and, as far as he knows, to Mark, too.

Stefan told himself that Mark was just busy, that he'd have a chance to catch up at Mark's birthday the next day. And then the next day came, and Mark made only the most cursory appearance at his own party. He talked to no-one but his dad, sliced off perhaps the smallest piece of cake physically possible, and disappeared back upstairs to his room, there to hide behind his blackout curtains with his computer and his plate of death-by-chocolate with sprinkles.

Stefan's thought about it every day since. Mark's been not just a science tutor to him, but also the older brother he never had—Stefan's sister is eleven years younger than him and just awful at physics. Mark's absences, more and more frequent this year, have been crushing. Mark's birthday was Stefan's last chance to see him before he left for university, and he didn't even look him in the eye.

8 NOVEMBER 2012 — THURSDAY

Russell's been out of school all week and no-one will tell Stefan why. He's texted, he's called, he's asked the head of year and the lunch lady; he's even stopped by the house and banged on the door for what seemed like hours.

Nothing.

So when his phone starts ringing and Russ's name comes up, Stefan doesn't care that it's almost midnight, that he has school tomorrow, and that he's royally pissed off with Russ for ignoring him. He picks it up before the third ring.

"Russ? Is that you?"

"Stef. I'm at your door. Can you come let me in? I don't want to ring the bell and wake your parents."

"Sure, Russ, sure. I'll be down in a second."

Normally, Stefan would argue: he's not allowed visitors this late. But Russell sounded so drained, so worn-out that he wants to see him in person just to make sure he's not deathly ill. He throws on his dressing gown and some winter socks and takes the stairs down three at a time. He practically drags Russell into the living room and deposits him on the good sofa, the one that still has a nice bounce to it.

"Russ," he says, "you look terrible."

"It's Mark," Russell says. "He's missing."

It takes a while and the intervention both of Stefan's parents and of two mugs of hot chocolate each, but Russell eventually gives them the whole story.

Mark hadn't originally intended to live on campus. The Royal College of Saint Almsworth isn't far out of town, and for a fraction of the money required to rent a dorm room, Mark could have bought a crappy car and commuted. But Mark wanted a fresh start—new friends. Russ doesn't know what happened with Mark's old friends, but they stopped visiting or texting a long time ago.

Mark went off to live in dorms and reportedly had an uneventful first month at Saints. But it wasn't long before his professors started to find him "disruptive" and "disrespectful"; he was asked to leave a lecture for the first time about a week before his disappearance, and by Friday had stopped even showing up.

Then on Saturday, he didn't return home to his dorm.

According to the police, Mark entered Legend—popularly considered the worst nightclub in Almsworth; also the cheapest—at 19.24 on Saturday, November 3rd, and left at 01.44 after collecting his coat. The attendant was the last person to see him.

"We've been waiting to hear something since Tuesday, when they told us he was missing. But they have no leads, no evidence, not even a fucking suicide note! Sorry, Mrs Riley."

"That's okay, dear."

"A suicide note?" Stefan says. "You think he might have killed himself?"

Russell shrugs. "That's what Dad thinks. I mean, he won't say it, but that's what he thinks. I mean, it makes sense, right? He's not been the same since Mum died, and then his friends stopped talking to him. Then he moves out to the dorms and he's *still* lonely, so he gives up. On everything." Cupping his second cooling hot chocolate in his hands, Russell finishes, "I just wish he'd talked to me first. I would've told him not to be so bloody stupid. And now he's probably dead."

It shouldn't make sense. Stefan should be arguing for him, telling Russell there has to be another explanation, that this is all just a huge misunderstanding. But he can't. Because Russell's right.

"Jesus Christ," he whispers to himself.

"Stefan Riley," his mum says, "you do *not* have the same leeway as Russell. You do *not* take the Lord's name in vain in this house."

"Sorry."

19 JANUARY 2014 — SUNDAY

Stefan's mum never remembers to buy the stuffing.

They've been eating on the cheap ever since Dad was downsized and Mum was forced to cut her hours or join him on the dole, and while as a family they've become expert at providing acceptable meals on a budget, every so often Mum gets nostalgic for a real Sunday lunch, and saves up until they can afford a proper roast chicken with all the trimmings.

Plus, this one's going to be a celebration: Dad might be going back to work!

But she always forgets the sage and onion stuffing mix. Just Stefan's luck that he happened to be hanging around the house with nothing to do; the perfect candidate for the half-hour walk to the big Tesco near the university.

He's waiting in line for the self-checkout machines, exact change in one hand and box of stuffing mix in the other, when he sees her.

Stefan doesn't normally talk to strangers. It's not that he's shy, necessarily, but he's not the biggest fan of being around people. He fidgets under inspection, and when people look at him for too long it makes him feel hot and uncomfortable. Pretty girls especially.

But this girl, one ahead of him in the queue and just now stepping up to a checkout, seems to be so anxious she's having difficulty operating the machine. The checkout next to her opens up and Stefan nips in and watches her scan her food with shaking hands, sometimes needing two or three tries to get things to register.

Poor girl. He wonders what she's so upset about.

He puts his stuffing through and is about to leave when she drops her debit card. When he scoops it up for her and holds it out, she looks at him like she's seen a ghost.

"Um," he says, still holding it out.

"Oh!" she says, coming to her senses. "Thank you."

God, but she's pretty. Bright blue eyes, a river of blonde hair that frames her face and looks like she put a lot of work into it, and a cute little nose that—

Stefan frowns. There's something familiar about her. Something he can't quite put his finger on.

The woman—Melissa Haverford, assuming it's her debit card in his hand—shakes herself, takes the card from him, smiles her thanks, and marches out of the store. She wobbles a little as she rounds the corner to the exit, as if she's not quite used to the modest heels on her boots.

Stefan watches her go, puzzling over the encounter. It takes him a moment to realise she left her shopping behind. He mutters a word he's not allowed to say in the presence of his mother, drops his box of stuffing into her plastic bag, slings the whole thing under one arm, and leaves Tesco at a jog.

She's not far down the road.

"Hey!" he yells, wincing at how loud and deep his voice is. "You forgot your shopping!"

She doesn't look around, starts walking even faster. Which turns out to be a mistake: the pavements are still slippery and the inevitable doesn't take long to happen. She goes down onto her butt; it looks like a pretty painful fall, but at least it gives Stefan the chance to catch up with her and return her groceries.

"Hi," he says, looking down at her. She looks every which way but back at him.

"Thanks," she mutters, and Stefan frowns. Even her voice is giving him déjà vu! She's said not three words, but something about her alto tone nags at him. Her face, her mannerisms…

He finally places it: she's just like Russell's mum! Her face and her voice are still etched into Stefan's memory. It's been a good few years since she died, but she always had a kind smile and a coke for him when he went over to see Russ and Mark. Suddenly, Stefan knows exactly why everything about this girl seems so familiar. He offers her a hand up, and as she takes it, he says, "Do you know Mark Vogel?"

"W— what?" she says, her face now pale enough that the blush on her cheeks looks almost comical.

"You look like him," Stefan says. "I thought you might be a cousin or something. Melissa, right?" She nods dumbly. "*Do* you know Mark?"

"Oh, um, I used to," she stammers. Her voice cracks a little, and Stefan scolds himself. She probably struggled with Mark's death the same as he did, and clearly didn't expect her Sunday morning grocery shopping to be interrupted by some pipsqueak fifteen-year-old unearthing buried grief.

"Shit," he says. "Sorry. If it's upsetting to think about him, I mean. I shouldn't have…Sorry…" He trails off, cheeks burning.

She doesn't look scared anymore; she's smiling, and it's horribly, wonderfully familiar, just like everything else about her. It's the same indulgent, patient smile Mark would turn on him when they went through Stefan's homework together, and Stefan made an obvious error.

"It's okay," she says. "He's been gone for a while now."

"Yeah. I miss him."

The girl, Melissa, puts a gentle arm on Stefan's shoulder, takes her shopping out of his hand. Gives him back the stuffing. Favours him with another smile. Broader; happy. Nostalgia grips him and holds him in place.

"I'm sure he'd miss you too, Stef," she says, and squeezes his shoulder.

She's halfway up the road and boarding the bus back to the university before Stefan realises he never told her his name. Confused, he watches the bus pull away, clutching his box of sage and onion stuffing, his shoulder still warm where she touched him.

14 SEPTEMBER 2015 — MONDAY

Stefan sits alone for his first class in AS English Language. Around him, his new classmates—some of whom he knows, most of whom he doesn't—settle into their chairs, chatting, laughing. He doesn't mind being alone; he needs to concentrate. His GCSEs were only average, so the next two years need to go well if he's to get into the Royal College of Saint Almsworth and qualify for one of their small number of assistance grants.

Saints has a fantastic and highly sought-after Linguistics programme, and Stefan curated his choice of subjects at AS-level to give himself the best chance possible: English Language, English Literature, German and Psychology. He doesn't have a second-choice university; it's Saints or it's nowhere.

He saw Melissa Haverford only once more, a year ago, outside his then-new part-time job at the Tesco. She didn't see him, or pretended not to, and climbed into a waiting car less than a minute after he spotted her. She looked different: more adult, more poised.

Stefan has a theory about that.

On his sixteenth birthday, his parents told him he wouldn't need a part-time job. Dad was working full time again and Mum had found a job she could do on a laptop from the front room, so she could keep Petra in her sight at all times. Enough money for the family *and* for an allowance! But he took a job anyway, because working at the big Tesco gave him an excuse to wander over to the Saints campus on his lunch break or on his way home, the better to look for Melissa, or Mark, or clues.

Mark isn't the only boy to have vanished. Stefan's painstaking research indicates that, going back at least two decades, between two and six boys have vanished almost every year while attending the Royal College. Like Mark, they rarely disappear on campus. Some go out into town and never come home; some leave campus at the end of term and never get off trains they were seen boarding; some leave suicide notes and vanish into the night. Unruly boys, most of them, with bad reputations around campus. A woman in the admin office implied, when Stefan pretended to be a reporter following up on the disappearances, that the school was better off without them!

Stefan's not convinced the school *is* without them, though. It wasn't hard to get pictures of most of the vanished boys, and after a few nights spent memorising their faces, he was pretty sure he'd recognise them even if they… looked a bit different.

So far, he's seen five. Six, if you include Mark—or Melissa. Five other girls, all of them so startlingly exact a match to their missing counterparts that they're either unusually similar-looking siblings, or could they *be* the missing boys?

Compared to the photos, some of them have definitely had some work done—a brow-reshape here, a tracheal shave there, in addition to a catch-up girl puberty—but if Stefan was given to gambling, he'd stake all his savings on them being the same people.

He's convinced *someone* at Saints is helping closeted trans women start new lives. And comprehensively, too: Stefan's looked it up, and the facial surgery he thinks some of the girls have had runs to thousands of pounds. And then there's the faked disappearances and the new identities they'd need. Maybe whoever is doing this prioritises girls escaping unsupportive families? It makes sense, thinking about Melissa: her dad's always been rough around the edges, and after his wife's death he became…well, Russ has always been reluctant to talk about it. His dad got moody, is all he'll say.

He's still pondering the question when he gets home. It preys on his mind as he collates his notes from the day's classes, as he showers, and as he sits up in bed, reading on his phone, too wired to sleep.

It lines up. Even the rumours of the boys being "unruly" prior to their disappearances; in that last year here on Rectory Street wasn't Melissa, when she was still Mark, so depressed as to be barely functional? Easy to imagine trans girls in similar situations expressing their frustration outwardly instead.

As for who is helping them, he doesn't have any names, but he has an address: all the girls live at Dorley Hall, an older dormitory on the edge of campus. It's reserved for girls from disadvantaged backgrounds, and if anyone qualifies as disadvantaged, it's trans girls so afraid of their families that they feel they have to pretend to *die* before they can transition.

Stefan closes the book on his phone—he wasn't reading it, anyway; he'll have to go back a couple of dozen pages to pick up from where his mind started to wander—and opens the camera app. He switches it to selfie mode and examines himself on the screen.

He *needs* to get into Saints. He needs to find whoever is doing this, whoever is helping these women, because his parents, well, they're nice enough, but they've always been religious and rather strict about it.

In the camera, he runs a finger over his pronounced brow, his masculine jawline, his high hairline, and sighs.

If there's one thing Stefan's sure of, it's that he's *not* a boy.

He sure looks like one, though.

12 OCTOBER 2019 — SATURDAY

He hates how fucking cold his room is. It's costing him almost £600 a month and the view out of his tiny window is mostly of an advertising hoarding but the worst thing is undoubtedly the way he has to do his assignments under the duvet if he doesn't want his typing fingers to seize up. It's not even that cold out! It's just that the shape of the building and the curve of the street together contrive to funnel wind right through the tiny window into his room, his bed, and his bones. He'd run his little oil heater all the time if he could afford it, but he can't.

He can't afford anything much anymore.

Two whole years at Saints, waiting fruitlessly to be found. Is he wrong? Was he imagining it all? Whatever mechanism the Dorley people use to identify closeted trans women clearly hasn't worked on him. And he's looked! He's looked everywhere. He spent all his spare hours searching, scouring, hoping, convinced there was some secret he hadn't found, some code word he hadn't learned, some sympathetic ear he hadn't caught the attention of. He even went to Dorley Hall and asked to see Melissa or to talk to someone who knows her, pretending to be on some innocent errand, but they turned him away. He wasted enough time on his search that he almost failed his second year and had to retake two exams over the summer, all the while staying in an overpriced, undermaintained house-share with people he barely knows. And he can't even go back and live with his family to save the money, because Dad got an amazing opportunity in London last year, and now his childhood home belongs to someone else.

It's not like he had much of a home to return to even before they moved away. His few acquaintances have all moved on, and Russ, the only one who hasn't, doesn't speak to him anymore. Shouldn't have told him he thought Mark was still alive. "People die, Stefan. Move on, Stefan. Get over it, Stefan. Leave well alone, Stefan! Shut the fuck up or piss the fuck off!"

His twenty-first was the most depressing birthday of his life. No Melissa or Mark or whoever; nobody at all. One of the girls at work gave him a cupcake and he ate it alone.

Worse: he had thought he looked unrecoverably boyish at sixteen, but it turned out puberty had a few more tricks left up its sleeve, and it deployed them at regular intervals. It's not that he's unattractive—before his third year at Saints, when he started wearing his bad mood on his face and not just under his skin, girls hit on him relatively regularly—but he's so… male. He knows that's not a very helpful way of thinking about it, but if what he sees glaring back at him from every mirror, window and piece of cutlery he encounters is at all accurate, then even the world's most accomplished plastic surgeon would have their work cut out. Probably a Nobel-worthy feat, carving an attractive, feminine face from his caveman mug.

"Not helpful," he tells himself again, trying to divert his thoughts from the track that usually ends in alcohol, Netflix and a perplexing inability to cry, even though sometimes it feels like he'll die if he doesn't. "Not fucking helpful."

He's given up. Officially. But it's harder than he expected.

It'd be easier if he could be certain. He's read about dysphoria, devoured every description of it he could find before he had to step away from the websites he found them on, lest he drink even more. These sites are full of people who are moving on and living their lives while he hides in a cold, drafty room and dreams of a friend who probably hasn't thought of him for years. He envies their certainty.

Although he's read about dysphoria, and while sometimes he thinks he can almost feel it, most of the time he just feels numb. And that's not something he can work with. Yes, sure, he's still pretty certain he's not *really* a boy—say it, Stefan: you're twenty-one now; it's not *boy* you're failing at, it's *man*—but he can't say, after all these years, that he's a girl. Without that conviction, that rock on which to rebuild his life, he's stuck. And all the time he's obsessing over what he can't have, he's missing out on what he can.

Would he be *happier* as a girl? Almost definitely. But he's had to admit that it's a dream, and he has to live in reality. Whatever happens in the shadows at Saints to give trans girls a new start has passed him by, found him unworthy, or never existed in the first place, and there's nothing he can do about it. It's time to make the best of what he has, and what he has is a masculine body and no money.

He's told no-one of his theory. Even if they—whoever they are—can't or won't help him, he wants them to keep helping others, and secrecy is obviously an important part of that. He thinks of Melissa in that Tesco sometimes—beautiful; scared—and for her, and everyone like her, he'll keep the secret.

Plus, if he told anyone, they'd think he was fucking crazy.

Fuck it. Stefan's housemates invited him out tonight and, as part of his deal with himself to get the hell over it, he's going to go. Surprise them all: the hermit gets drunk with other people for a change.

The party is on campus, in one of the new luxury dorms out where the old Psychology building used to be. The place was a building site for years, one he walked past almost every day during his first year at Saints. As he looks around, he keeps seeing things he half-recognises, altered, recontextualised.

Everything changes but him.

This was a bad idea.

But then someone from last year's Psycholinguistics class spots him, waves him over, offers him something to smoke, and he re-evaluates his plans to leave. Maybe he'll stay awhile, get high, and reconnect with people. If he's going to commit to his new goal, to just be a guy, or some approximation of one, then step one should be to stop being so fucking miserable all the time. Hang out with friends. Remember what it's like to be a person.

Forget his obsession with something that probably was never real in the first place.

He meets Christine an hour or so later. Auburn-haired and *seriously* pretty, she's sitting cross-legged on a snooker table, drinking from a bottle, laughing with another girl. A mutual acquaintance makes the introduction and after checking with her friend, she pats an empty spot of green baize, inviting him up. Feeling a little light-headed, he hops up on the table. He almost loses his balance finding a way to arrange his limbs without making potentially unwanted contact with the girl. A pointless exercise, since she giggles at him and stretches her legs out onto his lap.

No, she's not drunk, she tells him piously; she's *high,* and she's happy to share. They swap trivia about themselves as they do so, and he's pleased to find she's studying Linguistics, too. Planning to specialise in speech and language therapy. He's impressed, because she's much earlier in her degree than he is, and he doesn't have any plans at all. She encourages him to look into speech therapy. Very rewarding, she says. There's no money in it, but if it's money you want, piss off to the Business School and become a heartless bastard.

He laughs.

She hops off the snooker table and beckons him to follow, snatching a half-bottle of something alcoholic as she leaves the room. The building's unfinished, and dangerously exciting to explore together. They poke drunken heads into rooms marked as construction sites, stagger down flights of stairs that lead to doors that won't open. Eventually end up on the roof.

There's something calming about a clear, starry sky. The Royal College is far enough out from Almsworth proper that the light pollution from the town mostly doesn't reach it, and as he looks up into the infinite he feels, for the first time in a long, long time, almost content.

Maybe he can't be a girl. Maybe he shouldn't be. But maybe he doesn't have to be a guy, either. A thought for another day. What he *can* do is make friends, meet nice girls, and drink and smoke with them under the stars.

He tells her about his family, who still text all the time. His little sister's ten now, and learning to play the trombone; both existentially terrifying concepts. She laughs and, with only a little hesitation, kisses him on the temple. She's glad she took a chance on a good-looking guy tonight, she says. It's just a shame she has a lot of work on, or they could stay up all night.

He offers to walk her home, but she declines with a smile. She's not turning him down; she thinks she'd like to see him again. It's just that she lives on campus, and it's a very short walk. Whereabouts? Dorley Hall.

"Oh, hey," he says, warm from the alcohol and loquacious from the weed, "I know a funny thing about Dorley Hall…"

13 OCTOBER 2019 — SUNDAY

The bright overhead lights aren't the only reason he's got a pounding headache when he wakes up—that he imbibed basically everything Christine handed him last night is probably a major contributor—but they aren't fucking helping. Where is he, anyway?

He opens his eyes a crack, but can't see anything useful until he forces himself to sit up and angle his head away from the lights above. His fingers close around a thin, cold bedframe and through the glare and the headache he realises his bed for the night was a small, hard and completely unfamiliar cot.

Did Christine take him to her place? He looks around, but she's nowhere in sight. The room itself isn't much to look at: bare concrete walls on three sides, and a clear glass wall and door on the fourth. It looks like it leads into an equally bare, though less brightly lit, concrete-walled corridor, and when he stands up, staggers over to the door and leans on the handle, it doesn't move.

The floor is concrete as well, and cold against his feet.

Wait. Why are his feet cold?

He looks down: his shoes are gone. As are his socks and all his clothes except his underwear, replaced by a green smock that goes down to just above his knees and just behind his wrists.

He tries all the walls, the door again, the joins where glass meets concrete. He pulls the tiny mattress off the cot; he pulls the cot away from the wall. Nothing. Grudgingly he remakes the bed, sits heavily on it and cradles his headache in his hands, waiting for whatever is happening to happen. Perhaps it can bring him a painkiller when it does.

A few minutes later, the shriek of an intercom system obliterates the eerie silence, and a voice he doesn't recognise addresses him over a speaker he can't see.

"What do you know, Stefan Riley?"

2
Cell

13 OCTOBER 2019 — SUNDAY

"I don't know anything!"

"Don't lie to us, Stefan Riley."

"I'm not lying!"

"Tell us what you know about Dorley Hall, Stefan Riley."

"Nothing! Is that where I am?"

"Tell us what you *know*, Stefan Riley."

The voice is crackly and distant, like the hold music when you call a big company over a bad connection. It's probably a woman's voice behind the distortion but it's impossible to be certain. And, God, he wishes she'd stop using his name like that. Like punctuation. Like a club.

"Nothing!" He really yells it this time, breaking his voice and hurting his ears when the tiny concrete box echoes it back to him.

Stefan doesn't know why he lies. There are good reasons not to tell everything you know to a faceless person interrogating you over a loudspeaker, but none of them apply: he's not trying for leverage; he's not trying to avoid punishment; he's not trying to outwit his captors. If he were rational, he might make the argument that he doesn't know *who* captured him, and that if he reveals the scant information he's gathered over the years it could threaten the girls from Dorley Hall—if his theory is even right—but he's too tired and scared to look objectively at his thought process and start making excuses for it.

Simply: he's overcome with shame. Telling them his suspicions about Dorley Hall inevitably leads to him having to answer searching questions and ends with him confessing everything. And he's never opened up to anyone before; not to Mark, not to Russ, not even to strangers online or to a private diary. He's never so much as whispered it to himself.

Anything to avoid making it real.

Because he knows what he looks like. What he sounds like. In his mind, even the most compassionate person would laugh in the face of his confession. Laugh *at his face.* He *can't* be a girl. Can't be anything *other* than a man. To think otherwise would be ludicrous.

God. He hopes she can't see him.

The demands for answers don't stop coming, so he lies back down on the hard, cold cot and wraps the thin mattress around his head to block out the voices from without, and from within.

***

Tap tap tap tap tap.

The sharp, echoing sound intrudes on his dream, causing Stefan to react unexpectedly: he falls out of bed.

It takes him a few seconds to come back to reality, and when he does, he wishes fervently that he hadn't. He's still in a concrete box, still wearing an ugly green smock made from some of the itchiest material he's ever encountered, but this time there's no-one yelling at him over the intercom. Instead, an attractive woman taps idly on the glass door.

He's a little more ready this time. His hangover's retreated, and his shame and self-loathing have become less overwhelming, easier to deal with; easier to hide. Once more becoming one of those unpleasant things you learn to live with, like tinnitus or a persistent toothache.

He's not *on show,* is he? A quick check: no. The scratchy smock is making his genitals feel just as vaguely uncomfortable as the rest of him, but at least he's not flashing the girl.

Tap tap tap tap tap.

He hauls himself to his feet. Runs the back of his hand across his face. Stubble. Ugh. He hasn't seen a mirror since he got here, but it's inevitable that the late night, the alcohol, the bad sleep, the brief but potent anxiety attack, the inability to access a shower and—most pointedly—the concrete prison have him looking more or less as awful as he's ever looked.

The woman looks him up and down, so he looks right back. She's blonde, the sort of blonde that takes bleach to achieve, and wears her hair short in what Stefan thinks is called a pixie cut. He'd describe her as impish, but that might just be because of the hair.

He doesn't recognise her at all.

"Hello?" he says, after a while. He has the impression she's evaluating him, but for which traits or for what purpose, he can't even begin to guess. If he's right about everything, then it's a reasonable bet he's at Dorley Hall somewhere; does that mean she's one of the trans women they help?

If he's wrong, and the way she narrows her eyes suggests he might be, then he could be anywhere.

Shit. Maybe Dorley Hall really *is* just a dorm.

But then why was he interrogated so urgently?

"Was that you this morning?" he asks. "On the intercom?"

"No," she says. A deeper voice than he was expecting. It reminds him of Melissa's. And, God, about Melissa, is he wrong about her, too? He was so convinced, for so long. Is Mark dead after all? What the hell is he supposed to think? "Who spoke to you on the intercom?" the girl demands.

"I don't know. That's why I asked."

He immediately regrets even the slightest bit of impertinence. Whoever this girl is, he needs information from her, and the best way to get it is to play along without fuss. All she has to do is let him know what game she wants him to play.

"Eat," she says.

"Eat what?"

She rolls her eyes. Points down. On the floor, by the door, is a metal tray with a banana and a cereal bar on it. Either it came up from under the floor or through the door by itself somehow—unlikely; he can't see any mechanism by which that could have happened—or she walked in while he was sleeping and left it there.

"Right," he says, scooping up the tray. He places it carefully on the cot and starts peeling the banana. "Thank you," he adds. Keep her happy. Speedrun that Stockholm Syndrome.

She sneers at him and spins on her heel to walk away down the corridor.

"Wait!" he calls, slightly muffled by banana. When she stops, he swallows as quickly as he can. "What's going on? How long am I going to be here?"

She doesn't turn around. "You'll find out, in time."

"When?"

"Soon."

"You have to give me something!" he yells, his desperation not entirely played up. The thought of more time in this glass-and-concrete coffin is not an appealing one. "Anything!"

She hesitates. "Don't scratch your stomach," she says, and starts walking again. It doesn't take long for her to vanish from sight, but he can still hear her, even through the thick glass; her footsteps remain evenly spaced for about ten seconds. Maybe fifteen.

So, that's something to add to the puzzle of this place: he's at the far end of a long corridor. Not a super helpful fact in isolation.

He finishes the banana and the cereal bar. It's nothing like enough food, considering he's still recovering from his hangover, but it takes the edge off. He puts the tray back on the floor by the door and resolves to keep an eye on it to find out how they get the food to him.

It occurs to him, far too late to do anything about it, that the mysterious blonde girl might have drugged the food, but he dismisses the thought almost immediately. Why would they need to drug him? They've got him pretty comprehensively trapped already.

She told him not to scratch his stomach. Why?

He turns away from the glass door and lifts up his smock, runs a hand across his belly. It has that irritated feel skin gets when you wear scratchy fabric for a long time, sure, but nothing seems—

There. Right there. A raised bump, slightly smaller than his pinkie fingernail. A darker spot right in the middle. He's familiar with the sight: in the summer of his second year at Saints he got so listless that at one point he spent two straight weeks in bed. He only got out of bed when his leg started hurting and only left the house when his leg didn't *stop* hurting. The doctor prescribed a course of anticoagulants, and told him to move around more and maybe avoid taking all his holiday hours at once in the future.

A red dot in the middle of a raised lump: exactly what it looked like after he injected heparin into his stomach for a weekend.

He's been stuck with a needle.

Breathing heavily, barely even thinking about being seen naked any more, he lifts up the smock and searches his body for any other telltale marks. He doesn't find any until he pulls the garment all the way off and sees in the crook of his left elbow another red dot, this one in the centre of a flowering bruise. Like from a blood test.

They took some of his blood and they injected him with something.

What the hell are they doing to him?

* * *

He wakes to the same cold cell, to the same unpleasant smock, and to an itch around the injection site in his belly so overwhelming he immediately sinks his nails into his forearm to keep from scratching.

Searching for a distraction and finding nothing in the cell aside from the nasty little metal toilet in the far corner, he locks his limbs, closes his eyes, and goes over what he knows.

What he *thinks* he knows.

The Royal College of Saint Almsworth has a problem with boys who disappear. It's passed largely under the radar because the boys don't vanish on-campus, and because it turns out that *most* universities have people who end their lives or simply vanish. If Saints' tally is slightly higher than most? Put it down to a quirk of the local area.

He knew a teacher at his secondary school whose son had gone for a late-night stroll from his university dorm and didn't realise he was walking on a frozen lake until suddenly he wasn't anymore. There was a memorial in the assembly hall; Stefan got his mum to help him make an apple crumble. The teacher hugged him, thanked him, and wept on his shoulder.

These things happen.

All of that: fact. But Stefan's having to face that it's the only genuinely verifiable information he's got. The girls he's seen? That they look like some of the missing boys means little. They could be relatives. It could be coincidental. Or his memory could have played tricks on him, made him see similarities where none existed because he wanted it with all his heart to be true.

And the barest hints of rumours he picked up about Dorley Hall? They could so easily have been about something else entirely. This, for example: kidnapping random people and doing...what? Psychological experiments? Is there someone out there watching him on a screen, waiting for him to snap, timing him against the last person?

That's it, isn't it?

He clenches and unclenches his fists, stretches his back, and thinks hard. What have they done so far, really? They've put him in uncomfortable clothes, they've fed him, they've taken a blood test and they've (probably) injected something into his belly. He's supposed to think it's a tracking chip or an electric shock device or something; likely it's just saline. After a couple of days of this, there'll be a form to sign, a pat on the back and a small cheque.

It's just an experiment. It has to be.

He relaxes on the cot, satisfied with his reasoning. He was wrong about Dorley Hall. So what? He's no worse off than he was yesterday morning, and if he gets paid for his participation then he's actually up on the day. The unscheduled days off work might get him fired, but screw it. He hates that place. Maybe he'll go work at the retail park instead. They have a gym there; he can get in shape, start his new life properly.

Kidnapping? Fake injections? Interrogations by intercom? All very clever, for sure, but there's no sense letting the imagination run wild.

Stefan closes his eyes and gets some more sleep.

* * *

Clearly some part of this experiment has to do with enforced boredom. With no phone, no books and no TV, Stefan is probably supposed to be out of his mind by now, but he's survived twenty-one years inside this body randomly gifted to him by chance and genetics, and he's good at passing unwanted time. Meditation's fine. Sleep's better, if you can manage it. But yoga's best.

He's not done it for a while—his last year has been less about self-improvement and more about self-destruction; another effective way to pass time—but the mattress off his cot is thin enough to work as a mat, and there's enough space in his cell to stretch out in most directions. It's nice to get back to it. He has always liked the way it makes his body feel: not entirely like itself.

The blonde girl comes back with another tray of food, and due to the position he's maintaining he gets to watch her shift quickly from bored indifference to irritated astonishment.

"Hiya," he greets her, upside down.

"What the hell are you doing?" she demands, losing control of her voice and wincing when she does so. In Stefan's mind, he writes another note on the whiteboard: *bleach-blonde girl's voice gets deeper when she's annoyed.* He's not entirely given up on his original suspicions.

"Yoga," he explains, and carefully unfolds himself back into an upright position. Which ends with him facing away from her, so he turns with what he hopes is a gentle smile and adds, "It's relaxing."

"It's time to eat," she says, her alto lilt returning. "Step away from the door."

He does so, and she opens it, almost throws the tray on the ground, and closes it again. There must be a fingerprint reader or something; she doesn't have a key that he can see, but the locking mechanism is opaque, and he can't see the front of it.

"Thanks," he says.

"You're not fooling me, you know," she says.

"I'm sorry?"

"You know what I mean. Sociopath."

She's walking away when she says it, so doesn't catch Stefan's frown. "Sociopath" isn't accepted terminology, as far as he knows. He's no expert, despite his Psychology A-level and his single semester of Psycholinguistics, but he's sure of it. Shouldn't it be "antisocial personality disorder", or something?

Maybe part of this experiment, whatever it is, involves acting as unsympathetic—and possibly unqualified—nurses, to examine how people behave under misdiagnosis.

Shady.

Assuming it *is* an experiment, of course. Stefan's had a pretty good run of being wrong about things; it's important to remember his supposition is nothing more than a guess with a fancy name.

Well, he can't do anything about it for now. He looks over the lunch/dinner/breakfast on the tray and decides that the bowl of soup and glass of orange juice can wait a couple of minutes while he cools down.

***

The fading of the overhead lights brings Stefan back to awareness. Over the past few hours he's eaten his vegetable soup, remembered his way slowly and carefully through the plots of pretty much all his favourite novels, and obligingly stepped to the back of the room so the blonde woman can collect his empty tray.

It takes about half an hour for the lights to dim from their approximation of sunlight to a twilight glow, which brings with it some concerns. If they're lining up their fake day-night cycle with the real one, it means Stefan's been in here for only about a day; he thought it'd been nearly two. Clearly, his time-passing techniques aren't as good as he hoped.

He's cooled on his theory that this is all an experiment, but hasn't come up with anything to replace it yet, and can't forever block out the voice in the back of his head that's screaming at him to become seriously worried, perhaps even to panic. He quiets it for the moment—how would panicking actually help him?—by reminding himself that they've still done nothing but steal his clothes and isolate him. They've even fed him, and the hearty soup put paid to his worries that they're intending to starve him.

The bump on his belly is a concern, though. On cue, it itches. He digs his nails into his forearm again.

The lights in the corridor have dimmed as well, so it takes Stefan a while to realise that someone's watching him from the other side of the glass door. She's squatting, hands casually flopped over her knees, and she's frowning at him. The sudden presence of another person flips a few more of the "panic!" breakers in his head, but he closes his eyes for a second, concentrates on his breathing, calms himself, and stands. As casually as he can, he walks the length of the cell to meet the woman.

He squats, imitating her. As he does so she puts a phone on the floor, torch pointing up, providing enough light to see her face properly.

It's Christine. From the party.

"I've turned off the cameras," she says. "We need to talk."

3
Death by Chocolate

13 OCTOBER 2019 — SUNDAY

It gets easier every day.

She won't claim it's not hard, being out in the world as a girl, as a woman. But it's a thousand times better than what she used to be.

She used to be so *angry*.

She also, she muses as she drums the first two fingers of her right hand against the bench, used to smoke, and right now she's missing it more than anything else she's had to give up. She makes a fist, calms herself, and watches the horizon.

The Royal College of Saint Almsworth sits at the base of Almsworth Hill, a shallow bump in the landscape only worthy of a proper name because the surrounding countryside is so persistently flat, and Christine Hale sits at its very top, on a bench dedicated to someone whose name has long since rubbed off, waiting for night to fall. She has a marvellous view of the campus, but it's difficult for her to appreciate it properly right now.

Beware decisions made in haste. Something her father said a lot; mostly to the newspaper, occasionally to her, when she couldn't successfully avoid him. If he could see her now…

If he could see her now, the old bastard would probably have another heart attack. Absently she clicks her left wrist in remembrance of him. It still hurts sometimes.

But the man had a point, and Christine hates him even more for it: she made a rash choice, didn't think it through, and now she's made everything worse.

She'd *kill* for a cigarette.

Her phone screen lights up: it's Indira, her Sister. Her sponsor. God, won't *she* ever be disappointed if she finds out what Christine did last night!

"Chris-teenie!"

"You know that's not my name. You *picked* my name."

"Wow. You're in a mood."

"Just, you know," Christine says, "memories."

"Sweetheart! You're not…backsliding, are you?"

"No. God. Absolutely not." The thought of it is enough to cause Christine to shudder.

"Do you want me to come home and look after you?"

"I'll be fine. Really. Just thinking about Dad again. And I thought you were in London this weekend?"

"You know I'd come back for you."

"You're sweet."

"Always!"

"So," Christine says, standing up from the bench and stretching, "not that it's not lovely to hear from you, but…?"

"Why did I call? Aunt Bea texted: there's a new boy. Thought I'd warn you."

"Oh? Who brought him in?"

"Pippa."

He's not set up for an easy ride. Pippa's hardly the ideal sponsor, from what Christine knows of her, but she's also the only candidate left unassigned this year, and Christine happened to know she was at home last night, so manoeuvring poor, drunk Stefan Riley into the bushes outside the hall, within earshot of Pippa's open window, and screaming her best and most well-practised horror-movie scream… well, it had been the only workable idea she could come up with on such short notice. She could have gone straight to Aunt Bea, but there are unpleasant rumours surrounding the way she deals with threats to the hall. Better he only *wishes* he was dead, right?

Besides, he's *got* to have done *something*. In Christine's experience, most boys have.

It was God's own luck that it was Christine he ran into last night. He got only a few incriminating words out before she kissed him in a desperate attempt to shut him up, but he still managed to reveal way more knowledge about Dorley Hall than any outsider is supposed to have. Clearly, someone needs to have a talk with Aunt Bea about opsec.

"Poor lad," Christine says.

"Hey, Pippa's probably raring to go."

"I repeat: poor lad."

"He'll be right as rain in no time. Remember what you were like when you joined us?"

"Please, Dira, I thought we agreed Memory Lane was a bad place?"

"For you, not me."

Sun's going down. Time to move. "Look, Dira, I've got to go."

"Okay, sweetheart. You're sure you're okay?"

"I'm sure."

"And you've eaten?"

"Yes." She hasn't, but if there's one thing Dorley Hall isn't short of, it's leftovers to heat up. She'll take something up to her room later.

"Okay. Kiss-kiss."

Christine, feeling conspicuous, says, "Kiss!" but doesn't make the face to go with it, the one she knows Indira's probably making at her phone. It's hard not to feel like she's always being watched. An inevitable side-effect, Indira told her; either it'll go away eventually or she'll get used to it. She slips her phone into her bag and starts walking the shallow stone steps down the hill.

Saints, as a campus, is a slapdash mixture of styles, ranging from the very old—the entrance to the Student Union Bar looks like a village pub because that's what it once was—to the turn-of-the-millennium complex by the lake and the obnoxiously new Computer Science building. Christine gives *that* a wide berth; more bad memories. Dorley Hall isn't of a character with even the oldest buildings, having been here before Saints was Saints; it's a red-brick monstrosity, crawling with vines and wearing its origin as a private hospital on its sleeve. It looks, quite frankly, haunted and isn't actually on the campus proper, being set out at the edge of the grounds, where grassy scrubland meets dense woods, bracketed from the rest of the university by a thick semi-circle of empty land which, mysteriously, has never been earmarked for development.

It's home, and it looms reassuringly.

Two girls from the upper floors are vaping on the steps up to the main entrance, so when Christine lets herself in to the ground-floor kitchen she smells like strawberry bubble gum. There's no-one inside except Vicky, eating at the kitchen table. She smiles when she sees Christine, and surreptitiously drops the contraband paper bag that had been sitting on the table into her lap.

"I saw nothing," Christine says.

Vicky, through a mouthful of omelette, indicates gratitude, and Christine leaves her to her dinner, heading through the dining hall and, using her finger, through the locked door to the floor below.

The security room's empty. Not surprising for this time of night, this early in the programme. Everyone'll be studying or relaxing somewhere, with a laptop open if they have to monitor their charges. Christine ducks in and flicks through the screens and finds Stefan. Good: he's sitting perfectly still. Dozing, probably. She scrubs back through the footage, identifies a suitable start point, and taps the information into her phone. It's the work of another second to have her phone talk to her laptop, which is up in her room and already connected to the network, and loop the signal.

She loops the video for the connecting corridor and the stairs down, and disconnects the camera feeds for good measure. Her phone gets her through the biometrics on the door down to the lower basement and doesn't leave any trace of her in the logs.

You can take the boy out of the hacker, but you can't take the hacker out of the girl, no matter how many Linguistics lectures she attends.

* * *

"Where am I?" Stefan demands.

The girl, Christine, looks almost disappointed. "Where do you think?" She's wearing a light hoodie unzipped over a pale blue t-shirt, dark grey leggings and a pair of running shoes. Appallingly casual and comfortable-looking, compared to Stefan's scratchy smock. Like she's popped in to see the prisoner after a nice healthy jog.

"Dorley Hall?"

"Bingo. You're under it. Specifically, the lower basement. When all this was a hospital—" she waves a hand around her, causing the light from her phone to flicker eerily on her face, "—this place was the morgue. Or the laundry. I'm not sure."

"Did you bring me here?"

She looks uncomfortable. "Yes and no. It's complicated."

"Well, then—"

"I know, I know. I'm working up to it."

Stefan sits back from his squat, crosses his legs in front of him and rests his chin on tented hands. "I'm not going anywhere."

"Look. Okay. Look." She's strangely nervous for a kidnapper. "When you said to me, last night, that you know about Dorley Hall, what exactly do you know?"

"Ah. That was you on the intercom this morning."

"Yes. Please answer the question. It's important."

He could stonewall her, show her just how unimpressed he is to be on the wrong side of a cell door, but such an approach would only extend his stay, so he starts outlining his theory. As he does so, Christine's frown slowly deepens, and that's it. That's all the proof he needs that his earliest read, his first idea, was and is ridiculous.

He trails off, feeling *beyond* foolish.

"No, please," Christine says urgently, "finish. I need to know everything."

Stefan shrugs. "I mean, that's more or less it. I thought this was a place that helps trans people get away from unsupportive families. Helps pay for transition stuff. But it's not, is it? It's not, and I'm just an idiot."

"Why were you looking at Dorley so hard in the first place?"

"A friend disappeared," he says quickly. Best she doesn't get the opportunity to consider why else an apparent man would look so hard at such a place. "My friend's older brother. He was…kind of like an older brother to me, too." He smiles involuntarily, remembering Mark as he used to be. "When he came here, to Saints, he went missing one night. Officially missing; declared and everything. No leads. Just gone. But then, a year later, I saw him. I mean, I saw a woman I thought was him. She looked *exactly* like what he would look like if he'd been a girl. And I thought, maybe…maybe he was a girl all along? Maybe she pretended to run away so her dad wouldn't find her. Because, I mean, Russ didn't say it *out loud*, but I'm pretty sure he was—" Christine's staring at him now, expression unreadable, and he cuts himself off. "But I was fooling myself. Because he's dead, isn't he? And she was just some girl who looked a bit like him." He blinks rapidly; whatever this place really is, he's certain he doesn't want to cry here.

"Shit," Christine says, and flops down onto her bottom, unintentionally mimicking Stefan. "Shit, shit, shit, shit, *shit.* I'm an idiot, Stefan Riley."

He flinches. "Don't call me that," he says, before he can stop himself.

"Why not?"

"I don't like it."

"Whatever. Look. If you *promise* not to tell anyone what you just told me, *ever,* then I can get you out of here."

"Why? How?"

"*Why* is because the lives and freedom of a hell of a lot of people, including me and people I care about, rely on *no-one* ever knowing what you know, and *how* is because I put you in here, in a roundabout way, and I can get you out again."

"What do you mean, 'what I know'?" Stefan blinks. "I was right? It's *real?*"

Christine looks pained. "Yes and no. Look, do you agree, or not?"

It's real. It's fucking real! "Yes and no" could mean anything, but if *any* part of it is true, that means Mark—Melissa—might still be alive! And it means Stefan has to face up to his gender *fast,* whatever it may be, before all this slips away from him. Before Christine gets him out.

But he can't say it. He's never told *anyone* before. Hardly even admitted it to himself. And he's always been terrified that if he tells someone, if he comes out, if he actually tries to transition and it turns out he's wrong, if it turns out it was all just a fantasy, that he's not trans after all, that it was just a delusion by an ugly, idiot boy who hates his life and can't take responsibility for it, then he'll have nothing left to live for. It's the fear that eats him every night, the fear that's left him with nothing but an empty life, a cold, drafty room in a house he hates, and less than £16 in his bank account.

"Is it *real?*" he tries again.

She narrows her eyes. "What's up with you?"

Time to get to the fucking point, Stefan.

"Are you a trans woman?" he asks. It comes out more bluntly than he means, but he's overtaken by an urgency he hasn't known since he first saw Melissa, years ago.

Christine looks at him for a long time. "No," she says eventually. "Sort of. Not really. It's complicated."

"Stop saying that!"

She's frozen. He wants to reach through the glass and poke her. He waves at her instead, and the movement brings her back.

"I know, I know," she says. "I'm trying to decide how to say it. I'm not exactly fond of just coming out like—Oh shit!" Her phone is vibrating insistently, and she swipes it up off the ground, frowns at it. "I have to go," she says.

"What? Now? Why?"

"Someone's coming, and I'm *not* supposed to be here. Can you survive one more day down here?"

"I guess. Nothing's actually happened to me yet."

"Yeah, well. It might." Christine stands and bounces on the soles of her feet. Full of nervous energy. "Listen, you *can't* say anything to anyone about me—and that includes meeting me at the party—or about what you know about this place. You *have* to act like you don't know anything! And I'm sorry, but people here will think you're a horrible person."

"What? Why?"

"Just go along with it! Please! I can fix it all tomorrow! *Shit!*"

* * *

Christine ducks into the storeroom with only seconds to spare, and hurriedly taps through her home-grown app, re-enabling the cameras and cancelling the looping video. She brings up the direct feed and watches Pippa take the stairs at a jog and march past Christine's hiding spot without a glance.

Breathe out.

A bit of luck: if this had all happened even a few days ago, when some of the others were still in their cells, she'd never have been able to sneak around like this.

As she stands, she almost knocks something off a shelf with her elbow, something made so shapeless by time and neglect she can't tell what it is; an empty bottle of bleach, maybe? Carefully she puts it back and looks around the room properly for the first time. God, it hasn't been cleaned in—Are those bedsheets? Maybe this floor used to be the laundry after all. A shame; there's more symbolic weight to repurposing a morgue.

With Pippa in place and already berating poor Stefan, Christine quickly sets the stair cameras to loop for the next thirty seconds and legs it as quietly as she knows how.

Vicky's still in the kitchen, and this time her guilty expression has nothing to do with the paper bag in her lap and everything to do with the slice of chocolate cake on the table in front of her.

"Hi again," she says, grinning. There's icing on her lower lip, and Christine could just reach out and rub it off…

She takes a moment to compose herself. Most girls who graduate from the Dorley programme are attractive, but Vicky is something else. Christine carefully and firmly redirects her intense jealousy of Vicky's girlfriend to something much more acceptable. "Where did you get that cake? It looks amazing."

"I know, right?" Vicky says, slicing off a piece and holding it up. It looks like something off a baking show: four perfect layers in two shades of deep brown, clad in icing. "It's Death by Chocolate. One of the second years' bakes."

Christine laughs. "That's lucky for her sponsor."

"It's not as feminine as you're thinking. Aunt Bea was delighted when she heard; less pleased when she saw *how* this girl bakes." Vicky mimes someone engaging violently with a bowl of cake batter. "It's like a rugby tackle on the kitchen table."

Aunt Bea, current custodian of Dorley Hall, is a firm believer in the healing power of femininity, and applies it to her charges at every opportunity. Christine would have scoffed, once upon a time, but she's since had to admit that it does have beneficial qualities. Perhaps not when taken quite to Aunt Bea's preferred extreme, though. She winces. Memories. The programme can be tough.

Shit. The programme! Stefan bloody Riley's downstairs being softened up by Pippa right now! And *she, Christine,* put him there!

She shouldn't have panicked and done that to him. But what choice did she have? He came waltzing into her life just as she's finally starting to like herself, drunkenly babbling things no-one is supposed to know and unintentionally threatening not just her future, but the future of everyone she loves. What else could she have done?

Talk to him like a normal person, perhaps?

"Shut up, Christine," she whispers to herself.

"Hmm?"

"Nothing, Vick," she says.

"You're sure?" Vicky says, taking Christine's hand.

It's hard not to admire Vicky, who entered the programme the same week as Christine but graduated in an almost unprecedented two years. It was like she understood, from the first moment, what was being asked of her, and set out to achieve it as quickly and completely as possible. Her drive, her determination, her skill—her frosting-flaked lower lip—are all beyond impressive, and yet she's unfailingly kind, straightforward, and helpful. She still hangs around Dorley, but it's because she still has friends here.

And because she can steal estrogen for her girlfriend. Christine gave her the code for the secure medicine locker. Possibly the first thing she ever did in her life she can actually be proud of. She's pretty sure Vicky pretends to get it online.

"I'm really fine," Christine says. "Long day. Hey, how's Lorna?"

She's unable to stop herself smiling as Vicky launches into a delighted ramble. Her love for her girlfriend is infectious, and seems to have healed the last of the wounds Vicky suffered here. "She finally agreed to sing in front of me and, God, Tina, she's so talented. She hates her voice but she worked so hard on it and she sounds so *good* and I wish I could just put her inside my head so she could see what I see and hear what I hear and then she'd *know* she's the most wonderful girl in the world. With the sweetest voice! And we went shopping and I *know* I shouldn't, but I used some of my stipend to get some things for her and, well, um, it's a cliché, but 'dress go spinny'!" Vicky laughs and twirls a finger in the air. Christine rolls her eyes; Vicky should spend less time scrolling trans memes. "She looked so beautiful and so happy I had to kiss her right there in the changing room. Then we had lunch at this pub on the other side of town and these two guys came up and were hitting on us and we got to do that thing, you know, where you hold hands across the table and you're like—" she switches temporarily from her usual bubbly soprano to a husky drawl that does dreadful things to Christine's hindbrain, "—'Actually, we're together', God, I could have *died* laughing. Oh, and we went through our Brain and Behaviour notes together and she's *so* smart, Tina. I actually can't bear it. She asked after you, you know. She wants to know if you ever got round to playing *Bloodborne.* I said you haven't yet, you don't even have an Xbox—"

"PlayStation," Christine whispers, through her grin.

"—but maybe when you come over you can play on hers? She's set it up in the downstairs room at our new place but the other girls just want to play *Mario Kart.*" Christine nods, playing along. She's had a long-standing invite and, truthfully, she'd love to drop in to the house Vicky and Lorna recently started sharing with two other girls—another measure of Vicky's extraordinary success; Christine still feels uncomfortable away from Dorley—but if what she did to Stefan ever gets out, she'll be surprised if she leaves Dorley before 2025. "We've got the house looking really nice now and it would be *so* lovely if you visited. Maybe bring Indira, Paige and Abby along? I've told her so much about them and she *so* wants to meet them."

"I'd love to," Christine says.

"God, I really just talked all over you, didn't I?" Vicky pops the last bite of cake in her mouth and chews thoughtfully. "You know," she adds in a conspiratorial whisper, "I think there *might* be brandy in this cake."

"They're giving second years alcohol now?"

"I know!" Vicky squeals. "Doesn't seem fair, does it?"

It takes several more minutes for Christine to disentangle herself from Vicky's boundless enthusiasm, but she can't deny that she needed the pick-me-up. Up on the second floor, where all the third-year programme girls live, she bypasses the biometrics on her door out of convenience rather than subterfuge: she's got a plate of reheated curry in her left hand and chocolate cake in her right and it's just easier to speak a command to her phone than to find a thumb.

Inside, she sits on the bed and arranges her tools in front of her: curry, chocolate cake, huge water bottle—Aunt Bea insists all second years drink eight glasses of water every day for their skin, and it's a habit that's stuck—phone, laptop, nightly pills. She necks her estrogen and progesterone with a half-litre of water, deciding to be a good girl about it and dissolve them properly under her tongue *tomorrow*, and starts on the curry as she loads the security feeds on her laptop.

She's not a sponsor, so she's not supposed to be able to do this. It's lucky for Aunt Bea that she mostly believes in the programme, or she could send a whole lot of people to prison. *Starting with me,* Christine thinks, as she calls up the view of the boy whose kidnapping she's an accessory to.

Stefan Riley. She doesn't know what to make of him anymore. At the party, he'd seemed like a nice guy, a bit quiet and a bit shy, willing to let her take the lead in the conversation. He didn't undress her with his eyes and he even appeared, through the haze of alcohol and weed, to be genuinely interested in what she said. In all, the kind of man she felt the least uncomfortable around. Perhaps even the kind of man she might have taken an interest in independently, had Paige not encouraged her to talk to him.

Hah, "encouraged"! As if Paige hadn't painted her up, beautified her hair, squeezed her into a low-cut top, made cryptic comments about Christine needing to finally find someone she likes, and dragged her out to the party with the sole intent of shoving her in front of pretty people. At least she picked someone respectful.

And then he had to ruin it by knowing too much. Not enough to be right about Dorley, but enough to get them investigated.

Looking for his friend. Not even! Looking for the person who might as well have been his older brother. Did Stefan pick Saints for university solely to investigate a disappearance?

Shit. This is looking more and more like a colossal fuck-up. *Her* colossal fuck-up. She should have dismissed his theories, sent him off home and gone straight to Aunt Bea. But no, she had to go and drag him into the belly of the beast, via Pippa of all people.

He's lying on his cot with his knees under his chin and his arms curled around his legs. Foetal.

Christine scrubs back through the footage.

"I know about you, Stefan Riley," Pippa's saying. Christine zooms in, but the camera angle makes it difficult to get a read on her expression. Her voice is doing that too-level thing she does sometimes, when she's so angry she can barely hold it in. Christine remembers it well from when she moved up to the second year of the programme and Pippa, then in her third year, still argued with Aunt Bea. Most of Christine's memories of Pippa, now that she comes to think about it, are of her arguing with someone. She's always seemed so unhappy. "I know why you're here. Do you?"

"This is a School of Psychology thing, isn't it?" Stefan says. "A study on isolation, or something."

"Yes, that's good," Christine mutters. "Play dumb."

Pippa laughs. "Stupid boy," she says. "Do you know what toxic masculinity is?"

Oh, no. She's doing the whole spiel *now?* She's supposed to just psych him out! He's supposed to stew for *days* before she starts in on him! Is she that eager to berate some poor guy—?

"I'm an idiot," Christine groans. "God, and I'm repeating myself, too."

Pippa hated the programme. From what Christine heard from her Sisters in the year above, Pippa fought the hardest, spent the longest time in isolation, and had to be warned and restrained over and over again. And only someone very stupid would think her experiences, even now that she's come to terms with and accepted them as a necessary part of her rehabilitation, would leave her the slightest bit of compassion for a boy in the position she'd once been in. For a boy who represents the person she's grown beyond.

He's her sin in human form. She's going to *hate* him.

"What have I done?" Christine whispers to herself, watching the scene play out on the laptop screen. "What have I done?"

4
Room and Bored

14 OCTOBER 2019 — MONDAY

It's the intercom that wakes him, but it's not shrieking with feedback this time and the voice that comes out isn't shouting.

"Are you okay?" Christine whispers over the speaker. "Don't turn over. We're not supposed to be talking to each other. I've muted the microphone in your room but the camera's still active, which means someone's watching you right now. You're facing away from it; stay that way."

He doesn't want to say anything. After his interrogation and a night of some of the worst sleep he's ever had, all he wants to do is lie on the thin, uncomfortable mattress, stare at nothing, and slip in and out of consciousness. Maybe wrap the ugly, scratchy smock tightly around his own throat.

Stefan's never felt so horrifyingly *male* before.

The blonde woman lectured him for what felt like hours. Stefan kept silent as much as he could, but it seemed only to encourage her. Stubborn boy. Not listening. Pathetic. He was an insect she'd found on the sole of her shoe, and no matter how many times she stamped on him, he wouldn't cooperate and die.

She had treated him as if his body and spirit were interchangeable, both of them tainted. She had held his name against him with malicious glee, branded him with it, burned it into his skin. Treated his masculinity like a disease he was too weak to recover from, too stupid even to recognise. Accused him of wielding it as a weapon against all those around him.

Violent. Ugly. Dangerous.

Clumsy. Oafish. Graceless.

Over and over she put him in his body, exposed it to him, made him see his very nature as despicable.

Stefan had found it hard, in the end, not to believe her. So many of his own fears placed in her mouth and spat back at him. He wanted *out.* Out of this cell; out of this body.

"I'm not okay," he says, and at the sound of his voice—grating, dry, deep—he sinks his nails into his arm once again. This time, some of them break the skin.

"I'm so sorry."

"Why did she say all those things?"

"She's…very angry. At herself as much as you, I think."

"She *hated* me."

"It's not supposed to be personal. It's part of the programme here. Think of it like an entrance exam."

"An entrance exam *for what?*" He raises his voice, can't help it. If he could shriek loud enough to expel last night from his memory, he would. He itches in a way that has nothing to do with the smock.

"Don't turn over! The camera will see you talking!"

Stefan freezes. Keeps his eyes closed. Carefully moderates his breathing. Digs his nails in even harder; you can't obsess over your whole body if you're forced to deal with the one part of it that really, really hurts, right?

An old trick, one he keeps returning to lately. He wonders if someone who believes his life hasn't been defined by dysphoria, as he's always insisted, should have quite so many tricks like that.

Concentrate!

This place, whatever it is, has Christine so scared of being caught talking to him that she ran off to avoid his interrogator. So scared that she's hijacked the intercom system instead of coming down to see him again. Does the blonde girl, or whoever she works for, have power over Christine, too?

"I'm sorry," she whispers over the speaker. "I've made a huge mess."

He relaxes his hand. He doesn't look at his arm, though he can feel the wetness of blood under his fingers.

"What is this place?" he asks.

"Long story. Look, I'm going to get you out. Last night made that process…a little more complicated than it has to be, but mostly only for me. You *should* have just had another night of isolation and shit food. Another couple of days of it, actually. But I think she's accelerated the programme, and if she has, she might take you out of your room today, to visit the other boys."

"There are more—?"

"Please just listen. If she does, you *have* to continue to act like you don't know anything. It's awful, I'm well aware. And those boys, they've all done something. It's why they're here. Sometimes it's something violent, sometimes it's more like…social violence. They will think you're like them. Try to roll with it. And the girl who berated you last night, she thinks you're like them, too. It's part of why she hates you so much."

"She thinks I'm violent? Is that why she said all those things?"

"Yes. I mean, it's also because she's, uh, working out some issues. But yes."

"Why does she think I'm violent?"

"Because you're *here.* Good men don't end up here. Just go along with it for one more day, be the bad guy they think you are, and I'll come see you tonight and get you out. I have to go."

"Just tell me what this place is!"

"It's a long story and I don't have time. I'm still on the programme here myself, and I have an inspection any minute. Sit tight, and I promise you'll see me tonight."

"What do you mean, you're still on the programme?" Stefan says, but the slight hum from the intercom has ceased. She's gone.

***

Tonight's her last chance. The next step after the first session—the debasement Pippa subjected Stefan to last night—is to introduce him to the other boys. The point is to move fast, to keep him off-balance. He'll be shown the locked doors, bare little dining area and utilitarian bathroom facilities, and he'll be made to understand that it will be his home until Pippa says otherwise. And then he'll go back to his cell for one more night to stew, to get scared, to build up in his head the horrors that await him that have, up to that point, been only artfully implied.

It'll be her last chance to catch him without anyone else around. Her last chance to get him out, to lead him quietly past every lock, to erase his data from the system. The implant in his belly will dissolve in a month or so. At most, he'll feel a bit tired.

But Pippa is a problem. If she really is stepping up his introduction to the programme, then by tonight he will have seen the faces of all the other men taken this year. He'll have seen the faces of several sponsors and possibly even their names. And he'll know the exact layout of the cells and the common area and the bloody utilitarian bloody bathroom!

If only she'd gotten him out last night. She's got a plan to fashion a believable system glitch that takes out the cameras and the locks. She could have *Jurassic Park*'d him out through the darkness. Kept him quiet with half-truths about the programme, maybe promised to find his friend. Photoshopped the face on the records, changed the surname, erased the video files…It would have been messy, risky as hell, and she would have had to be extra careful to erase all traces of her clandestine movements from the logs, but it *could* have worked.

Nothing on the technical side has changed. But after today, when she gets him out, Stefan will want to go straight to the police. Men kept against their will? A whole underground facility? They look like a bunch of kidnappers! Worse: they actually *are* a bunch of kidnappers.

There's only one solution: she'll have to convince him of the worth of the programme *before* she walks him out. Make him understand it's best for everyone if those boys stay put. God, it's a big sell. Can she even be convincing enough? She believes in Dorley, sure, but does she believe in it enough to make an ironclad case for it? Does she *really* think every single one of her Sisters benefited the way she did? Does she genuinely, in her heart of hearts, believe the boys down in the basement will be better off?

"Or are you just saving your own hide, girl?" she whispers to herself.

Shit.

Shit shit shit shit shit shit *shit.*

On the screen, Stefan is still facing the wall. He might be shaking. Last night hit him hard, harder than she expected, even when she saw how Pippa was going at him. Mostly the boys are indignant, defiant, like she had been. What's different about him?

Maybe it's just that he's the first innocent to be inducted into the programme. Well done, Christine.

The sound of the door just down the hall from hers makes her jump; they're done with Paige's inspection. Quicker than she expected.

She shuts down the monitoring software she very much is not supposed to have, and takes stock: is she ready for this? No more or less than usual. Her room is in its normal state, tidy enough for anyone not pathologically obsessed with cleanliness, and therefore probably worth a grudging C or C+ from Aunt Bea. Her laptop and phone are both innocently idle, all unauthorised software closed and lurking in a hidden partition, and her binder is open on her bed with the notes from her last Language Acquisition lecture written out in the looping handwriting that Indira, with some exasperation and amusement, encouraged her to adopt.

Ah, but she's wearing her habitual casual clothes: a loose scoop vest, shorts, and white ankle socks. That's going to lose her some points. Too busy worrying about Stefan to change into something with flowers on. Hopefully the glittery fabric of the vest will be worth something, at least.

Too bad she has to go right after Paige. Paige, who already has thirty thousand followers on Instagram and a wardrobe full of influencer outfits. Paige, who very nearly graduated early, like Vicky, and was foiled only by a loss of composure near the end of her second year. Paige, who has blonde extensions down to the small of her back and a heartbreaker smile. Next to her, Christine might as well be a donkey with a wig on.

Just as the lock on her dorm room door buzzes—in their default state, the biometrics are quite loud—she quickly dashes to the cupboard, pulls out her plush pink penguin and tiny fluffy rabbit and practically throws them at the pillow, adopting an innocent, "just studying" pose mere moments before the door opens and Aunt Bea strides in, followed by Abigail Meyer.

Christine relaxes slightly. If Abby is standing in for Indira and acting as her sponsor today, this might not be so bad.

"Christine!" Aunt Bea says, opening with a smile of the sort you might find waiting for you in a dark forest. "How are you this morning?"

Christine ostentatiously puts down her binder and places her hands carefully in her lap. "I'm very well, Aunt Bea."

"Such a shame you are still in your pyjamas."

"Oh, um," Christine stammers, "this is just what I'm wearing today." As soon as the words leave her mouth, she realises Aunt Bea was offering her an out: "Oh, yes, Aunt Bea, I was just about to get changed into my prom dress or my pink blouse or my pretty bloody pinafore; you simply caught me amidst my morning ablutions," or some shit. Too slow, Christine.

"Hmm. Rather…boyish, don't you think?"

Christine affects a pout and stands up to look at herself in the full-length mirror they all have in their rooms. "Do you think so?" she says, injecting disappointment into her voice. "I was going for playful."

"A lot of girls on campus wear very similar outfits," Abby says, winking at Christine from out of Aunt Bea's line of sight. A brave move: it's never been proven that Aunt Bea doesn't have eyes in the back of her head.

"I'm sure you're right, Miss Meyer," Aunt Bea says to Abby, and returns her appraising gaze to Christine who is still making a show of inspecting herself in the mirror. "You look *quite* charming, Christine."

"Thank you, Aunt Bea," Christine says, hoping her smile of relief passes for genuine gratitude. And Abby gets to be "Miss Meyer", does she? The privileges of rank.

"You've returned to classes, have you not?"

"Yes, Aunt Bea." First year Linguistics. Her second shot at a degree here at Saints. Many girls who return to classes do so in the same subject they initially studied, relying on time, a second puberty, and surgical alterations to avoid being recognised. Not Christine. Computer Science was judged to be one of the things she would have to let go. Too much of a contributor to her malfeasance. She's not sure if she misses it or not. At least her new courses are interesting.

"Would you mind summarising your most recent lecture?"

"Of course, Aunt Bea," Christine says, bobbing down by her bed to collect her notes. She takes them to the dainty little folding chair by her desk and starts reading through, making sure to gesticulate in an expressive but feminine manner with her free hand, and carefully angling the page so everyone can see how beautifully curly her lettering is.

Aunt Bea listens attentively. She doesn't carry anything on which to make notes, but Christine can almost see the pen and paper in her head, marking off delighted check marks or disappointed crosses depending on the performance of the girl in front of her.

The custodian of Dorley Hall looks immaculate, as always. Her dress is modestly beautiful, her hair is artfully styled, her makeup is subtle and elegant. How much of the persona she presents to those still in the programme is an act, Christine doesn't know, but she's chosen not to try and find out. In Christine's first year here, down in the basement, the boy who is now Jodie Hicks called Aunt Bea a MILF to her face and earned a week back in the starter cell. Christine's always wondered if she still holds it over the poor girl. Jodie has the first room on their floor, so she's always first in line for monthly inspection; did Aunt Bea look her up and down this morning and ask, in her prim and proper pronunciation, "Do you still consider me a 'mother you'd like to eff ewe see kay', girl?"

Christine never considered the acronym appropriate, anyway: she can't imagine Aunt Bea doing something so vulgar as fucking.

"Christine?" Aunt Bea says. "Are you still with us?"

"Oh! Sorry." Christine glances over her notes, buying some time to come up with an excuse for zoning out. "I was just remembering something funny the lecturer said, Aunt Bea."

"That is quite all right," Aunt Bea generously allows. "I'm pleased to see you so absorbed in your studies. Would you mind repeating the joke? Assuming it is appropriate, of course."

"Yes. Right!" Christine racks her brain. "It was, um…How much do you know about the history of Linguistics?"

"For the purposes of this conversation, assume I know nothing."

"Okay. Of course. Chomsky, he's a linguist, among other things, and he concepted something called a 'Language Acquisition Device'. It's heavily contested these days, but it still has its adherents, and, um, Professor Coleman, he said they occasionally produce pamphlets about it that have, he said, exactly as much educational value as any other 'LAD mag'. We, um, we all laughed."

Christine holds her breath. The story's true, except that Professor Coleman immediately afterwards had to explain to a silent lecture theatre that back in the nineties there were things called "lad mags". Magazines for men, he told them. Rather unpleasant, he told them. And the Chomskyites, he told them, *their* opinions are worth about as much as—

He let them out early.

"I see! Well. Thank you, Christine."

Behind Aunt Bea, Abby has to bite her lip to stay silent while her face creases up, and Christine has to look back down at her notes to maintain her composure. So she misses it when Aunt Bea reaches out, and almost jumps when she crooks a finger under Christine's chin and lifts her face.

"Let me look at you, girl," Aunt Bea says.

Levity forgotten, Christine struggles against the urge to screw her eyes shut and to go stiff. This is always the worst part: she didn't ask for this body, and now she's being judged on her upkeep of it.

"You have beautiful skin," Aunt Bea says. "Although you really should try to get more consistent sleep. Drink more water, perhaps."

"Or get better at concealer," Christine says, taking a risk, hoping Aunt Bea takes it as a mild joke.

She does. Or she smiles, at least. Sometimes Christine thinks she appreciates the effort more than the result.

"Quite."

A gentle pressure on the back of her neck urges her to stand. She does so, and Aunt Bea moves her hand to Christine's shoulder and pushes lightly, encouraging her to turn around, to give the woman the full 360.

Christine does better than that. When she has to, she can move her body like a dancer.

"Beautiful," Aunt Bea says. "Your mannerisms have come along wonderfully."

"Thank you, Aunt Bea," Christine says. Her voice doesn't shake.

She's asked herself how she feels about what was done to her. Whether she approves of the changes that, eventually, she agreed to participate in.

One night, early in her second year, when she was still developing, she investigated herself. Lying in bed she raised her elegant hands to the starlight and winked out the heavens, finger by finger; she stretched out her legs, hip to toe; she explored her sore, growing breasts and her arched back. That night, alone in her room, one finger at a time, Christine discovered herself.

She likes who she is. Genuinely. Not just her new shape but her new mind, too. Christine is a better person to be around and a more enjoyable person to be than the boy who woke up in Cell One more than two years ago. At a critical point she was given the choice they all were, to accept the programme or to wash out, and when she properly examined what was being offered, she took it without hesitation.

The boy was miserable. The boy hurt people. The boy cultivated solitude. The boy, ultimately, had no future. The girl, the woman, is someone new. Someone better. And the girl is *her* creation. The sum of *her* choices. The life she now lives is hers alone. The boy might have been given the map, but it was Christine who made the journey.

But it's hard to remember all that when Aunt Bea has a hand on her. It's hard to forget how angry she was to be caged.

***

"Get dressed, Stefan Riley."

Stefan hadn't noticed the blonde girl walk up, hadn't even noticed the glass door opening and closing, but now, on the floor by his cot, there's a pile of clothes. Workout stuff, by the looks of it: loose joggers and a hoodie.

Was he asleep? Or did he just zone out that hard? Something about the last day or so has obliterated his coping strategies. Maybe it's the isolation or the strange hours; maybe it's the wild hope, still alive in him despite the bewildering circumstances. It's all mixing together, leaving him adrift and losing time.

Wake up, Stefan. Pull yourself together. Christine said he was going to be introduced to the other inmates, yes? He'll finally get to find out what happens here.

He swings himself off the cot, picks up the clothes and looks pointedly at the blonde girl. "A little privacy?" he says.

"You have nothing I haven't seen before."

At least he can turn his back. But he still feels her eyes on him as he pulls off the smock and starts getting dressed. There's a t-shirt in the pile, and he can hardly put it on fast enough.

Even under the best of circumstances, Stefan does not enjoy being seen naked.

"Before I open this door," the blonde girl says, "there are some things you must know. One: every woman you see is armed, including me. Two: our weapons are locked to us and us alone; useless to you. Three: all the doors are locked and this whole area is monitored remotely. Four: if you are compliant, you will be rewarded. And five: violence against our staff will not be tolerated. Every year, there are washouts. Those who wash out are never heard from again. Attempting to hurt any of the women in this institution is the quickest way to wash out. If you have aspirations to one day see the sky again, you will be docile and you will follow instructions. Say you understand and agree."

Christine said he should be the bad guy everyone else thinks he is, but how would a bad guy even behave in this situation? Yell and scream? Bang on the glass door? Try to disarm someone? Unattractive options. And someone could get hurt.

Aren't bullies known to back down at the first show of strength? He'll be the bully. He'll back down.

"I understand and agree," he says. He doesn't have to fake his nerves.

The blonde girl smiles. "Then welcome to Dorley Hall, Stefan Riley."

"Dorley Hall?" he says, remembering to feign ignorance, as the door buzzes and slowly swings open again. "On the edge of campus?"

"Under it."

He steps out into the corridor. The blonde girl and the two others who are with her—tasers held casually in their hands, he can't help but notice—put their backs to the wall and give him space. They indicate for him to walk past, so he does, hands in the pockets of his hoodie, broadcasting an absence of hostile intent as hard as he can.

He *really* doesn't want to get tased.

***

After what seems like forever, Aunt Bea finally congratulates Christine on her dedication and steady progress and, with a silently acerbic eye aimed at the untidy pile of textbooks by the desk, leaves. Christine holds her breath, waiting for her footsteps to fade, waiting for the buzz of the biometrics at the end of the corridor. When finally it comes she almost collapses.

The tension exits her body along with all her air, and Christine laughs until her chest aches.

"Oh my *God,*" Abby wheezes. She sits heavily on the folding chair and takes off her glasses to clean them. "The pyjamas thing! I thought she was going to make you strip, there and then!"

That'd be nostalgic. "I almost pissed myself," Christine says, falling backwards on her bed and narrowly missing her laptop. "Thanks for the save, by the way. I was *not* prepared."

"I think it helped that I'm having a slob day, too." Abby pulls on the fabric of her loose yellow t-shirt. It says *Saint Almsworth Hockey — GO SAINTS!* on the front, and her dark skin shows through in several places where the much-loved shirt has become threadbare. "Hard for her to get on your case when I'm wearing *this.*"

Christine sits up, puts on her best lecturing face and wags a finger. "You're setting a bad example for the younger girls, Abs." A giggle breaks through her stern frown. "How will we learn to dress like princesses and dance like angels when you keep reminding us of the existence of full-contact sports? And—" she fake-gasps, "*—t-shirts!*"

"Just be glad Liss isn't here or you *know* Bea would have picked her instead of me."

Melissa Haverford had been the star of her graduating class: too damn pretty and too damn well-dressed for her own good. Or, to be precise, for the good of every girl around her.

"It's not fair," Christine says. "I can be pretty! I can wear nice things, if someone else picks them out for me. I even kinda like it! I just…" She sags as her mood collapses. "I don't like doing it for *her.*"

"Hey," Abby says, picking up the folding chair, moving it closer, and taking Christine's hand; unlike with Aunt Bea, this is contact Christine doesn't shy away from. "You're doing great. And you've not got long to go until you can be pretty when you want and slobby when you want." With her free hand she poses, fingers under her chin as if she's posing for a selfie. "Just like me."

Christine grins at her. "I'm going to be like Paige and Melissa: perfectly pretty all the time. I'm going to be *so* annoying."

"I'll believe it when I see it," Abby says. She hooks an arm around the back of Christine's head and gently draws her closer. Touches their foreheads together for a moment. "I'm proud of you," she whispers. "And I know Dira is, too."

Closing her eyes, Christine absorbs Abby's touch. Abby, Indira, Vicky, and Paige; Christine feels indecently lucky. Their friendship, kindness and patience still seem like things she hasn't entirely earned. If she has to live by Aunt Bea's strictures for another year, well, perhaps it's a small price to pay if she gets to stay with the first true friends she's ever had. And her third year at Dorley has been by far the least onerous. The relatively casual monthly inspections are preferable to the constant moral inventory she was required to maintain in her second year, to say nothing of the need to keep herself appropriately feminine.

A shame she can't be like Vicky, already accorded the trust due all graduates; trust she immediately started abusing to supply HRT for her girlfriend. But with Vicky it had been as if the programme simply discovered the girl who'd been inside her all along; Christine had to go looking for hers.

Abby lets go of her hand and sits back. Christine instantly misses her touch.

"How's Dira?" Abby asks, reaching over to Christine's desk and stealing one of her bottles of Evian.

Christine raises an eyebrow and holds out a hand, refusing to respond until Abby hands her a bottle. Aunt Bea's orders, after all. She cracks the bottle and takes a swig. "She's good. Down in London for an audition, and visiting family."

"God," Abby says, "imagine being cleared to see your folks."

"No, thank you."

Indira's parents and older sister were, a little under a year ago and after extensive lobbying from Indira and several other Sisters, visited by an associate of Aunt Bea's and led to believe their "son" had always been a trans woman, and had chosen to disappear because she feared how her family would react to her transition. As a friend, the associate explained, they were willing to act as go-between on Indira's behalf, and perhaps arrange a meeting in a neutral location. Somewhere safe for their first time seeing their new daughter.

At the meeting, her family embraced her with open arms. They scolded her for vanishing for years and giving them the shock of a lifetime, and dragged her back home for a whole week, culminating in a party to which they invited several Dorley girls as well as, seemingly, the entire street. It had been Christine's first trip outside Saints as her new self, and the first time she'd felt like she might be able to make it in the world as Christine, after all.

Indira's sister took them both out shopping for something to wear to the party. Christine keeps hers safe in a dress bag in the back of her wardrobe; a memento from one of her first genuinely good memories.

Visit any time, they'd said.

"You don't miss your parents?" Abby asks sarcastically. She knows she doesn't.

"Mine aren't like Dira's."

"Are anyone's?" Abby says with a giggle.

"Did you see Dira's mum on the news last week?"

Indira's mother, now a minor social media celebrity thanks to her enthusiastic public support for her younger daughter, has been on Channel 4 News twice in the past year, first for an interview about her mother-daughter reconnection and more recently to provide the counterpoint to some new "gender critical" celebrity on a post-cancellation media tour. Dira proudly sent Christine a screen grab of her mother in the chair opposite Krishnan Guru-Murthy, with the strapline, *Aasha Chetry: Social Media Mum & Trans Rights Activist.*

"Yeah, we had it on in the common room on third. She's just fantastic." Abby bites her lip. "So, did you get the latest update pack on your family?"

"About a month back." Christine gestures at a folder on her desk. "I don't open them anymore; they're all the same. Dad's still sick and Mum's still caring for the old bastard. No contact with the authorities. It'd be nice if they acted like they cared I'm gone, you know? Just a little bit." Abby reaches out, takes Christine's hand again. "How about you?"

"They're still looking for the old me. They've got a private detective and everything. I've asked Aunt Bea if her 'contacts'—" two manicured fingers make an air quote, "—can put out feelers. Assess their mood. She said she'd think about it."

"You're thinking of doing a Dira?" Christine asks, surprised. Is this going to be a thing from now on? Dorley graduates getting back in touch with their families?

"Maybe. I don't know. I'd like to! I'm sure they'd be okay with it. With me." Abby sighs heavily, scrunches her fingers up in Christine's. "I'd hate to have to lie to them all the time, though. Not about who I am; you know how I feel about that." Christine nods. Abby's thoughts on gender have very much influenced her own. "But about where I've been, and stuff. I can't say I've been *here* all the time, right? Indira had to pretend she spent a year couch-surfing, and Aunt Bea's worried about bringing too much attention down on us."

"Better to lie than never see them again, right?"

"Yeah. Right."

"How's work?" Christine says, to lift the mood.

Abby's worked for the local paper for a couple of years, which is why she still lives at Dorley Hall and picks up some extra cash part-timing as an administrator for Aunt Bea. Whoever owns the *Almsworth Gazette* clearly believes young journalists need experience and exposure more than food.

"It's good!" Abby says, smiling again. "I pitched a piece deep-diving into the pay dispute at the council. You know, history of low wages, understaffing, inflation reducing the actual pound value of the work year-by-year." She pauses, building anticipation. "She said yes!"

"Oh my God!" Christine yells. "Congratulations!" Abby's been trying to get her byline on something real for a while.

They hug, and Abby fills in a few more details, including the interviews she's got lined up with various local notables. "Actually," she says, "about the paper, I wanted to ask you a favour?"

"Anything."

"You can still get at…things you're not supposed to, right? On our network?"

"Yes," Christine says, grinning, "but shush."

"There's a new boy, right? Downstairs? Do you have his profile? I want to keep us in the loop if he gets reported missing and we hear something at the Gazette, and since I'm not *technically* a sponsor any more I'd have to submit an official request, yadda yadda yadda…" She curls up her nose. "Paperwork."

Christine nods, freezing her smile in place while her heart sinks. She calls up Stefan's information on her laptop, using the app she's shown to a select few of the Sisters, the one that implies she has access to only the less vital files.

There he is. Stefan Riley. He still looks kind of sweet. Christine swallows against the guilt.

"You're kidding," Abby says. "Tell me you're kidding. Christine, you're *sure* this is the guy?"

"Hundred percent."

"Fuck *me,* Chrissy. That's Melissa's friend!"

"You're not serious? The kid? The one she always talked about?" Stefan *did* say he was looking for someone; Melissa?

Stupid, stupid. Christine should have started looking for a way into the unredacted graduate files as soon as he told her. Or she should have asked for a bloody name! This is why amateurs shouldn't kidnap people.

But the timeline works out. Melissa was drifting away from Dorley while Christine was still in the first year of the programme, so she doesn't know her particularly well. They've barely talked at all, and when they have it's been awkward, like at last year's disaster of a Christmas party, when a drunk Christine spent half the conversation calling her Sabrina; Melissa looks a lot like the girl from the nineties version of *Sabrina the Teenage Witch.* But Abby's stayed in touch, and talks about her a lot, even if things have been a little strained between them lately.

"She always said he was the sweetest kid ever," Abby says. "Said he wouldn't hurt a fly, even if it wore a *Kick Me* sign and peed in his cereal. What *happened* to him? What did he do?"

"Do you…want me to try and find out?"

"I don't know," Abby says, hesitating over the laptop. "No. We shouldn't. We're not his sponsors." She looks to Christine for reassurance. "It shouldn't matter what he did. It *shouldn't.* Whatever it was, whoever he's become…he's here to heal from it, right? It'd be wrong to pry, right?"

"Right," Christine says, pouring as much enthusiasm into one syllable as she can muster.

"Right," Abby repeats, nodding, still unsure.

Shit!

5
A Machine Made of Meat

14 OCTOBER 2019 — MONDAY

Stefan's not surprised to see other cells, identical to his, lined up on his left as he walks slowly down the concrete corridor towards the double doors at the end. Each one has the same glass wall, the same cot, the same thin mattress, like the world's least hospitable capsule hotel. He counts ten, and an eleventh room of a different sort; an interrogation room? He cranes his neck by the dirty window set into the door and sees nothing but shelving units and dust.

Ten cells, then. What kind of place is this, that it has ten copy-pasted concrete boxes in which to throw people? What horror show has he stumbled into? And how is Melissa involved?

"Stand aside," the blonde woman commands. "Face the wall."

He complies, still playing the obedient but bewildered boy. Not much acting required! The lock triggers with a hideously loud buzz, and then he's being ordered through doors that have now swung open. On his way past—"Turn right! Be quick!"—he gets a look at the mechanism: what looks like a fingerprint reader attached to a lock the size and shape of a brick.

There's another one just like it on every door in the corridor he finds himself in. He hopes Christine is genuine in her insistence that she can get him out, because it's clear he's not going anywhere without her help.

He's willing to bet that with all this concrete you could scream and shout for hours without being heard from the outside.

Chilling.

Christine said she was still in the programme here; does that mean she's walked the same walk? Did she wake up in a similar cell? What did she do to end up there? The boys—the *other* boys; whatever—are all here for "violence or social violence", she said. Did she hurt someone?

Try not to let your imagination run too wild, he tells himself, as the blonde woman opens another set of doors, leading into what looks like a common area. Before he can go through, one of the other women taps him on the shoulder, motions for him to stay.

"Stefan Riley," the blonde woman says, and he's too distracted even to notice she's full-naming him again, "you're not going to cause me any problems, are you?"

"Hm?" Stefan says, watching the men in the common area turn curiously to watch him. "Oh. No. I promise."

She rolls her eyes. "You're remarkably docile, remarkably quickly."

"Thanks. I try."

She gestures at him with her taser, and he regrets being flippant. "Don't be clever," she says.

"Sorry."

"In you go, then. Have fun with the other *boys.*"

He nods, puzzling over the emphasis on the word, and walks carefully through the double doors.

The common room reminds him of prisons he's seen in movies, with three exits: the one he just came in from, another to his right, leading to what might be a lunch room, and another to his left, labelled *Showers.* There's a handful of metal picnic-style tables in the centre of the room, each with their own metal chairs attached, some with threadbare cushions. Around a TV bolted high up on the far wall, there are a few sofas, and most of the men in the room are lounging on the ones that provide the best view. There are metal storage cupboards, with large locks and red lights that suggest they're controlled remotely, and behind him as he enters are a half-dozen women, all armed with tasers and batons, standing by or sitting on another cluster of sofas near the door. Most of them are also looking at Stefan, waiting to see what he does.

"Would you look at that?" one of the men says, waving. "Someone new!" His cheerful mood seems out of place.

None of this, aside from the ubiquitous concrete walls, is what Stefan expected.

The one who spoke gets up from the sofa and approaches him, hands in the pockets of his hoodie, walking with a hesitant gait that makes Stefan think of a small prey animal emerging from its den.

"Sooooo," the man says, stretching out the vowel, "when did *you* get here?"

"Yesterday," Stefan says, frowning. "Or possibly the night before. I'm sorry, but what's going on? Who are you people?"

"Oh, we're just a ragtag family of naughty kittens, here to be neutered, clipped, tagged and released back into the wild."

"Uh. What?"

"It's Woke Jail," says one of the other men. "What thoughtcrimes did *you* commit?"

"It's not Woke Jail, Will," another one says quietly. "He keeps calling it that," he adds, looking somewhere around Stefan's feet and speaking quickly, like he's pre-empting an interruption. "It's ridiculous. I keep telling him."

"Tell him what *you* think it is," Will says, smirking. When the other man doesn't cooperate, he continues, "*He* thinks these girls are part of a secret underground ring, working for the shadow government, and they kidnap men to drain us of our—sorry, what did you say it was called?"

"You're saying it wrong," the quiet one says.

Will turns away from Stefan to address the quiet one directly. "No, it just sounds stupid when you hear someone else say it."

The two of them bicker between themselves in low voices.

"What's happening?" Stefan says to the man still standing with him.

"Ignore them. They're a double act we're all *fucking bored of*—" he twists around to yell at Will and his friend and then turns back to Stefan, "—but it's okay because neither of them has managed to say a single thing of value since they got here. Hi. I'm Aaron. I was here first. Welcome to Woke Jail."

He holds out a hand and Stefan, still confused, limply takes it. "Hi."

"And…?"

"What?"

Aaron retrieves his hand and uses it to articulate his next sentence, which he enunciates like a primary school teacher: "My name is Aaron and your name is…?"

"Oh. Sorry. Stefan." His stomach clenches when he says it. He doesn't like the blonde woman calling him that and he doesn't think he'll enjoy the sound of it in Aaron's mouth, either. "How long have you been here?"

Aaron blows out through puffed cheeks. "Two weeks, nearly? I think? They fake the day-night cycle in here—I'm sure you've noticed—but assuming they're not playing games with that, about two weeks. I didn't even get to the start of the semester before the cartoon shepherd's crook found me and…*fwwwp!*" He mimes being dragged away by his neck. "Woke up in one of those fun little cells."

"In your cell, did you get the whole…?" Stefan doesn't know how to ask what he wants to ask without sounding silly, but Aaron seems to understand, anyway.

"The 'men are evil and so are you' lecture? We all did. And then we all came stumbling in here and sat around all confused, asking each other the same questions over and over: 'Did they put *your* dick in a vice, too? Yada yada yada.' I was here already so I just watched."

"They put your dick in a vice?"

"It's a metaphor, Stefan. They lectured us all about toxic masculinity, chastised us for not regularly imbibing the 'respect women' juice and threw us in here to get on each other's nerves. So? What did you do?"

"What did I do?" Stefan asks.

"Leave him alone!" shouts one of the men who hasn't spoken yet. "He doesn't have to tell you anything!"

"Shut up, Murderer Moody!" Aaron yells back. "No-one cares what you think."

"I'm sorry," Stefan says, looking back and forth from the man, sitting by himself in a sad little curl on the floor by one of the cabinets, to Aaron, "but who is he and what do you mean, 'What did you do?' "

Aaron looks at him for a second. "Right! Okay! You're confused. Understandable! Sit." He sits at one of the metal benches and slaps the table. "Sit! I'll introduce you. Give you the full tour. First things first: we're not *just* in here because of our 'toxic masculinity'—" finger quotes, rolled eyes and shrugged shoulders leave Stefan in no doubt as to what Aaron thinks of the concept, "—or our poisonous Y chromosomes or our big meaty dicks. We all did something that caught the attention of this bunch of—" He pauses and rolls his eyes. "Don't zap me, Maria!" he adds, facing the women near the doors and holding up both hands. "I didn't say it! I just thought it really, really loud."

Stefan glances back at the women, but if one of them is Maria, she doesn't react.

"So, if everyone here did *something*," he says, "what did *you* do?"

"Sorry," Aaron says, and makes a game show-esque 'you lose' sound, "you've failed to unlock my tragic backstory. Besides, I've given you the lowdown; you owe me a funny story. What horrific crime against the female gender did you commit?"

"Nothing!" Stefan insists.

"Ah. You're an innocent, are you? Like Raph."

"Fuck you, you piece of shit channer," says a man reading a magazine on another bench, without looking up.

"Raph here insists on his innocence! But we all know why he's here, don't we, boys?"

"Fuck you," Raph says again.

"Our man got a girl pregnant when they were both *seventeen,* then made her get an abortion when she wanted to keep it. *Then* off he fucks to university and cheats on her with every Stacy he can get his hands on, which was a dumb fucking move because of course she finds out. It takes her two years but she does, and someone here gets word of it and snatches him up and now, here he is!"

That's…it? Stefan got the impression from Christine that every man here would be dangerous, poised on the verge of violence, but what Aaron's describing is so mundane! Cheating is awful, and forcing your preferences on a pregnant woman is worse, but he can't discern a legible moral calculus that imprisons a man because of it.

On the other hand, there's a wrecked life between the lines of Aaron's glib summary, and there's almost definitely more to the story, so maybe this guy, Raph, deserves…whatever this place is.

Stefan's forming a new theory, and he refines it while Aaron babbles on, arguing with Raph about the exact nature of his transgressions: it's a scared-straight programme. Take bad, bad people, and lock them away for a while. Teach them that actions have consequences. Maybe there are talks or classes; lectures on how to be a better person. Keep them here until whoever runs the place considers them ready to go back to the world. Supervised for a while after, maybe; Christine, after all, attended a party and got high despite still being "in the programme" in some sense she hasn't yet defined.

Unfortunately, there's no space in this for his theories about trans women, and especially not for Mark/Melissa. Probably he was completely wrong about her. Christine's answer to his blunt question about her gender was noncommittal, after all. Hell, he might just have confused her. Certainly none of the men down here seem like trans people looking for help.

He puts his half-finished theory aside and refocuses on what's happening around him.

"Plus," Aaron's saying, "we all know Raph has rage issues. I bet plenty of those girls he fucked woke up the next day with a few extra bruises. Am I right, Raphael?" He grins sardonically and holds up a hand as if awaiting a high five.

"I don't have rage issues, shithead!"

"What do you call that?" Aaron says, pointing.

There's a dent in one of the metal cabinets. It's deep and many-faceted, made by multiple strikes. Stefan looks hard at Raph, pictures him kicking it. He's a big guy.

Stefan shudders.

"I call that, 'fuck off or you're next'," Raph says.

"Ooh, scary," Aaron says, making a mocking gesture. "Come at me. Please, I'd love to see you get tased again."

Raph replies with a middle finger and returns to his magazine.

"Well!" Aaron adds, turning back to Stefan with a wild grin. "That's Raph. Who's next? Oh, yes, the double act. Will and Adam. I still don't know what dreadful things they did but they're really fucking annoying, so Maria and her pals probably did the world a favour by locking them up down here. Love you, Maria!" he adds, blowing a kiss in the direction of the women by the door. One of them, an East Asian woman, idly waves a taser at him. "She loves me, really. But, yeah, unless you want to go completely insane or you want to know everything there is to know about who *really* did 9/11, stay away from Adam and Will." He drops into a whisper. "Apparently it was demons. Demons did 9/11."

"Which one is the demon guy?" Stefan asks, losing track. "Adam?"

"Does it matter?"

"Fuck you, Aaron," Will says. "You're right, new boy. *He's* the demon guy."

"I'm not!" Adam says, in a quiet but insistent voice.

"You said yesterday that demons make people gay."

"No, I *said* that demonic influence in secular culture is responsible for the glorification of homosexuality." The line sounds rote, practised, and Stefan wonders whether Adam read it online or was fed it by someone in his life.

"Fucking Westboro freak."

"I'm not a freak!"

"Aww, they're fighting again," Aaron says. "And yet they always sit together! I think it's wuv."

"Who's left?" Stefan asks, wanting nothing more than to get this over with. Everyone here seems deeply unpleasant, with the potential exception of the women, the ones with the tasers.

"Those two," Aaron says, pointing to two men who've been ignoring the whole spectacle in favour of some TV show, "are Declan and Ollie. That one hit his wife, *that* one hit his girlfriend. No; other way round. Sorry. Fun fact: Ollie there has been zapped sixteen times!"

"Why?"

"He thinks if he can get a weapon off one of the girls, he can escape. But it's pointless. They're locked to their fingerprints, or something. And there are a couple of really big guys knocking around somewhere, waiting to jump on us if we need jumping on. Declan grabbed one of the girls last week and got fucking dogpiled."

"Oh my God," Stefan says. "Was she okay?"

"What? Uh, yeah. I guess so? Declan got the crap beaten out of him, although personally I think they should have hit him hard in the head if they wanted it to stick. Watch for his limp, it's hilarious. Okay, okay, who are we missing? Oh, yeah. Murderer Martin Moody. The fucking sad case over in the corner there. If you ever need him just listen for the soft weeping sounds." Aaron switches to a whisper. "He's the only one with a body count. Like, a directly-attributable-to-his-actions body count! No, 'Oh, he ruined my life and now I can't go on' shit,'" he says in falsetto, resting his palm dramatically on his forehead. "He's the only genuine cold-blooded killer here. Unless you are, too. No judgement if you are!"

"A body count? What did he do?"

Aaron mimes pouring a bottle down his throat. "Drink driving. Killed a guy, injured his wife. Got off with a fine, which the queen bitches—Sorry, Maria! Which our *benevolent captors* didn't like. So! Here he is."

"I didn't 'get off'," the man mumbles, just loud enough to hear. "My family leaned on the court. I wanted to—I *needed* to pay for what I did."

"Congratulations!" Aaron says, grinning wildly. "You're paying for it now, and we're stuck paying for it with you. I'm sure even the people you *didn't* go so far as to kill while you were drunk are grateful to be rid of you. As for everything else—" he starts pointing around the room, "—toilets and showers are through there, TV's there, dining room's *there*...And that's that! Unless you want to tell me what you did?"

"Nothing," Stefan repeats.

"Suit yourself. Ah!" He points through the thick glass doors that separate the common room from the lunch room, in which a woman is laying out plates. "Lunch time!"

* * *

Stefan's surprised by the burgers—they look really good—but not by the plastic cutlery.

Aaron swings onto the chair next to him, apparently keen to keep exploring a bond Stefan would rather not develop. *Good men don't end up here,* Stefan remembers, and tries not to think about what Aaron might have done. The list is bad enough already: two men who hit their wives or girlfriends, a cheater who forced his girlfriend to get an abortion she didn't want, and a drunk driver. Not to mention whatever the two guys at the end of the table, Will and Adam, did, although given both the subject and tone of the running argument they've been having for the last several minutes, he'd rather not speculate.

Carefully, Stefan looks at each one of the men in turn, fixing in his mind what he knows about them. He doesn't want to forget who they are, even for a moment. Of all of them, the drunk driver, the one who's actually killed someone, might be the least objectionable. Not a conclusion Stefan enjoys coming to. Maybe it's just that he's quiet.

"Don't get too excited about the burger, mate," Aaron says. "It's veggie. Everything here is."

"Meat's too masculine," says Raph, the cheater. "Too raw."

Stefan very carefully does not make the obvious observation that eating raw burgers is unwise and might explain Raph's deathly pallor. Instead, he attempts to spear a chip with his plastic fork. It bends.

"You can thank Declan for the plastic cutlery," Aaron says. "You've seen that bump on your stomach? Well, so did he, and he got hilariously butthurt about it."

"Why? What is it?" Stefan says.

"It's an implant. Releases a drug called Goslafin."

"Goserelin, you fucking imbecile," Will says. "It's a drug for men with prostate cancer. It lowers testosterone. It's to make us less aggressive."

"Does it work?" Stefan asks.

"Fuck no," Aaron says.

"Shut up," Will says. "Of course it does! Your body's a machine made of meat. You can't act like medication just doesn't work on you."

"Sure I can."

Will says to Stefan, "Ignore him. My dad is the toughest man I know, and when he was on it, it made him tired and depressed. You've been on it longest—" he points at Aaron with his plastic fork, "—so you should be the most *emasculated* one in here."

"Whatever," Aaron says, turning away from Will, who theatrically rolls his eyes and returns to his discussion with Adam. "*Anyway,* Declan over there found out his boy juice was being interfered with and tried to dig it out with a spoon."

"Did it work?" Stefan asks, trying not to think about the idea that the thing in his belly might be suppressing his testosterone. It's almost too good to be true.

"Hah!" Will says. "No. I *told* him it wouldn't."

"Fuck you, Will-i-am," Declan says. He's alone at the far end of the table, picking his burger apart with his fingers, eating only the bun and the cheese.

"And now we have plastic forks," Aaron finishes. "Thanks, Declan."

Stefan tries his burger. It's pretty good. "So," he says, swallowing, "now I know why you're—why *we're* all here; what is this place, anyway? What's it *for?*"

"Are you slow?" Aaron says. "Think about it for a second! It's a masturbatory fantasy by insane feminists who want to believe they can take ordinary guys and make pussies out of us. But it's just all a big show. It's fucking *theatre.* They get us all down here, put anti-cancer drugs inside us so we're tired and depressed and floppy dicked. They spend a few weeks lecturing us about what big bad boys we are, and then we're supposed to go free as changed men. It's not going to work, of course—"

"Why not?"

"What do you mean, 'Why not'? It's bullshit! It's a fucking psychology experiment or something. Someone's grad paper on masculine aggression. Someone found this bomb shelter or whatever under a girls' dorm and had an idea that really impressed a grant committee and now we're stuck with it. We probably can't even sue; I bet they had all of us sign something when we were high or drunk or, I don't know, just really fucking sad like Moody over there. Where were you when they got you?"

"Uh, I was at a party," Stefan admits.

"There you go. They'll have got a girl to chat you up and make you sign something and then the next thing you know, concrete walls, veggie burgers and—and fucking weepy boy in the corner." He throws a chip at Martin Moody.

"He's just guessing," Martin says, ignoring the chip. "He doesn't know."

"And *he* just wants this place to be, I don't know, fucking purgatory."

"This is my chance, Aaron. Leave me the hell alone."

"Cry more, murderer."

Stefan takes another bite of his burger and tries to avoid listening to the conversation. One thing seems certain: if there's anyone who understands less about what's going on under Dorley Hall than Stefan, it's the men sat around the table with him. Their theories all suggest something new and temporary, but if it's connected to the missing boys Stefan's been investigating, this place has been going for years.

He feels eyes on him and looks up, sees the blonde woman out in the corridor, staring at him through the reinforced glass doors. He smiles and shrugs at her and she glares back, frowning slightly, like he's a puzzle she can't solve.

There's a lot of that going around.

* * *

After lunch and a few more abortive attempts at conversation, Aaron seems finally to get the idea that Stefan isn't particularly interested in talking, and joins Will and Adam on the sofas near the television. Most of the other men drift over to join them over the next few minutes, leaving Stefan and Martin alone together at the dining table.

"My name's not Moody," Martin says.

"What?" Stefan snaps, irritated to be distracted from his thoughts.

"My name's not Moody. It's Holloway. That little shit, Aaron, coined it on my first day out of the cell. 'Moody Martin the Murderer'. And that's who I am now."

"Was he right?" Stefan asks. "Did you kill someone?"

He nods. "I didn't mean to. But you don't mean to do a lot of things when you drink, and I was *always* drinking." He talks without emotion, but there's something in his voice, a hard edge that comes up occasionally, that reminds Stefan of how Mark and Russ sounded, reading from the letters their mother left them after her death. "I thought I could drive home. Just two miles. But I lost control. Left the road right as they were leaving the restaurant. Their anniversary dinner. He didn't make it to the hospital, but she survived. A broken leg. He pushed her out of the way. Saved her. From me."

"Jesus…"

"My family has money. Influence. Hired the best lawyer they could. Said I was a young man who'd lost his way. Said it wouldn't be fair to snuff out my potential over a mistake. Even found a criminal record for the man I killed, to make him look like less of an innocent victim. And I got off light. I was supposed to go back to rehab, but I couldn't hack it. Not until Pamela brought me here. *Made* me dry out."

"Pamela's your…?"

"My sponsor. And those guys, they're all wrong. This is no experiment, and it's not Woke Jail or whatever stupid thing Will Schroeder's going on about. Something happens here. They keep us locked up, they suppress our testosterone, they take blood samples… Something happens here."

"What do you think it is?"

Martin meets Stefan's eyes. An unpleasant experience. "I don't care," he says. "Whatever it is, I deserve it."

Stefan doesn't find himself able to contradict the miserable man. He just stares back at him, feeling almost more uncomfortable in his presence than he had when the blonde woman was needling at every aspect of his supposed masculinity. Eventually Martin takes the hint, swings around on his chair and returns to the common room, leaving Stefan to push his empty plate aside and lean his forehead carefully on the table.

Jesus, these people. He's tempted to ask Christine, when and if she gets him out tonight, to lock all the doors behind them and bury the key.

He gets almost a minute alone before the door through to the common area buzzes, locking him in the dining room. The blonde woman enters from the corridor, pocketing a remote.

Stefan can't stop himself saying, "Oh, thank God."

"What?" the blonde woman says, stopping before she sits down and giving him a quizzical look.

Fuck it. Tell the truth. "I was expecting another one of them. Another horror story with a face. But it's just you, the woman who yells at me."

At the door, another woman takes up a relaxed but ready position, taser in hand. The blonde woman nods at her, and sits. Steeples her fingers.

"Do you not like your new friends?" she says.

"They're all awful."

"You should fit right in, then."

Stefan swallows his reply with a cough, remembering the role he's supposed to be playing; although he's not sure, anymore, why he's playing it. Surely all he has to do is tell this woman he's not anything like those men?

But she won't believe him, will she? Just like Aaron. He saw someone like him and so does she.

"Can I ask your name?" he says.

"Why?"

He shrugs. Affects indifference. "You know mine. I know theirs." He nods towards the common area. A few of them, Aaron included, are watching his conversation, but presumably can't hear anything. "I'd like to know yours."

She glares at him. Eventually: "Pippa."

"Hi, Pippa," he says, smiling.

His smile sets something off inside her. "Don't think for a *second* that this is working on me," she snaps.

"What do you mean?"

"You know exactly what I mean. The whole act. *This.*" She gestures in Stefan's direction, her mouth curled into a sneer that suggests she doesn't like what she finds there. Well, ditto, lady.

"I don't understand."

"The nice guy act! The smiles, the friendly chatter, the polite questions, the—the flipping yoga! You're nothing but an act, Stefan Riley, and when girls fall for it, that's when you get them."

"I 'get' them?"

She hits the table. "Stop acting clueless! I've *seen* this before! I've seen how it ends! And it won't work on me but it *will* piss me off! You're as bad as the rest of them. Maybe worse."

"Worse than the drunk driver? Or the ones that hit their wives? Or that little scrotum, Aaron?"

Pippa rubs her hand. "Potentially. That's the thing with guys like you: you're all cute and cuddly right up to the moment you're not, and then…then you're capable of *anything.*"

He can't win with her. He needs to stop trying.

"So, what's my future here?"

"That's up to you. I heard one of the others telling you about your implant. He's right: it's there to make you calm. If you choose to remain in the programme, if you agree to commit to your rehabilitation, it will be re-administered whenever it runs out, and you can expect other treatments in due course."

"Do I get to know what those are?"

"No."

"Right."

"This programme has one goal and one goal only: to protect people from you. You're a threat, Stefan Riley. You leave when we decide that the threat you represent is neutralised. What *you* get to decide is *how* you leave: either by completing the programme and becoming a new person, or by refusing to participate, in which case we will wash you out. And—"

"Those who wash out are never heard from again," Stefan says. "I remember. What do you do, send them on to a private prison or something? Put them in the veggie burgers?"

Pippa stands, suddenly all business. "Above my pay grade," she says. "Now. Come with me. You will be shown the rest of the facilities and returned to your cell, where you will remain until the morning. You have a lot to think about, Stefan Riley."

* * *

At some point on the way down the stairs, Abby's hand found Christine's. Looking for reassurance. Because Melissa is precious to Abby—Christine didn't know just how precious until about half an hour ago, though she had her suspicions—and Stefan is precious to Melissa. And so they talked about Melissa, about what she should know about Stefan and when she should know it. Before Christine knew what was happening, Abby had talked herself into a comprehensive invasion of what passes at Dorley for Stefan Riley's privacy.

Christine should never have let on about even a fraction of what she can do. She managed to talk Abby into a delay, but sooner or later, she's *going* to tell Melissa.

One of the hardest things to accept, for many of the girls in the programme, is the requirement that they never see their family again. It's not something that's ever bothered Christine—residual guilt about leaving her mother with her father notwithstanding, though *she* chose *him* over her son/daughter/whoever, and the memory of that day plays out in Christine's nightmares with some regularity—but it's been particularly difficult for Abby.

Family photos fill her room. Letters she's never sent spill out of her dresser drawer. And now she's telling Christine she's considering petitioning Aunt Bea to let her follow in Indira's footsteps and reconnect with her parents? The more she thinks about it, the more Christine's convinced the request will be denied. Aunt Bea will tell her to move on, to forget them as best she can, and Abby will be sanctioned if she ever goes against this instruction. The hole in Abby's kind soul that is her past, her family, continues to grow, continues to hurt her.

And now a piece of the past sits in a cell in the lower basement. Stefan's not part of Abby's past, sure, but he's part of Melissa's, and to Abby that's just as important. A connection to something lost, something yearned for. But it's a broken connection, fucked up and soured by the unavoidable conclusion that Stefan, if he's *here,* grew up to be a bad man. Not true, of course, but it would be the cherry on the shit sundae to drag Melissa back into it all, on the night Stefan gets out.

Assuming Christine can even pull it off. The number of people involved keeps multiplying.

One mistake begets a thousand. She's considered owning up, telling Aunt Bea everything, but she's not sure what will happen to Stefan if she does. She never did find out what happens to the washouts, but it's undeniable that after Craig from her intake washed out, he really was never heard from again.

It was the first thing she checked when she was allowed back on the internet.

Abby releases Christine's hand as they buzz into the ground floor kitchen. Time to look casual.

"Hi, everyone!" Abby gushes, waving at the women gathered around the kitchen table. They look, variously, exhausted, annoyed, and amused. They'll have just got done supervising lunch downstairs, making sure their charges don't cause trouble. Unlikely, given that the precipitating incident prompting them to switch out the metal cutlery happened early this year, but not impossible. Christine immediately finds Pippa who is sat at the end of the table with a laptop open and a hot chocolate in front of her.

Marshmallows *and* chocolate sprinkles. Shit. The full calorie bomb; must be a difficult day.

Christine accepts a hug from Maria and a shoulder-pat from Harmony, two of the older women who both have responsibility for one of the reprobates in the basement. Maria in particular she hasn't seen for a while except on the cameras. She looks tired. Her guy must be a pain in the neck.

Abby bustles her way to the table, pulls up a chair next to Pippa. Immediately she cranes her neck to look at the laptop screen. "Oh!" she says. "Is that the new boy?"

It's probably a good thing working for the local paper doesn't require acting skills. Christine adopts an expression of indifferent curiosity and walks around behind Pippa so she can see the screen, too. Stefan's back in his cell, doing stretches.

"Fitness buff?" she asks, as innocently as she knows how.

"He was doing yoga when I came to see him one time," Pippa says. Half to herself, she mutters, "I can't work him out..."

Abby swivels the laptop and watches Stefan carefully. It'll be an interesting moment for her: for all Melissa's talked endlessly about him, she's never before had a chance to see him, except in old photos on Riley family Facebook accounts. Christine glances at the screen; Stefan's touching his toes.

"What's he like?" Abby asks.

"He's different than I expected." Pippa takes a long sip of her hot chocolate. Slurps up a marshmallow. "If he wasn't, you know, *here,* I'd say he was just a guy. A bit quiet. A bit weird. Pretty cute. Kinda sad? God, it's so effed up; I want to *like* him!"

"That's a bad thing?" Christine asks, playing dumb.

Christine shouldn't be interacting with sponsors like this. It's in the rules, the real actual rules of Dorley, printed out and kept on a shelf in Aunt Bea's office. The idea is that, despite being on a long leash and having had most of her freedoms returned, she's still in the programme. Getting to see how the sausage is made—or unmade—is perhaps counterproductive, when you are, in a sense, the sausage.

She frowns. Bad metaphor.

It doesn't work that way in practice, anyway. Dorley isn't all that big, and the job of acclimating Sisters to their new lives is, by necessity, communal. Rumour has it that under Aunt Bea's mysterious predecessor, "Grandmother", things were more rigid and formalised, but few remain from that time, and none of them have ever spoken of it in front of Christine.

Rather more reliable rumour says that Aunt Bea herself was one of Grandmother's subjects, and Christine is more inclined to believe that one. It would explain the way Aunt Bea occasionally allows herself to be compromised by compassion for her charges. Turtles all the way down; did someone once make Grandmother out of some unfortunate boy?

So Christine and the other third-year girls come and go as they please, hang out with the sponsors, and have access to most of the inner workings of the programme. Christine's assumption is that this is at least partly to ensure they begin to think fondly of a programme by allowing them this freedom rather than making them spend *another* year shut inside, amassing resentments.

It's still amazing that the place works at all. Christine half-expects one day to open a random cupboard and find a big box labelled *Assorted Mind Control Devices (Point Away From Face).*

"Yes, it's a bad thing!" Pippa shouts. "I need to *hate* him!" She bangs on the table and winces. Maria frowns at her. "Sorry, sorry. Damn; Christine, can you get me some paper towels?" Christine obliges as Pippa quickly rescues the laptop from a slowly spreading puddle of spilled hot chocolate.

They mop up the mess together. Abby starts massaging Pippa's shoulders.

"It's so weird," Pippa says, when things are back to normal. "I gave him the first-contact spiel and it was as if it genuinely upset him. And I don't mean the way it does with most of the guys; he didn't get angry, or try to attack me through the glass, or call me a feminazi or a you-know-what. It was like...You ever make a joke that's in questionable taste, like a dead baby joke or something? And then it turns out someone in the room had a miscarriage, and they're trying to hide it but you can tell they're really genuinely upset, and you feel like the worst person in the world? It was like that. I didn't even get through the whole thing because I started worrying I might be about to cause a suicide attempt before I even got him out of his cell! And then, just now, when I took him to lunch and to meet the other guys, it was like he'd just—just forgotten it all!"

"What do you mean?" Maria says. She and the other women are watching Pippa intently now, and Christine remembers that Stefan is Pippa's first subject. Is she being evaluated, too?

"It was like he hit the reset button overnight. Back to the personable, pleasant guy. No, wait; he was fine again until he met the other guys. Then he almost shut down. They *really* got to him."

"So you have a lever," Maria says. "Actually, it sounds like you have several." Levers are one of the things the sponsors look for: sore spots, sensitive issues; anything that can be used to promote a change in behaviour. You grab something the boy doesn't want grabbed and you twist for all you're worth. Only extremely rarely is it something physical.

"I'm not sure I want one. God help me, Maria, I almost want to unlock all the doors and let him go."

"Well, look," Maria says, "it sounds like you need to adjust how you see him before your next session. Harmony said she watched how you were with him during the tour, and she thought you did okay; what were you thinking about then?"

"My cousin," Pippa says, "and everything that happened with her. I tried to see, you know, *him* in Stefan, and it helped."

Maria reaches for her hand. "Well done," she says.

"I can't keep doing that. I don't like thinking about him."

"Then just try to remember, we've had these oh-so-charming types in before. They're always looking to get your guard down. What he did? Keep it in the front of your mind. It can help."

"What *did* he do?" Abby asks, clearly unable to contain the question any more.

Christine doesn't close her eyes and bang her head against the wall, but she wants to. She knows where this is going. Letting Stefan out tonight is going to look like a fucking nuclear-level disaster. It was never going to look good—*What* was *your plan, exactly?*—but this is just awful. The entire current sponsor team knows him, and not just by sight; they're actively discussing his fucking psychology!

Try thinking before acting next time, Christine.

"He was with this girl, right near the dorm," Pippa's saying, "and she starts screaming. Like, full-on, 'Get off me!' stuff. I look out the window in time to see her take off and he looks like he's about to pass out in the flower bed. So I went down, grabbed Raj from the breakroom so he could watch out for me, and the guy, Stefan, is fully asleep by that point. I find his wallet, and by this point I don't know what to do with him. Like, he's asleep and I've got Raj with me so he's not a threat, but the girl he was with sounded distinctly *not happy* with him so I kind of don't want to send him on his way without checking him out. So Raj watches him and I look him up. His file's—well, look." She spins the laptop around so Maria can see it. "It's sealed. And they only do that when there's been litigation to cover up something nasty."

Or when someone hops on the system five minutes earlier, does a bit of creative writing, and changes a single field in a spreadsheet from *no* to *yes.* The university has reasonable network security, but the weak link is *always* the office staff. Every year there'll be some poor fucker in IT pulling their hair out when they realise the class lists are in Excel *again.*

Maria reaches over, pulls the laptop towards her, scrolls around. "There are all these comments," she says, discovering Christine's hurried bout of creative writing. "Kind of suggestive, no?"

"Exactly," Pippa says, sounding relieved.

"Did we ever ID the screaming girl?"

"No. Camera deadzone. We have a couple of shots of her running away, but she has her back to us in all of them."

Nice to have confirmation that Christine did *something* right, at least.

"So," Maria says, summing up, "we have a screaming girl running away from a drunk guy. We have locked records, indicating some major incident that's been made to go away. And a tonne of comments on his file that stop short of anything actionable but paint a picture that says, if you read between the lines, 'Don't leave him alone with women.' It sounds pretty conclusive, Pip; you've got a real dangerous arsehole there. And you *know* Aunt Bea's looked at this same information and approved his stay. I mean, sure, it wouldn't stand up in court, but—"

"But we're not a court," Pippa finishes. "I know. God. I feel stupid. I fell for his act, didn't I? After everything, I fell for it. Flipping, flipping—*Fuck.*"

"It's okay. It happens. The important thing is, you talked to us about it. And you always can, you know?" Maria smiles warmly.

"I know," Pippa says, nodding. "Thanks, Maria."

"You're going to be okay?" Abby asks her.

"Yeah. I've got this."

"Then *we*—" Abby points at herself and Christine, "—have some late lunch to steal. Anything good?"

"There's cauliflower casserole somewhere in there," Harmony says, waving at the fridge.

"Yum," Abby says, smiling at Christine and making prompting motions with her eyebrows.

"Thanks, Harmony," Christine says, clenching her stomach. The "suggestive" comments she left in the open sections of Stefan's file had felt like such a good idea at the time; now it seems all she did was hand his executioner a bigger axe.

Three minutes of microwaving later and they're bounding up the stairs to Abby's room on the third floor. Christine always feels a little strange coming up here, given that most of the girls from third on up are ordinary university students with (probably) ordinary genders and she's always waiting for one of them to catch her out, but today she's got more on her mind. She smiles absently at a pair of women watching TV in the common area and lets herself be bundled into Abby's room, noting once again how strange it is that none of the dorms on this floor have centrally controlled biometric locks.

"Fuck, Chrissy!" Abby says, dumping her plate on her desk and ignoring it. "Fuck! I don't know what's going to break Liss's heart more: that Stefan is here, or that Stefan *deserves* to be here!"

"Maybe he doesn't!" Christine says, too quickly.

"You *heard* Maria!"

Christine takes a deep breath and lets it out slowly, giving the appearance of composing herself so she can think through what she wants to say. How can she divert Abby from making a decision that will make things even worse? "You know what Maria's like," she says, "always ready to see the worst in people."

"In *boys,*" Abby inserts, though without much feeling.

Christine nods, conceding the point. "In boys, yes. But her evidence is flaky as *hell,* Abs. His file is closed, and suggestive comments in the notes are just…suggestive. Even the girl yelling and running away, yeah, *sounds* bad, but it's all circumstantial. Even Maria said it wouldn't stand up in court."

"I can't stand the thought of the innocent boy I heard so much about going through what *we* went through." Abby wrings her hands. She doesn't talk about her time in the programme much; Christine's got the impression her sponsor went particularly hard on her. Trying to imagine Abby as a boy, let alone a bad one, is so absurd it makes Christine's head hurt. "But I also can't stand the thought of that kid just being *gone.* Replaced by a dangerous creep. And—And what if it's because of *us?* Chrissy, *we* took Liss away from him!"

"Tell you what," Christine says quickly, before Abby can dive for her phone again, "why don't I look into it? I said I could try and find out what he did, and I meant it. I bet I could get his file open. I mean, even back then I never went *that* far into the university system—" *Lies upon lies to tarnish my soul,* she thinks, "—but Saints is hardly GCHQ. And then you can know for certain. And if it's nothing, if he was brought in for no reason, if this is all just a big misunderstanding, well, then we go to Aunt Bea."

Abby's eyes, which are reddening, light up. "You can do that?"

There. That's the exit strategy. A trusted programme graduate asks her to pull out the old black hat one last time, and Christine reluctantly agrees. She then finds a totally innocuous incident on Stefan's file and an innocent explanation for all the sinister notes, and together they go to Aunt Bea to exonerate him. Maybe he can sign an NDA, or something; surely nothing too dreadful can happen to him now he's had so many eyes on him?

"Yeah," Christine says. "I can do it. Give me a day, and I can do it."

15 OCTOBER 2019 — TUESDAY

She doesn't know why she bothered setting her phone alarm, since she's been running on adrenaline and caffeine since yesterday, but at the very least it startles her out of her reverie. It also gets *I Knew You Were Trouble* stuck in her head.

Five hours ago, when she set the alarm, she'd thought the song an amusing joke. Now, after a night spent worrying, it feels inappropriate, and not just because she's been guiltily weighing the pros and cons of just leaving Stefan down there and saving them all the hassle. If everyone else she knows benefited from the programme, then who's to say he won't, too?

The answer to that was drilled into her head the first time she got hassled by another student. "A quick basement job," she had suggested to Indira. "No-one has to know." And Indira had to tell her that Dorley found out the hard way that not every boy is suitable. You can't just go dragging people in off the street; you have to be selective.

Otherwise, she said, it's just torture.

She taps her phone to silence it. Checks the laptop for the locations of the sponsors; all are in bed. She flips through the cameras just to be sure: the night-shift guys are dozing lightly in their break room on basement one, the security room's empty, and no-one's roaming the corridors or the central staircase.

She throws on a shirt. It can get cold down there, especially at two in the morning.

Let's go see Stefan.

Early in her second year, Christine discovered that the electronic locks on all the doors could be cycled slowly, making them virtually silent. She even tested a script that would hook into the system and quietly lock every door except the ones closest to her phone, allowing her and only her to walk around Dorley Hall and its basements unimpeded. It worked perfectly, but she's never used it since: one person trying a lock and finding it broken can be explained away as a glitch, but if a dozen people do so then it's fairly obvious someone's just ratfucked the network. The script is the sort of thing that's only truly safe to use if you don't plan on ever coming back. And where would Christine go?

She settles for locking Pippa's door only, looping as few cameras as she thinks she can get away with, and activating the alert script on her laptop. It'll ping her phone if any of the biometrics activate. She should have a few hours; more than enough time.

She goes down the back way. Her route takes her out through one of the hall's back doors and past the fire escape for the basement, concealed rather clumsily as a garden shed. She has to tramp through the woods for a couple of minutes, but it's been dry enough today that her trainers don't even get dirty. And then she's at the back entrance to the long concrete slope that takes her back under the hall and deposits her at the end of the residential corridor. She doesn't enjoy going this way—she has to pass good ol' Basement Bedroom 3, her home away from home for one difficult year, which now houses some guy called William—but it's by far the least populated route, and she's more than earned a little discomfort.

Stefan's waiting for her in his cell. Remarkably composed, which is a trifle irritating. At least he's not doing handstands.

"Hi," he whispers.

"You can talk normally," she says. "I switched everything off."

She sits, feeling the lack of sleep in every bone in her body, and he follows suit, crossing his legs under himself. If it weren't for the glass door, they'd be close enough to touch each other.

"Okay," he says. "Are you going to tell me what's going on?"

"God. I'm not even sure where to start."

"Yesterday, I asked if you're a trans woman. You didn't really answer me. Maybe start with that?"

This is it. The point of no return. Shit. She's been dreading this part.

"What I am," she says, "and *who* I am, it's all bound up with this place, and what happens here. When I came here, I was…very different. Angry, afraid, and—" she recalls a phrase of Indira's from her very first evaluation, "—capable of acts of great cruelty when I felt trapped and lonely. I was never physically violent, but I hurt people all the same." *This is not who you are any more. This is not who you are any more. This is not who you are any more, Christine!* "And it's because of that, because of the things I did, that I was brought here. For rehabilitation. Because that's what the programme does, Stefan. That's what it's *for.* It takes dangerous men, men like, well, the ones you met today, and it turns them into…into…"

She can't say it. It's just too fucking much and she can't say it. So she just holds her hands out in the classic magician's *ta-da* pose. Stares into his eyes as she does so. Can't look away.

Don't judge me. Please don't judge me. Even though, God knows, I deserve to be judged.

"You mean, you were—"

"Yeah," she says.

"You really—?"

"Yeah," she says.

"But you're so—"

"Yeah," she says.

"You're a *man?*"

Now she breaks eye contact. "No."

"But you said you're not trans. Or 'sort of' or something."

"My gender isn't the issue here," she says, holding herself still, willing herself not to react, even as her belly fills with bile, even as old wounds open all over her, even as memories she despises overwhelm her.

The confession and the location mingle. Suddenly she's two years younger and screaming at Indira from the other side of a glass cell door, screaming and crying and ashamed of both. She can't stop it coming out: "But if you call me a man again, *I'll walk away from this cell and leave you to rot!*"

Christine clamps a hand over her mouth. Stupid. So, so stupid. Then and now. "Sorry," she says, through her fingers. "Sorry, sorry, sorry, *shit!* Sorry!"

His eyes are on her, on the boy she once was, cruel and lonely and sad and scared. She's changed, she wants to say, to herself as much as to Stefan, but the boy will always be where she came from. The monster she's forever trying to escape.

"It's okay!" Stefan says. "I'm sorry. I didn't mean to—Oh, God, you're crying! I'm sorry, Christine, that was—I shouldn't have said that."

She screws shut her eyes, wipes them with her sleeve. "Don't be *sorry!*" she hisses. "I put you here! And I was just like those fuckers out there!" She presses her hands, balled up in her shirt, to her temples. "*Hate* me!"

"No!"

"Stefan, I—"

She hiccups, the way she does when she's about to collapse into floods of tears, and the discomfort breaks through her misery enough that she can hold her breath, count to ten, and regain control.

The shame. God, the shame. Still overwhelming, years later.

Christine didn't expect coming out to Stefan to be so painful. With Indira's family it had been different, so she hadn't thought about it much—truthfully, had deliberately avoided thinking about it—until it was time to say the words. Foolish. Indira's family believe her to be a trans woman, just like their beloved recovered daughter; a convenient lie, and one she can live with, take pride in. But as much as she wishes Indira's family were right about her, they aren't. She has nothing to be proud of. She didn't choose this, didn't fight for her own self-determination. She was captured and transformed against her will; a woman made out of a man so repugnant that someone took a long, hard look at him and decided the world would be better off if he simply ceased to exist.

And now Stefan knows.

"Christine," he says, quietly, full of concern, and God, she doesn't deserve that name. Doesn't deserve to hear it spoken softly.

"Please," he says, and she looks back at him, there on the other side of the door, stuck in a prison she put him in, and he's holding a hand up to the glass, pressing it there like he wants her to reach forward and—

"Christine," he whispers.

She holds up her hand. Places it against the glass. Closes her eyes.

It's almost like they can feel each other.

"Shit," she whispers, relaxing her shoulders. There's moisture on her cheeks. "I'm sorry. I, uh, I wasn't prepared for how hard that would hit me. Jesus, I thought I was over all that."

"You want to talk about it?"

"No," Christine says, and sighs. "But it's part and parcel of Dorley, so I guess I kind of have to." She drops her hand, curls it in her lap, cradles it. Watches the tendons twitch with an exhausted curiosity that finds her sometimes when she's emotionally spent. Be kind to yourself, Christine. "The Sisters of Dorley. That's us. Remade, all of us. Reshaped. Made better."

"Made into women," Stefan says. Not a question.

"Yes."

"All the guys out there. It's going to happen to them, too? Like it did for you?"

"That's the idea."

"Does it work?"

"Worked on me."

"For everyone?"

"No."

"The washouts."

"Yes."

"How many are going to wash out?"

"It varies. This looks like a particularly shitty batch, for what it's worth."

"What happens to them?"

"I don't know."

"Do they die? Or just get moved?"

"I don't know."

"And still you brought me into this."

"Yes. I panicked. I'm sorry."

"I don't blame you. Not really. I spent years investigating this place. I wanted to find out everything about it. Even if I was, in the end, completely wrong about it."

"I'm going to get you out. Tonight."

Stefan doesn't say anything for long enough that Christine finally looks up from her lap again. He's looking her over. Examining her. For what? He doesn't look critical; just curious.

"I have a few questions," he says, when he realises he's got her attention.

"Okay."

"Melissa Haverford? She's…Mark? Mark Vogel?"

"I never knew her by that name, but, yes."

"Is she okay?"

"She's okay."

"Does she…ever mention me?"

"All the time, I'm told."

"You don't know her personally?"

"Not really. We've talked a little."

"Can I see her?"

"She doesn't live here anymore."

"No, I mean, do you have a picture of her? Like, a file photo or something. I only have what's in here—" he taps the side of his head, "—and it's been a long time."

"Oh, uh, yeah," Christine says. "Give me a second. Abby sends me pictures. Better than a file photo. Here."

She holds her phone up to the glass. On the screen, Abby and Melissa are posing, four times over, in a strip of photobooth shots: laughing; sticking their tongues out; Abby planting a big kiss on Melissa's cheek; bunny ears. Stefan touches his finger to the glass.

"It's really her," he says. He loses his voice on the last syllable, and everything else comes out in a whisper: "She's really alive."

Christine loses control again. Here's Stefan, staring at pictures of his old friend, his almost-brother, his lost sister, and she can't help but give in to the pressure inside her. She never had that kind of connection with anyone, not until she came to Dorley, and the thought of having that and it being ripped away is beyond heartbreaking. She had looked up their respective ages, back in her room; Stefan thought Melissa was dead—or gone, at the very least—for *seven years.*

At least Indira taught her how to cry openly, how to draw strength and pride from her emotions.

"We need to get you out of here," she says, sniffing and putting her phone away. "And about Melissa: I can send you some more pictures, once you're safe, but it'll need to be a while before we can think about putting the two of you in contact." She stands, brushes out the folds in her shirt, wipes her cheeks again. "Aunt Bea's going to be antsy about you knowing as much as you do about this place, so you probably won't be able to meet Melissa in person for—"

"I want to stay."

He's still sitting on the floor, looking up at her with desperate need. She has to replay what he said a few times in her head before she gets it.

And it still doesn't make sense.

"You want to *what?*"

6
When I Get A Round Tuit

15 OCTOBER 2019 — TUESDAY

She's wearing sleeping clothes: a long nightgown with a cutesy pattern, leggings, and an open shirt, loose enough to hang off her shoulders, with the now-damp sleeves rolled a little way up her forearms. Her mid-brown hair, which hung around her chin when he first met her, is now brushed messily out of her eyes, with the longest strands gathered in a small ponytail. And her face, still slightly wet, shines red around her cheeks.

He can't remember the last woman he saw who was so beautiful.

To recentre himself, Stefan pulls back his sleeves and scratches at the back of his hand. An old habit: usually he hides his hands from himself under shirts two sizes too big, pulled so far over his fingers that he wears out the fabric in weeks, but sometimes, when he needs the self-control, he'll expose them. Pick at the flesh at the base of the thumb. Examine the tight skin, the stubby nails, the veins that lace elbow to knuckle.

Self-hatred as self-indulgence.

When he was younger, a teacher had caught him stabbing himself in the palm with a compass. Sent him to the head of year for punishment. He hadn't been able to tell her why he was doing it, only that he felt compelled to. He doesn't know why he never connected these feelings, this catalogue of revulsion, to the concept of dysphoria, except that perhaps he'd known that to acknowledge them, to dignify them with analysis and categorisation, would make them all the harder to live with.

Christine's hands, so graceful compared to his, are currently clasped in front of her, fingers intertwined and fidgeting, and they betray her mood as surely as his, now buried again in his lap with the sleeves of his hoodie pulled tight, betray his.

"Stefan?" she says. "What do you mean? You can't seriously want to stay?"

Even the way her lips move…

"I need a moment," he manages to say, pulling out the words like staples.

She nods. Raises a finger to tuck a lock of hair behind her ears, bites her lip. She's worried about him, and he should be grateful for her concern, but all he can see in her now, all he can think about, is the girl he could become.

Come clean, Stefan, while it's not too late. Admit to yourself once and for all what you've been denying since you were old enough to sort men from women. Trust the part of yourself that knows you well enough to realise that this place, obscene though it seems, is the only place left that can help you.

What are your doubts? Really? That you've never been able to say, with no caveats, even to yourself, *I am a woman?* Does that even matter? Say *I want to be a woman* instead, because that fits, and you can go from there. Even *I don't want to be a man* is enough. Why would it need to be more? Who's judging you, really, apart from yourself?

You think you'll be ugly? Unpassable? Does that even matter anymore, in the face of the losing battle you're fighting with yourself? Besides, if you're going to use this place's resources for yourself, well, *every* woman you've seen here is beautiful. Surely some of them must have started out like you.

You think you can't do it? You think you're not strong enough? Then what better place for you than right here, where they will *make* you do it?

Stefan swallows. Incredible that it takes a place like this to make it all so simple. Assuming he believes Christine, of course. Her claims, while they—somewhat perversely—explain the whole setup he's seen down here, describe something so absurd he can still barely grasp at it. She's a woman who was once a man, brought here against her will and...changed.

And so is Melissa.

He can just about imagine Christine as a trans girl who caught her testosterone puberty early enough to negate or mitigate the worst of its effects, or who got a very lucky play in the genetic lottery. It's harder to imagine her as being like one of the men he met before, swaggering around the basement, revelling in unpleasantness.

She got upset when he called her a man. How can someone be transformed so completely?

Stop.

Think.

What do you know, Stefan Riley?

Mark/Melissa was very unhappy for her whole last year of school and, looking back with adult eyes, for a lot longer than that. At the time, he'd believed she was just lonely after her friends moved on and she didn't replace them. With hindsight, it reads as dysphoria. But what if it was something else? Something darker? What if she came here to Saints, alone, and did…something? Something bad enough to be taken by the Sisters?

No. He *knows* her! No matter who she became in that time, she wouldn't hurt anyone. Ever.

He only realises he's shaking his head in disbelief when Christine says, "What is it?"

"I can't believe you," he says.

"*What?*" It bursts out of her as she spins on her heel and walks away from the cell a few paces, towards the far wall. "No," she says, turning around again and pointing at him, "you *have* to believe me. Do you know how hard it was for me to just—just fucking *tell* you my history? You think I *like* talking about it?"

"Christine," he says, pushing himself back up the wall, leaning on the concrete for support, not trusting his shaking legs, "none of this makes any sense! I mean, *look* at you!"

"Yes?" she says, frowning. "So what?"

"When we met, I thought you were a cis girl. And I can believe you're trans and just like, *really* lucky. Or incredibly rich. But then you tell me you're a—"

"*Careful,* Stefan."

"And Melissa?" he says. The dizziness is back; if he could dig his fingers into the wall he would. "You expect me to believe she did something so awful it warranted *kidnapping* and *transforming* her? She's not like that, Christine! She's a good person. She was never *anything* but kind to me!"

"She—" Christine starts, but she interrupts herself. Slaps the glass wall. "Shit. I should have guessed this would be a sticking point." She glares at him. "Why do you want to stay, Stefan?"

"I'll tell you when you start making sense!"

"I could just drag you out of here, you know." She pulls her phone out of her pocket and waves it at the lock on the door. It buzzes open, startlingly loud even compared to their raised voices.

"I'll shout!" Stefan says, desperate. "You're not supposed to be down here, right? I'll raise hell! Everyone will come running!"

"Shit!" She kicks the glass. "What if I just leave you here to rot? You'll find out just how much fun this place can be."

"*Good!*" he yells.

Christine near-screams in frustration, then slaps a silencing hand over her mouth. Swears under her breath. Closes her eyes and leans against the far wall. Her chest rises and falls.

When she opens her eyes again, she says, "Let's talk."

"I need to understand this place," Stefan says, unprepared to back down just yet, "and you. And Melissa." He realises he's taken several steps forward, and carefully he steps back to the support of the wall, before his adrenaline collapses and takes him with it.

"Okay," Christine says, making conciliatory gestures with both hands, "but you have to know: we're running out of time. If I don't get you out of here in the next hour or so, that's it. You're here for good. And 'for good' means two years at the *very* least. So ask your questions quickly, and don't waste time bugging me if there's something I won't answer."

"Why wouldn't you—?"

"There are a lot of secrets here," she says, "and not all of them are mine to share."

"Okay," Stefan says. "I get it."

"Can I trust you, Stefan?" she says. When he nods, she pushes open the unlocked door and joins him in the cell, sitting heavily on the concrete.

It's the first time he's been in the same space as her since the party. Her shampoo smells of strawberries. He sits opposite her, cross-legged. Less than thirty centimetres between them.

"All the raised voices," she explains, pushing the door shut with a toe. "It makes me nervous. If I'm going to shout again, I want another layer between us and everyone else." He nods again. "You want to understand Melissa?" she says. "How she ended up here?"

"Yeah. I can't believe she became like Aaron or Will or Martin. Never in a million years."

Christine nods and starts tapping on her phone. "This is a *huge* no-no, by the way," she says. "When someone leaves the hall—or is on the verge of it, like me—her past is *hers.* It's another country. Another planet. She's someone new, with her own choices to make; the…the man who was here before is, for all intents and purposes, dead. And good riddance. This whole place fails otherwise."

"Got it."

"But I need to make you understand Dorley, so, for you, I'm breaking that rule just this once. And only because I think Melissa will understand. Okay," she adds, after frowning at her phone for a moment, "I've found it. Abby's final write-up. *Highly* confidential. You need two-source authorisation to get at this." She grins. "Or you have to be me. Good news: she didn't do anything violent. Abby doesn't go into all the dirty details—those'll be in the intake files in the office upstairs; they get purged from the database every couple of years—but it looks like Melissa was starting to go down a dark path. Isolated, self-destructive, yadda yadda…" She twirls a finger. "Nothing we haven't seen before. After years of watching men like that grow up and seeing the things they end up doing, Aunt Bea started recommending we take them. Ah, and there might have been some kind of accident, reading between the lines."

"Accident?"

"It won't have been a serious one," Christine says. "Maybe a near-miss? Something that could have gone bad but didn't? No-one was hurt, whatever happened; the basic personnel files are marked if there's been death or serious injury, and we generally don't bring killers in, anyway. Yes, I know about Martin, but it wasn't deliberate. Abby is being her usual self here—the woman could see the good in the devil, I swear—but reading through…Yeah, I'm pretty sure I have the picture now. We get people like her occasionally: nihilistic, lonely. Walking time bombs, basically. She must have done or said things to make one of us think she was potentially dangerous in the future, but worth saving. So we brought her in. And if that sounds thin, I've been reminded that we're not a court of law, we're a secret extrajudicial dungeon; our evidence can be, like, bad vibes." She shrugs. "Anyway, that's why we brought her in. To save her. That's why we bring anyone in, really."

"Changing a man into a woman is about *saving* him?"

She looks at him like he just questioned the colour of the sky. "Well, yeah. Saved me."

"And all those guys out there? They're worth saving?"

She nods. "Aunt Bea thinks so, and, officially, so do Maria and Harmony and the rest. I mean, those guys are *definitely* all awful people, right? I wouldn't be sorry, personally, if every single one of them washed out. Which is why I'm not and never will be a sponsor. Although I think we may have bitten off more than we can chew with some of these guys; wanting to change, wanting to be saved, is a part of it, and not everyone does. Sometimes someone is just too big a piece of shit, too invested in their own supposed masculinity, too unable to see over their massive dick."

"Jesus."

"Yeah, well. Noble goals. Unpleasant methods."

"I'm getting that."

"You believe me now?"

"Maybe."

"Enough to answer my question?"

"Maybe."

"Please, Stefan," she says. "I have to understand why you want to stay. I know I come off like a bit of a mean bitch, but I can't stand the thought of leaving someone down here who doesn't deserve to be here."

"You don't come off like a bitch."

"Oh?"

"I've been thinking of you as pretty kind, actually."

She laughs. It's cynical and over almost as soon as it starts, and when it's done she's not looking at him anymore. "Thank you," she says quietly.

"As for why I want to stay..." he says, and lapses into silence. He considers prefacing his statement with the usual justifications he marshals when he imagines this moment: stories from his childhood and difficult teenage years, his litany of self-loathing. But it's finally clear that those are all just excuses. A pre-emptive defence against his gender being considered ridiculous, disgusting or impossible. It's bad enough for a boy to claim to be a girl; for a particularly masculine-looking boy to do so...

He bites his tongue to stop himself spiralling and the pain returns him to the present. Christine's looking at him again, her earlier irritation and anger replaced by honest interest. He briefly tries to imagine her here. Waking up in the cell, as whoever she was back then. As a man.

Almost impossible.

Except...she's almost exactly his height; a couple of centimetres taller, maybe. He noticed when they were standing, yelling at each other. Noticed when she kissed him, when they first met. A single small way in which, despite the gulf between them, they are more or less alike.

Maybe womanhood isn't so unobtainable, after all.

"I want to stay because I think I want to be a girl," he says quickly, before he can think any more about it. And winces; he managed to force equivocation in there, anyway. A little doubt, a little wiggle room, enough to let him take it back, should he need to. Fuck that. "I *am* a girl," he says. "A trans girl," he adds. "As in, I'm a—"

"Understood," she says gently, smiling, and then she blinks and her eyes widen. "Shit. It makes sense now. That's why you were looking for this place: you were looking for Melissa, for your friend, like you said, because you thought she was trans, and…God…"

"Yeah," he says, matching her smile, "I thought you lot helped her transition."

"I mean. We did. Just. You know. Not like *that.*"

"I was genuinely looking for her, as well," he says. "It's true that I wanted Dorley's help, but I wanted to see her again, too. I miss her." Warmth spreads in his chest as he remembers the last time he saw her close-up, pictures the smile on her face as she gave him back his absurd little box of stuffing, outside the Tesco. "I miss her so much."

Christine holds out a hand and Stefan, after a moment's hesitation, takes it. Her fingers are warm. Christine blushes, withdraws, and says, "So, uh, to be clear, because I think in this situation we need to be *incredibly* clear, you're planning on undergoing biomedical and possibly surgical treatment to become a girl, yes? And yeah, I know, 'become a girl' is cissexist framing, but—"

"It's okay," he says. "It's the easiest way to be sure. Draw the stick figures first, paint on the detail later." He giggles, feeling dizzy again, still looking at Christine. He wants what she has, wants it so desperately and completely it's a challenge to think about much else; in her presence, his lifelong doubts are made ridiculous. Now all he needs is to make sure she doesn't send him away. "Oh, sorry," he adds, seeing her frown, "that's just something Melissa used to say, when she helped with my homework."

"Abby says something very similar, sometimes," Christine says. "Probably got it from her too."

"They're close, are they?"

Christine rolls her eyes. "Incredibly close. We often bond with our sponsors—Indira, my sponsor, is like my older sister—but they're closer than most. Abby was a *mess* when Melissa moved out. And they talk constantly. Like, if you're in a room with Abby and you hear her tapping away on her phone, odds are she's talking to Melissa. Sometimes she shows me the terrible memes they send."

"Good," Stefan says. "I don't like to think of her being lonely. And, to answer your question: yes. I want to become a girl. Hormonally, surgically, whatever. In any and every way possible."

"Then this is the wrong place for you, Stef," Christine says, switching to the more gender-neutral version of his name. "We're not set up for actual, real trans girls, and I have *no* idea what Aunt Bea would do to an outsider who knows so much about us. She might be benevolent and give you everything; she might honestly kill you, just to keep the secret. I'm scared of her, and I'm not the only one. Like I said, we don't know what happens to the ones who wash out. God," she adds, rubbing her face, "this whole situation won't stop getting more fucked up. I'm so sorry I dragged you into this."

"I dragged myself into this," Stefan says. "And, besides, I don't intend to *tell* anyone."

"Please don't tell me you're saying what I think you're saying."

"I'll be one of the arsehole guys," Stefan says, spreading his hands out.

"Stef, that's *insane.* They're already set up to think of you as a terrible person—a terrible *man*—and if you stay here, that's how you'll be treated. We go *hard* here. Dorley Hall is where toxic masculinity comes to die. To be killed. By *us.* We hammer at them, over and over, because the men we bring down here, most of them cling to their masculinity like—" she hesitates, then laughs weakly, "—like it's a piece of driftwood in the middle of the ocean. Even as they get farther and farther from shore, they can't bring themselves to let go, because they've never known anything else. We have to pry their fingers off, one by one. Force them to learn how to swim." She looks away again. "That's something Dira said to me. *Several* times."

She's resting her forearms on her knees, staring at the wall. She's repeatedly flicking her forefinger against her other thumb, and she's picking at her lower lip with her teeth. A collection of nervous habits; a picture of grace. Stefan balances jealousy with disbelief.

"You keep saying you were down here," he says, "that you were a… not like you are now. I'm trying, but I still can't picture it."

"Good." She shudders. "I don't want you looking at me and seeing *them.* Even though maybe you should." Before Stefan can interject to contradict her, she continues, "I know what I said, about saving them, but the guys down here, right now, are nasty, bigoted, small-minded, and either so astonishingly sexist they're incapable of thinking of women as real people, or so blisteringly nihilistic they're practically solipsists. And all of them have hurt people. Mostly women but not all. This place, Dorley, what it does…it makes *people* out of *bastards.*"

"By turning men into women."

"By taking away their masculinity," she says, prodding a finger into the floor with every word. "Their driftwood. These are men who have only one lens to see the world through, and it's a fucking distorted one. A lot of them don't even realise how skewed their view is. It's perfectly possible to be masculine and a good person, but the official position here—explained to me *at length*—is that it's almost impossible to reform someone whose masculinity has…curdled. It's poisoning them and everyone around them, but they don't know it. Or they know it, but they don't care. It has to be completely excised from their psyche with a scalpel, layer by layer, until there's nothing left but whoever existed before they were poisoned. It, uh, doesn't always come out cleanly."

"I can't believe it's the only way to change them."

She doesn't get frustrated this time. She smiles wryly, like she thinks he's naive. "Then you try it," she says. "Fix them. Take one of those guys and fix him without changing anything else. And do it before he hits a woman." She scowls. "Or hits *another* woman. Because almost none of them will reform on their own, not in a country so in love with toxic pigs that it puts them in government. So, actually, don't try it. Leave them here, and hope we can change them. But *you* should go."

"I can't."

"Stef! This place will treat *you* like *them.* It'll paint you with all their sins and their arrogance and their cruelty and it'll punish you for it! And I saw how hard you took it when Pippa was giving you the spiel; that was just a *taste.* She went easy on you."

"She did?"

"Yeah. She thought she was triggering you in a way she wasn't *trying* to, so she laid off. Which I'd think was a good omen for your future wellbeing except the other Sisters, the more experienced ones, told her you were putting it on, that you're one of those guys who acts vulnerable to get women to let their guard down, and she should treat you just like them."

"Do I really come across that way?"

"No! God, no, not at all. You seem, I don't know, like a nice girl. Kinda sad, maybe—"

"Please don't do that."

"Do what?"

"Don't call me a girl."

"But you *are* a girl. You said—"

"I don't deserve it."

She gapes at him for a moment. "Stef, that is super fucked up. You don't have to 'deserve' your gender." Christine frowns as she says it, trips up a little in the middle of her sentence. "It's just your gender," she adds. "It's yours."

"Maybe that's the wrong way to say it," he says. Thinking it through as he goes, he continues, "I don't like who I am now. Who I've been for the last, I don't know, five years? More? I'm not dangerous, not the way the guys out there are, but I'm not anyone I can be proud of. I've never *grown,* Christine. I've wilted. I'm barely alive. And I don't want this *guy*—" he jabs himself in the chest with an aggressive thumb, "—to be someone I carry through into my future. I want to start again. To become someone new. And if you call me a girl right now, it taints who I want to be. If that makes sense?"

"Yeah," she says. "It makes sense. A scary amount of sense. Which it shouldn't, because my gender was formed *here,* in this…pressure cooker."

"You think it's that different out there? For a closeted trans girl?"

She's been leaning forward, and she catches herself, bites her lip again, and sits back. "Yeah," she says slowly. "I don't know. I never was one. But yeah. Maybe it's not. And, uh, if you don't want me calling you a girl, should I start calling you Stefan again?"

"Stef's fine. It's better. Melissa always called me Stef."

"Okay. Good. I still think this is the worst possible place for you. I know you can look at Melissa or Pippa or even me and think that because we turned out okay, you can, too, but we were *very* different from you when we came here."

"I can't leave," Stefan says.

"This place will *hurt* you."

He smiles. It all feels so simple now. Awful, when he considers the years of wasted time, the scars he's left on himself, but simple.

"I think you need to understand where I'm coming from. I've been denying myself for almost as long as I've been alive. There was always a reason: maybe every boy feels this way, I thought; maybe I'm not like those other trans people, the *real* trans people. And then later, as I grew up, the reason became: I'm too masculine-looking to transition; I'm not strong enough to transition."

"Okay, but—"

"Listen. This is important. I've *always* known. And I've *always* denied it. And every year I've denied it, it's gotten worse. Every year, I've made it harder for myself. And not just because I've got more and more masculine, although I have. Because I've got weaker and weaker. Less and less able to cope with just living, let alone transitioning! It's like there's a cliff in front of me, and it keeps getting taller and the handholds keep getting farther apart. I know I should have started climbing years ago, but I've never even tried because I know I'll fall."

"I can help you," Christine says, almost pleading. "I'll get you out of here and then I'll help you."

"You can't help me enough. Not unless I'm in here."

"This place will *kill* you, Stef," she whispers.

He laughs. It's sudden and far too loud and deep and he surprises himself with it. But the adrenaline's back, and it's carrying him through this bizarre confessional with a forthrightness he hadn't imagined himself capable of.

"I won't pretend dealing with Pippa wasn't hard. But if I know what to expect, I can prepare for it."

"It's more than just what she said to you. It's a total psychological invasion. And if your time down here is *anything* like mine, there'll be whole *months* where we make you feel shame for the changes we're putting your body through. I'm still not quite over that myself!"

"You can't make me feel shame for changes I want."

"Yes, but…"

"What kind of changes are we talking about?" he asks. "HRT?"

"Um. Yeah. That's already started, actually, with the antiandrogen implant. You'll get a new one every so often. They dissolve."

The little bump on his belly. Stefan places a protective finger over it. "How long on just the implant? And do they ever do anything to make the implant…not necessary anymore?"

"They'll start you on estradiol in, like, a month? Two months? It depends. And, uh…" She trails off, then shakes her head. Looks irritated with herself. "Yeah. Orchiectomy at the six-month mark. Sorry. I wasn't going to tell you. It's kind of my default to assume anyone down here would find the idea terrifying. I did."

"How did you deal with it when it happened to you?"

She bites a finger while she considers what to say. Inspects the tooth imprints. "Some of the others got really angry. I just shut down. Hid in my room. Wouldn't talk to Dira for a couple of weeks." She looks away, rubs at her face. "Paige helped. A lot. But it was Vicky who talked me around in the end. The way she did for all of us, really."

"Vicky?"

"She was in the programme with us. I don't know what for, to this day. But she *got it,* right from the start. Where I was at the end of the first year, that was her after, like, a month."

"Is she trans?"

"She says she isn't. Just adaptable. And very eager to leave her old self behind."

"I'm sorry it was all so hard for you," Stefan says. "I know how it must feel, me coming here asking for all this."

"No, no no no no," Christine says. "You don't need to apologise. I *needed* remaking. It hurt, but…" She sniffs. "I deserved a little pain. And I don't resent you or anything. I understand why you're here. I just think you're making a huge mistake."

"I disagree," Stefan says, returning to his point. "What else did you get? Hair removal?"

"Yeah. Laser for me, electrolysis for the blondes and the redheads, like you. I'm, uh, glad I didn't have to get electrolysis. I'm told it *sucks.*"

"Facial surgery?"

"Yeah, for most."

"You?"

She glares at him. "Yes," she snaps, and then holds up a hand in apology. "Sorry. Sore spot. But you should know, I guess. I, uh, had this bit shaved down—" she runs a finger across her forehead, "—and got a nose job. Oh," she adds, rubbing at her neck, "and a trach shave. I used to look like a giraffe that swallowed a tennis ball."

"What about your voice?"

Her smile returns. "Oh, that's *all* me. Hours of practice, every day. Even got singing lessons. I know all the words to almost everything Taylor Swift's ever recorded."

"Huh. Thought you'd got vocal surgery or something. How did they make you do that?"

"What? Oh. They didn't. I was cooperating by that point. More than cooperating; couldn't wait to be a new person. Practically begged Dira to let me start the lessons early."

"And that happens to everyone?" Stefan asks.

"Most. After a point, if you don't get on board, you get put back to the start, or you wash out, and that's that. We don't all proceed through the steps the same way, though; every sponsor is different, every girl is different."

Stefan nods. "So," he says, leaning forward, "how much do you think all that cost?"

The question surprises her. "I don't know," she admits.

"Last time I looked I had less than twenty quid in my bank account. All that stuff? I couldn't afford it in a hundred years. So, let's math it out, yeah?" Christine looks suddenly like a small forest animal caught in the headlights of the night bus. Stefan starts counting on his fingers. "Hormones, that's, what, fifty a month if I buy them online? At a guess?"

"Maybe?"

"And as for FFS, I know some girls don't need it at all to pass, but I've spent a lot of time looking at this face. I'm under no illusions: I need *the works.* Brow job. Nose job. Hairline. Jaw work. Chin work. Trach shave. Tens of thousands of pounds. And electrolysis? Chuck another grand on the pile."

"What about—?"

"The NHS? Maybe I try it. Get hormones and bottom surgery for free. But they don't do FFS and even speech therapy is hard to get, and the whole process is, from what I've read, frustrating, humiliating and dehumanising. And do you know how *long* the waiting list is?"

"Yes," Christine says, nodding, clearly on firmer ground. "Vicky's girlfriend's been waiting for years. She gets her HRT out of our supply." She bangs her head against the glass again. "Shit. Stef, I did *not* just say that. It's a secret. But that's it! I can do that for you!"

"You can get me free hormones?"

"Yes!"

"Free facial surgery? Free electrolysis?"

"Well. No."

"Pay my rent? Buy my food?"

"No."

"Because I need *all* that stuff. I don't have a wealthy and accepting family backing me all the way. I don't have friends; I don't have anything. I'm falling apart, Christine. All that's left of me is the front I put up. I'm probably already fired for missing work, but I was on the way there anyway, and even *with* my job, I can't make rent for much longer. And maybe I could have done better—got more hours at work, got a better job, tried harder in classes, whatever—but it takes everything I have just to keep putting one foot in front of the other. Forget transitioning; I can barely survive. And if I *somehow* got on hormones? It wouldn't fix anything else. Except now I'd be a *complete* hermit, because I know I'm not strong enough to transition out in the world. I don't know how other trans women do it; I just know I can't. The thought of people *looking* at me..."

"Hey." Christine takes his hand again. He's shaking, he realises. "Stef. It's okay. Breathe."

He almost snaps at her, but it dies in his throat. He takes a deep breath instead. Lets it out slowly. "And then there's Dorley. Everything I need, all in one place. Wasted on guys like Aaron and Will and that drunk-driver piece of shit."

"Not wasted," Christine says. "It wasn't wasted on me. Or Melissa."

"But you didn't ask for it, did you?"

"We needed it."

"So do *I!* And so do any number of trans people."

"I know!" Her shoulders slump. "God, Stef. I know. Don't you think I'd love to just give our shit out to every trans person at Saints?"

"I'm not accusing you. But you can imagine what it's like, yeah? Seeing this…this *bounty* get handed out while I can't even afford a bloody estrogen pill?"

"I get it," she says. "I wish it was different. But I'm not in charge; I just live here."

"Christine," he says, raising his voice, "I don't understand; how are you not completely miserable? How are you not clawing at your own skin? You say you're not trans, but they *made* you into a girl! I don't even know your real name!"

"It's Christine," she says, hardening.

He really is a stupid boy, isn't he? "Sorry," he says. "I didn't mean it like that. Or maybe I did, but you're making my head spin. I'm having to make myself remember that you're…you know. You seem so normal and nice and then it hits me again and…I don't get how this isn't a living nightmare for you."

"Why would it be? Being a girl isn't so bad."

"But—"

"I don't think it's the same for me as it is for you."

"It can't be that simple."

"It isn't, not really, but we *don't* have time to get into it. For now, Stef, you'll just have to accept that I'm fine. I'm happy! And so is Melissa. So's Abby, so're my other friends. Even Pippa."

And there's his opening. "I want to be happy, too," he says. "Please, Christine, help me be happy."

She raises a finger. Lowers it. Contemplates it for a moment. "Shit," she says. "Shit, Stefan. I give in. Your…financial conclusions are impossible to argue with. We have obscene resources here, and it's only right you should benefit from them. And you know what's going on in your head better than I do. If you really think you can survive this place—"

"Honestly?" he says. "I don't know if I can. But I know I won't make it out there. This is my last chance, Christine. I have no money. No friends. I'm struggling in my classes. I need, at the very least, *major* facial work done—"

"You're not being fair to yourself with that," Christine insists. "You never know what HRT will do."

"Oh? Now that I've seen you, do you think I could be at all happy out there, rolling the dice, hoping against hope that hormones will plump up my face enough to disguise all this?" He waves a contemptuous hand at his face. Can almost feel the ugly contours in the air that passes under his fingers. "You're gorgeous, Christine. Absolutely beautiful. Don't scowl; you are. And if I stay, I don't just get to transition, which may very well save my life, I get the chance to be beautiful, like you. Out there, *even* if I start on HRT immediately and *even* if it ultimately changes my face beyond my wildest dreams, I've still got to live long enough to get there. Months and months. Years, maybe. Finding ways to make money, to go to classes, to struggle along with life, and those are all things I've *already* failed at. It's terrifying, Christine, and I just can't face it. I want—I *need* what you have."

"Even if you have to go through hell to get it?"

"I'm *in* hell," he says. "At least your hell has catering."

***

"Christine, dear. Weren't you endeavouring to sleep?"

Christine raises her head from the kitchen table and on the second try successfully props it on what is currently her most reliable hand. In front of her, in assorted states of focus, are an empty coffee mug, a half-eaten croissant, a half-dozen other girls looking on with concern and/or amusement, and Aunt Bea, standing in the double doors and frowning down at her. It feels like the Queen of Hearts has swept into her court and found it packed with Mad Hatters, Alices, and rodents hiding in her teapot.

At least two of the Alices escape while Aunt Bea's attention is on her.

"I endeavoured," Christine says, wincing at the gravel in her voice, "I really did. It didn't help. And I have classes today."

"Your studies are important, of course," Aunt Bea allows. She makes a beeline for the coffeemaker. "A refill, perhaps?"

It's not like Aunt Bea to wait on her girls. At least, she doesn't think it is, Christine hasn't exactly spent a lot of time with her socially. "Thank you, Aunt Bea," she says, holding up her mug and regretting not picking something daintier and more feminine than the chunky grey *Round Tuit.*

Aunt Bea pours coffee and oat milk, and grins at Christine's choice. "Ah," she says, "always a favourite of mine. A fun joke."

On the other hand, maybe Christine picked exactly the right one. Boomer humour! She smiles her gratitude and immediately drains half the mug, taking care not to slurp. Stef kept her up until five this morning, arguing, brainstorming, and eventually just talking. He might be an idiot for wanting to stay, but he's an enjoyable conversationalist. For a moment Christine wishes that, on the first night they met, they had both been what they appeared to be. Cis girl and cis boy, meeting at a party. For an hour or so, she'd felt normal.

Aunt Bea hands out coffees to all the Sisters in the kitchen, picking only the most dubiously funny mugs off the mug tree. Pippa's has a repeating pattern of cartoon ants and bees around the rim, which takes Christine a second to get. Blearily she looks down the row of coffees on the table, all provided by the custodian of Dorley Hall in novelty mugs. Christine blinks. One of them says, in thick black letters, *You don't have to be a girl to work here, but it helps!*

Aunt Bea must be in an unusually good mood.

Christine concentrates on her coffee.

"Hi, all," Pippa says, marching into the kitchen from the hallway and looking disgustingly chipper, like she's just woken up from nine restful hours of dreams about how super horrible she's going to be to Stef. "Oh, Christine, you poor thing. You look terrible."

"You're so kind," Christine mumbles.

"I'm actually very mean," Pippa says, pulling out the chair next to Christine and bumping gently against her arm as she sits down, "and you know it." Christine grimaces at her, prompting Pippa to rub her shoulder in gentle encouragement.

Christine hasn't been in the third year of the programme all that long, and spent most of that time with Indira, Abby, Paige and Vicky. Maybe everyone from Aunt Bea on down suddenly being super nice to her is just what happens when you're no longer a second-year scrub. Now you're just one of the girls.

Actually, she remembers, Vicky's been hanging around with the other Sisters since she started her second year. Possibly they've all been waiting for Christine to stop being quite so consistently antisocial, then.

"Yes, you're very mean," Christine agrees. They inhale their coffee in silence for a little while, until Pippa pulls out her phone and starts scrolling through her notes on Stef, which reminds Christine that she has an obligation to fulfil before she leaves for her Linguistics workshop. "Um, Pippa," she says, "I wanted to talk to you. About the disappearance. Have you done it yet?"

As Stef noticed when he started his investigation, everyone inducted in the programme disappears, presumed dead. Engineering the circumstances of their disappearance and ensuring no suspicion falls on Dorley Hall is the responsibility of each sponsor. It hadn't occurred to Stef that he would be required to disappear, too, and the thought had made him quite distressed; just because he wasn't close with his parents, he insisted, didn't mean he wanted his family to think he was *dead.* But no sooner had Christine thought she'd found the motivation that would wake him from his madness, the little shit came up with an idea, and an irritatingly good one, at that. If Christine had been half as together in *her* first week…

"Not yet," Pippa says. Her eyes dart to Aunt Bea, who is buttering toast and paying no apparent attention. "I was just going to have him vanish on the way to work, you know? Keep it simple?"

"What if he doesn't have to 'disappear' at all?" Christine says, leaning hard on the caffeine and wishing there was considerably more of it in her blood. "I had an idea. It requires his cooperation, but I don't think it'll be difficult to get it."

"Oh?" Aunt Bea says. "Why would he cooperate so early in the programme? He's been here less than a week, has he not?"

"Days, Aunt Bea," Pippa says. "I accelerated his induction to bring him in line with the schedules of the others."

"Wise. So, Christine, why do you think he will cooperate?"

There's that adrenaline rush. Christine swallows, and locks her legs so they can't run away without her. "I know him a little," she says, and runs through the story they concocted together. "He takes Linguistics, like me. Different years, but a girl in my advanced unit knows him pretty well from a module they did together last year. She, uh, wanted to set me up with him, actually," she adds, laying on the shyness as thickly as she dares. If she could force a blush, she would, but the capillaries in her cheeks are as tired as the rest of her. "We talked a couple of times, and I kinda liked him. Not, like, *that* way, but I thought he was sweet. I was surprised to see him in here; he didn't seem like the type."

"They often don't," one of the others at the table says. Edy. Nice girl. Tall. Drinking from a mug that says, *Retail therapy is better than regular therapy* (the word *Retail* has been scribbled out and *Hormone* has been written on in its place). Borrowed one of Christine's skirts once. Never gave it back. She's sponsoring someone this year; is it Adam? The quiet, heavily religious one?

"What's your idea?" Aunt Bea asks, with every impression of encouragement.

"I think he should 'go travelling'." Christine air quotes with just one careful finger; she needs the rest to keep her head steady. "He's been having problems with his classes and with at least one of his professors. He had resits over the summer. Everyone knows he's not been happy. It wouldn't be hard to create the impression that he's decided to just forget everything and take a year or three off. Go off-grid, backpacking around Europe or something."

"If everyone knows he's been unhappy," Aunt Bea says, "why not take the suicide route? It's considerably simpler."

"Suicide means attention. Sometimes even more attention than a disappearance. And we've got a big haul this year; I've heard people talking about missing boys." If Stef noticed, others could, too. They need to be more careful, both with who they haul in—the "evidence" she manufactured for Stef isn't even the sketchiest she's seen on her trawls through the network—and with how they handle the cover stories. With any luck, she can prompt a rethink. "He's not all that close with his parents, but he has a little sister, and when he talks about her, he lights up." She can't help smiling; the video he showed her on his phone, back at the party, of his sister playing the trombone, was adorable, and his love for her had been so obvious that she'd just had to—oh, God, she kissed him, didn't she? Several times. No more alcohol for Christine for a good, long time.

"Christine?" Aunt Bea prompts.

"Oh," she says, and shakes her head, making a show of clearing it. "Sorry. I was just remembering a conversation we had about her. He really does love her. And if she thinks he's dead? He'll hate it. He'll fight it. Might even resist the programme just because of it. So, instead—" she's becoming more animated, fatigue forgotten, "—you offer him an out. You outline the way things would *normally* go—maybe dwell on his family having to have a memorial service, or the years and years of trauma for his little sister—and then you say, there's another way." She points at an imaginary Stef in the middle of the table. "All he has to do is hand-write a couple of letters, one for his family and one for the guys he lives with, saying he's gone travelling. Gone to find himself. He can include a bunch of authentic personal details to really sell it. And then, no police. No investigation. No-one showing up at his family's doorstep to tell them he's 'missing'. And his baby sister won't have to grow up with a dead older brother, always wondering what happened to him." Her phrasing is deliberate: Pippa has a cousin whom Abby says she misses dearly. "Sure, eventually he doesn't come *back* from Europe, but we don't tell him that part." Actually, Stef insisted to Christine that he can just leave once he's got everything he needs from Dorley, go see his sister in person. And if Aunt Bea deploys the usual threats to stop him, he can ask to have his records unsealed and show her that he—by then, Christine assumes, *she*—was kidnapped on a lie. Will it work? Only God knows.

Aunt Bea hums in thought. "It's a workable plan," she says, and Christine carefully doesn't show her relief, "but it does tip our hand as to how long we expect him to stay with us. That information is up to the sponsor to deploy or withhold. It's information he might pass on to the others. What do you think, Pippa? He is, after all, your charge. The buck stops with you."

"Doe," someone corrects unhelpfully.

"We'll have to pretend he has a chance to see his sister again," Pippa says, frowning, "but that's probably a useful lever. Yes." She nods to herself. "Once he's written the letters, I can hold them over him. Say I'll release information to his family that suggests he's died while backpacking abroad unless he cooperates fully. Carrot and stick. Handy for some of the more…complex elements of the programme."

Christine sips some more coffee so she doesn't snort in amusement; if Pippa's thinking about the orchi, she's not going to have any problems with Stef on that front. The boy's ready for the snip right now.

"And I doubt he'll tell the other boys anything," Pippa continues. "He hates them. A lot more than I expected." She looks thoughtful. "He might not like seeing himself in them. Hmm. Anyway, I can make his silence a requirement." She stops contemplating her mug and looks up at Aunt Bea. "It's a good idea."

"Excellent, Pippa," Aunt Bea says. "Proceed with my blessing. And well done, Christine."

In a perfect world, Christine would be allowed to faint as the adrenaline leaves her system, but she has a subterfuge to maintain and a Linguistics workshop to get to. She takes a second refill offered by Aunt Bea instead, downs it, accepts a hug from a grateful Pippa, and manages not to stagger from fatigue until she's halfway along the path to campus and safely out of everyone's sight.

***

He's not *trying* to antagonise Pippa by being caught in yoga poses whenever she visits him, but there's nothing else to do in his concrete box besides sleep or grudgingly operate the horrible metal squat toilet. Nothing except, perhaps, panic, and that's possible to route around, now he has a better handle on what's going on.

Pippa glares at him and he glares back, trying to communicate nonverbally that if she doesn't want to find him with his feet over his head, she should provide magazines.

She looks good, though.

Stefan's sample size of Dorley women is currently at two, with background data provided by a few glances at the one he thinks is Maria and some others whose names he doesn't know. He can't help but be intrigued at the way these women who were once, supposedly, ordinary cis men—men who were extremely unpleasant!—choose to present themselves. Christine seems usually to dress in simple, comfortable, unfeminine clothes, with little to no makeup, as Stefan might expect from a newish woman still acclimatising to her role. The only exception was the night they met; her friend Paige dressed her up for that, Christine said. Pippa, by contrast, seems to live in dresses. Today's is dark green, gathers around the mid-calf, and bears a pattern of roses down her left side. She wears heeled sandals—which, he notices as he stands to meet her, elevate her to almost exactly his height—and a simple, handmade bracelet around her right wrist; it looks old and well-loved, and she's worn it every time he's seen her. She accentuates her pale skin with dark eye makeup that stands out brilliantly under her bleached pixie cut.

He wonders if he could get away with complimenting Pippa's eyeliner, because it's great.

He remembers, moments before he opens his mouth, that he's supposed to be confused, disorientated, and extremely unhappy to be locked in a basement. At least he has Christine's reassurance that Pippa's been primed to see him as ingratiating and manipulative, and while it doesn't make him feel good, it is at least easy to play. He can thus bank his energy towards enduring her next attempt at wearing him down.

The memory of the last time is vivid enough that it flickers a frown onto his face for a moment.

Perfect. Use it.

"Pippa," he says.

"Well?" she replies. "Have you made your decision?"

Straight to business. "Stay or wash out, yes? And the washouts are never heard from again, correct?"

"Those are your choices."

He shrugs. Pretends indifference. "Then I choose to stay." He can't resist adding, "You can't keep me locked up forever, after all."

Pippa fails to control her smirk at Stefan's rebelliousness. "Good," she says. "Come with me."

Out of the cell, Stefan keeps his distance. Pippa doesn't have guards this time, but he doesn't doubt he's being watched on the monitors by women with tasers and batons and other things he doesn't want pointed or swung in his direction. There are male guards, too—trained professionals—but Christine said they don't like to bring them in unless they have to, preferring to keep them as ignorant as possible about what really goes on here. Wise: in Stefan's experience, men are very protective of other men's masculinities.

They round the corner and pass the doors to the communal rooms. Aaron, clustered around the television with some of the others, watches him pass through the reinforced glass set into the doors, and fires finger guns at him with a wink that Stefan does not respond to. At the end of the corridor, opposite the entrance to the communal bathroom, there's a pair of opaque double doors, solid and metal and much more like Stefan's idea of a security door, though they currently sit open. Behind them lies another concrete corridor, painted in the duck-egg off-white he associates with cheap rental flats; colour theory for "you can live here, but you won't like it". There's an emergency exit at the far end, described by Christine as leading to two more sealed "airlock" rooms and a long passageway that eventually opens into a pair of bunker doors out in the woods, biometrically sealed and only to be used in, presumably, very slow-moving emergencies. Lining the walls are ten doors, five to each side. They look like ordinary bedroom doors that have just materialised inside a concrete bunker, and absurdly out of place. They all have the bulky biometric locks, but in deference to a more homey atmosphere, they've also been covered in wood-effect laminate.

The door at the end is open and Pippa guides him into an ordinary dorm room, similar to the one he had in his first year at Saints. Slightly nicer, even. There's a generous bed, a wardrobe with full-length mirrors, a set of shelves, a metal desk with a computer—bolted down, on closer inspection—and a utilitarian-looking vanity and chest of drawers. There's even a phone sitting by the computer, presumably with its cellular radio neutered.

Still no windows. Stefan makes a mental note to ask about vitamin D supplements.

Snaking out from under the bed and nestling in the middle of the duvet is something Stefan's first dorm room definitely didn't have: a pair of handcuffs on the end of a heavy chain.

Pippa's been standing in the doorway, and when he sits on the edge of the mattress and weighs the cuffs in his hands, she says, "Behave, and you'll never have to put them on. You can tuck them under the bed and it'll be like they're not even here. Antagonise me, and they go on and *stay* on until I—" she clicks a device Stefan hadn't noticed, and in his grip the cuffs pop open, "—say they come off. So don't piss me off, Stefan Riley."

He puts them carefully back on the bed. "Understood," he says, and unconsciously massages his wrists.

"We have more to discuss, but first, you need a shower."

"Now?"

She wrinkles her nose. "Now."

"Oh. Right. Sorry. Must have gotten used to it."

Pippa directs him to a bag of toiletries on the vanity, and fetches him a clean towel and a dressing gown out of the wardrobe. She escorts him down the hall to the communal bathroom and snorts when he asks for some privacy.

When he saw the bathroom yesterday, on his short tour of the facilities, it put him in mind of the changing rooms from his old school, transplanted underground, shrunk a fair bit, and heavily cleaned. There's a full-length mirror by the paper towel dispenser, and while normally Stefan would avoid his reflection, today he follows an impulse to examine himself. If, in the hands of Pippa and the Sisters, his body is going to be remoulded, he wants to familiarise himself with the starting state of the clay.

He disrobes, down to his underwear, and slings the dressing gown around his shoulders. Stefan wonders where he'll see the changes first. In the rough edges of his face? In his veined, wiry arms? In his taut, waxy belly, a legacy of poor diet and persistent poverty? He runs a hand through his hair, spills ginger strands across his forehead. Counts the freckles on his cheeks. His finger brushes against his stubble, which breaks the spell; that, at least, he can take care of on his own, right now.

He keeps looking at his reflection as he unpacks the little battery shaver. He's been used to viewing himself, his body, his face, as aberrations, mutations forced onto him by a puberty he didn't want. Now? They're still just as ugly to him, but perhaps they no longer represent a trap he can't escape.

God, he even smells different. He's been marinading in his own sweat for almost three days, and the odour isn't at all what he's used to. Is that even possible? After just days of having his testosterone blocked?

Maybe. Maybe not. Wishful thinking, perhaps.

The one called Will interrupts his thoughts, ducking out of the shower annexe and rubbing his hair with a towel. In the small mirror over the sink, shaver in hand, Stefan can't stop himself from staring; Will is well built and completely naked.

"What are you looking at, homo?" Will says.

Ah, yes. He's also a prick.

Stefan buzzes the shaver and starts working on his whiskers, turning his back so he can't see Will in the reflection. He doesn't reply. Doesn't trust himself, because now he can't stop picturing on Will's body the eventual effects of testosterone blockers, estrogen and a spot of surprise surgery to the nether regions.

When the man finally leaves the bathroom, visibly irritated, Stefan loses all control, and laughs so hard he drops the electric shaver in the sink.

***

She should be sleeping. Goodness knows she needs it! But Christine is glued to her laptop screen. It's a pivotal time for Stef: not just his longest conversation yet with Pippa, but the one in which they discuss the content of the letters he's going to write. He's playing his part tolerably, sitting cross-legged on his new bed and idly turning over the cuffs in his hands as he pretends to think about Pippa's suggestions. To Christine, he comes across as far too innocent, but institutional inertia is working in their favour. He must be bad: he's at Dorley!

Pippa's behaving a little strangely around him, though. She's not being nice to him, heaven forfend, but the edge of controlled anger is gone from her voice. Good news for Stef, probably, as long as Pippa doesn't figure him out.

Pippa keeps playing with something on her wrist. Suddenly Christine gets it: Pippa's thinking about her cousin, the one who made the bracelet she never takes off. Shit. Playing on Pippa's weak spot to get her to agree to the plan seemed like a good idea at the time, but Christine should have considered how much it would upset her.

She marks another check on her mental list of people she's hurt as she flails around, attempting to clean up her own mess.

Christine slams the laptop lid shut. "Be kind to yourself, Christine," she mutters. The hard part's over! Stef's in place, Pippa's going along with it, and Aunt Bea approved the letter idea. Another normal year begins: eight boys in the basement, one of whom is handily already a girl; six newly minted girls on the first floor, one of whom is apparently a capable and strangely violent baker; and six completely and utterly normal young women on the second floor, one of whom is currently chewing on the end of her finger.

She rubs at the tooth imprints and dries it on a tissue.

Everything's fine. Not so much for Stef, but at least he's getting what he asked for, even if he's not going to enjoy what it takes to get it.

"Relax," she says to herself. When that unaccountably doesn't work, she adds, "Relax, idiot!"

She's still a mess, so she puts on *1989*, pulls out her phone and starts going through her week planner. She moves her shoulders to the music, lets her tension out with the beat. She laughs, as she always does, at the one-minute-thirty-five mark: *Everybody here was someone else before*. It hasn't yet stopped being funny.

Christine sings.

Four tracks in, her intercom goes off. She scrabbles to pause the music and check her room for incriminating evidence, then almost trips over a pair of shoes on the way to answer it.

It's Abby.

Shit.

She forgot: she has one last obligation to discharge before things are genuinely back to normal.

"Chrissy!" Abby hisses, as soon as the door closes behind her. She wastes no time: "What did you find out about Stefan?"

"Okay," Christine says, bouncing back onto the bed, "I have *so* much to tell you. But I might be getting a little manic from fatigue? If I get weird, or fall asleep mid-sentence, just poke me."

Abby pokes her, but Christine's complaints fizzle out when she hands her a can of Red Bull. "I came prepared," Abby says.

"God," Christine says, downing half the can and deciding that with its help she can probably hold off unconsciousness for another hour or two, "thank you. Are you ready for something really complicated and *really* weird?"

Abby nods, sitting down on the chair she dragged over from Christine's desk. "I came back to Dorley Hall. I *live* for complicated and weird."

Christine belches, and grins at Abby's mock-censorious eyeroll. She's the only one here who doesn't try particularly hard to get her to be more ladylike. "I thought you came back here so you wouldn't have to pay rent?"

"I can have more than one reason. So? What's going on with Stefan?"

Christine launches into the story she agreed with Stef. Helpfully for her tired mind, it's very close to the truth. Stef didn't want Melissa's best friend thinking ill of him, and Christine assured him that she was trustworthy. They did, however, alter certain details so Christine doesn't come off—in Stef's words—like a psychopath. "He's *not* a bad guy. Not Dorley material at all. No history of violence. No antisocial behaviour. He's not here because he's a bastard, Abs. In fact, you were right: you said it was our fault he ended up here, and it kind of is. Because, years after Melissa vanished, he *saw* her."

"He *saw* her?"

"Yeah."

"He saw *her?*"

"Yeah." Christine smiles. "They were buying groceries at the same time. And, uh, that's probably something we should be more careful about in the future? Just passing that up the chain."

"I mean, it's kind of a unique set of circumstances. Do you know *when* he saw her? What year?"

"Uh, yeah. About…two, no, three-ish months into her second year. Would've been early 2014."

"Well then," Abby says, crossing her arms, "she was only half-done with transition. *And* Stefan knew her basically all his life, and lived close enough to randomly bump into her. *And* she looks more like her old self than most of us because she barely had to get any work done. She was always beautiful, even before." Abby coughs and looks away from Christine. "So, uh, it's a perfect storm, really," she continues briskly. "We'll just be more careful when the girl is local. I don't even know if it's ever happened before, actually. I should check—"

"Can I finish my story?"

"Oh. Yes. Sorry." Abby taps her temple. "Work mode."

"You're not even a sponsor anymore," Christine says, to be pedantic.

"It's the sponsor brainworms," Abby says. "There's no cure."

Christine pats her on the back of the hand. "Poor thing."

Pushing her away, Abby says, "I thought you wanted to finish your story?"

"*Fine,*" Christine says. "Okay, so they recognise each other. And they both *know* they recognise each other. She tries to play it off like she's someone else. That she's just related, or something, but she knows his name. And that sort of clinches it. He starts researching us."

"Us?"

"Us. And he's, what, fifteen at the time, so this is early work, but he's a precocious brat."

"Brat?" Abby says. "Isn't he your age?"

Christine shrugs. "Yeah, I guess, but, like, I'm almost done with the programme and he's just starting. It's weird to think that we're both twenty-one. Anyway. Stop interrupting me!" She swats at her Sister.

"You interrupted yourself!"

"Then stop encouraging me!" she says, laughing and belching again.

"God, Chrissy, you're so feminine."

"I know. I'm an example to the other girls. Okay. Right." Christine closes her eyes for a moment. Tamps down on the hysteria that's been building inside her. Too much Red Bull. She finishes the can anyway. "So he researches us. Figures out we have kind of a vanishing problem here at Saints. Thinks maybe Melissa disappearing wasn't just some fluke accident, maybe it's part of a pattern. Yes, I know, we don't exactly come off as a competent operation in this story. I can see on your face that you want to say something, but don't, because I'm not done. He looks into Saints, picks the degree he thinks he's most likely to make the entry requirements for, and studies his arse off. And he gets in! Starts attending classes, starts looking for Melissa. It takes him a long time to narrow it down to Dorley, though, so, you know, we're not *that* sloppy."

"All the same…" Abby says, knotting her eyebrows. "I think I might tag Maria at the weekend and review some procedures."

"Good idea. So now he knows about Dorley—not all the facts, but enough that we're his natural focus—and he goes looking for help on the Dark Web." Christine resists the urge to wiggle her fingers in a spooky fashion. Invoking the sinister "dark web" had been her suggestion. Stef's original idea had been, "I don't know, Bitcoins or something." "He finds a hacker, they doctor his records so he looks shady as fuck, and he stages an incident. Below Pippa's window, it turns out! And voilà; he's inside and ready to start investigating this place, looking for Melissa. But—"

"But she's not here!" Abby finishes. "Is all this really true?"

"As far as I can tell," Christine says. "I checked up on his Dark Web stuff. It looks legit."

"So he's stuck here. Oh, God, Chrissy, we've got to get him out!"

"Yeah, that's what *I* said. But—" Christine pauses for effect, "—he wants to stay."

"*What?!*"

"That's *also* what I said. He's trans, Abby."

Abby almost hiccups. "*Really?*"

"Yeah. He's a trans woman. He hasn't been able to transition yet because he says he needs FFS and all that stuff and he's too broke even to buy hormones. He's desperate and actually kind of pissy about how we have all this money that we very deliberately don't use on trans people except, you know, accidentally. And he has a point, there, Abs." She has to admit, he took the words, had she ever had the courage to put them to Aunt Bea, right out of her mouth. Since Vicky started dating Lorna, it's rankled that all their resources remain pointed stubbornly basementwards. "He wants to game the system. He'll pretend to be like, well, *us*, at least until he's gotten everything he needs."

"That's crazy," Abby says.

"I thought so, too. But he really, genuinely believes he has no other option, and I've argued with him for ages about it and not changed his mind. He won't let me take him out of here—he threatened to scream—so what choice do we have? We either tell Aunt Bea, or we don't. And, Abby, I'm a bit scared of what Aunt Bea might do if we tell her."

"You don't think she'd wash him out, do you?"

"I don't know that she *wouldn't.* You know what she's like, Abs. I know you're closer to her than I am, but—"

"No," Abby says, "no, you're right. I don't *think* she would, but I don't know it, either."

"So we stay quiet?"

"We stay quiet."

"I mean," Christine says, tapping her nails on the empty can, "ultimately, it's his risk to take. All we have to do is pretend we don't know anything."

"God, this is fucked up."

"I know."

"He really can't transition away from this place?"

"I went through it with him," Christine says. "Numbers and everything. Honestly? I think he's right. It sucks, but he's right. Or right enough, anyway. You know how long Vicky's girlfriend's been on the waiting list?"

Abby nods, and goes quiet for a moment. Taps her thumb on the crook of her elbow, thinking. Then she smiles. "At least he's going to get the care he needs. Even if it's not in an ideal form. And we can help him quietly, and— Wait! Shouldn't we be calling her, well, *her?*"

"He asked me not to. Had a whole thing about it, which I won't break your brain with. For now, he asked me not to change pronouns. He likes it when I call him Stef, though. Apparently it was what Melissa always called him."

"That's right," Abby says, frowning in concentration and whispering, "Not Stefan. Stef. Stef. Stef. Stef." She looks up, embarrassed. "Just making sure I don't get it wrong if we ever talk."

Christine giggles. "I remember you doing that with me."

"I did?"

"Yep. It was, like, a day or two after I moved up onto the first floor, and I was in the kitchen. Dira was supervising as I made breakfast, but got waylaid by a bunch of third-year girls and it was all really noisy and intimidating. I ended up just kind of huddled in the corner, feeling like one of the rabbits from *Watership Down* shortly before everything goes to shit. Then you came in and squatted down beside me, all, 'I don't think we've been introduced!' And you gave me your name like you'd never seen me before, so I gave you mine. You were the first person I told after

Paige and Vicky. And you talked to me, Abs. Kept me company for like an hour. Made me feel like I wasn't just some…some broken ex-boy." Christine reaches out a hand. Abby takes it and squeezes her fingers. "How are you always so sweet?"

Abby looks at her, very seriously. "I eat a lot of sugar."

The distance between them is suddenly too great, so Christine steps off the bed and pulls at Abby's hand. Abby joins her in the middle of the room and they embrace, arms locked around each other, Abby standing on tiptoes so she can rest her head on Christine's shoulder.

No-one ever really held her until she came here.

"Thank you," she whispers. "For everything."

"You're my sister," Abby replies, and stretches as far as she can so she can kiss Christine gently on the forehead. "I love you."

Christine steps away and wipes her face with her sleeve. "Love you too, Abs." She kisses Abby on the cheek and goes to sit down again. Abby takes a step forward, offers her arm as support until she's steady.

What was that about being indecently lucky?

"I meant to ask," Abby says, returning to her chair, "how did you talk to Stef?"

Too tired and too buzzed to make anything up, Christine says sheepishly, "I figured out how to hack the biometric locks a while ago. I waited until everyone was asleep and just visited him in his cell. Please don't be mad at me?"

"*What?*" Abby says, almost shouting. "Christine!" She flaps her hands for a second, momentarily too overcome to speak, and then leans forward and adds in a whisper, "That's *amazing!* What else can you do?"

7
Consensus

15 OCTOBER 2019 — TUESDAY

Dear Mum, Dad and Petra,

I know what follows might sound bad, so I'm telling you upfront: I'm okay. I'm BETTER than okay! Happier than I've been in YEARS. But my degree isn't working out, and I have to do something about it.

Things have been getting harder and harder for me. I know, I SHOULD have told you. But we haven't seen each other much, especially since you moved away. For a long time I blamed you, but if I'm honest with myself, it's MY fault. MY choice. I think I didn't want you to see me so unhappy. You know how I struggled after Mark disappeared, and from there things kept getting worse. I started having trouble concentrating. I lost my motivation. I spent more and more time on my own.

After he was gone, I threw myself into my education. And that, I've only just realised, was the WRONG choice. I know my third year of uni is a BIT late to realise this, but at least I'm finally THINKING! It's not even that I don't like my degree. I do. But I'm burned out. I've been working hard for so many years that I don't have any hard work left in me. I need a break.

So I'm taking one.

I've had to do resits but never actually had to repeat a year, so if I suspend my studies now, I can still access student loans when I return. And yes, I said return. Because I'm going on a trip.

I'm getting out of the country for a while. A year. Maybe two. I'm going TRAVELLING! I want to see Spain, Italy and Turkey. Maybe I'll stay on somewhere, maybe I'll keep going. I haven't decided yet.

I won't be taking my phone. I haven't been able to afford credit for the thing for a while now, anyway.

As soon as I made this decision it felt like a weight I've been carrying for years just fell off my shoulders. I feel hopeful for the first time in a long time!

I have a chance to find the real me.

This is goodbye for a little while. But NOT forever. When I come back—and I will—I hope to be someone you can be proud of.

Petra, I love you SO much. I've seen your music in the videos Mum sent. You're SO good! You inspire me, and not getting to see you for a while is the only dark cloud on my horizon. I'll write again in a little while and tell you EVERYTHING I've been up to. Keep practising your trombone, work hard (but not too hard) at school, and we'll see each other again before you know it.

All my love,

Stefan.

"Happier than you've been in years?" Pippa had said when she read it back.

He'd shrugged. "I'm selling it. They have to believe I'm serious, right? And, look, about Petra, I've said I'll write. Can we do that? Every few months? Just so she doesn't worry."

"I don't see why not," Pippa said. "If you behave." The whole time they'd been going over the letter she hadn't looked at him much. Seemed more interested in playing with her bracelet. A nervous tic?

"If you let me write to her," Stefan replied, "I'll do whatever you ask."

Her little smile had been unmissable.

She left him alone after that. Said dinner would be delivered to him later, and suggested he use the time until then to get acclimatised to his new room. Stefan had been surprised to be left alone again so soon, but it makes sense: if the programme is about gradually eroding his supposed masculinity with a mix of hormones and manipulation—and surgery, eventually!—then it can't be antagonism all the time. He needs time to stew, to catastrophise. He wonders how the others reacted at this point; taken from a bare cell to a fully furnished room, shown the washing facilities and the limited entertainment options. It must have dawned on them that they're in for a *long* stay. Away from friends and family. Away from the sun. No control over your meals, or your movements. Locks on every door. Handcuffs under your bed.

None of them seem to have even the slightest idea what's actually going on here. The weirdo who thinks it's demons is probably closest. When it finally becomes clear, how will they react? It seems suddenly like something he needs to know; if Stefan's going to get through this, it's his fellow inmates he's going to need to understand and predict, not Pippa.

God, Pippa. Who did she used to be? He's given up questioning that every woman he's seen since waking up in his cell has gone through the whole process themselves. Now he's more interested in how they feel about it, having "graduated". Christine is *fiercely* defensive of her gender. Proud of it! How does Pippa feel about hers? Does she truly not resent being grabbed off the street and forcibly remade? Christine said they get orchiectomies after six months. For someone who doesn't want it, that's mutilation! Did Pippa wake up one morning, slowly come to understand that something was terribly wrong, and start grabbing in pain and fear at her—

No. Horrible thought. Abandon it.

He had laughed at Will. It doesn't seem so funny anymore: they're going to castrate him. First chemically, which is reversible, then with a scalpel.

Stefan balls up the duvet cover in his hands. He has to stop worrying about what happens to these people because not only is he powerless to stop it, he's not sure that he would if he could. Wife beaters, drunk drivers, misogynists. *Bad* men. Bad, at least, for now. Because that's the other thing: believing Christine means believing that most of the men down here will eventually come to embrace the new lives that are going to be forced on them. They'll be rehabilitated. Christine insisted that was the purpose of this place: bad men, made better. She's ashamed of having been like them, once. Both her womanhood and her contempt for her old self, whoever he was, make a compelling argument that the programme works.

Except for the washouts. But, from the point of view of this Aunt Bea person—definitely the sort of name you'd adopt if you had a basement full of kidnapped men and wanted to add an air of respectability to the whole deal, while remaining comfortably anonymous—the washouts are probably a key part of the plan. You take X bad men, you put them through the wringer, and by the end of the programme you have (X minus Y) women, reformed and ready to start new lives, where Y represents the men too bad, too stubborn, too inflexible to change. However large a number Y is, you've still removed X bad men from the world. Win-win.

Forget the morals for now. He can always blow the whistle on this place when he's free, assuming he can find a way to do so without endangering Christine or Melissa. Or Pippa. Or any of the other graduates, probably.

God, will he even want to, when he leaves? Will this place change him like it changed Christine? Will he leave not only as a woman but as a true believer?

"Shut up," he hisses to himself.

If the point of leaving him alone in his room is to make him spiral, then he's right on schedule. Time for a distraction.

He takes inventory, which didn't pass much time when he was in his cell, but there's considerably more stuff here. The room is unglamorous but comfortable. The wardrobe, which Stefan half-expected to be full of dresses, is mostly empty, with a few sets of near-identical outfits: hoodies, t-shirts, jogging trousers, socks, in a handful of neutral shades. The shelves on the wall and the drawer in the bedside table are empty, and the vanity contains only a plastic hairbrush and his wash kit. There's a small cabinet set into the wall by the door. There's a small green light beside it, which Stefan correctly surmises means it's unlocked. On opening, he finds a box of cereal bars and a large water bottle. It rocks slightly under his touch as he removes the food, and he updates his assessment: it's a dumbwaiter.

There's even a rug on the floor between the vanity and the bed, and its slightly rubbery finish suggests it'll make a serviceable yoga mat.

He laughs, remembering the look on Pippa's face when he said this room was considerably nicer than his house-share.

He fetches down the water bottle and a cereal bar, pulls the wooden chair over from the vanity to the metal desk, and starts investigating the computer. There's a shortcut on the desktop labelled *Message Sponsor,* which loads a chat interface called Consensus. He can customise his name so he deletes the last two letters before he tries sending a message.

Stef
just checking to see if this does what I think it does

Pippa
Yes. It does.
Another privilege. It will be taken away if you abuse it.

Stef
define abuse please
is asking for things or making suggestions abuse?

Pippa
Abuse means if you use it to be rude to me.
I am also free to ignore you. You are not the only thing in my life.

Stef
naturally
I had a suggestion, if it's okay
to do with my "going travelling"

Pippa
Okay?

Stef
I assume you have my debit card
since I had it on me when you brought me in
disappearing like this, so suddenly, leaves my housemates without help with the rent
my last pay from work will come in this friday
my pin is in my wallet
when my pay comes in, can you take everything out of my account and put it in the letter for my housemates?
it won't cover everything but it's better than nothing
it means holding onto the letters for a few days but I think that's probably okay?

Pippa
Yes.
That's fine.
What about the stuff in your old room? While we're thinking about your housemates.

Stef
it came furnished
there's very little in there that's mine
just my garbage old laptop and my clothes
they can keep the laptop if they need it
and donate the clothes I guess

Pippa
We'll take them all, actually. To support your story.
We'll do it on Friday. Empty your account and leave the letter with the money on your bed.

Stef
how can you do that?
oh I suppose you have my keys too

Pippa
Of course.

Stef
fyi the front door key is the one on the frog keychain
you might have to jiggle it a bit
and my door is the elephant one
could you keep the keychains somewhere for me?

Pippa
Why?

Stef
presents from my sister
I don't care about any of my other stuff
but if you could find a shelf for them or something

Pippa
I'll keep hold of them.
For now.

Stef
if I'm good, right?

Pippa
Right.

Stef
I'll be good

Pippa
We'll see.
Do you have any other questions? I have notes to write up.

Stef
oh cool, what are you studying?
wait
never mind
sorry
no more questions
thanks

Pippa
Good afternoon, Stefan.

"Idiot," he tells himself, as Pippa's icon switches to idle. "Stop trying to be her friend."

In search of further distractions, he browses through the directories on the PC, finding TV shows and movies (mostly romantic comedies), a large library of books (also mostly romances) and a handful of games: *Stardew Valley, The Sims, Tetris,* that sort of thing. Absorbing and, unless there's something about *The Sims* he doesn't know, largely nonviolent titles. The music folder is mostly women artists, biased towards pop, and everything bar the games seems to be accessible through the phone.

He finds a pair of chunky, weathered headphones on an extremely long cable and plugs them into the PC, picks out a movie at random, and settles down on the bed.

* * *

There's a kitchen on every floor at Dorley, bar the first: the second-year girls who live on the first floor are confined to a self-contained dorm-within-a-dorm, behind heavier locks than anywhere else above the basement, and are expected to use the ground floor facilities under supervision. The kitchen on the second floor—a short walk around the U-shaped corridor from Christine's room—is particularly nice and has many advantages: low traffic, minimal chance of an Aunt Bea sighting, plenty of Weetabix and a nice view out into the woods. What it doesn't have is a surfeit of leftovers, which is why Christine finds herself once again pushing aside the double doors into the ground floor kitchen on the hunt for something to heat up.

It feels like she's spent more time here in the past week than she did in her entire second year. Still, with all her obligations discharged and Stef apparently settling nicely into his room, Christine will have time to do her own shopping again, and go back to preparing her cheap little meals for one in the blessed almost-solitude of the second floor.

It's quiet down in the main kitchen for once. There's only Maria, eating dinner at the big table and leafing through a binder, and some faint conversational sounds from the dining hall next door. Christine realises as she relaxes that she'd been hunching her shoulders, and smiles sheepishly in Maria's direction. Maria answers with a pinkie wave, so she doesn't have to put down her fork.

"There's salad," Maria says, "and this sort of mushroom pie thing that I'm having, which is pretty good. And something with beef I'm not sure I can recommend."

"Thanks, Maria."

Christine's still got her head in the fridge when someone grabs her from behind and hugs her hard enough to lift her slightly off the floor.

"Hi, Dira," she wheezes, when her sponsor Sister puts her down again.

"Hi, Teenie!" Indira says, taking Christine gently by the shoulders and turning her around. "Sweetheart!" she exclaims, when she gets a proper look. "When's the last time you had any sleep?"

In Christine's head, the guy from *The Office* wipes the number clean from a whiteboard that says, *Number of hours since someone told me I look like shit.*

She submits to the follow-up hug. "Last night," she says, "but I don't think it counted. It was like four hours. I have big plans for tonight, though." She pulls away from Dira's hug and smiles at her. "Big plans."

"Cancel them," says Paige, marching in from the dining hall and almost running up to Christine and Indira. She sings, "We got per-miss-ion!"

"Permission for what?"

"Aunt Bea said we can take you off-campus tonight," Indira says, shutting the fridge and offering a steadying arm to Christine, who evidently looks like she might fall over at any moment.

"Off-campus?" Christine says, allowing herself to be steadied. Indira guides Christine's bottom gently towards the kitchen table, where it parks itself without Christine's conscious attention. "Where?"

Off-campus means being out among people who don't know who she used to be, and who won't be minded to grant her any slack.

"Don't worry, Teenie," Indira says, tucking back a stray lock of Christine's hair. "We're going with Vicky and Lorna and some of their friends. You'll just be one of nine or ten girls; no-one will look at you twice."

"Thanks a lot," Christine mutters.

"I mean," Paige says, grinning, well aware of Christine's ever-faltering confidence and having none of it, "if you *want* them to look at you, we can make it happen. Make you look *stunning!* You'll have to beat the boys off with a stick."

"That's Maria's job!" Indira giggles. Maria, who up to this point has been ignoring the commotion, laughs and nearly chokes on a mushroom.

"I don't want that," Christine whispers, stiffening up, half-wondering if she's going to leave fingerprints embedded in the kitchen table.

"But you're so pretty, Christine!" Paige insists. "You could be gorgeous if you just let me at you."

"I did let you!" Christine says, unwilling to give Paige any slack. "Just last week!"

"And you looked great." Paige takes the victory and presses home her advantage. "You even pulled! What happened to that boy, anyway?"

"Oh, uh," Christine stammers. Stalling, but also panicking. Idiot. Why bring up the party where she met Stef? She doesn't want *anyone* thinking about that. "I kissed him, I sent him home. He was nice, but I'm not really ready for boys, you know?" *Please don't remember him, please don't remember him!*

"Wait," Dira says, "she *pulled?* A real-life *boy?* Tell me *everything!*"

"There was a party on Saturday," Paige enthuses, interpreting Christine's silence as permission to just bloody well spill everything, "in that new dorm building. Just a little thing; some people from the SU set it up. And you *know* I've been trying to get her to come out with me since forever."

It's true. Paige, social butterfly, has been cursed to be friends with Christine, the social equivalent of one of those burrowing creatures who only show up after midnight to eat the grubs the above-ground varmints don't want. She persists in trying to drag Christine out of the dorm anyway. Probably because the only other options on their floor are all non-starters. Jodie, who dresses like Morticia Addams and who Christine only sees when she happens to catch her livestreamed *World of Darkness* games, has never willingly opened her door to Paige lest she be forcibly de-gothed. Vicky is already stunning, sociable, and capable of dressing herself and doesn't technically live at Dorley anymore. And Julia and Yasmin are both already trying to put their time in the programme behind them, having found jobs instead of returning to classes. Once they've been officially released, Christine expects never to hear from them again.

"What did she wear?" Indira asks Paige, fully aware that Christine would prefer to die of anxiety or embarrassment than engage seriously with the question.

"I had a box come in from that place I was telling you about, and they had this *beautiful* scoop-neck brown top—I know, brown, but it was broken up with an off-white floral pattern that was just *gorgeous*—" Paige makes gestures around her chest to indicate that that wasn't the only reason she liked the top; she has an obsession with getting Christine to show off her breasts, for some reason, "—so I put her in that with some Converse and a lovely loose cardigan in the same shade as that old skirt I've been carrying around with me since forever, you know the one, and I did her hair and face. Hang on; I have pictures."

Christine leans heavily on the table as Paige scrolls through her phone for a delighted Indira. She knows the pictures Paige will be swiping through for Indira, because Paige begged for permission to put them on her Insta and looked tremendously put out when she refused.

Christine did get copies, though. Proof that she really can look good, when someone *else* tries.

"Teenie," Indira says, "you look *fantastic.* You should dress up more often."

Christine, wearing shorts, vest and shirt, nods silently. She's not wrong. It's just that when she applies makeup, everything looks too bold, and when she chooses clothes, everything looks too showy. Trying to be beautiful and getting it wrong is so much more frightening than just throwing on a hoodie and putting up with the occasional boy asking her if she has a skateboard.

"Tell her about the *boy,*" Paige says, dragging Christine back into the conversation after a few more excitable back-and-forths with Dira.

Oh, well. At least she can drop some misinformation. "He was, um, tall," she says. "Blonde. White. I liked his glasses."

"And she talked to him *all night,*" Paige adds triumphantly, apparently not realising that of all the attributes Christine supplied, only his skin colour was correct. Stef's shorter than Christine, doesn't wear glasses, and is strikingly ginger. Christine wonders if she should have given decoy-Stef a beard. Perhaps an eye patch or a pirate's hat. It's not that Paige is actually *likely* to remember the face of the boy Christine kissed at the party, or connect him to the trans girl currently making terrifying decisions in their basement, but you never know.

"You kissed, right?" Indira asks, and as much as Christine loves her, she wants to look away because she knows the next thing she says will put Indira's energy level through the roof.

"A bit," she admits, and tries not to grimace when Indira squeals and hugs her again. Ever since Dira started seeing her childhood friend Hasan, she's been romance crazy, and desperate to start matchmaking for Christine. Christine doesn't see what the rush is; she's only been a woman for a year, and has spent most of that time inside. "He, um, didn't really do anything for me," she adds, silently apologising to Stef.

"You think maybe you might want to meet a girl instead?" Indira asks.

"I don't know yet," Christine says with a shrug.

"Then that's *exactly* why it's good that you're coming out tonight," Paige says. "You're going to have fun with your friends—" she points an aggressive finger at herself and Indira, and a questioning one at Maria, who shakes her head and points to the binder next to her plate, "—and you're going to dance with hot people and see if any of them float your boat."

Christine declines to comment on the state of her boat and whether it is capable of floating. She has more pressing things to worry about: "What if they, you know, *know?*"

Paige rolls her eyes. Indira performs an exaggerated gasp. Maria puts down her fork, swallows, and says, slowly and patiently, "Christine, you could strip down to your underwear in front of anyone you care to name, and they wouldn't 'know' anything. You have nothing to worry about."

"They'd know you're beautiful," Indira insists, stroking Christine's temple, "and sweet, and kind, and intelligent, and—"

"They'll know all that just from seeing me naked?" Christine says. Dira frowns at her; she's told her off before for masking insecurity with bad jokes.

"Okay," Paige says, "then they're going to know you have killer tits." She bites the tip of her tongue at Christine.

Indira's eyes flicker to the entrance from the dining hall and Christine turns her head in time to see Aunt Bea step delicately inside, presumably to find out what all the noise is about.

"Aunt Bea!" Christine says, as a desperate last resort. "Help! They're being mean to me!" Maybe she can still get washed out.

"Oh?" she says, packing a great deal of scepticism into a single syllable.

Indira leans on one of Christine's shoulders, Paige the other. They both smile ingratiatingly at Aunt Bea. "We're being very nice to her," Paige says, "and paying her lots of compliments."

At the table, mouth full, Maria silently nods. Aunt Bea's face assumes the pinched expression it often acquires when her charges are being playful: like she can't quite believe her girls are so carefree; like she's proud that they are.

Either that, Christine thinks, *or she's just going to the mental place boomers go when the kids are having too much fun.*

"You're going out tonight, I understand," Aunt Bea says.

"We are," Indira says.

"Take care of each other, then."

"We will."

With a satisfied nod, Aunt Bea returns to whatever she's up to in the dining hall; paperwork, probably. She doesn't like to eat in her office, and doesn't stop working ever. Some of the still-new second-year girls are probably also being supervised alongside her. Her dislike of boys seems to extend to avoiding them as much as possible until they have become girls—nominally, in the case of the new second years—but once they are, she likes to be involved.

"See?" Indira says. "Official seal of approval."

"I'm doomed, aren't I?"

"Yes," Paige says, pulling on Christine's wrist. "Now come upstairs and we'll help you make yourself all pretty again."

***

However soundproofed the basement is from the outside, the walls between the bedrooms are obviously thinner: when Stefan removes his headphones after a marathon of honestly quite entertaining Meg Ryan movies he hears thumping from next door. Someone hitting the wall in the bedroom next to his. It's faint, but just about audible.

Intrigued, he puts his ear to the wall and listens. The thumps pause after a few more seconds and then, at the very edge of legibility, a ragged voice practically screams, "You won't keep me down here forever, you fuckers! You can't cage me! I'll get you! I'll get all of you!"

Optimistic.

It must be disorientating, to be stuck down here for weeks and still not know what's going on. Stefan can't find it in himself to sympathise with the guy, but he'd like to know who's in the room next door so he knows under which name he can add *impromptu outbursts* to the notes he's assembling on his fellow basement dwellers. His information is currently very thin.

He slips his headphones back on, leans over to the computer, and cues up another movie, starting something called *The Princess Switch.*

It feels indecent to be so relaxed, and not just because of the commotion next door. Christine talked this place up as a house of horrors! And for her it undoubtedly was. But for Stefan, the pressure's off. No more testosterone. No more trying to remain conscious in a lecture the morning after a late shift at work. No more work! No more bills. Sure, there are downsides, like the total lack of freedom, but Stefan's never felt all that free, anyway.

Barely ten minutes into the movie—a second Vanessa Hudgens has just entered the frame, which is probably the most exciting thing that's going to happen to Stefan for the rest of the day, unless the magical old man who is definitely not Santa shows up again—it pauses and minimises itself, revealing a pulsing chat icon.

New User 63
Hello, Stef?

Stef
who is this please
?

New User 63
It should say.
Oh.
Drat.
Sorry.
Christine set this up for me.

Stef
You know Christine?

New User 63
Yes.
Hold on, I think I've worked this out.

> **New User 63** has changed her name to **Abby**.

Abby
How's that? 😀

Stef
abby, hi
aren't you the girl in the pictures with melissa?
oh shit should we even be talking about that on here

Abby
Christine says we won't leave logs, and neither of the cameras in your room are angled so they can see the screen. So as long as you close the chat window when we're done, you're fine. You can say whatever you want.

Stef
there are cameras in here?

Abby
There are cameras everywhere. It's kind of our thing. In your room, there's one over the door and another over the wardrobe, pointing down towards the bed.

Stef
I can't see them
I believe you though
so that was you in the pictures?

Abby
Which pictures?

Stef
the photobooth

Abby
Oh! I know the ones. 😋
That's me, yes. I went to see her back in August.

Stef
where does she live?
what does she do?

Abby
Questions I can't answer, I'm afraid. Not without her permission.
And Christine has persuaded me that it would not be wise to bring her up to speed just yet.
Two of us knowing is enough.
Plus, she would come racing back here and demand to see you and probably blow the whole thing. Liss is many things, but sneaky is not one of them.

Stef
she'd really come straight here just for me?
she still cares about me?

Abby
She thinks the WORLD of you.
You were always the boy who could do anything if you would just put your mind to it.
Oh. Sorry.

Stef
don't worry about it
up until recently I was a boy
still am one now
kind of
not really?
it's difficult to talk about
I wasn't exactly an egg but I was in deep denial

Abby
Christine told me some of it.
I'm so sorry this place seems like your only option.

Stef
hey it doesn't seem all that bad so far
getting yelled at and stuck in a building with people I hate
it's like being at work
except you guys are going to pay me in
idk
tits and orchiectomies instead of not enough money

Abby
Christine told you about the orchi???

Stef
yeah
but I mean
I'm fine with it
I want it

Abby
Ah. Yes. True.
Sorry. It's throwing me for a loop. I've been here a while, and my expectations for what someone so early in the programme will be like are fairly well established.

Stef
christine said something similar
and hey if you want your expectations satisfied the guy next door to me was banging on the walls and screaming just a few minutes ago
so
you know
you can be reassured you girls are still scaring the living shit out of people

Abby
Cool!

Stef
I don't suppose you have any suggestions for speeding up the whole process though
like somehow getting pippa to arrange my orchi for next week or something?

Abby
Not without tipping your hand, no.
And that would be a very bad idea.😯

Stef
maybe I could give her the idea subliminally
adopt a very orchiable pose every time I see her
like sit on the edge of the bed with my legs apart
no
actually, that could work
it'd look like manspreading
I bet that's a dorley no-no
do you punish manspreading here?

Abby
It's not a primary objective, no.

Stef
you could probably go viral if you did

Abby
I hope you're not this cheeky with Pippa.

Stef
don't worry, when I'm around her and those guys it's not too hard to act appropriately intimidated
especially when I'm around those guys, jesus
they made me want to have a shower more than going a bunch of days without having a shower made me want to have a shower

Abby
The other boys are going to be a problem for you, you know.
Shit. Sorry. Not the "other" boys.

Stef
seriously don't worry about it
I know I'm sequence breaking here
glitching through the floor and skipping straight to the lava temple

Abby
I have absolutely no idea what that means. 😅

Stef
ask christine
she said it to me in the first place

Abby
I mean it, though. Watch out for the men down there.
Not everyone reacts the same way to the programme but violent outbursts are common, especially early on. In theory, the girls will protect you, and we have two professionals on standby at all times. In practice, someone could come at you in the shower, or simply on the other side of the common area if they don't care about getting tased immediately after, and no-one could get to you in time.
We've never had anyone die that way, to the best of my knowledge, but we've had some bad moments.
As distasteful as I know it must seem right now, I suggest you make a friend.

Stef
I really don't want to

Abby
I know.

Stef
they're all complete arseholes

Abby
They won't be forever.

Stef
how do you know??

Abby
I was like them, once.

Stef
see, you and christine keep saying stuff like that and as hard as I try I can't imagine it

Abby
Well, I'm glad about that.😘

Stef
she's been so kind to me

Abby
I'm glad about that, too!
Instead of trying to imagine us when we were more like the boys out there, you should think of us as proof that change IS possible.
And that not everyone out there will be an arsehole forever.

Stef
unless they wash out I suppose

Abby
True. Best hope none of them do.

Stef
honestly abby right now I hope all of them do
I can't imagine willingly spending time with any of them
how am I supposed to pick the least objectionable prick from a basement of objectionable pricks?

Abby
Then perhaps you should pick the one least likely to do you personal harm.
I looked over the reports on these boys, and I suggest Aaron.

Stef
aaron?
that little shit?

Abby
I know. He's abrasive, misogynistic, self-obsessed and practically an incel. But he has no history of physical violence. And if you stick with him, well, two targets are a lot less appealing than one, to the bully looking for an outlet.

Stef
I'll think about it

Abby
I should go soon, but do I have your permission to contact you again? I admit, I'm quite curious about Melissa's Stef.

Stef
go ahead
I'm not going anywhere
I want to talk to you about melissa too
I understand you're limited in what you can say but I miss her so much

Abby
I will answer any questions to the best of my ability. 😌
Be safe, Stef.

> **Abby** has signed off.

* * *

The explosion of noise from Indira when they open the door to Christine's dorm room and find Abby sitting cross-legged on the bed, futzing on a laptop, has the same effect on Christine's limbic system as a tin of Red Bull and a kick in her sensitive parts. Indira, it turns out, missed Abby.

The two of them exchange hugs, greetings, and gossip about Dira's boyfriend and Abby's still unfortunately tragic love life while Christine balances herself carefully against the headboard to check the laptop screen and make sure Abby closed the chat app. Relief: yes, she did. Abby throws her a smile and a wink when Dira temporarily diverts her attention to pulling something out of her bag, and Christine lets some of her tension earth itself in the bedsheets.

Either their conversation diminishes in volume or some of Christine's senses check out for a while from exhaustion, because she manages to get in six whole minutes of something almost like sleep before Paige comes piling in with an armful of clothes and a determined expression.

"Okay, girlie," she says, when Christine has been successfully roused, "get up and let's make you look gorgeous."

"I thought I could just go, you know, as I am," Christine says. "Girls wear shorts to clubs, right?"

"Not like those," Dira says, laughing and trying to poke Christine in the thigh.

"Christine," Paige says, marshalling all of her six feet of height to look as unstoppable as possible, and borrowing Aunt Bea's diction, "you are a beautiful young woman and I will *not* have you slobbing around in shorts for the rest of your life."

"What if we make a deal?" Christine says. "I start wearing dresses again when I'm thirty?"

"No."

"Just give me nine more years."

"Absolutely not."

"Christine," Indira says in her "sponsor" voice, which Christine's always thought makes her sound like the beleaguered oldest sister in a certain kind of family sitcom, "Aunt Bea's noticed the way you've been dressing."

Christine's fingers twitch. She couldn't have mentioned this before? "Shit," she says. "What did she say, exactly?"

"She reminded me," Indira says, rolling over on the bed so she can be closer to Christine, "that the freedoms granted to third years are conditional on their 'continued feminine development'. I'm sorry, sweetheart; I was trying to be quietly encouraging—you know, positive reinforcement, carrot instead of stick and all that—but it's time."

Christine decides her brain needs a jump-start, or possibly to be jolted right out of her skull, so she bangs the back of her head on the bed frame a few times. "Shit," she hisses, in percussive accompaniment. "Shit, shit, shit."

"Oh, Teenie, no," Indira says, and immediately starts gently stroking the back of Christine's head, "you don't need to worry *too* much. She's not mad. She's not intervening. She's just…paying attention. She's still leaving it up to me, for now. But she *did* like the idea of you coming out tonight."

Christine attempts a smile, but it doesn't come out quite right, so she shuffles up on the bed and gathers her knees under her chin. Sometimes the impulse to take up as little space as possible is too strong. "I just want to be *done*, Dira," she says.

"I know, sweetheart, I know."

"I don't see what's wrong with me right now."

"I know."

Paige sits back heavily on the bean bag chair. "You know what you have to do, then," she says. "You suck it up."

"Paige," Indira says sharply.

"I get it," Paige says. "You want to be done, yesterday. And all of this? Aunt Bea's expectations? Everything? It's hard. I *get* it. You just want to be *you*, right? Then *this* is what you have to do." She leans over and lifts Christine's all-but-abandoned makeup box up off her desk. "This—" she taps the box with an impeccably manicured nail, "—is the last wall you have to climb. The final class. *Advanced Woman in the Modern Age.* Makeup and nice clothes and smiling and looking pretty and going out and meeting boys. And doing it all *yourself.* You had Indira and Abby and Vicky and me to help you out with it last year, but ever since we stopped, you've given up. And that's bullshit, Christine. Because you *know* you've got to learn this stuff. And don't—" she points, sensing Christine's imminent objections, "—give me all that shit about how this isn't how girls have to be. No-one knows that better than me." Christine doesn't miss Paige's wince, quickly hidden though it is, and remembers what happened at the end of their second year in the programme. Paige thought she'd changed enough. Thought she was ready. Rebelled against Aunt Bea's requirements. It got her locked in her room for over a week. Privileges revoked. Freedoms curtailed. Almost like being back in that cell again; almost like she hadn't changed at all. "You don't have to agree with Aunt Bea to understand her point of view," she adds, "although lately I have to admit, I've come around on it."

Of course you have, Christine thinks sourly. *Instagram queen.*

Immediately she's glad she didn't say that out loud. It's unfair. She, Paige and Jodie talked with each other about the restrictions imposed on their presentation, but only Paige was brave enough to take it to Aunt Bea. Later, Christine learned from Abby that something similar happens every year. All of them making the same mistakes. All of them walking in the groove their Sisters laid down in the years before them.

Dorley Hall has more powerful rituals than the Catholic church.

The logic of Aunt Bea's position is clear enough: she wants her girls to have access to all the skills they might need in their lives, not just the ones her charges happen to believe are relevant at the time; and she believes that because her girls were raised as boys—if *raised* is the term for the neglect many of them suffered—then the things that girls are taught as children must be learned *now,* with no exceptions.

And you can argue, as Paige has, that the expectation that girl children learn to dress in a feminine fashion, experiment with makeup, and so on, is sexist. Backwards. Slowly losing relevance. You can argue that many of those children hate it, are harmed by it. And you can find large numbers of children raised that way who are not girls at all, just as you can find many girls, cis and trans, who describe wholly different experiences. Surely, then, to become a girl, to become a woman in the modern age, should not require these things.

But Aunt Bea's girls will have *every* chance when they leave her care, because she is *not* sloppy with her rehabilitation. Her girls *will* know how to make themselves look feminine and beautiful even if, the very moment they leave, they decide to cut their hair short and wear only overalls. Her girls *will* understand the demands made of women, even if some of them come eventually to realise that they are not girls after all. Her girls will be in a position, when they graduate from the programme, to make the *choice.*

Christine had been surprised to learn that not every graduate remains a woman. Apparently none have ever become men again, but Abby said their graduate pool probably has a higher incidence of nonbinary people and non-gender-conforming women than almost any random, age-appropriate sampling of the greater population. And Aunt Bea, with every appearance of joy, welcomes those people back when they visit. Christine saw it at the holiday bash where she met Melissa: Aunt Bea, fearsome custodian of Dorley Hall, laughing with a nonbinary graduate, chatting with them about their job and their partner, and agreeing to wear a pronoun pin. Never once messing up using their new name. Never once misgendering them.

The hardest thing for Christine to grasp, when she remembers being locked in a cell, or waking up after her first surgery, or listening to Paige cry through a door she didn't dare unlock, is that Aunt Bea seems genuinely to care for all of them, in her way.

"Don't forget," Paige says, "the goal is to be yourself. *Fully* yourself, whoever that is. You've gotten rid of the armour—" that's always how Paige describes her former self: a scared child, clad in armour that was forced upon her, believing those who promised that it would make her invulnerable to pain or consequence, "—but you haven't yet explored who you are without it. You don't know what you can do, because you're still too scared to experiment."

"Paige—"

"This is me tough-loving you, Christine. Put on the fucking dress and come out with us."

Indira's holding Christine's hand, and she squeezes it as Paige finishes her speech. Christine tries to imagine a flow of energy between them, reinvigorating her just enough to say what she needs to say, because she's got to push back. Not against the clothes or the makeup, but the timing. She almost smiles at how mundane it is.

"I'm exhausted, Paige," she says. "I can't even describe how tired I am. I *want* to come out with you—" half a lie and half not; Christine really doesn't want to be a hermit forever, "—but I've had almost no sleep. Since, I think, Saturday? Can I come along next time, instead? I know it won't be such a big group, but it might actually be better for me if it's just us four and maybe Vicky and Lorna. Please? I'll dress up, I'll do my makeup. I promise. I just can't do it tonight."

Abby, still on the edge of the bed with her feet up on the hamper, meets her eyes. Christine tries to emphasise, in the moment of that brief connection, just how much she needs the rest.

"Dira," Abby says, "you've been away for a few days. You don't know what's been going on with her. I think it's just stress from classes—" *God bless you for lying for me, Abby,* Christine thinks, "—but you know how these things snowball. She had an evaluation with Aunt Bea—more stress—and it's all piled up. I think we should give her a break."

Indira, pulled between her responsibilities as sponsor and her affection for Christine, hesitates.

"I need a time-out, Dira," Christine says quietly.

"Are you sure?" she says, concern flooding her eyes.

"I'm sure."

Long ago, before Christine graduated to the second year. Before she was named, when first she flickered into life inside the spiteful, hurt boy who'd come to Dorley, Indira had sat her down on the bed in her awful little bedroom and laid it all out. Soon there would be no more concrete walls; no more communal bathroom; no more unwanted surgical interventions. Her first taste of freedom was coming. But it came with responsibilities, which must be lived up to. And when she outlined them and scared the nascent and still-to-be-named girl to the bone, Indira had moved right next to her on the bed and taken her hand, slowly and carefully so as not to scare her—because when she first arrived in the basement she flinched away from all contact—and had made her a promise:

I'm not just your sponsor anymore; I'm your Sister. If ever it gets too much, if you need a break, if complying with a request of mine will hurt you more than it will help you, and if you understand that there are expectations upon me to ensure your progress and commit to helping me fulfil them, then all you need to do is ask. Ask, and I will do everything I can to help you. If I have to, I will move this whole building to keep you safe.

"Then you're getting one," Indira says. "Paige, Abby, go meet with Vicky and have some fun. Christine and I will stay here—"

"No," Christine says, "I don't want to spoil your night. You only just got back today. You should have fun."

"I can have fun with you," she insists. "We can watch movies. You won't have to talk."

"I'll be fine. I promise. I'm just tired. So tired I can barely think. I need to switch off, hopefully sleep, and get ready for classes tomorrow."

Indira squeezes her hand again. "Okay, Teenie. You'll come with us next week?"

"I will."

"We'll all go out together."

"I'm looking forward to it."

"I'll talk to Aunt Bea."

"Thanks, Dira."

"Be kind to yourself, Christine," Indira says. A refrain as old as her name. Dira kisses her on the temple, pauses over her for a moment to stroke her cheek, then hops off the bed and silently gestures for Paige and Abby to follow. Abby offers a little wave on her way out; Paige mouths an apology. Christine smiles at all of them, watches as they close the door behind them, and rolls over into the warm spot Indira left behind. She buries her face in her pillow, and she lets go.

***

She's been meaning to come up here since she moved to the second floor and legitimately was granted the run of Dorley Hall and, in theory, the whole campus. It's been doable ever since she cracked Dorley's security, but the roof has only one exit, so it's not somewhere she ever wanted to get caught. Not unless she very quickly developed a talent for climbing down six storeys of vine trellis without breaking something, and even last year's Christine had better self-preservation instincts than to test that.

There are two other people on the far side of the roof—two women, presumably, given that it's Dorley (premier women's dormitory on campus, please don't ask about our wine cellar)—so Christine gives them their space. She settles for the observation bench at the front of the building, which affords a wonderful view of the university grounds in general and the Student Union Bar in particular, its village-pub frontage cast in rainbows from the garish cursive *Saints* sign on the roof. The neon lights of home.

Dorley Hall's roof is laid out a bit like a Zen garden—an unknowingly ironic reflection of its basement—but Christine has no idea if it's authentic or not. The central gravel square doesn't seem to have any intentionality to it, being that its contents escape its boundaries on all sides, and she remembers reading somewhere that real Zen gardens are supposed to reflect nature, which this one decidedly does not, so she settles on fake. There's a set of white plastic garden chairs scattered haphazardly in the middle, anyway. The gravel square isn't covered but does have four brick pillars at its corners, and Christine's heard that before the insurance got too expensive, they used to drape a tarp over them and host informal gatherings up here.

There's a wide pathway around the central square, in which lurks the occasional clump of potted plants, picnic tables, and benches, each dedicated to a famous or notable alumni, all facing outwards.

Indira says you can have a wonderful picnic up here in the summer.

Christine hopes Dira and the others are all having fun right now, dancing, drinking; she regrets missing out on the chance to see Vicky's girlfriend Lorna again. Partly because she's very sweet and partly because now Christine's taken responsibility for a trans girl of her own, she would love to ask Lorna a few discreet questions. Care and feeding, etc.

God, she wishes she was out there with them. Being normal. She pulls her hoodie tight, leans forward on the railing and stares out into the night.

She doesn't know why she isn't better at being a girl by now. There's nothing mechanically *hard* about applying makeup or wearing a dress, and goodness knows she's dressed up for parties and Dorley social events before. Almost her entire second year was spent prettied up at the hand of someone or other. And it's not that she's got any hang-ups left about participating in her own gradual transformation, either, because what was voice training if it wasn't Christine enthusiastically embracing her new self, and the things she was required to do?

The first two fingers on her right hand twitch, and she curls them into a fist to keep them still.

It's fear.

Well, no. Not precisely.

True, she has no confidence in her ability to make herself look feminine without the help of her Sisters, she remains steadfast in her belief that, left to her own devices and ordered to choose her own dress and makeup, she will render herself unavoidably clownish. Probably that's a large component of what Paige called the last wall she has to climb.

But it's not just that. It can't be.

Maybe she's just scared to let this place go. Becoming a free woman in the eyes of Dorley, in the eyes of Aunt Bea, means becoming a woman in the eyes of the world, too. And she wants that. God, she wants it! She stretches her left arm out in front of her, the sleeve of her hoodie pulled up, and smiles at the graceful fingers with the scrappily painted nails, at the beaded bracelet she made with Indira as part of a matched set, at the smooth skin that shines softly in the light of the stars and the Student Union's neon sign. She *made* this woman, from top to bottom, and she's proud of her. The world *should* get to meet her.

But she fears it, too. Because what if, without the looming presence of Dorley behind her, encouraging her—forcing her—to be and to remain the woman she's become, she loses her? What if her womanhood crumbles and Christine dies and that boy, that vicious, lonely, evil little *thing*, rises again in her place?

"You're being stupid, Christine," she whispers to herself.

Maybe she's just scared that without Dorley to tell her who she is, she won't know at all.

Makeup, clothes, and the lessons in feminine grace they were all subjected to: Paige likes to call them her tools. She didn't get all her tools from Dorley, she says, but Aunt Bea gave her a lot she didn't have before, had never even thought about acquiring. And you can't build yourself back up from nothing without access to *all* the tools available to you.

Put on the fucking dress, Christine.

"Hi," someone says. "Are you okay?"

Christine doesn't jump. It's the girls from earlier, and she smelled them coming. They've been smoking, and an ex-addict never gets fully desensitised. Can't sneak up on someone when you reek like yesterday's ashtray.

She sits back and smiles at them. "I'm okay," she says.

"It's just," the other one says, "we heard crying."

"I wasn't—" Christine starts, and then touches the back of a hand to her cheek. "Oh. Yeah. I was." Too tired even to spot emotions when she's having them; she's supposed to watch out for that. "Long day. Long week! Bad memories. I'm fine. I promise."

"Good," the shorter one says. She sits down on the bench next to Christine and pulls back her hood, revealing short black hair, golden brown skin and deep brown eyes. Christine can see the reflection of the neon pub sign in her irises. "I'm Naila and they're Ren." Naila smiles, the sort of beautiful, easy smile Christine always finds enviable.

"I'm Christine," she says, and because she didn't miss the pronoun Naila used for her friend, she adds, "she/her."

Naila's smile broadens. Ren, leaning their back against the railing, says, "I like your dress."

Christine had almost forgotten about it. Paige had left the pile of dresses behind when she left, likely hoping for Christine to try some of them on. Feeling guilty, Christine had rummaged through them, looking for something she liked and something she wouldn't feel too self-conscious in: a Venn diagram with a very small intersection. She chose one that falls to the mid-calf and doesn't show off too much skin, and then she put a hoodie on anyway and half-covered it up.

"Thanks," she says. "It's not mine. My friends were trying to get me to go out with them but…I just wasn't feeling up to it."

"They're in there?" Ren asks, nodding their head sideways at the bar in the distance.

"No. Somewhere in town. Paige thinks I need to meet boys for some reason."

"Oh!" Naila says. "You know Paige? From the second floor?"

"The floor with all those weird locks on the doors?" Ren says.

Christine's fingers twitch again. Idiot. Giving away too much information, always. Perhaps *this* is why she's scared to leave the programme; she'll meet someone socially and the first words out of her mouth will be, "I was force feminised in a secret basement and all I got was this lousy novelty mug."

"Oh, yeah. I forget about the locks, honestly," she replies. "I think they're a legacy thing."

"I was wondering if we can ask the uni to pay for uber-locks on the fifth floor, too," Naila says.

"You want to keep me out *that* much?" Ren says.

"They steal my cereal bars," Naila stage-whispers to Christine.

"I'm a criminal," Ren says. They sit down heavily on the other end of the bench, with Christine between the two of them. Christine gets her first clear look at their clothes.

"I like your skirt," she says. Ren pulls at the hem in response, showing it off. It's dark blue, almost black, with repeating patterns that look like tattoos would, if you could tattoo fabric.

"Thanks," they say, beaming.

"They made it," Naila says, "like, a week ago, and wouldn't shut up about how awesome it is for *days,* so thank you for another few hours of—" she opens and closes her hand, like the mouth of a Muppet, "—sound and fury."

"Signifying fashion," Ren says.

"I hate to ask," Christine says, having finally given up wrestling with temptation, "but can I bum a cigarette?"

Ren's face falls. "Damn. You can smell it?"

"From a mile away. Sorry."

Naila shakes a pack in front of Christine, dislodging a cigarette. "I told you deodorant doesn't work," she says to Ren, who rolls their eyes.

"Uh, can I get a light as well?" Christine asks sheepishly. "I'm supposed to have given up, like two years ago now, but…"

"Bad night," Ren finishes.

"Bad week," Naila remembers, sparking her lighter.

Christine ignites, inhales, and sighs. The smoke dissipates the neon light, casting them all into shimmering shadow for a moment. "I'm going to get *such* a headrush."

"Just don't fall off the roof," Ren says.

"No promises," Christine says, and inhales again.

"We have to go, actually," Naila says, checking her phone and making significant eyes at Ren, "but it was nice meeting you, Christine."

"You too."

"Drop by the fifth-floor common room if you want to say hi."

"Or if you want to bum any more of Naila's cigs," Ren says.

Naila and Ren interlock fingers and return to the stairs. They respond to Christine's wave by waggling their joined hands at her, before shutting the door and leaving her alone on the roof.

"See?" Christine mutters at herself, wreathing her head in smoke. "They both seemed nice and together and normal. Why not be like them? Which one?" She giggles, on a mild cigarette high. "Pick one!"

She winces as the promised headrush is joined by a momentary stab of pain above her eye; exhaustion making itself known. She should probably sleep soon.

But not yet. It's not even midnight, and her first tutorial isn't until eleven in the morning. She's got time.

Time to figure herself out. Time to ask herself the questions she's been putting off answering. Time to lay it all out and get truly analytical. She takes a deep drag from her cigarette, watches the paper burn down, takes it in and holds it in her lungs. Lets it warm her, suffuse her, invigorate her, poison her.

Finally, chest burning, she releases it, and the smoke cloud catches the wind, rips itself to shreds, and billows away across the green.

"What do you know, Christine Hale?"

8
Midday on Mercury

16 OCTOBER 2019 — WEDNESDAY

I did it. I came out to Christine. And to her friend, Abby, as well. Abby, the one who knows Melissa. Who bloody SPONSORED her! Which is really weird and circular. But, I guess, thinking about it, there are only eight of us down here, and if there were similar numbers in previous years and they all stay in touch then, the chances of interacting with someone new doesn't—

Stefan irritably hits delete and starts again. This isn't what matters; it isn't what he needs to be thinking about.

I want to be a girl. I've never written that down before. Barely even thought it. And I know I should be thinking more like, I AM a girl, but I don't know how I can KNOW that unless I've actually tried it. That's not how I've seen trans women—OTHER trans women—describe their experiences, but maybe there's different ways to be trans, or I'm just less trans, or—

Delete. He's been down that road before.

Christine. I don't know what to think of her. On the one hand, she's been understanding, and didn't freak out when I told her I'm trans (okay she DID freak out but it was a concerned-for-my-safety freakout, not a bigoted one), and she's the reason I'm actually finally going to transition, and do it right. I mean, I've seen her, Pippa, Maria and about half a dozen other girls now, and even knowing what I know…it's hard to see. It's also completely fucking RIDICULOUS that, supposedly, none of them are/were trans. (Are they even trans now? Christine says she's not, but do they wake up each morning and feel about their bodies the way I do about mine right now? Again, Christine says no. Which makes NO SENSE. Maybe I should ask Abby about it. Get a second opinion. Oh, that'll go well, won't it. "Hi, Abby, Stef here, I want to ask you some really personal questions about your gender! What's that, you say? 'Fuck off'? Okay!")

But that's just me looking back to what this place apparently DOES. Because on the OTHER hand, Christine's first response to someone knowing about Dorley (even if I was wrong, or right in a really, really wrong way) was to fucking kidnap them and bring them here to the place where men are basically tortured.

She's wrapped up so tight in this place you can almost see it on her. The way she talks about how all these guys are going to be "helped" creeps me out…Even if sometimes I do kind of think they deserve it. I mean, they're all really bad guys! God, "bad guys", that's an infantile way to talk about them. They're misogynists, woman-beaters, and drunk drivers with fatalities to their name. Taking these guys out of society until they can be reformed? A good thing, unequivocally. (I guess? I don't know. Am I pro-carceral justice now? What even ARE ethics?) But THIS? I guess I can see that if you want to reform a misogynist then ONE way to do it is make him truly understand and empathise with the subject of his contempt, and how better than to become it? But that can't be THE ONLY way. Is it???? If Christine and Abby have been telling the truth, maybe it is?? God, I've been down here half a week and already I'm starting to be all, "maybe the kidnappers have a good point?" And what ABOUT Christine, anyway—

He's getting off-topic. And it feels wrong, somehow unfair, speculating about Christine like this, when they've had only two actual conversations. Two conversations if you don't count the night when they met, anyway. The night they kissed, the night Stefan was pretending to be something he's not. The night that marked the end of everything he knew.

He clears the screen and tries again.

Today is the first day of the rest of my—

Fuck it.

The phone bounces as it hits the mattress and slaps screen-first into the concrete wall. For a rebellious second he leaves it where it lands, face-down. A moment of contempt for Dorley Hall's vaunted programme, for not being what he hoped it was, for leaving him out there alone, for taking Mark from him and for keeping Melissa from him. He should break *all* their shit.

But then he remembers that only Christine and Abby know why he's *truly* here, and that if he doesn't want to piss Pippa off, he probably shouldn't chuck the phone she gave him across the room. Thankfully, there are no scratches or blemishes. Funny; last year, when he dropped his own phone less than half a metre out of a chair, the screen spiderwebbed into near-illegibility. The phones here are obviously just better.

Like the mattresses. He hasn't slept so well in years.

He's a little startled a moment later when the phone wakes itself for an 08.00 alarm and starts playing a Taylor Swift song. As he silences it, the thin red LED strip above him, the one embedded into the ceiling over the bed, which he'd assumed was just a nightlight, increases in intensity.

That'll be the morning routine here in the basement then. He gets comfortable on the bed and waits for whatever comes next, half-expecting all the rest of the lights in the room—the bedside lamp, the desk lamp by the computer and the four small lights embedded in the ceiling—to come on at once at maximum brightness. He imagines Pippa in some control room upstairs, cackling, turning a dial from *pitch black* all the way up to *midday on Mercury.*

Nothing happens. Apparently, it's up to him to decide what to do next.

Not something he has a great deal of experience with.

He lies in the near-dark for a few more minutes, illuminated only by the soft red glow of the light strip and the dull green LEDs on the locks for the door and the little dumbwaiter next to it. He taps through the quiescent phone and makes sure all traces of his attempts at a diary entry are gone; anything he saves to the thing will almost certainly be readable by Pippa and God only knows who else. The last thing he wants to do, when Christine's gone to so much trouble to obscure his origin, is accidentally be himself anywhere it might be seen.

So, how the hell is he going to track his transition?

The best he can do, he decides after a little more thought, is to take a daily photograph in the full-length mirror on the wardrobe door and use the timestamps to track his physical changes. If Pippa confronts him about them, he can pretend to be concerned about the effects of the Goserelin implant on his beloved male body. As for the emotional effects, he'll just have to do his best to remember them. Far from ideal, but the best he can do under the circumstances.

He doesn't look at the picture when he takes it; instead he drops the phone back onto the mattress and concentrates very hard on getting dressed, because just a glimpse of his near-naked body is enough to bring bile to his throat.

There are violent things he would very much love to do to his body right about now, and only the promise that soon it will be fixed and that someday in the future he'll stand next to Christine and Pippa as an equal and not as this *thing,* is enough to stay his hand.

God, but he wants to. So. Fucking. Much.

He settles on pinching himself. Upper arms. A couple of times on each side. It's far from enough, but a little control is better than none at all.

He glares at the marks as they form on his skin. They could be redder. They could be deeper. He could have broken the skin again. He could just—

He could just fucking stop. He shakes his head, irritated with his lack of self-control, and busies himself hunting around for something to keep his hair out of his eyes. There's no product in the dresser so he slicks moisturiser through his fringe, which works well enough and the task is sufficiently distracting that by the time he's done, the worst of the revulsion—and the compulsions that come with it—has faded.

"Took you twenty-one years to call it dysphoria, didn't it?" he mutters to himself, with enough presence of mind to face away from where Abby said the cameras are. "Idiot."

One more pinch.

* * *

Dorley has a lot of rules. They drop away as you move through the programme, but even graduates are still restricted in certain ways: no contact with family or friends from before Dorley; no contact with the new boys until they become new girls unless you have explicit permission from their sponsor or Aunt Bea; no deviating from your agreed NPH, or New Personal History. It's up to the individual whether they want to present themselves as a trans or cis woman once they leave, but it's a decision that can be made only once.

Early in their second year, when they were all of them still fresh in their new names and identities, and only Vicky seemed truly to have a handle on things, Paige wrote *The first rule of forced-fem club is: do not talk about forced-fem club* on the recipe board in the kitchen. Aunt Bea, quite unexpectedly, loved it. For a while, she talked about getting it printed on a novelty mug, but either she relented or she keeps it locked away in her office. If it's bad opsec to list your crimes on a coffee mug, it's worse to be caught drinking out of it. Not that that's stopped whoever it is who keeps ordering all the other dangerously on-topic mugs that keep popping up in cupboards and mug trees across the lower levels of the Hall.

Christine has her own list of unofficial rules, designed mostly to give her some semblance of a quiet life in a building that seems orientated around the exact opposite. The one in force this morning: *If you think you might be under suspicion of backsliding, put on a nice dress and stay in your room with the door open, so you look like you have nothing to hide.* So, Christine, who declined last night to dress up and go out, despite receiving Aunt Bea's explicit permission—and thus her implicit instruction—to do so, has been up since seven-thirty, with another of Paige's dresses on and the door and window open, watching the late summer breeze play with the pages of her textbooks, and practising her eyeliner.

She's only poked herself in the eye three times so far; an improvement on last time. She's wiping off her latest failure when Vicky pokes her head around the open door.

"Hey, Vick," Christine says, holding up her pencil. "Come to see me suck at makeup?"

"I just came by to see how you are," she says, and then drops a gym bag off her shoulder with a guilty grin. "*And* to pick up a few things."

"Is there anything even left in your room that's actually yours?"

"The essentials," Vicky says. "And, uh, a pile of dirty plates. Don't tell anyone."

Christine zippers her lips.

Officially, Vicky Robinson still lives in the dorms, two doors down from Christine. Really, she lives off-campus with her girlfriend, and returns only to visit, steal food and clothes, and to sneak out estradiol for Lorna. With Vicky's room mostly empty, Paige got permission to get her thumb added to Vicky's lock, and uses the room as a walk-in wardrobe that just happens to have a bed and a desk in it; handy also for Vicky and Lorna, who are both only a couple of centimetres shorter than Paige and thus haven't had to go clothes shopping for months.

What Aunt Bea thinks of the arrangement she hasn't said, but she wouldn't have let Vicky graduate early if she didn't think that Dorley's rules, besides the obvious ones around disclosure, had become completely unnecessary for her.

One of many things about Vicky to be jealous of.

"Are you okay?" Vicky says, stepping over her gym bag and perching next to Christine on the bed.

"Yeah, Vick, I'm pretty okay."

"Only pretty okay?"

Christine makes herself look away, because the shape Vicky's lips form when she says *pretty* is not something she can witness and remain a hundred percent on-task afterwards. "Dira and Paige had a mini-intervention last night. Aunt Bea has been making comments about my 'continued feminine development'."

"Oh," Vicky says. "Oh *crap*, Tina."

"It's okay, kind of. I mean, we're not at drastic steps yet. But I'm behind everyone else. Not just you and Paige; everyone. Even bloody

Jodie's *My Immortal*-ass fashion sense is more developed than mine. I've been officially noticed."

"Is that why you're dressed up this morning?"

Christine nods, and leans back on the bed, inviting inspection and trying to stop her heart from fluttering. Vicky fucking Robinson is looking at *her*…

"What do you think?"

Vicky laughs. "I think when you bite your lip like that, you could have anyone you want."

Christine swallows. Can almost feel the Adam's apple she once had bobbing in her throat. "I mean, um, about the dress." She billows out the fabric around her thighs and kicks her legs lightly; it's a shortish dress and Christine's quietly proud of her legs. Comfort isn't the only reason she habitually wears shorts.

"It looks lovely on you," Vicky says.

Vicky and Christine have never kissed, never touched each other except platonically. Vicky's never done anything with anyone from their intake, choosing instead to wait until she could go out and meet someone healthy and normal from the outside world. But she had no peers among them, so why would she? By the time Christine and Paige were indulging in faltering experiments in horny and strangely adolescent denial—"I'm a straight guy," Paige had said, although that wasn't yet her name, "and so are you, but if we let ourselves forget what we know about each other for just a few minutes…"—Vicky had already booked her facial surgery, persuaded her sponsor to let her name herself, and been allowed up to the kitchen to meet the second- and third-years at least a dozen times.

Difficult not to dwell on possibilities, though, when a beautiful woman says you look lovely.

"Um," Christine says, and marvels briefly at her own eloquence before regaining full control of her mouth and continuing. "Thank you. Paige picked it, but I, um, put it on. I mean, she brought over a bunch of clothes—" she flails an arm at the pile, "—but it was me who decided, hey, I like green today." She touches the back of her hand to her hot cheek and looks away. "Sorry. I'm an idiot. And now I'm embarrassed."

Vicky puts a hand on Christine's knee. "Don't be. You're beautiful. You should be confident, too."

Christine picks up the eyeliner pencil again and twirls it between her fingers. "Working on that."

"You want some help?"

"It's tempting, but I can't." Christine drops it back on the bed and blows a strand of hair out of her eyes. "I got help all through second year, and that's why I still suck. I never learned."

"Well, if you need to borrow anything, my door is always open," Vicky says, and scowls. "Literally. Paige never locks it."

"You know, I might take you up on that."

"Can I give you some advice?" Vicky says, removing her hand and lowering Christine's heartbeat out of the danger zone. "Aunt Bea likes effort. Results are best, obviously, but trying and getting halfway there? Almost as good. All she'll need to see, at least for now, is more variety in your clothes and a spot of makeup. A bit of eyeshadow, maybe. You don't need to worry about eyeliner that could kill a man just yet." She grins and pokes Christine in the hip. "And dresses like this? Good choice."

Christine sighs. "I'm going to miss my shorts."

Vicky laughs and hugs her. "I won't."

Fending her off, Christine says, "Just eyeshadow?"

"For now. Maybe add a bit of lip gloss. But practise *everything.* Every day. Do a full face every morning. You don't have to keep it on through the day if you do it before your shower. And it doesn't matter if you look like an idiot if you wash it straight off."

"And here I thought I was almost getting away with just eyeshadow."

"It's what I did, and it worked out for me. I think it will for you, too. It's better than Paige's approach." Paige had become an expert on every makeup type and tool individually, with hours of YouTube tutorials and written guides and whole evenings dedicated to, say, lip liner. Vicky continues, "You never saw how silly I looked every morning, those first few months of second year. Every week, I'd pick a look off Instagram, just something I liked, and I'd spend an hour each morning trying to replicate it. By the end of each week, I'd have it, or I'd be close enough."

Christine is saved from having to point out the flaw in Vicky's idea—that she is Vicky and Christine is, regrettably, merely Christine—by an interruption.

"It's good advice," Aunt Bea says, from the doorway.

"Aunt Bea!" Christine says, feeling suddenly like she's talking too loud but unable to hear herself properly over the rushing in her ears. "Hi!"

"Good morning, Christine, Victoria."

"Hey," Vicky says with a smile. "I'll leave you two alone, shall I?" She stands, squeezes Christine's shoulder, and retrieves her bag from the floor. "Oh," she adds, "Lorna and I are going to the protest this afternoon. Want to come? She missed you and she's giving a speech, so you can make up for last night and support her at the same time!"

"Oh," Christine says, "uh, sure. I'm done with classes after lunch. Who or what are we protesting?"

"Professor Frost," Vicky says. "If that's okay, Aunt Bea?"

Vicky's not in the programme anymore and doesn't need permission to do anything, but Christine does. Aunt Bea grants it with a nod. All programme members, once they are judged to look different enough from their old selves that no-one who knew them before would recognise them, are cleared for social media—Paige was pleased to get clearance before anyone bar Vicky, months before Christine, seeing it both as proof that her old self was so buried that not even her own mother could find him, and as tacit approval to begin spamming Instagram and accumulating industry contacts. Protests, though, where one might be filmed saying or doing something particularly notable, are a different matter.

So is Professor Frost.

"Feel free to ruin her day," Aunt Bea says, smiling.

Aunt Bea reserves a particular hatred for Professor Katherine "Oh, do call me Kat" Frost, author of *Gender Dysphoria: the Psychological and Physiological Mutilation of Our Children,* and Christine's never quite decided if it comes from allyship, personal affront, or the fact that the quality of Professor Frost's published writing is considerably more mediocre than her ascendant media stardom might imply. Months ago, when Professor Frost's book first landed on shop shelves, Aunt Bea's reaction had been spectacular. "Her *supposed* book!" Aunt Bea had howled. "It contains many of the attributes of a book, in that it has front and back covers, paper between, binding, and even endorsements from academics who should know better, but it lacks the quintessential feature that separates *books* from *bricks:* insight!" Christine had immediately set up a search alert for the words "Professor Frost" and "disappeared", hoping to get out in front of any difficulties Dorley might experience if Aunt Bea ever followed through on her invective and found the spotlight-hungry History professor a new home in their basement.

"Thanks, Aunt Bea," Vicky says, and throws a quick wave to Christine. "Three o'clock, Tina!" she shouts from the hallway. "Outside the Anthill!"

Aunt Bea shuts the door behind her, enclosing them in a space that only ever feels small to Christine when she's alone in it with the woman who is still, technically, her captor. Bea settles on the little sofa on the far side of the room from the bed, farthest from the door.

"How are you feeling, Christine?" Aunt Bea says.

Easy questions first, then. "Good. I finally got some sleep."

"So I see," Aunt Bea says with a smile. "You're getting along with your studies?" To Christine's confused frown, she adds, "Yes, yes, I know we talked about that the other day. But that was *routine.* An inspection. This, I assure you, is off the record. I just want to talk."

"I'm enjoying Linguistics," Christine says, nodding, still confused. "It's more interesting than I expected. I can see myself finding a career in it, I think."

"Once you have graduated from our programme," Aunt Bea says, "I think we may permit you to indulge your computing interests, if you would like. Some elective modules, perhaps?"

"Oh. Um. Thank you, Aunt Bea. But I'm not sure I would choose to. I don't think it would be a good idea."

"I see. You believe you might find yourself open to temptation once more?"

"No!" Christine says quickly. That she might even *think* about hurting people that way ever again...The very idea is an insult to everything she's become. She grips the bed to keep herself from shaking. Feels the pressure of her whole body in her knuckles.

"I apologise," Aunt Bea says. "A necessary question."

"I'm not *him* anymore, Aunt Bea," Christine says, losing control of her voice. "Not just because I don't look or sound like him," she continues, pausing for breath every few words, "but because he's gone. And I don't want him back. And he's not in danger of *coming* back. Going back to those lecture theatres would bring up bad memories, that's all." She pushes against the bed frame and empties her lungs, slowly, carefully. "When I've graduated. From Saints, not from the programme. I might look into it elsewhere. But. Not here. Sorry."

"You've done no wrong, Christine," Aunt Bea says. "I apologise again. I should not have asked. In fact..." She shifts her weight on the sofa, leans forward. "When Indira came to see me last night, to ask me to grant you some time to work on yourself at your own pace—a request I am minded to honour, especially in light of your conversation with Victoria—I took the opportunity to ruminate."

Oh no, Christine has time to think, before Aunt Bea continues.

"And I realised, we haven't really touched base, have we, you and I? You were, in every sense, a typical product of our programme: you were angry and bitter in all the ways I expected, rebellious in all the ways I expected, and ultimately compliant in all the ways I expected. And thus unmemorable to someone like me, who has seen many dozens of young women bloom. Even for your intake, you were unremarkable: Paige fought me harder; Victoria flowered considerably earlier; Yasmin and Julia acquiesced more quietly but are more isolated. And Jodie, well, she is, perhaps, cheekier." She holds up a finger to forestall whatever objections Christine might have; Christine, for her part, is busy struggling for words. "We have engaged with each other formally, at inspections and during your reviews, but Christine, I don't *know* you. And that is *entirely* my failing."

"Aunt Bea, no—" Christine says, following her instincts, all of which are screaming at her to contradict any self-deprecation the woman attempts in her presence.

"I want to know you," Aunt Bea presses on. "And I want to know how you feel. About all of this: the programme; me. You. And I want you to be honest. Absolutely honest, with no regard for my feelings."

Ah, Christine thinks, *my strongest suit: honesty.* "I don't know where to start."

"You dislike your former self," Bea says, "with more vehemence than most of your cohort. Perhaps you should start there?"

" 'Dislike' is too weak a word," Christine says, deciding to let Aunt Bea have all the honesty she wants on this subject, at least. "I hate him. He…hurt people."

"Try talking about yourself in the first person," Aunt Bea suggests quietly.

"I *hurt* people!" Christine says, trying hard not to grit her teeth. "And I know Dira says it's because I wasn't loved, because my father hated me, because he hurt my mother and she *still* chose him over me. And that's all true, but it's all…justification. Explanations after the fact. At the time, I was in control. I knew what I was doing. I just told myself it didn't matter. I told myself I was getting something back from the world. What I was *owed.* I—" Christine jabs her finger into the mattress with each word, "—did those things. And I didn't care who I hurt."

"Indira would also say—"

"—that I was trapped and lonely. Also true. God, Aunt Bea, I was *so* lonely. I made my first real friends here, you know? And found my first real family. I almost had to learn how to talk to people from scratch!

But those are excuses. I was angry and I was hurting, and I made it everyone else's problem."

"You're not angry anymore?"

Christine smiles. "I'm a little angry at you," she says. "And a little angry at Dira. For doing all those things to me."

"If you were given the chance, would you go back? Instruct your former self to stay away from this campus, or refrain from your… activities for a time, so you wouldn't be taken?"

"No," Christine says quickly. "Absolutely not." She meets Aunt Bea's eyes for the first time since they started talking; Bea's still leaning forward on the sofa, chin resting lightly on her hand. Looking for all the world like she gives a shit. "I was hurting people. And I was only going to escalate. I've *seen* what happens when people like that, people like me, don't get corrected. Sooner or later, I was going to hurt someone in a way they couldn't come back from. God, I still worry that I already did." She chases the thought away, because she needs to be present for this, and when she dwells on that possibility it often takes her out of the world for hours. "I needed erasing, Aunt Bea."

"You're wrong about that. You needed *help.*"

"You say *potato…*"

"We've covered your past," Aunt Bea says briskly. "How do you feel about yourself now?"

"Not bad," Christine says, ignoring the twinge of Stef-related guilt. He *wants* to be here! Be *kind* to yourself, Christine! "I'm… someone I can be now. If you know what I mean."

"I do."

"I mean, I like who I am," Christine says, before Aunt Bea can move on. "I'm proud of myself. I'm sorry, it's just, 'I'm someone I can be,' sounded so much like, 'Oh, well, if I must,' and that's not it. I'm *glad* to be me."

"Glad to be a woman?"

"Yes."

"Proud to be a woman?"

"Yes. God, Aunt Bea…This life, this second chance, it's a gift. It's a future."

"Do you mourn the man you might have grown to become? Absent your difficulties, of course."

"No. He's a fiction. A fantasy. Hmm. Give me a moment?" Christine raises a finger, and Aunt Bea nods. When Christine continues, she takes her time, chews over every word. "I can imagine a version of myself, taken out of my life when I was a child and placed elsewhere. I can imagine him growing up, going to university, getting a job, getting married. I can even imagine, if I were taken out of *myself* and placed into *him*, inhabiting him without complaint or inhibition. Living his life, quite content. But there's no path from *here* to *there*, you know? There's no way for me, as I am now, to become him, not without becoming someone I no longer recognise as *me*. And if you were to tell me you have impossible magic that can make it happen, I think I would refuse. Because I don't know him. I know me. And, when I let myself forget all my bullshit, all my guilt…I *like* me. I hope that all makes sense."

"It does," Aunt Bea says, smiling. "And yet, you are still angry at me."

Christine snorts. "Well, you *did* cut my balls off. *Without* permission."

"Would you have granted it?"

"I definitely would not have."

The orchiectomy—the castration, the mutilation, as Christine thought of it at the time—had been a turning point. A whole swathe of possibilities for her life going forward felt like they had been cut away. There was suddenly no going back, and the changes she'd seen in her body would only accelerate. She lost whole days to a depression that threatened to consume her entirely. But she recovered—with help from Vicky, who'd been waiting for this operation with obvious and increasing impatience, and Paige, who dealt with the loss of her testes with the same methodical thoroughness she applied to every other aspect of their imprisonment—and eventually allowed herself to consider the options that remained. A roadmap, which eventually she followed, seemed to sketch itself out in front of her.

A common inflection point, she learned later. And not entirely a coherent one: testosterone injections could have given back most of what had been taken from her. But no-one thinks about that in the immediate aftermath. It's too visceral, too much of a shock. It's not that the programme hinges on it—there are other ways to part a man from his masculinity—but it's where most of them pivot, all the same.

Christine remembers chastising Indira for robbing her of the opportunity to have children; remembers Dira smiling and reminding her of the comprehensive "health tests" they all had during the first few weeks underground. Christine can still have children one day, if she chooses. And that moment, that realisation that there were paths that had deliberately been left open for her, that it was not *just* about punishment but about building a new, different, better future, was when Dira began to reach her. And when a newly receptive Christine understood on an emotional level not just how much pain she had already caused, but how much damage she had been on course to inflict, her manhood, not a small price to pay, felt irrelevant weighed against the opportunity to throw away her old life, with all its mistakes and cruelties, and start again.

Masculinity had never been much help to her, anyway.

Aunt Bea looks thoughtful. "Indira and I spoke about your daily presentation. And, as you know, I overheard your conversation with Victoria. At the risk of putting words in your mouth, I don't believe your reluctance to dress in a feminine manner comes from, shall we say, a masculine reticence to indulge in femininity."

"Absolutely not," Christine says.

"When someone else helps you dress nicely, someone you trust, like Indira or Abigail, how does it make you feel? Take your time."

"I like it. I really like it, actually. Aunt Bea, it feels like…It's so *different.* Not just to how I was before, but to how I am the rest of the time. It's not all good—I don't like attention from men; most men, anyway—but it's quite…liberating? I think? I wouldn't want to do it all the time, given the choice; sometimes I feel more like I want to wear shorts and a top. That's not a laziness thing, that's a…I don't know, a *me that day* thing? Sometimes I *want* to look how I always look, but sometimes I don't, and…"

"And you're frustrated that you have the skills to fulfil only the former desire, and not the latter?" Aunt Bea finishes, surprising Christine, who wasn't entirely sure how much of that she'd said out loud.

"Yeah," Christine says, and adds with venom, "I look like a fucking panto dame when I try it myself. Sorry."

"Don't worry," Aunt Bea says with a smile. "Informal, remember? Just try to stay away from the c-word."

The confirmation that Aunt Bea even knows about the c-word is enough of a shock to coalesce some of Christine's scattered thoughts into something approaching legibility. "I hate feeling reliant on the other girls," she says, "so I don't ask for their help anymore. And when they offer, I usually refuse. And then I feel like a fake girl surrounded by real ones."

"Understandable, but not insurmountable," Aunt Bea says. "It will take some hard work on your part, but it is nothing compared to what you have already achieved. I trust you to pursue this, in your own time and way, although I recommend the approach Victoria suggested. Don't be afraid to ask for advice, and call on me should ever you need to."

"I will, Aunt Bea."

She nods, and adopts a grave expression. "There is one more thing. This morning, before leaving my office, I looked over your file. Start to finish. And I believe there is something you should know. Ordinarily this is information we withhold until graduation, but I believe it would be beneficial to air it now."

"Okay?"

"The women you contacted before you arrived here, the women whose testimony ultimately brought you to us, are none the worse for wear. They were reimbursed, which I think you know—mostly from what remained of your funds—and all of them are aware that your former identity is…erased, as you said. Two of them expressed sorrow that your former self could not be helped before it was too late, so I believe they would be satisfied with your current status." She smiles, stands from the sofa and crouches in front of Christine, putting herself on the same level. "You are not and never will be blameless and the harms you inflicted were real, but they were not lasting. They have healed and moved on. You should, too."

Oh, God.

She remembers their faces. How could she not?

"They're all okay?" Christine asks, through a throat suddenly dry.

"They're all okay. In fact, I would suggest that if they were offered the opportunity, most of them would forgive you. Especially in light of your reformation."

Oh, *God.*

Christine fades out for a while.

When she returns, she almost jumps at the realisation that Aunt Bea is sitting next to her on the bed, exactly where Vicky sat, and has an arm around her shoulder. Christine herself is leaning on Aunt Bea's arm, and the fabric of Bea's suit jacket is wet with Christine's tears.

She pulls away, and Aunt Bea passes her a tissue.

"God, I'm sorry," Christine says, blowing her nose and wiping her eyes.

"It's quite all right," Aunt Bea says. "I thought it important that you know."

"Thank you," Christine manages to say. "Yes. It's good. I should know. Shit. God. I've been dreaming about them, you know? Not every night, not anymore, but for *years.* God, that's…"

"A weight off your mind?"

"I hope so. Too early to tell, I guess."

"Indeed."

"I'm not…" Christine starts, but she can't finish, because she wants to say, *I'm not bad, not anymore,* but can't summon the conviction. Perhaps it will come some other day.

They sit in silence for a minute or so while Christine dries her face and collects herself. Aunt Bea graciously spares her from active attention, busying herself with emails on her phone. When Christine has recovered, Aunt Bea stands, and beckons her to stand, too. Momentarily scared that another hug is approaching, Christine is relieved when Bea takes her hand and holds it between them both, almost like she's about to kiss it.

"I'm very proud of you, Christine," Aunt Bea says. "I'm proud of all my girls, of course, but you…You are quite something. There is a thoughtfulness in you that I, to my shame, never noticed."

"Thank you, Aunt Bea," Christine says automatically. Something inside her makes her curtsey. Embarrassing.

"But there is something I wish you would try to internalise," Aunt Bea continues. "Sometimes you think *too* much. I can see you blushing, and yet your curtsey was both appropriate and well-performed. The only person who is embarrassed…is you. I submit that this applies to more in your life than your curtsey."

"I…Thank you, Aunt Bea," Christine says again, injecting more warmth into her voice.

Aunt Bea releases her hand. In the doorway she pauses, looks back, and with a smile, says, "Smoking while on hormone replacement therapy is very bad for you."

"Really?" Christine says innocently, suppressing an urge to cough. "Is it?"

"One of our girls, years ago now, resumed her habit when she moved to the second floor. For three months she smoked nearly twenty a day, and only quit when, very early one morning, she woke screaming from a pain in her calf muscle so excruciating she could barely communicate her needs. Unable to speak properly, she rolled aside the duvet to reveal to us a swelling that was the size and shape of a Cumberland sausage. We took her to hospital immediately. Just something to think about."

Can Aunt Bea smell the smoke lingering on last night's dress, hanging up by the window? Or does she just *know?* "Was she okay?"

"Yes. Monica was lucky. We all were. Good morning, Christine."

* * *

"Hey! New boy! You up?"

It's a male voice, shouting through the door, disturbing Stefan in his amateurish search through the computer for some hidden folder in which to hide a diary.

"Yeah," he says, deliberately not shouting; he can't stand the abrasive edge his voice takes on when it gets loud. Christine said she trained hers, so maybe she can give him some tips. Not on *actually* developing a new voice. Not yet, not while he's down here playing at being the bad little cis boy, but perhaps there's some prep work he can do. Some exercises to expand his range. *Anything* to reduce the amount of time he has to spend listening to himself sound like *this*.

Anything for a crumb of progress.

Whoever it is raps on the door. "Come out and get your healthy breakfast!" Another knock. "It's part of a complete, balanced diet!"

Stefan checks himself over quickly, with the sideways, fleeting glances in the mirror that are necessary on days like this. He hasn't done anything daft like tuck his trousers into his socks, and his hoodie isn't too obviously stretched from pulling the sleeves down over his hands.

It's fine. He's fine.

He fetches the phone from the bedside table and tries to open the door. It doesn't cooperate.

"Uh," he says, through the door, "how does this work?"

"It's a door," the voice says. "Just pull on it and watch the magic happen."

"Yeah, okay, *not* working."

"Did you unlock it?"

"The light's green."

"Your new best friend didn't explain how it works?"

"No? It's a door. I think she assumed I'd seen them before."

The voice mutters something too quiet for Stefan to hear, then continues in a lecturing tone, "You see the little black square under the green light? That is a fin-ger-print rea-der. Put your fin-ger or thumb on the rea-der and the door will o-pen."

Stefan scans his thumb. The door makes the now-familiar ear-assaulting buzzing sound, and clicks open a couple of centimetres. Pulling it the rest of the way reveals the too-bright ceiling lights of the residential corridor and Aaron, dressed similarly to Stefan though without the hoodie, affecting an expression of rapturous joy. "You see what can happen if you just *believe?*" he says, imitating an American preacher.

The urge to tell the little shit to fuck off is reasonably strong, but Abby's right: Stefan needs to make a friend.

"Thanks," Stefan says. "How do they know my fingerprints?"

"Well, I'm *guessing*—and this is just a guess, you understand—they took them when you were unconscious."

Stefan probably deserves the sarcasm; it was a stupid question. He smiles to show he's taken it in good grace, and asks, "So, what does the green light mean, if it doesn't mean the door's already open?"

"It means *you* can open it. You're only actually locked in if it's red; that's when only your specially assigned girlfriend can let you out. Red light means it's piss-in-a-bottle time."

"They really expect you—us—to pee in a bottle when they lock us in?"

Aaron shrugs. "Who knows? Half the fun of this place is figuring out the rules as you go along, and getting tased or at least very heavily bitched at when you guess wrong. We've only had a lockdown once so far, when Declan went digging for Nazi gold in his nasty little Nazi stomach."

"Wait. Declan's a Nazi?"

"I dunno. Maybe. He seems like the type. Long, goose-stepping legs; a tendency towards sudden and irrational acts of violence. Does it matter?"

"Yeah, kind of."

"Don't talk to him, then," Aaron says. "I don't, if I can avoid it. He's a fucking weirdo, anyway. But! My point: *he* does the whole belly-button fandango, *they* take him away to get patched up. They probably bang him around a little, too. I mean, I would." He slaps the air in front of him, and shouts, " 'Stop! Being! A! Weird! Little! Dick!' They took him away so quick, I didn't even get to see the wound. Anyway, we were only in lockdown for an hour or so, and the only one who genuinely did piss in a bottle was Adam, and he probably does that all the time anyway, to cleanse himself in the eyes of the Lord. Or to give himself something to drink after lights out. Oh," he adds, pointing at Stefan's phone, "put that in your pocket, and leave it in your room next time, or they'll take it away. Common room's all about socialising."

"Okay," Stefan says, pocketing it. "Why?"

"Why do they want us to socialise?" Aaron says, pushing on the double doors to the dining room and walking over to the seats nearest the entrance. On the table, there's a box of Weetabix, some oat milk, and a pile of plastic spoons. "Haven't you been paying attention? They're trying to rehabilitate us! Get us all together in one room and have us waggle our dicks at each other for a couple of weeks until we're good boys. Just like boarding school."

"You went to boarding school?" Stefan asks, frowning.

"You're thinking, 'he doesn't sound like a posh lad,' aren't you?"

"Yeah," Stefan admits, Weetabixing one of the plastic bowls.

"Dad got his business bought. Suddenly we're rolling in money, and he's too busy for me and Mum. Suddenly we're moving from a two-up two-down to a big new house in a big new town and suddenly I'm being sent off to a big new school where all the Hooray Henries and Chinless Charlies go to learn how to tie their shoes and spell their names without smiley faces in the Os and run the country. And don't *they* have a fun new target? That was a glorious five years. Believe it or not, I think this place is a lot nicer: it's warmer than the coal shed the posh boys liked to lock me in, and there are hot women to look at, even if they do all have tasers and hate me."

"I'm sorry," Stefan says. "That sounds awful."

"Aww. Did I tug at your heartstrings? Did you hear a little violin playing? If I want your pity, I'll ask for it."

"It's empathy, not pity."

"That's just 'pity' with more letters and a fucking viral TikTok account," Aaron says, stabbing his breakfast with a plastic spoon and not making a dent. "Inspiring videos of girls with too much money breaking down crying when they think about three-legged cats and the coming climate apocalypse."

"Is he whining again?" Will says, from the other end of the table. He and Adam are the only others in the room, carrying on the same variety of murmured argument Stefan saw yesterday. Possibly, it's the same argument.

Stefan needs to make his decision. If he's going to befriend someone—and he's got to befriend *someone* or he'll end up like Declan's belly—then it'll be one of the three men in this room. The other ones, based on his limited observation and Aaron's introduction, are each some combination of unpredictable, violent or apathetic, none of which are useful to Stefan right now. Of the ones who remain, Adam seems to believe in some wild shit, and Stefan's spent under two hours total in Will's presence and has already been called a homo. Better the devil you could fold up and put under your arm…

He takes a side.

"What do you care?" he says to Will, affecting a sneer, which comes easily enough. "I'm talking to him, not you."

Not the *most* ringing endorsement of his nascent friendship with Aaron. Baby steps.

"I *don't* care," Will says, matching Stefan's contempt and returning to whatever he's talking about with Adam. Demons, or being a massive homophobe and how cool that is, or something.

"Idiot," Stefan mutters, and catches Aaron looking at him strangely for a moment, before returning to his stubborn breakfast.

"So," Aaron says, around a mouthful of dry Weetabix, "are you ready to tell me your crimes, yet?"

"Are *you?*"

"I feel like you'll judge me. Will you judge me?"

"Yeah, probably," Stefan admits.

"Hah! You *are* like Raph. He judges me a lot, too, but I'm, like, seventy-to-eighty percent certain he's knocked a bunch of women around, which is way more extreme than *my* thing. Except getting him to admit it is like pulling Goslafin implants out of Declan's stomach."

"It's *Goserelin,* you fucking imbecile!" Will shouts, from the other end of the table.

"You're doing that on purpose, aren't you?" Stefan whispers.

With a finger to his lips, Aaron replies, "Shush. Watch."

Stefan looks back over. Adam has put a hand on Will's wrist to quiet him. Will waits a second before shaking it off. Adam looks put out for a moment, but keeps his hand on the table next to Will's, just centimetres away. Their conversation resumes.

"What do you think?" Aaron says quietly. "Closet cases? Or just really, really repressed? Adam's from this freaky Christian sect, the New Church of Something-or-Other, and William is a truly massive wanker."

"The idea that all homophobes are closeted gay people is just a myth," Stefan says. "A couple of big-name arseholes getting exposed doesn't make it a pattern."

"Whatever. I think they want to touch dicks." He slaps his hands against each other a few times.

"That's not how gay men have sex, Aaron."

"Sounds fun, though, right?" Aaron says, grinning. He adds, "Boarding school," by way of explanation, and shovels more dry Weetabix into his mouth.

"Why haven't you put milk on that? Wouldn't it make it easier to eat?"

"It's oat milk. And this is Weetabix. I won't pour oats onto oats. It's perverse!"

"Weetabix is made of wheat, Aaron. It's in the name. There's even an oat version. Called Oatibix."

"Oh. Never mind, then. Don't tell Will I said that."

"I heard, idiot," Will says. "I wasn't going to dignify it with a correction. Some things are just too stupid to bother with."

Aaron shows Will his middle finger and turns back to Stefan. "So! How was your first evening at Hotel Feminazi?"

"Relaxing," Stefan says, to be annoying.

"Well, good, because you're going to be here a while."

"What can I expect from this place? You know, day to day?"

Aaron adds milk to his bowl as he talks. "Boredom. If you're down on your masturbation quota for the decade, this is a good chance to, you know—" he rubs a near-closed fist up and down the handle of his plastic spoon, "—catch up. It's a shame Maria took away my Fitbit or I could make my steps at the same time. They get judgy about sticky sheets, though, so you may want to nominate a sock to be your new bedtime pal."

"What, they just leave you alone all day?"

"Mostly. I know, I was hoping for more, too, because Maria's opening speech to me was highly enjoyable as far as failed attempts to make me feel guilty go, but there's been nothing since. Maybe they're hoping we'll resort to cannibalism just for something to do. It'd make a change from Weetabix."

"So? What do I do?"

"You don't listen, do you?" Aaron says, mouth full. "You wank, you watch some TV, you wank some more. Sooner or later you get big angry sores on your dick so you give the wanking a rest for, I don't know, the length of a movie." He pushes his bowl aside. "Oat milk on Weetabix is fucking disgusting. Come on, let's go watch some TV, and then we can turn away from each other and be very quiet and respectful of each other's privacy for, say, five minutes."

* * *

The Anthill: a turn-of-century lecture theatre complex built as part of the campus expansion into its then-newly acquired lakeside land, the heart of Saints' new campus-within-a-campus, an architectural marvel of interlocking brown domes and circular green skylights that has, since opening to the student population, been known as the Arthur Nathan Turner Halls on paper only.

Arthur Nathan Turner reportedly was not happy with the nickname, but expired before he could remove the Royal College from his will. Presumably he would have had much to say about Saints' quarterly cultural newsletter, which since 2004 has been titled *News from the Anthill.*

Christine's seen the Anthill from above, via drone camera, and thinks, as nicknames go, it could have been worse.

"Teenie!"

Poking out above a sea of student faces is an arm wearing a beaded bracelet that matches Christine's, so she heads for it, and gets engulfed by Indira and her sign. It reads *Protect Trans Kids!* and is almost as big as she is.

"Hey, Dira!" Christine says, accepting her embrace. "I didn't bring a sign. Is that okay?"

"You can yell, right?" Vicky says, joining in the hug from another angle. Christine, in the scrum, manages to nod. "Then that's fine!"

"I'm so glad you could make it!" Indira says, squeezing hard. "You're feeling okay? You got some sleep?"

"I'm good. Aunt Bea came to see me."

"Vicky said. How did it go?"

"Pretty good, actually," Christine says, as the three of them disentangle themselves. "She put my mind at rest about a few things, and endorsed Vicky's suggestion on how to proceed with—" Christine hurriedly edits what she's about to say, remembering just in time that she's in mixed company, i.e. people who came about their current gender in one of the more usual fashions, "—you know, that thing I need to get better at."

Indira squeals and kisses Christine on the cheek. "Proud of you," she says, as she steps back.

"Thanks, sis," Christine says. They trail their hands against each other's for a moment.

"Hi again, Christine," Lorna calls, and Christine looks round to see her at the edge of the crowd, standing next to Vicky and playing nervously with a much smaller sign. She's changed a lot: where once she was all angles, she's now filled out, and she doesn't look as lost as she used to in clothes that, yes, have definitely been stolen from Paige's second wardrobe. She's becoming strikingly beautiful; a good match for Vicky.

"Hi," Christine says, stepping closer so she doesn't have to shout. "I wanted to ask you something, actually."

"Maybe later?" Lorna says, and points at a picnic table a couple of people are carrying over. "I'm doing a speech soon and I'm kind of nervous? But I'll be back down after, and then we're going to the SU when the protest winds down?"

"Perfect," Christine says. "Good luck with your speech! You'll be amazing! When does the professor get here?"

"In about five minutes, supposedly. But people are saying she might not show."

That might be preferable. Professor Frost's public appearances are generally heralded by a flock of middle-aged busybodies whose favourite trick is to point their phone cameras at the trousers and skirts of all the women in a crowd of protesters and look for folds in the fabric they can draw red circles around and claim on social media are totally, definitely, one hundred percent positively erect penises, and that's not something Christine wants associated with her own personal crotch. Self-consciously she swings her shoulder bag around from the side to the front, just in case.

Her trepidation can't last long. The energy of the crowd is undeniable, and Christine finds herself buoyed up by it. She joins in a couple of chants, returns to Indira and links elbows with her, and excitedly greets Ren and Naila, who notice her from across the way and unwisely get within range of Indira's hugging arm. They introduce the newcomers to Vicky and then all of them get caught up in the loud cheers for Lorna, who's been clambering up onto the picnic table in front of the crowd.

"Thank you, everyone!" Lorna says, accepting a microphone from someone with rainbow fingernails and wincing as it feeds back. "I'm so happy to see you all here today! And we all know why we're here: Professor Katherine Frost!" She pauses for boos, then opens up the script on her phone and starts her speech: "*There was a time when Saints University used to stand for the truth…*"

"Isn't she fantastic?" Vicky stage-whispers in Christine's ear.

"She's amazing!"

"I'm going to marry her, you know."

"Really?"

"She doesn't know it yet, but I do. I know it. She's just…she's perfect, Tina. I can't imagine ever wanting anyone else."

Christine lets her heart squeeze, just a little, before she replies. "I'm really happy for you," she says, with all the warmth she genuinely feels. It's not that she's jealous of Lorna or Vicky, for all that they are both breathtaking, but she longs to have that kind of connection with someone.

Vicky bumps shoulders with her, to say thanks. "Oh," she adds, "if you're still serious about coming out next week, we have something planned."

"I am."

"Good. Lorna's got a date for FFS and we're celebrating."

"Oh! That's fantastic!"

"I don't think she needs it, but I've, uh, stopped telling her that. She got kind of upset with me."

Christine thinks of the look on Stef's face when he asked why he should put up with anything less than what Christine was given. "Yes," she says, "I think I get why."

* * *

> **WELCOME TO TRANS YOUTH UK! (Not affiliated with the Egg Society of Great Britain.)**
> All the usual Consensus rules apply. Click **>here<** for server rules. Obey them or begone!
> There are no stupid questions. Only stupid answers! Please refrain from giving stupid answers.
> Message **Diamond In The Ralph** for moderation. Message **GAYBOT III: THE BOTTOMING** for automated server functions.

Christine
Hi

Far and Away
Welcome!

Quite Contrary
Hiya.

distilled
who are you

Girl Alex
You're so rude, Penny, WOW.
Hi, Christine. Welcome to the server.

Christine
Before I start I should say
I'm not here for me
A trans friend of mine -- my friend's gf -- gave me the invite because
Well
It's complicated!
I've made a new friend, and she's a trans girl just starting out, and she's in a hostile environment that she can't leave, and I want to know what I can do to support her
Also I've had two drinks, I'm not drunk but if I typo, it's the drinks, I'm a v good typist normanly

Far and Away
Okay.
First things first: this server is private, for reasons of both safety and comfort. You are of course welcome here, but we don't advertise this place for a reason.

Christine
Understood
I'm good at secrets

distilled
oh yeah
name five

Girl Alex
Please ignore them. They just can't help themselves.

Christine
Understood

cicada
hey all, can't stay, just saying, I know Christine, I gave her the invite, I also bought her those drinks!! She lived with Vicky for I think two years, she's

really good people and SUPER sweet and Penny if you're mean to her I will fight you

gotta go bye!!!!!!!!

distilled
well
ok
guess you're vouched for then
also if I can't be mean to you I guess I'll be double mean to alex
get ready bitch I'm going to make so much fun of your terrible boyfriend

Girl Alex
Can anyone hear a sort of high-pitched screeching sound? Like a really loud but dumb bird? Coming from the Nottingham area?

distilled
eeeeeeeeeeeeeeeeeeeeeeeee

Girl Alex
I'm getting a headache.

distilled
eeeeeeeeeeeeeeeeeeeeeeeee

cicada
oh yeah the protest went REALLY well, I'll post pictures later and I'll circle Christine for you
(but I drew trans flags on her cheeks so you'll recognise her easy anyway)
ok bye!!!!!!!! but for real this time

Christine
Oh no there are pictures

distilled
gutted

Quite Contrary
You really have trans flags on your cheeks?

Christine
I do
They won't rub off
So I guess they're a part of me forever

distilled
you're one of us now
you've been transed against your will

Christine
Yes

Quite Contrary
What would you like to know, Christine?
Between us we have quite a lot of experience at being trans in hostile environments.

Far and Away
Understatement.

Christine
I don't know
Just like
Okay so she's only come out to me and my friend and she wants to keep it that way for now
And she lives with a bunch of guys who are really not very nice

Quite Contrary
Family?

Christine
Other students.

Far and Away
Like in a dorm, then?

Christine
It's definitely a dorm-type situation, yes
Seven boys, the youngest is 19, the oldest is 24

She's 21
And they're all kind of
Dickheads?
I feel like that's not a strong enough word
It's not only an environment in which she can't come out, it's an environment in which she can't afford to appear, I don't know, weak? Unmasculine?
There's a sort of low-grade hostility from them all the time, and a couple of guys who might opportunistically hurt her if she doesn't act "right"
Or if they just get bored enough honestly

Far and Away
The long dark school changing room of the soul.

Christine
Exactly
There's actually communal showers so it's even more apt than you think

Far and Away
You're describing a fairly harsh environment.

Quite Contrary
Not an unfamiliar one, though.

Christine
How can I support her?
The more I think about it the more worried about her I am
I can't even imagine spending any time down there myself and I'm not in her situation
Like, I think it's going to be triggering as hell to be in that environment with those guys

Quite Contrary
Maybe, maybe not.
I can only speak for myself, but I find it hardest being among girls.
With girls, I'm made very, very aware of what I don't have. The way they move, the way they talk, the way they are with each other. There's a

community I'm completely locked out of. Sometimes it can be hard to even look at them.

With boys, I can switch off. It's not pleasant—it's actually horrible—but it's manageable. It doesn't hurt to be around them, unless they actually physically hurt me.
Around boys it's like nothing matters. You do the boy act until you don't have to anymore. Simple.
Around girls it's like the volume's turned all the way up and everything matters WAY TOO MUCH.
I think the big problem is going to be, how does she find HER inside herself, when she's had to be HIM all day? I think that's where she's going to need help.
Because that's my problem. I'm ALWAYS him. Never her, not anymore.
And he's like this disease inside me that keeps getting worse and it's never safe for me to even address the symptoms.
It's getting hard to remember what being her was even like.

Girl Alex
I'm hugging you, Mary.

Far and Away
As am I.

distilled
I'm waving respectfully

Quite Contrary
Sorry, that became mostly about my thing.

Christine
No, no, it's actually very applicable
And I'm really sorry that has to be your life for the moment

Far and Away
Does your friend have somewhere private she can be herself? Perhaps with your help?

Christine
No
She is, in every sense of the word, trapped

She can't dress up or go out as herself or anything
Idk if that's important, is that important?

Girl Alex
It can be helpful.

Christine
Shit

Quite Contrary
If you and your friend are the only people who know her, then maybe the best thing you can do for now is talk to her.
Be available to her.
Be someone she doesn't have to keep secrets from.
That's why I come here. There's no-one like that in my life otherwise.

Far and Away
We can get her an invite code for here if having other trans people to talk to would help.

Christine
It would, probably, but she can't get online like that

Far and Away
Then it seems like she's going to have to rely on you.
Does she have plans for her transition? Does she need financial help?
Between us we can boost GoFundMes pretty hard.

Christine
No, that's all covered
It's a bit of a weird situation
But thanks
What I'm getting from this is that what she needs is emotional support more than I guess anything I can physically do
If that makes sense

Far and Away
It does, but,
If you can think of anything you can physically do, definitely do it.

If you can find a way for her to wear affirming clothes, do it.
If you can get her bits of makeup and that's what she wants, do it.
Even if she has to hide it, and can use it only rarely, it can help.
And if you care, give her something so she knows you care.
It doesn't have to be anything physical, although that's good if you can, and if she has somewhere safe to keep it.
But if her environment really is that hostile, give her a totem. Something to look at, or something to think about or look forward to. A beacon.
Take it from me, it can make all the difference.

Quite Contrary
Listen to her. Talk to her. Be her friend. Remind her it won't always be the way it is.
Sometimes just hope is enough.

Christine
Thank you, everyone.

Girl Alex
Good luck.
And do point her our way if there's even a chance she can get online.

Christine
I will
If it's okay, I'd like to stay on this server for a while
In case I have any questions

Far and Away
I'll give you the role of Cis Ally then.

distilled
you'll be our first!

Christine
Thanks
I'm going to go talk to my friend

* * *

Christine
Hi, Stef
Sorry I didn't say hi before
Been kind of knackered

Stef
oh it's completely okay
I've been very busy
making friends with terrible people
getting good at suppressing the urge to throw up just from association
I'm fine

Christine
Jesus Stef was it that bad?

Stef
actually it was mostly boring
and sort of morally reprehensible

Christine
Yeah that's kind of our thing

Stef
no I mean from my end
abby suggested it would be safest to make a friend
so I've been making a friend
I wish I knew what he did because I feel weird cosying up to a guy when
I don't know why he's here
abby said he wasn't violent but that's all I know

Christine
I can find out
It'd be a huge breach of trust, but fuck it, right?
Which one are you talking to?

Stef
aaron

Christine
Oh, I know that off the top of my head
He's Maria's boy
She complains about how annoying he is
It's dick pics
That's what he did
Like, a BARRAGE of dick pics
And sexual harassment as well
He had a particular thing for a girl from one of his lectures, and forgot to anonymise his shit properly one time
Put his name to like a dozen pictures of his scrawny little incel peen
So we brought him in

Stef
I keep being surprised at the level of guy you bring in
dick pics and sexual harassment, they're really bad but surely there are channels?
are they really a kidnapping matter?

Christine
Little shit's got rich parents
And he was warned
A LOT
Kept it up anyway
Aunt Bea's opinion on that is, it's only a matter of time before that kind of behaviour, left unchecked, degrades from sexual harassment to sexual assault
And I've seen the proof of that in the records
We haven't always brought in that kind of guy
Dorley has sort of ebbed and flowed in its recruitment methods over the years

Stef
recruitment!
that's a bloodless word for it lol

Christine
Or whatever you want to call it then
I've seen it when guys like that get to grow up

They mostly don't change
And what they turn into
They hurt women, Stef
We stop that

Stef
I forget you're a true believer

Christine
Sometimes I do too
I guess if there's one thing to understand about me, it's that this place?
It's my normal
It's the baseline from which I judge everything else
And this place is, I'm sure you're noticing by now, fucking bananas

Stef
yeah I noticed a bit

Christine
How are you doing, Stef?

Stef
I mean I'm not enjoying myself
honestly I don't know
this place is fucked up but
fucked up is MY normal
I'm used to it
I think I'm just impatient to start actually changing, you know?
I know what I want
I know how I'm going to get it
and now I'm just
waiting
can we not just sound the forced fem alarm and have pippa and maria
and the others break out the scalpels?
I was having mixed feelings about what you're going to do to those guys
before and I suppose I still am but if you offered me a pussy tomorrow
I'd feed them all into a woodchipper feet first
is that bad?

Christine
I actually kind of get it
Vicky wanted nothing more than to race through the whole thing
She was so impatient she even managed to hurry us along with her a little bit
I'm glad she didn't feed us into a woodchipper

Stef
I mean me too
then you wouldn't have been around to kidnap me
I still don't get why you're not freaking out all the time about what was done to you
and I absolutely can't imagine aaron or will becoming completely normal seeming women like you, that's fucking out of this WORLD
Christine

Christine
I'm normal-seeming?

Stef
actually you're weird
it's not a bad kind of weird!
mostly not anyway
you're probably the most interesting person I've ever met

Christine
I'm in a good mood so I'm taking that as a compliment

Stef
go for it

Christine
Then, thank you
Look, I want to try and make this all easier for you

Stef
why

Christine
Guilt

But also, I like you, Stef
You say I'm interesting?
You refused to be unkidnapped
You're pretty interesting yourself!
What I'm saying is
I'm making myself available
You can talk to me
Not just about the programme or anything
But like, about everything
If you need to vent, if you've had a bad day -- worse than normal -- or if you're feeling especially dysphoric, you can talk to me
Only on here, for the most part though
It's difficult for me to get down there a lot

Stef
there is something actually
I want to track my transition
but I'm guessing my phone and things are all pretty closely monitored?

Christine
Everything but the logs between you and me, and you and Abby

Stef
can I use you as
I guess
a sort of transition journal?
if I write things out in here that I want to remember, maybe with pictures, you can maybe save it somewhere safe?

Christine
I can absolutely do that
I've just made a hidden folder for that
And I know for a fact that we didn't strip the built-in zip function out of the phones we give you
So put your pictures and your diary stuff in a zip file and password protect it
And upload it to me through here
And delete your original
I won't even be able to look at it without the password
(Well okay I definitely could crack it but I promise I won't)

You'll have a private diary, just saved on my computer instead of yours
And any time you want something out of it I can send you the zips

Stef
thanks
like really thanks!!!
that's actually a huge relief
I was just going to take pictures and rely on the timestamps
which sucks
but wait, even if I delete stuff, won't they know?

Christine
Probably not
We're not very sophisticated and there aren't that many of us really
There's no active monitoring of your devices
Just file dumps and stuff
Make sure you don't have anything saved that you don't want them to
see by midnight each night and you're fine

Stef
right
thank you
GOD thank you
this is earning you back a lot of karma points from when you
kidnapped me
if you want to help other ways
you can keep me company
remind me there are good people in the world

Christine
I qualify as good to you?

Stef
well no
I mean see above re kidnapping
but you're not like THEM
I used the word empathy in front of aaron and he looked at me like I
just pulled a trout out of my top

Christine
Well like I said
Any time you want to talk
And I'm not, like, actually in a lecture or something
I'm here

Stef
cool
um
christine
I can do this, can't I?
I can be a girl, can't I?

Christine
Fuck yes you can, Stef
I did it and I was a complete basket case
Literally all my friends did it
You can do it, too
And Abby and me, we're going to help you any way we can
You've got this

Stef
thanks
seriously
thanks christine
I think it's just
there's a whole lot of concrete down here and nothing else to look at but arseholes, right?

Christine
Right

Stef
so tell me about the other guys
what are they in for?

Christine
I don't actually have that in front of me
I can go find out if you like

Stef
no it's not important
I already know I hate their fucking guts
and if the worst aaron is going to do is send me dick pics
well he already mentioned his dick or other people's dicks about thirty times today so I'm
you know
prepared

Christine
Most of them will be in for the same old same old anyway
From what I remember from a glance at the files, a decent proportion of them this year have actually been physically violent
Wholly unoriginal
But still actually physically violent so be careful
We only had one washout in my year but with your lot I'm guessing 2-4

Stef
do you make bets on that up there?

Christine
I refuse to answer on the grounds that it may incriminate me

Stef
lol
I'd love to know what's an original way to end up down here
other than the way I did, I mean

Christine
Well okay
A few years ago we had a guy who invested thousands of pounds in DurstCoin, the Limp Bizkit-themed cryptocurrency
The coin crashed like it was always going to and his "investment" was wiped out
All his savings
Apparently he got mad and started a fight when he was telling his story and someone else at the bar told him to "keep on rollin', baby"

Stef
you're making that up
there's no way that happened

Christine
Okay busted
Sorry

Stef
it's fine
lying is like
the least of your crimes

Christine
True

Stef
it's been really nice to talk to you
it actually really has
I didn't know how I felt about you
is that rude to say?

Christine
Probably but I don't mind
It's hard to say I haven't earned it
And it's been nice to talk to you, too

Stef
I kind of want to keep talking
I'm enjoying this little island of normal
normalish, anyway
but I'm tired
got a long day tomorrow in the lady dungeon
need my beauty sleep

Christine
Okay
Sleep well, Stef

And let me know if there's anything you need
I have some tricks up my sleeve
If you need it bad enough, I can have a go

Stef
I'll remember
thanks
nn christine

9
Vertigo

25 OCTOBER 2019 — FRIDAY

"Best behaviour, ladies," Indira says to the assembled Sisters in the ground floor kitchen, a mix of second years, third years, and sponsors. "We're going to have a guest."

Hasan, Indira's childhood-friend-turned-boyfriend, has been imminent for over a week, constantly delayed by work and—as Indira has told Christine in a slightly anxious whisper—contributing to her growing sexual frustration. But this morning he went to his boss and demanded a four-day weekend so he could visit his girlfriend and see the sights in sunny Almsworth. He had a birthday party to get to, he said.

Paige and Christine have snagged two chairs at the kitchen table, not ordinarily a precious commodity but in short supply this afternoon, as various second years mill about, preparing dishes, talking quietly to each other, and snatching the occasional shy glance at the third years. Christine, watching them, wonders what they think of her: do they see another woman? Or are they still fighting the programme, still viewing themselves and everyone around them as men too weak to stop themselves from being permanently altered?

"Yes," Paige says, elbowing Christine suggestively and jolting her out of her introspection, "I'm sure we're going to see *so* much of Hasan."

"What do you mean?"

"You *know* how she feels about him," Paige whispers, and adds an almost-too-quiet-to-hear impression of squeaking bedsprings. Christine, lightly and with love, hits her.

"Now," Indira's saying, ignoring Paige's commentary, "you should all have had the standard visitor protocol explained to you. Yes?" Christine nods, prompting the second-year girls. After a few seconds, most of them start nodding, too. "Good. The only slight wrinkle is that

Hasan believes Christine and I are transgender women, which means he might say something that suggests he 'knows'. I promise you, that's *all* he knows. So don't panic. That's Christine there, by the way." She points. Six second years stare.

"Hi," Christine says, waving with crooked fingers and wishing she'd worn a hoodie so she could cover her face and conceal her blush. She shuffles closer to Paige and whispers, "Hide me." Paige, amused, just pokes her with an elbow again.

"Is he right?" a second-year girl says.

"Right about what?" Indira says.

"That you're a trans woman?"

Indira smiles. "That's closest to how I view myself, yes. It's also how I've chosen to present myself to the outside world."

"Wow," the girl whispers.

"What about you?" one of the second years asks.

"Oh, uh, no comment," Christine says.

"Christine is still in her third year here," Indira says, "and has not yet been required to define her NPH; that's her New Personal History, if your sponsors haven't covered that yet." Her frown at the confused faces in front of her suggests they should have. "So don't hassle her about it. But she and Hasan have met before, much earlier in her transition, so for tonight, and whenever Hasan is around, she's a trans girl and so am I. He shouldn't cause you much trouble, anyway: Aunt Bea and your sponsors will be available to help you, and for the most part you will be separated from him. Hasan will be with me, and my group. Paige, don't complain."

"I wasn't going to!" Paige says, with an edge of sulk to her voice.

Paige collects fringe gender theories like Aunt Bea collects amusing coffee mugs, and the presence of an uncomplicatedly cis man inside the hallowed walls of Dorley will put a fairly large and unaccustomed restriction on her mealtime topic selection. Christine knows for a fact that Paige has spent hours this week listening to a podcast by a guy who claims there is only one gender, that it is the gender of angels, and that men and women are merely aspects of it. Paige has been waiting to talk about it with Abby, who is out of all of them the happiest to discuss gender apocrypha, but who has been away all week at her "real" job. Having to leave it until after Aunt Bea's big birthday dinner, when they'll all be too tired and sleepy to concentrate will be torture for her.

Paige's sponsor, Francesca, has told her off several times for cultivating so many unorthodox interests, to which Paige generally responds that the purpose of Dorley is to create *women,* not *boring* women. And besides, of the two of them, who has thirty thousand Instagram followers and who has sixteen?

There's a reason they don't socialise together.

"Think of it as good practice for being cisgender," Indira says, and Paige sticks out her tongue in response.

Paige explained to Christine a while back that she's stuck with her identity as a cis woman, that she ended up railroaded into it before she had a chance to think properly about the choice. When Christine asked why, Paige replied, "Marketability." Her Instagram followers and the fashion industry contacts she's accruing are her ticket to a future in which she will, she hopes, be able to do whatever she wants. It's too important to risk. Later that night, however, a drunk and talkative Paige cornered her, looked deeply and unsteadily into her eyes, and explained that her cisgender façade runs only as deep as it needs to, and that once she finds a partner she can trust, she will reveal herself absolutely and completely to them. "Assuming they don't already know everything about me," she added with the intense seriousness of the very drunk, just before a distraught look plastered itself to her face and she rushed off towards the nearest bathroom. Christine followed her and spent the next half hour holding Paige's hair out of the toilet.

One of the second years puts up her hand.

"Yes," Dira says, "Faye, is it?"

The girl called Faye takes a moment to reply. "Oh. Yes. Um. Who is this man, please? Has he come to evaluate us?"

"No," Dira says, laughing. "He's my boyfriend."

Faye and the other second years take an understandable handful of seconds to process this. Christine hasn't been keeping the closest eye on their development, but as far as she knows they completed the move up from the basement to the first-floor dorms shortly before the start of the semester. The slowest of them will have spent barely two months above ground. They'll still be coming to terms with their new identities, might still be mourning their old ones. They may well be capable of understanding that the third-year women looking up at them from the kitchen table with amused smiles (Paige) and worried frowns (Christine) are merely versions of them who have had longer to explore their womanhood, but the extra leap needed to understand that a woman who has gone through the very same programme is comfortable enough with herself to have a *boyfriend* from *out in the real world* is clearly one most of them are having trouble making.

"You should see them together," Christine says, to fill the silence and let the girls off the hook. "They're adorable."

"Thank you!" Indira beams at her.

"You won't have to talk to him," Paige says, with a meaningful glance at Dira, "if you don't want to. He's just here to see his girlfriend and eat a nice meal. And then you won't see hide nor hair of him for the rest of the weekend."

"How come?" asks Faye, official spokeswoman for her group. "If you don't mind my asking," she adds. She seems to have a bit of reflexive politeness going on.

"He's her boyfriend," Christine explains, hoping she doesn't have to go into any more detail.

Realisation—and fascination—dawns. "You're *allowed* that?" one of the girls says. Christine's pretty sure she hears another one whisper, awed, "*Sex? With an outsider?*"

"Of course we're allowed!" Dira says.

"Indira graduated years ago," says one of the sponsors Christine doesn't know very well. "When you graduate, you will regain all the freedoms you had before, including the freedom to associate intimately as you choose."

"And you will be in a position to use your freedoms *responsibly,* unlike before," Indira says, unwilling to be outsponsored.

"And you're really like us?" another second-year girl asks. "You really used to be a—?"

"Yes."

"Gosh," she says, and sounds both so innocent and so awed Christine can't stop a snort from escaping.

"I'm sorry," she says, "It's just, I remember being you. Everything's new and strange and, just when you're starting to get some kind of a handle on everything, my lovely Sister here—" Christine directs a meaningful thumb at Indira, "—goes and drops a bomb like that on you. It's a lot to take in."

Indira blows Christine a kiss, which Christine fends off, and the chatter in the room moves on. Most of the second-year girls return to the dishes they've been nursing, but one of them steps closer.

"It gets easier, right?" Faye asks. Christine finds in Faye's voice memories of waking every morning in her new bedroom, looking out at the world through real windows, and wondering how she was going to learn to face the world as a woman when, after a year underground, even the idea of going outside was extraordinary.

"It does," Christine says, putting all her conviction into it. "I promise." She smiles, half to reassure the girl and half because she can't help thinking of Stef, a little over a week ago, asking if he can be a girl. Different journeys, same destination.

"You're Christine, right?" Faye says. Christine nods. "Do you…like your name?"

"I do. She gave it to me—" she gestures at Dira again, "—and it didn't take me long to get used to it. A new name means no baggage, you know? It helps with sorting out who you're going to be from now on. It helps you move on. Of course, it helps if you *want* to move on."

Faye nods slowly. "I do," she says. "I do want to."

"Good," Christine says. Then, to cement in the girl's mind that the two of them are the same, that Christine is living proof that everything will be okay if she just keeps going, she adds, "So did I."

"You're very pretty," Faye says, smiling shyly and curling a stray strand of hair around her finger.

"So are you," Christine says. "You're beautiful, actually." Because she is: Faye's jaw is still a little swollen from recent-ish facial surgery and her hair is still growing out, but she has the kind of girl-next-door beauty Christine has, on occasion, been told she possesses herself.

The girl's smile broadens and she takes another half-step towards Christine before freezing in place, perhaps feeling like she almost crossed a boundary. Christine closes the distance between them, and pulls Faye into a quick, tight hug, trying to express with her body the things it might still be too early to say out loud: *It's okay to express your emotions. It's okay that you stopped fighting this. You're strong, not weak. Brave, not cowardly. You have a future. And it's okay to be happy when someone calls you beautiful.*

"You're going to be okay," she whispers to the girl instead, pulling back to look right in her shining eyes before releasing her.

***

"God, I hate this show."

"Why are you back for it every day, then? I have a distinct memory of you practically skipping over here not twenty minutes ago."

"What else am I going to do down here? Besides, *you* were already here, so my choice was either come over here and gradually expire from boredom in front of the telly or stay out there and die very, very quickly when one of the wandering dickheads decides it's time for a spot of kicking practice."

"You could just lock yourself in your room and wank. I thought that was your thing."

"Didn't I tell you about the friction sores? I'm sure I told you about the friction sores."

"It's possible I've deliberately forgotten."

"Well, okay, when a boy and his cock love each other very much—"

"Stefan, will you please shut your boyfriend up?"

"Aaron. Be quiet and watch your favourite show."

"God. Fine. Whatever. I can't wait to see if the guy will like the jacket."

The common room has acquired a small pile of beanbag chairs and some large, only moderately uncomfortable cushions, fetched from the storeroom by Maria after Aaron refused to spend any more time in the vicinity of Declan unless he was forced to take more regular showers, which neither his sponsor's powers of persuasion nor her taser have proved adequate for. The beanbag chairs, Aaron argued, would allow him and Stefan to position themselves far away from Declan's odour wherever it may appear. Maria eventually relented, returning from a side room with enough squashy living room furniture to furnish an Ikea, much of which has ended up spread around the common room and inhabited by Declan and his fellow unfortunates, but some of which remains localised by the TV. Aaron also asked for a can of air freshener, which Maria refused. "Probably because it's highly weaponisable," Aaron said at the time, describing, largely with mime, the process of fatally decontaminating Declan in such a ridiculous manner that Stefan, despite himself, laughed.

There are times, when Aaron goes whole hours without saying anything more than mildly objectionable, that Stefan has to remind himself exactly what the little shit did to the women of the Royal College, because God help him if Aaron isn't growing on him.

"Of course he'll like the jacket," Will says tiredly. "They always like the jacket. They don't know how to dress themselves; they'll like anything that doesn't make them look stupid. It's the same every time. R/MaleFashionAdvice crap. Why do we watch this again?"

"Because we don't control the TV," Adam says mildly.

Stefan doesn't know exactly how the four of them became a unit oppositional to the others, but after the run-ins some of them have had with Declan, Raph and Ollie over the past week, he's grateful. Very nearly grateful, anyway. By unspoken agreement they pee, wash and shower in pairs: usually Stefan and Aaron, Will and Adam. It took a couple of days for the group properly to coalesce, but after Ollie had another go at getting his sponsor's taser off her and got thrown in the cells, after Raph threatened Aaron in the bathroom because he claimed Aaron looked at his dick, and after Declan threw a plastic dinner plate at Adam's head and bruised him quite badly, it was difficult not to acknowledge that there was strength in numbers, especially if those numbers comprised the most calm and least murderously unpredictable people in the basement.

Martin, the drunk driver, has been almost entirely absent, holed up in his room, indulging in his own self-pity. Stefan would have been surprised at his sponsor letting him skip the socialisation element of his rehabilitation, but on the few times he's observed them together it's been obvious that Pamela, Martin's sponsor, despises him. Probably hoping he washes out, whatever that entails; despite his two informants upstairs, Stefan still doesn't know. Everyone claims ignorance.

"What do you think I'd have to do to get Maria to give me control over the TV for one day?" Aaron says. Stefan, lying upside down with his head resting on a beanbag chair and his legs dangling over the backboard of the sofa, can feel the vibrations of Aaron's voice in his ribcage: Aaron's lying lengthways, with his feet tucked under Stefan's back. The boy's toes get cold, apparently.

Aaron's surprisingly tactile, Stefan's noticed, provided he's the one who initiates it.

"Reform," Stefan says. "Pledge never to send another dick pic or harass another woman as long as you live."

Aaron laughs. "I don't think she'd believe me. And I still don't get how you guessed that I did that."

"You just look the type. Something about you says, 'I send unsolicited photographs of my penis to random women.' "

"He's right," Will says. "You really do look the type."

Stefan bites the inside of his cheek for a moment. That pronoun's getting harder to deal with. But he's talked it over with both Christine and Abby, trying out alternatives like *they/them* and *zie/hir* and even, at Christine's insistence, consenting to be *she/her* for a night, but there's nothing that doesn't make him feel like an imposter.

He's a *he* until he's not, he told Christine, which seemed to piss her off enough that it was days before she contacted him again.

"Eat me, William," Aaron says, showing him the finger.

"Shut up, Aaron."

"I'm so glad we're all getting along," Stefan says. Aaron turns the finger on him instead. "Now will you shush and watch the show? I'm invested."

"How can you even see like that?" Aaron says. "You're, like, upside down."

"He can see fine like that," Adam says before Stefan can say anything. "I used to watch videos that way all the time back home."

"And where *is* home, Adam?" Aaron says, folding his arms.

"Just home."

The three of them have been trying to nail down Adam's origins all week, but they haven't managed to gather anything more than Aaron told Stef on his first day: Adam was raised in a church that may or may not be a literal cult, and it's called the New Church. Stefan asked Christine to look into it, but she didn't even bother Googling: "Do you know how many religious institutions are called 'The New Church of Something Something'?"

Adam's childhood was clearly both sheltered and religious enough to inculcate in him the belief that the "sins of the flesh" originate in demonic temptation, but for all his apparent beliefs he's surprisingly soft-spoken, preferring to keep himself mostly to himself, though his near-whispered arguments with Will have occasionally expanded to include the others. A few days ago, unable to contain his curiosity, Stefan tested him, claiming as part of a story he was telling to have kissed a boy once, after school, but instead of the condemnation—or possibly the exorcism—he expected, Adam merely asked, neutrally, if he enjoyed it. But then there's the fact that sometimes, when Adam talks, when he says something in his soft voice that chills Stefan to the core, he sounds like he's reading aloud from a book only he can see.

At least Will is simple. He's a walking Reddit post who went home for the holidays after his first year at Saints and found out by accident that his younger brother was gay. So Will beat the shit out of him. Simple, but not actually pleasant. Tabitha, his sponsor, thinks he's an idiot and delights in antagonising him. She's been pressing him about his brother: yesterday she told Will he'd been declared officially missing, and that his brother had been seen to breathe a sigh of relief. Will didn't take it well. That night, Stefan was subjected to another hours-long session of yelling from the room next door, which didn't interrupt his movies but did give him a few extra things to write in the notes he keeps on his fellow prisoners.

The show wraps up, and Aaron takes it as his cue to roll off the sofa. "I need a piss and a shower," he announces, and grabs at Stefan's arm. "Come on, stop sitting like a weirdo and come with."

They collect their washing kits, towels and dressing gowns from their respective rooms and meet up in the shower annexe, where Aaron startles Stefan by facing him and disrobing, underwear and all.

"Uh," Stefan says.

"Look at me," Aaron says.

"Why?"

"I want you to be honest: is the Goserelin having an effect on me?"

"What kind of an effect do you think it's having?"

Aaron taps Stefan lightly on the cheek, to get him to stop looking away, and cups a hand against his chest, just under where a breast would be, if he had any. "Am I growing tits?"

"*What?* Why would you possibly think that?"

"Will said it lowers testosterone," Aaron says. "So, am I growing tits?"

"Aaron," Stefan says, "the implant's not going to make you grow breasts. It's just to, you know, calm you down."

He doesn't actually know for certain whether blocking testosterone results in breast development; when he tried to research HRT he barely got beyond the basics before it seemed better for his immediate mental health to close the laptop and continue to deny everything. But it doesn't *seem* likely.

"In *Fight Club*," Aaron insists, "the guy lost his balls, and grew tits."

Stefan turns away from Aaron, his non-existent breasts, and his naked body, and throws his robe and towel over the rail beside one of the shower heads. "I haven't seen it," he says. "But it's a movie, right? Not known for being medically accurate."

"But—"

"Will said his dad was on the stuff. Didn't say anything about growing breasts, and that seems like the kind of thing he would mention."

"Listen—"

"Stop showing me your cock and have a shower."

"I'm not—"

"I can hear it slapping around between your legs. Shower. Now."

Stefan stares at the reassuringly plain tiled wall while he undresses, shutting out any further babble as best he can. It's not *pleasant* to think about Aaron being changed against his will, even though he's done awful things and, up until now, escaped the consequences. And if he's to take Christine at her word, for all that she sounds occasionally a little too much like she's in a secular cult of her own—the Cult of Dorley—unchecked, people like Aaron have a tendency to escalate. Maybe it *is* better to catch them early?

Stupid to think about. Stupid to dwell on. Who cares if this is a good place or not? Who cares if there's another way to reform these men? All that matters is that Stefan, who hasn't harassed, hit, manipulated or run anyone over, gets what he needs. Screw these guys. Best to believe Christine: they deserve this, and they will, ultimately, be helped by it.

Unless they wash out.

He rinses out the shampoo, holds his head under the water for longer than strictly necessary. The water's slightly too hot and he luxuriates in it, feels his skin tingle under its heat, feels his flesh begin pleasingly to numb, and breathes steam, exhales hot vapour. For a little while, the shower becomes his world.

And thus he completely misses Declan entering the shower annexe.

He only realises something's happening when Aaron hits the floor by his feet.

"What the fuck?" Stefan yells, stepping back.

"Stef-an!" Declan yells. He's wearing trousers and socks but no top, giving Stefan a first look at Declan's figure: he's built like a guy who drinks beer every night but gets a lot of exercise. Literally barrel-shaped. You see a lot of guys like that if you live near a certain kind of pub; you don't often see them this young, though. "Nice of you to join us! I was just telling Aa-ron here about my plan."

"Uh—"

"Don't ask him about his fucking plan," Aaron mutters, scrambling to his feet and nearly slipping on the wet floor. He grabs Stefan's upper arm to stay upright and his dick slaps unwelcomely against Stefan's thigh. The combined weight of them both makes Stefan unsteady, and for a moment the tiled floor wobbles in front of him. "And, yeah, welcome back," Aaron continues. "You were seriously zoned out."

"What's going on?" Stefan hisses. Declan's walking away from them both, towards the other end of the shower annexe, and sticks his hand under Aaron's still-running shower on the way, washing a dark liquid off his knuckles. Stefan makes the connection, takes Aaron's jaw in his hand and turns it around, inspecting him: blood on his temple, a trickle out of his nostril. "Jesus, Aaron, did he hit you?"

"God," Aaron says, "you really *were* out of it. Yes, he fucking hit me!"

"Aww," Declan's saying, as he makes an obscene gesture, "look at you two. You're so cute! Do you sleep together, too?"

Stefan, sure now that Aaron is steady enough on his feet that he won't fall, carefully removes Aaron's hands from his upper arm and steps back, away from the running water. "What are you on about, Declan?"

"Sitting together," Declan says. "Showering together. Only one thing left."

"Declan, you imbecile," Stefan says, hoping to draw out this conversational break in the confrontation long enough for Pippa or Maria or *someone* to see them on camera, "this is a comm-un-al show-er." He spaces out the syllables the way Declan does when he says someone's name. "We have no choice but to shower together. It's just like after PE at school. You remember school?"

"Fuck you, you patronising prick."

"You're antagonising him!" Aaron whispers.

"What's your plan, mate?" Stefan says, ignoring Aaron, who closes his eyes in frustration, but it's either keep Declan talking or deal with whatever happens when he stops. *Where are you, Pippa?*

"Oll-ie keeps going for the girls," Declan says. "Stupid. Instantly piled on. Instantly taken out. But if he went for you instead, the girls' favourite little pet, and got a hand round *your* throat, they'd *have* to let him out."

"Me?" Stefan asks. "Why me?"

"You're too nice," Declan says. "Everyone else, even this little shit—" he gestures at a defiant Aaron, who is holding onto a pipe to stay upright, "—talks back to the bitches. Few of us got zapped for it. You? Not even the drunk and the weirdo are as nice to them as you. You *love* them. They love you. You're their spy. You work for them. They protect you."

"They haven't tased me, and that makes you think I work for them? I just haven't done anything to make them have to! There's no point trying to fight them: they have weapons, Declan, and there are locks on all the doors. There's concrete walls and no windows. It's a prison. You don't escape a prison with a clever plan. They're built so you *can't.*"

"That is *exactly* what their little bitch would say."

"Nothing's going to happen here, Declan," Stefan says, taking another step away from the shower, towards the entrance. "Just calm down."

"Fuck you," Declan says, and rushes artlessly forward. Stefan tries to step out of the way, isn't quite fast enough, and could have been badly hurt if Aaron hadn't collided with Declan from the side. They struggle to stay upright: Stefan staggers back into the wall, Aaron drops onto one knee and starts massaging his shoulder, and Declan slams into the side wall. It looks like he's going to get his balance back first, but before he can do anything, Monica, his sponsor, steps into the annexe.

"Okay, Declan," she says, sounding very tired. "Stop fucking around."

"Can't shoot your taser in here, Mon-i-ca," Declan taunts.

"Hence this," she says, unclipping her baton from her belt. "You two: scram," she says to Stefan and Aaron.

"You sure?" Stefan says. "You going to be okay with him on your own?"

"I'm not going to be alone in a few seconds—" her eyes flicker down, and she smirks, "—so if you don't want any other women seeing your junk, I suggest you robe up and leave."

"Right," Stefan says, and pulls his robe over his shoulders. Aaron's is lying on the other side of the bathroom in the middle of a large puddle of water, so Stefan throws him his towel. Aaron's still tying it closed when Pippa and Maria follow Monica into the annexe.

"I didn't start it, Maria," Aaron says.

"I know," Maria says, as Stefan catches Pippa's eye and shrugs. "Go to your rooms and get dressed."

"Have fun with Declan," Aaron says, and Stefan puts a hand on each of his bare shoulders and pushes him out of the annexe.

"Three strikes, Declan," Monica says, "and—"

The closing bathroom door cuts her off. Stefan doesn't want to speculate on what "three strikes" means for Declan. Doesn't want ever to have to think about him again, if he can help it. All he wants is to get to his room and collapse onto his bed.

Unexpectedly, someone else had the exact same thought.

"Aaron," Stefan says, settling onto the edge of the mattress and not bothering even to try to kick him out; it would be far too much effort, "why are you in my room? Correction: why are you in my room, naked?"

"I'm not naked! I'm wearing a towel. And don't worry, I'm not all lewd under here; my dick is securely tucked back. It's hiding, actually. Trauma reaction."

"What? To Declan?"

"Yes, to Declan! Don't make him sound so trivial. Remember, he was the one who tried to fillet himself? Maybe if you'd seen it, you wouldn't be so fucking blasé about him."

"I'm not blasé," Stefan says, leaning forward and fishing a pair of trousers and a hoodie out of his wardrobe and passing them to Aaron. "Look," he says, holding up a shaking arm. "I was just trying to keep him talking until help arrived, or at the very least get farther away from him to increase the chances of him slipping and braining himself on the tile before he got to us."

"Don't say that," Aaron says, dropping the towel on the floor, "he tripped me, remember. While you were off in your mind palace, or whatever. That could have been *me*, braining myself on the tile."

Aaron doesn't turn around to get dressed, so Stefan, judging himself steady enough to stand, picks out fresh clothes and faces the wall while he pulls them on, trying to make himself believe that just because he's now seen Aaron's penis twice, it doesn't necessarily mean there's going to be a third time. A delusion, obviously; Aaron's genital obsession borders on the pathological. No wonder he took all those pictures.

"Look on the bright side," Stefan says, flopping back onto the bed. "If you die down here, no more women will have to be subjected to your…amateur photography."

Aaron joins him on the bed, perching on the end nearest the door. "My what?"

"Your dick pics, Aaron."

"Oh." He laughs, still apparently unrepentant. "Those."

"For fuck's sake, Aaron," Stefan says, grabbing the box of tissues from the bedside table, "you're still bleeding."

"Uh, what? Where?"

"Sit still," Stefan commands, and when Aaron complies, he dabs at the cut near Aaron's eyebrow, cleaning the wound as much as he can with the wadded tissue. He takes another one out of the box, spits on it, and works on cleaning the blood off Aaron's cheek and upper lip.

"This is weird," Aaron says, watching Stefan with careful eyes.

"Grow up," Stefan mutters, wetting another tissue, "and *stay still*." Aaron fidgets, so Stefan stills him with a hand on his shoulder. Has he never been taken care of like this before? He's acting like—

"Ahem."

Stefan doesn't jump, but Aaron does, and it smudges some of the remaining blood in a line along his jaw. Under Pippa's gaze, Stefan licks his thumb and wipes it off. She doesn't bother hiding her amusement.

"Hey, Pippa," Stefan says, "can you look at this cut? I don't *think* it needs stitches, but I'm no expert."

She rolls her eyes, yanks Aaron's head roughly to the side and peers at his wound. "He'll be fine." She releases him and steps backward, flexing the hand that touched him. "Since you're both here, I can save Maria a job: you're all going to have medical examinations tomorrow, so be ready and don't muck around."

"That sounds ominous," Aaron says, raising a hand to dab at his wound and flinching when Stefan slaps it away.

"Don't mess with it!" Stefan whispers.

"It's nothing to worry about," Pippa says, before Aaron can complain. "You'll have a physical exam, there'll be some questions to answer, and we'll be taking some blood—so drink the bottle of water that will be in your dumbwaiter in the morning. You'll need to provide a sperm sample, so, Aaron, Maria said it would be best if you left your penis alone for the night."

"No promises," Aaron says. "What's the blood test for?"

Pippa recites, rote: "We'll be checking your general health and ensuring your Goserelin implants aren't causing you any problems."

"Yeah, what's with that, anyway?" Aaron says. "Maria says it's to help keep us calm."

"It is," Pippa says.

"Yeah, well, it's not working on fucking Declan, is it? It's not the first time he's come at one of us."

"Monica will deal with Declan. Now go away. I need to talk to Stefan."

Aaron stands up and steps unsteadily around Pippa. "Don't hurt him too badly," he says, before winking at Stefan—an utterly baffling gesture—and departing. Pippa shuts the door with the back of her foot and leans against it.

"Jesus Christ," Stefan mutters, throwing the dirty tissues into the bin and lying back on the bed, trying to force the tension out of his shoulders. When it's just him and Pippa in the room, he feels safe: the worst she's ever done is yell at him—and, yes, trigger a very bad dysphoric episode, but she didn't know that was what she was doing—whereas the men, even Aaron, still have him on edge. Declan, today: a reminder of what most of them are capable of.

"What's your deal, Stefan?" Pippa says.

"I have a deal?" Stefan props himself up on his shoulders and looks at her.

"Playing mother hen with the boy flasher there."

"Oh, right." He drops back down again and starts stretching his fingers and toes. "I think I've adopted him."

"You've adopted him."

"Like a puppy. One of those ones that hasn't yet worked out that nibbling on the other dogs is bad."

"You let him in your room."

Stefan shrugs. "I didn't mean to. He just followed me in. And then he was bleeding, so I cleaned it up. Is there any reason we don't have first-aid kits in these rooms?"

"Yes. Look, you *know* he's dangerous."

"To women. Not to me." It hurts to say.

"What do you mean?"

"He's a sexual harasser, right? He's not sexually interested in me, so—"

"It's not about that, Stefan," Pippa says, briefly closing her eyes. "Sexual harassment…it's about power, it's about the thrill. The target often doesn't even matter. And it escalates: just flashing people and sending them pictures isn't going to satisfy him forever."

"I get that," Stefan says patiently. "I know he's a piece of shit. And I know he needs to change, and you hope—somehow—to change him down here. But he isn't harassing me, and he literally doesn't have a way to send me pictures here. I'm safe with him, I think."

"Stefan," Pippa says, perching on the chair by the computer and addressing him like an unruly child at his first detention, "we watch him on the cameras. He's flashed you. Multiple times."

"I mean, twice, maybe, but that's—"

"Half a dozen times, actually. And that's if you don't count just getting undressed in the shower without turning away."

"Oh. See, I *was* counting that," Stefan says. Pippa shakes her head, and he adds, "Why does he do it?"

"Who the hell knows?" Pippa says. She breathes out heavily through her nose. "These guys, they're just…They're all nightmares, at least for now."

"Yeah," Stefan agrees, without thinking, "for now."

Pippa nods, fidgets with her homemade bracelet. And then she blinks, straightens her back and glares at him. "You know that's you, too, right? You're here for the exact same reason."

"What?" Stefan says, caught off guard by the change in Pippa's mood. "Flashing?"

"You're *dangerous*," she says.

"Oh. Yeah. Right. I'm dangerous." Stefan digs his head a little deeper into the bed covers. "It's too easy to forget that, when you're talking to me like a normal person."

"You don't like the reminder?"

"Not really."

***

It's Aunt Bea's birthday and, true to her habits, she has the second years making a huge celebratory meal. Also true to her habits, there's a point to it: to assess how well the girls are settling into their new identities. Because it's one thing to sit quietly in your room and be comfortable; quite another to participate in a stressful and often confusing multi-person, multi-hour endeavour—like, say, preparing a four-course meal for your notoriously critical and highly intimidating schoolmarm-cum-kidnapper—without reverting to old, toxic patterns of behaviour.

And it is *hot* in the kitchen. Four ovens, eight pans bubbling away on two hobs, and a dozen bodies milling around will do that, especially when protocol dictates that they're not allowed to open the main doors, lest one of the second years makes a run for it. The small windows, high up and discreetly barred, are barely adequate ventilation on an ordinary day; today, they might as well be decorative.

Christine, ducking back into the kitchen long enough to manoeuvre around a panicking second year, steal a Pepsi Max from the fridge, and wink at Faye on her way out, is sweating by the time she makes it back to the relative serenity of the dining hall. She's also a little tense; she knows from last year just how badly the cooks are overheating.

In the dining hall—the opulent opposite to the functional kitchen—various Dorley women gather in loose groups, awaiting the arrival of Aunt Bea. Abby, Vicky and Paige have claimed a small table in a quiet corner and Christine joins them, dropping into a chair next to Abby and cracking open her can.

"Jesus, it's hot in there," she says.

"Right?" Vicky says. "Remember when that was us?"

"I remember my soufflé collapsed."

"No, no," Paige says, "it was *my* soufflé that collapsed. You did the casserole that was cold in the middle and crunchy at the edges, and Vicky made all those parsley puns."

"You're right," Christine says, and takes a large swig. "As usual." She wonders how Aunt Bea feels about having her birthday catered every year by a gaggle of newly-in-knickers second-adolescent twentysomethings whose ability to cook an edible dish was not on the list of criteria for kidnapping. At least one of this lot can bake a credible cake. "When're Dira and Hasan getting here?"

"Any minute," Abby says, looking up from her laptop, "but it's been 'any minute' for about the last twenty." Christine cranes her neck to look at her screen: Dorley admin stuff. Nothing she hasn't seen before on her occasional trawls through the secure files.

"There was a signal failure," Paige says, tapping on her phone. "Minor delays."

"Remember, Tina, you're a trans girl tonight," Vicky says, reaching around Abby to poke Christine in the shoulder.

"I know," Christine says. "We had this conversation already."

"Actually, why *are* you trans to Dira's family but cis to my girlfriend?"

"Poor planning."

"Really?"

"Exceptionally poor planning," Abby says, peering through her glasses at the laptop screen and not looking up. Christine ignores her and drains her Pepsi.

A sudden crash from the kitchen forces a surprised belch out of her, and one of the second-year girls bursts through the double doors, runs through the dining room and out into the corridor on the other side.

"Wait," Christine says, "was that Faye?"

Before anyone can answer, Nell, Faye's sponsor, follows her halfway through the dining room before stopping, throwing up her hands and turning around. "I have *had* it with that girl tonight!" Nell shouts.

At their table, Paige clenches her fists and looks away. Her reaction pushes Christine to her feet in less than a second; if there's one thing no-one at Dorley needs, it's an authority figure in a rage. Nell is pacing back and forth in the dining hall, working herself up as she goes, so it's easy for Christine to plant herself in Nell's path, stopping her short without having actively to grab her attention.

"What? Yes?" Nell snaps. "Christine, isn't it?"

"Yeah," Christine says. Back in the corner, she sees Vicky hugging Paige, who has sunk into her chair and is looking everywhere but at anyone. "I can go talk to Faye."

"How would that help?"

Christine shrugs, affecting uncertainty. "I think she would benefit from talking to someone closer to her own age. And we already talked a little, earlier."

"I remember. You think one hug is enough to build a rapport?"

"I'm an outside voice. A new face." Out of the corner of her eye, Christine sees Pippa exit the kitchen, take in the scene in the middle of the room and walk over to Abby and Vicky, who are still comforting Paige.

"You're still in the programme, aren't you? You're not qualified for this; what will your sponsor say?" Nell makes a show of looking around. "Is she even *here?*"

"It's fine, Nell!" Abby yells, closing her laptop and taking off her glasses, the better to glare. "Untwist your undies and let Chrissy talk to the girl!"

"I still don't see what good it will do," Nell says.

"I *was* her, only a year ago," Christine says, choosing not to be visibly annoyed by Nell's attitude. She is *not* this woman's inferior just because she isn't technically free yet. "I think I can relate to her on a level you, perhaps, can't."

"You won't—"

"*Nell,*" Abby says, in her sternest voice.

"Fine," Nell says, stepping aside. "She's all yours. Knock yourself out on her thick fucking head."

"I will," Christine says, "just as soon as I check on my friend."

Paige looks up as Christine approaches, and nods: she's okay. Vicky's holding her hand and gently stroking her upper arm, and Abby's been having a whispered conversation with Pippa.

"Hi, Christine," Pippa says, "I think this was partly my fault."

"She's having problems with Stef…an," Abby says, just about managing to add the extra syllable to Stef's name in time.

"I'm not having problems," Pippa says. "That's the flipping *point.* He's so…I want to say docile, but that's not it. He's nothing but friendly to me, and now that he's spending time with some of the other boys down there, he's started, well, needling them."

"Needling them how?" Christine says, looking behind her at Nell, who has declined to resume pacing in favour of glowering at her.

"He's worked out what Aaron did to get here. Most of it, anyway. And he keeps *bringing it up.* Just throwing it in Aaron's face all the time, like he's trying to get it to sink in that what he did was wrong."

"So? That's good, isn't it?"

"I don't know! And he's too damn *kind.* I walked in on him patching Aaron up after the little sod got in a fight! And you *know* how long it normally takes them to get to that level of empathy. Not to mention the physical intimacy involved!" She kicks lightly at a table leg. "I feel like I don't understand him at all. And I need to, so when the treatments start—and they start *soon*—I have an idea how to coerce him, how to control him. I'm flying flipping blind, Christine!"

"You still have the sister thing," Christine says. "Pretty potent means of control. Look, I'm sorry, but I've got to go talk to Faye before her bitch of a sponsor gets impatient and goes after her. Pip, why not ask Abby to go down and talk to your boy? She's got the sponsor experience, and she's a blank slate as far as this intake is concerned. She'll be a good second pair of eyes. Maybe she can see something in him."

"That's an *excellent* idea!" Abby says, beaming, radiating such absolute certainty that Pippa starts nodding before Abby even finishes speaking.

"We're good?" Christine says. "Good. And don't tell Nell I said she's a bitch." And she flees, following Faye into the rats' nest of corridors that form the back half of the ground floor.

***

What is Pippa's deal, anyway? He'd love to turn her question back on her, find out why she seems offended by his refusal to be confrontational, but he's not sure the answer is worth pursuing: if the clues he's picked up about the coming year are anything to go by, every woman who's been through Dorley has a period of pretty serious and sustained trauma in her recent past. Risking triggering Pippa just to satisfy his own curiosity would be cruel; it might also get him tased. And, as Declan pointed out, Stefan's on a good run of not getting tased.

Hell, maybe if he does something provocative enough to get her to zap him, it might relieve her of some of her obvious tension.

The sound of the biometric lock startles him, and he has time to wonder whether Pippa really has come back down to give him a quick tase just for the fun of it when an entirely unfamiliar face appears around the half-open door.

"Hi! Can I come in?"

No, not unfamiliar. It's Abby. She enters in response to his confused nod; less than a fortnight in a basement and already he's completely unused to the idea of someone asking for permission to enter his room.

She's not dressed anything like she was in the photobooth pictures, though. Instead of casual clothes, a bare face and tied-back hair, she's wearing a loose black and white dress with a repeating monochrome dandelion pattern that inverts at her waist as it crosses the matching belt. Her skin glistens and glitters around her eyes and her hair hangs in tight curls around her face, brushing her bare shoulders as she walks.

Stefan takes a breath and forgets to let it out for a few moments.

"Hi," he says eventually.

She closes the door behind her and settles carefully on the chair by the computer. "Hi, Stef," she says, reminding him what a genuine, warm smile looks like.

On the bed, Stefan retreats behind his knees, wrapping his arms around his shins. Faced with such beauty, Stefan feels exceptionally ugly. "You look…*seriously* good," he says, pleased to manage the whole sentence without the thick feeling in the back of his throat impeding him too much.

She smiles at him again, and he swallows before envy chokes him.

"Before we say anything else," she says, pulling a remote just like Pippa's out of her purse, "let's get some privacy." With some ceremony she taps two buttons on the remote, and the light strip on the ceiling goes from red to green.

"I, um, didn't know it could do that."

"No cameras," she says, "and no microphones. Real privacy."

A ball of tension Stefan's been carrying for over a week escapes him in a laugh, sharp and loud and ugly, and he buries his head in his knees to stop it. "Sorry. That's just a weird concept right now."

"I know," Abby says. "I remember." He stares at her for a moment, making room in his head, as he has for Christine, Pippa, Maria and the others, that this relaxed, stunning woman was once imprisoned down here. The concept is yet to become any more believable. "It was a bit different, though, in my day," Abby continues. "The beds were smaller and nastier, and we didn't have PCs, just those wifi video player things. They were *awful.* They used to lose connection all the time."

"When were you down here?"

"Ten years ago, I think?" she says, uncertain, looking up at the ceiling as if something there might jog her memory. "Yes. Ten years. We'd redecorated by the time Melissa came through."

"It's completely mad, you know," Stefan says. "You and Christine are both so normal, yet you both talk casually about the time you spent down here, in this bloody dungeon."

"Christine not always so casually, I imagine," Abby says, frowning and crinkling one side of her mouth.

"Yeah. That's true."

"It's fresher for her. And, Stef, I want to say, now I finally have the chance to tell you in person: thank you for not revealing our secret. Frankly, you could have broken us."

Her fingers sit curled in her lap, the nails painted to match her dress. He clenches his own until the knuckles crack. Feels like breaking them one at a time.

"Sometimes I still think I should have," he says. "This place isn't exactly ethical, is it?"

"No, but—" Abby starts.

"—it works," Stefan finishes. "Sorry, but I know." His throat swells and his voice shakes, but he continues, monotone, "I've heard it from Christine. And from you. Dorley works. Everyone gets better. It's worth it in the end. Every fucking girl I meet down here is stunningly beautiful, fully invested in the betterment of mankind, and thinks torture is completely and totally justified."

"Are you okay, Stef?"

"Fuck, don't…"

"Stef?"

"Please don't call me that," Stefan whispers, unable to look at her anymore. Her presence, gorgeous and carefree, is a weight pressing down on him, a greater torture than anything the sponsors can devise. He's crushed, broken, and more aware of his body, of his shape, of the feel of his skin as he's ever been.

Misshapen and ugly.

Abby stands, or he thinks she does; he's not looking. She makes noises consistent with standing, at any rate: the silken whisper of expensive clothes, worn well. Makes it worse.

"What should I call you?" she says.

"Nothing."

"But—"

He has to make her understand so he glares up at her and sees only kindness and concern returned; undeserved but offered nonetheless. His anger and his shame fail him, are burned away, and he bites his lip until blood comes.

She reaches for him and that's when it breaks, the thing that's been keeping everything locked up all these years. Stefan doesn't cry, can't cry, has never been able to push out from himself the despair that consumes him, but by holding his hand, by sitting with him, by giving him permission, Abby finds the barrier and she breaks it. Stefan cries.

Impossible to say where he goes, but sometimes being looked upon kindly is the worst thing anyone can do to him.

The first thing he feels when he starts to come back is her arm around his shoulders. She's resting her chin on the top of his head and gently stroking the back of his hand. When she feels him move, she releases her grip on him, but he doesn't want her to let go, not yet, so he pushes back against her, asks silently for a few more minutes of real, human contact.

She keeps hold of him as he blows his nose, cleans his face, checks to make sure he hasn't dirtied her dress—no; he pulled himself up so tight that he cried almost entirely into the fabric of his trousers and the sleeves of his hoodie—and, eventually shrugs his shoulders and moves away, releasing her.

"Sorry," he says, backing up against the headboard.

Abby returns to the chair by the computer. "It's quite all right."

"I think I needed that."

"I could tell."

"It's been a while."

"You poor thing."

"And you can call me Stef. I was just being— It's fine. Really."

"Okay, Stef. Thank you. Are you ready to tell me what hurt you so much?"

He forces a smile. "You. You're beautiful. All the women here are, but since Christine they've all been…neutral towards me, at best. Which makes it a little easier to deal with, being around them when I have to be like this. But—" he holds up a hand when she opens her mouth, "—don't apologise. It's just my idiot brain doing cartwheels and landing on its arse."

She nods. "I feel like I should know just what to say here," she says, "but I don't. You don't respond like anyone we've ever had come through here. For all my experience, I'm at a loss."

Stefan laughs. "I'm kind of pleased to be an enigma."

"Well, you're definitely confounding Pippa."

"Oh?"

"She's why I'm here, actually. She doesn't know how to control you. Came upstairs complaining about how lost at sea she is. Christine suggested I offer Pippa a second pair of eyes and I jumped at the chance. I wanted to check in on you in person. See how the subject of our little conspiracy is doing."

"I think we've answered that," Stefan says. "Not great. How is Christine, anyway? We don't talk as much as I thought we would."

"She's been busy. Aunt Bea noticed she's been slacking on some aspects of her development. So she's been working hard on that."

"Huh. I thought she was basically done with this place."

"There are a few hoops she has to jump through before she can graduate. Most of them she's been dealing with fine on her own. She's very independent, but in a good way. Indira has the easiest sponsorship since, well, me."

"Melissa didn't give you trouble?"

"Almost none. When she came here, she was falling and she knew it. She just didn't know how to stop. I…caught her, and the rest is history. She was never aggressive with me. Mostly just confused."

He wishes he had a copy of the photobooth pictures, or any other picture of Melissa, but he can still remember her face, and he finds it difficult to superimpose his memory of Mark onto the person who came to Dorley, years ago. Better to think of her happy, anyway; graduated from this place, off in the world somewhere, living life.

Abby, wanting to talk about Melissa as much as he does, fills in the story behind the photobooth pictures; it's amusingly, delightfully mundane. Stefan follows up with some stories from his childhood, from back when Melissa was still around (and still Mark), and after a while they settle into an easy back and forth. He hadn't realised how much he missed having a normal conversation with a normal person. And Abby, like Christine, is shockingly normal, once you allow for the fact that her calibration for *normal* is balanced at least partly around her obvious belief in Dorley Hall.

They agree on the story Abby will take back to Pippa: that Stef is compliant and helpful because he wants to be treated well, because he considers himself "better" than the other boys—Abby's going to hint at a superiority complex—and because he's worried that if he isn't, Pippa will follow through on her threat and tell his sister he's dead. It's little more than a restatement of the information Pippa already has, but coming directly from Abby instead of Pippa's own limited experience. "It'll be enough," Abby says confidently, patting Stefan's hand.

He asks her about the impending medical examination and she fills in a few vital details: it's to establish a baseline for their upcoming estradiol injections; it's to make sure the Goserelin hasn't had any unexpected side-effects; it's to provide sperm for freezing.

"We want you to be able to have a child, in the future, if you want one," Abby says, and Stefan shakes his head at the sheer absurdity of it: it really is possible to believe that Dorley wants nothing but the best for its residents, as long as you squint enough that the full year of torture, the nonconsensual surgery, the complete isolation from your old life and all the other indignities and violations fade out of focus.

Abby excuses herself not long after—it's Aunt Bea's birthday dinner, and she can't miss it—but hugs him again before she leaves. It's all he can do to maintain his composure.

"You're very sweet, Stef," she says. "Melissa was exactly right about you."

"Thank you," Stefan says.

"Oh, and one more thing before I go," she says, holding up the remote. "You're going to be *so* pretty."

She grins and reactivates the surveillance before he can respond with the disbelief such a ridiculous statement clearly deserves.

***

It doesn't take Christine long to find Faye: people don't normally come back here unless they're making use of the extremely barebones gym room or fetching something from long-term storage, and very few people are audibly crying when they do so.

There's a small conservatory at the back of Dorley's ground floor. It's poorly positioned and poorly insulated, having no view to speak of and no time of year in which it is pleasant to inhabit, so it's become a storage room for old furniture, old books, old appliances, and anything else rarely or never used.

Faye, tear- and mascara-stained, sits cross-legged on a dust sheet that covers what probably was once a valuable chaise longue before it was skeletonised by moths. She's kicked off her shoes—heels far too high for her height, and the sort of thing only the stupid or the terminally glamorous would choose to wear while preparing a meal—and she's holding her ankles tight enough in each hand that the skin has whitened.

"Hi," Christine says quietly, because Faye hasn't noticed her yet and she doesn't want to scare her.

"Hey," Faye says, following up with a revoltingly liquid sniff before continuing, "unless you brought Nell, in which case, uh…"

"No Nell. Just me. Can I sit down?"

"Sure."

Christine sits on the other end of the chaise longue, leaving a whole person's-worth of space between them. She has no idea how comfortable Faye is with her body yet so, this afternoon's brief hug notwithstanding, any physical contact has to come from her.

"Did Nell pick those shoes out?" Christine says, pointing a toe at the ridiculous pumps.

"Yeah."

"Bad choice," Christine says, forcing a smile out of the girl. After a few more seconds of silence, she asks, "What happened?"

Faye's grip on her ankles tightens. "I was stirring the batter, like Bex said to—"

"She's another girl in your group?"

"Yeah," Faye says. "She's my…friend." Christine nods, encouraging her to continue. "I was stirring it, and then someone I don't even know, came charging into the kitchen, and she was angry, and it made me nervous, and you know how there's just *no* space in that kitchen, and I think I took a bad step on those *stupid* heels because the next thing I know there's a broken bowl on the floor and batter on Bex's skirt and Nell is yelling at me and I couldn't take it anymore! She's been such a— such a—"

"Bitch?"

"Yes! It's like she still thinks of me as her enemy. And I'm not. I *swear* I'm not. Not anymore."

"You used to be?"

"Yeah. I hated her so much." Faye sniffs. "But I guess I was kind of everyone's enemy. I was just so angry, you know? All the time."

Christine nods. "I was like that, too."

"You?" Faye says, staring as if Christine had said she used to be bright green.

"Me. I…did things to end up here. Same as everyone."

"Wow. I can barely even believe you're like me."

"Someone else said that to me, recently," Christine says, smiling. "I'm getting better at believing it. I used to think I was…stained. That no matter how much I changed, there'd still be bits of the guy I used to be, riddled through me. But I changed even more than I ever expected, and the guy, he's just…gone. I think you've changed, too, am I right?"

"I have," Faye says, nodding. "I'm not like that anymore. I just want to get on with people. I…I *like* it when I get on with people, you know? It makes me feel normal. But *she*…she won't let me be normal. She shouts at me and sometimes I can deal with it but sometimes it's like she flips a switch and wrecks everything. Like, the world gets louder and sharper, but everything's also faded and further away. Like I'm on top of a high wire looking down and the ground is swinging back and forth underneath me. So I panic. And when I panic…" She looks away, grasps her ankles even tighter. "And I've asked her to stop, to just say what she wants from me, but she's all, what do *you* know?"

"Faye?"

"Yes?"

"Let go of your ankles, please."

"I can't."

"Why not?"

"Because if I do, I feel like I'll lose control again."

Christine says, "Again?"

Faye sighs deeply, wetly, moving the mucus around in her sinuses. When she speaks, she interrupts herself with sniffs, trying to clear her nose and restore her normal speech. She's got that one-month-of-voice-training timbre, and Christine knows that at this stage it's difficult to keep hold of the voice you want when your breathing is misbehaving or when your system's all stuffed up. She's still trying for it, though, and hasn't reverted to her old voice. An excellent sign.

"You know those videos where the cat has its back arched up?" Faye says. "And it's hissing and padding around all over the place, and then suddenly, completely predictably, it just leaps forward and *goes* for someone? That was me. That was how I felt. That's what Bex said about me." Faye blushes for a second, and Christine bites her lip to control a wistful smile. "I was angry and I'd try to hit people," Faye says. "And *every* bit of progress I ever made got wiped out whenever something new happened. I'd go *right* back to being him. When they started the shots, I snapped. When my breasts started to come in, I snapped. When they took my— you know, after the orchi, I snapped. Every time. But Nell calmed me down, every time."

"How did she do it?" Christine asks, leaning forward.

"By being the biggest bitch I ever met," Faye says, smiling. "She'd yell at me and slap me and push me down. She'd put me in those cuffs.

She'd tell me that if I didn't learn to control myself and stop snapping over every little thing—" she pauses to laugh again, but it's a laugh that scratches her lungs, "—then I'd wash out. And it worked, I guess. I went months. And then, one day, a few months ago, all my old anger came back, and Nell wouldn't stop coming at me, you know, and before I knew it, I hit her. In the stomach, not anywhere dangerous; I had *some* control. She still put me back in the cell for a week."

"Jesus," Christine mutters.

"I know. I was so ashamed. I still feel like such a fucking…I don't know. I don't know *what* I feel like."

"I don't mean you," Christine says, "although, yeah, kind of extreme behaviour. But you really think you've got it under control now?"

"Most of the time," Faye says, nodding.

"I mean, she's clearly setting you off. Making you regress whenever she's like this, because you've changed, but she hasn't. And maybe you haven't changed as much as you could have because she's being stubborn. Your sponsor is supposed to modify their approach to you as you move through the programme. By this point it's not meant to be such an oppositional relationship."

"You mean, she's still treating me like I'm in the first year?"

"Exactly."

Faye turns the thought over. Flexes her fingers against her ankles; they're probably getting tired by now. "Okay," she says slowly, "but if that's true, what can I do about it?"

"I can ask Abby to talk to her. She won't listen to *me*—I'm still in the programme—but Abby's quite senior."

"Will she do it? She doesn't even know me."

"She knows *me.* And she's one of my best friends."

"You're friends with a sponsor?"

Christine grins. "Abby's not a sponsor, not anymore. But I'm friends with Indira, too, and she *is* my sponsor. I know she's, like, officially my Sister, but she's also my *sister.* Her and Abby and Vicky and Paige. We're a family. Formed right here, under this roof, in this weird fucking house." Christine pauses for laughter, and gets it after a moment. "It doesn't have to be the way it is between you and Nell."

"That's a nice thought," Faye says.

"So," Christine says, "the question is, if I talk to Abby, and Abby talks to Nell, and Nell lays off, maybe treats you more like a girl and less like an unexploded bomb, what will *you* do?"

"Stay calm?"

"Attagirl," Christine says, smiling. "Shake on it?"

She shuffles closer on the chaise longue and holds out her hand. Faye will have to release one of her hands in order to shake, and eventually she does so, stretching out each finger as she lets go, loosening her elbows and shoulders and rolling her neck. Eventually they meet, shaking hands, and it becomes a hug, tight and warm. As Christine shuffles backwards, releasing her, Faye leans upwards, towards Christine's mouth.

"No," Christine says, gently pushing Faye away. "That's not what I'm here for."

The girl returns to herself instantly, eyes widening. "Fuck!" she says, and shrinks away, steps off her seat to stand in the middle of the room, bisected by moonlight, clasping her hands in front of her. "I'm sorry. I'm so sorry."

"Faye, it's okay."

"It's just, with the other girls…God, you think I'm weird, don't you? A pervert. A fucking rapist or something."

"No!" Christine says. "No." She claps her hands together, hoping the sharp sound will break into what looks like the beginning of the sort of spiral she'd hoped to avoid. The way Faye jumps suggests she's at least partially successful. "Absolutely not."

"I shouldn't have kissed you."

"You didn't," Christine says, smiling gently.

"I tried! And, um, with the other girls, I've done more than that."

"Did they agree?"

"Yes!"

"Then that's okay."

"Is it? We're— we're *men!*"

"Are you?"

"I mean," Faye says, on less certain ground, "we used to be."

"Does it matter?"

"Yes!"

"Whatever you are, whatever you used to be, looking for pleasure with someone is never wrong as long as it's consensual."

"Fuck," Faye says. "No. God. That's not— I didn't mean it like that. Shit, I sound so homophobic now. I didn't—"

"What did you mean?"

"Can I have a second?"

Christine smiles. "Take your time."

Faye nods and walks around the room a little, clenching and unclenching her fists. A minute or so later, she stops, sits back down on the end of the chaise longue, a chaste distance from Christine, and says, "I was a straight guy. Completely ordinary that way. Not in a lot of other ways, but I was straight. And when I look at you, or my— my Sisters, I see women. And even though I *know*, it's like I don't know. Or I can forget. You know?"

"I know," Christine says. "I was the same."

"You were?"

"While I was still getting used to this—" Christine indicates herself, "—getting used to *me*, this new body, this new identity, in my head I thought, I can be with the other girls and just not acknowledge who I've become. They're women and I'm…me. And there was another girl who, for a while, thought the same way. I'm not telling you who," Christine adds, grinning, remembering. "And it helped. It was a route to figuring out who I am *now*. One of many. And pleasure's never a bad thing, if you both ask for it."

"You, uh, don't do that anymore?"

"No. My…partner and I, we didn't need the escape anymore. Because that's what we were doing: escaping from ourselves. And when we both became new people, new women, suddenly we had nothing and no-one to run from." Christine leans her chin on her palm, following her old self through memories. "If my first year here, down there, was about letting go of my old self, about accepting that, by the rules of this place, I needed to become a woman in order to truly kill *him* off, then my second year was finding out who *she* is, and becoming her. You know? Learning to live *as* her instead of *in* her." She laughs. "You get the body before you get the soul."

"I don't feel like a girl yet," Faye says, half to herself. "Bex says she does, but I don't know if she's serious or just trying to convince herself."

"Do you still feel like a man? I know you called yourself one, before; do you *feel* it? Or is it just habit?"

Faye crosses her legs again, leans back against the dust sheet. "I would have said yes a month ago. Maybe two months. But now…it's weird. In some ways, I don't feel any different. But, at the same time, I really don't feel like a man anymore. And it's not from looking like this. I don't think so, anyway. A guy at my school was trans, and he always said that even though he had to see a girl when he looked in the mirror, he knew who he really was. I'm kind of jealous of that certainty now."

"Were you friends with him?"

"No. I was a bastard to him." Faye laughs. "A bitch, now, I guess. I don't know. I feel like I've been emptied out. I'm no-one."

"You won't always be."

"Is that *really* possible? Can you really…*become* this? Not just accept it?"

Christine shrugs. "You can embrace it. It's a choice, like everything here. And, sure, the alternative choices are not enjoyable ones. But it's a choice, nonetheless. What do you think, Faye? How are you going to choose?"

"I don't know. I think…this? Being a girl? Like, even if I never feel it, there's…" She scratches her chin, covering her hesitation. "There's ways to live like this even if I never get there. I've been talking with Bex and we have some ideas. About the future. What we want to do."

"Oh?" Christine says, radiating interest.

"Well, I'm good at, um, art, and she's good with numbers, and Bella, Bex's sponsor, she says we don't have to do the same degrees we were doing before, so I'm going to do graphic design and she's going to do accounting and we're going to go into business together."

"That's great!" Christine says warmly. It's a good plan; better than hers, anyway.

"It's just," Faye says, deflating a little, "I don't know. It all seems so…unfair?"

"I know, sweetie," Christine says. "And it kind of is. We didn't bring this on ourselves, after all. This was, clearly, something that was *done* to us. But I was a bad person. And so were you, if you're honest with yourself." Faye nods. "And that was unfair, too, on everyone around us."

"Was this really the only way?"

"I don't know. Maybe. Maybe not. I definitely needed a hell of a kick to get out of all my bad habits, and there's almost no bigger kick than this. And it's worked. For me, for my Sisters, for my friends. I'm a better person now." *Say it again like you mean it, Christine.* "And I'll always be a better person."

Faye, biting the end of a finger, nods again, and then blinks, reanimates fully. Gently she pats her face, feeling her damp cheek with the back of her hand. "Fuck!" she says. "I've ruined my makeup. I don't care what Abby says to her, Nell will kill me for this."

"Actually," Christine says, "she doesn't have to see." She pulls her phone out of her shoulder bag, drops into the group chat and types out a quick message. The reply comes back instantly, and she grins. "Why don't you come up to my room and let Paige get you all fixed up? You'll be even more beautiful than before. You can really show off in front of Bex."

Christine watches a blush bloom on Faye's cheeks, and the girl knows it, because she tries to hide behind her hand. *Busted, girly,* Christine thinks.

"But wait," Faye says, frowning, "I'm not allowed upstairs."

"I'm saying you are," Christine says. "Just for tonight. And it's my room, so what I say goes."

"I'll have to go past Nell, anyway," Faye says glumly, "and she'll see."

"No," Christine says, "you won't."

In every building of Dorley Hall's age and pedigree, there are grand and open staircases for the masters of the house and narrow and winding staircases for the servants, and it's to one of the latter that Christine leads Faye. It'll take them to the second floor with no diversions and no witnesses, and though it's behind a locked door, all she has to do is…

She holds up her phone again, brings up her private app, scrolls through until she finds the reference for the door, and taps. In front of a wide-eyed Faye, the lock rolls over and the door swings quietly open.

Christine raises a finger to her lips. "Ssshhhh," she says.

10

Butterflies

25 OCTOBER 2019 — FRIDAY

Paige is waiting for them outside Christine's room, holding her clutch in front of her and tapping her fingers on the leather. She's leaning against the wall with one foot raised, the skirt of her butterfly-patterned dress flaring out against her thigh, and when she hears them approach, she pushes away from the wall, causing the spiderwebs of gemstones in her stockings to catch the ugly yellow light from the sconces and throw it out in rainbow colours at the walls, the floor, and Christine and Faye.

Christine's used to Paige, used to her effortless elegance and frankly unfair level of beauty, but Faye's sharp intake of breath and embarrassed squeak remind her of how she used to be around her, back when Paige was flourishing and Christine was still learning the basics.

Just once, it would be nice to get that kind of reaction out of someone.

"Hey, Paige," Christine says, taking the hand Paige offers and squeezing it gently. "You okay?"

"I'm fine," Paige says quietly. "Nell just set me off."

"I'm sorry," Faye says. "This is all my fault."

"No," Christine says, "it's Nell's. I'm going to talk to Abby about her." She unlocks her door and kicks it open, wishing she hadn't left Paige's dresses in such a messy pile. "Don't say it, Paige. I know. I'll take better care of your shit."

"It's fine," Paige says airily, retrieving the dress bags she hung from the light fitting in the corridor and throwing them onto the bed as she marches in. "I have new things for you. For both of you."

"Me as well?" Christine says.

"Yes, you as well! You need to change; you have sad girl on your dress. No offence, Faye."

Faye bites her lip and shakes her head. The reality of Paige—six feet tall, incredible dress sense, Instagram looks and practical attitude—can be overwhelming for people who haven't yet been exposed to her, and that's before she dresses them, puts makeup on them, or starts enthusing to them about her latest hyperfixation. Christine, by contrast, comes in a neat, instantly comprehensible little package. Just add anxiety.

Paige sits at Christine's vanity and starts sorting through her makeup. "You don't mind if we give Faye a few things, do you?" she says. "Eyeliner and stuff. You have a *lot.*"

"As long as they're not already open, you can do what you like. Aunt Bea added me to the accounts." This means Christine can order as much makeup and as many clothes as she feels she needs, within reason. A privilege Paige has never had, which is probably why Dorley Hall is still intact and not crumbling under an apocalyptic pile of dresses.

Paige nods and continues dividing Christine's makeup into piles. "How did you get up here, anyway? You came from entirely the wrong direction."

Christine laughs and pulls off her dress—which, yes, does turn out to have sad girl on it, just under her bust, where she couldn't see. "We came up the back stairs," she says.

"Aren't those normally locked?"

Damn. Of course Paige knows that. Below the general-purpose floors, the ones with the odd actual cis person on them, most doors are kept locked. Graduates and third years have access via the thumbprint readers, but the stairs from ground to second host four easily broken single-pane unbarred windows over an old water tank in the courtyard, and thus are subject to an extra layer of security. An uncomfortable reminder that Faye is still a prisoner.

"They were unlocked," Christine says, smiling and dropping her soiled dress into the hamper by the bed.

Paige turns a sceptical eye on Christine, which only briefly flickers down to her chest. *Gotcha*; the old game of near-naked chicken. Christine doesn't get to win often.

"They're *never* unlocked," Paige says.

"Ask her," Christine says, sitting down on the beanbag chair and pulling her legs up under her.

Both of them look at Faye, who is having multiple reactions simultaneously: to the size of the room, possibly—the second-floor rooms are much bigger than the ones Faye and her cohort will recently have moved into, and have their own bathrooms—or perhaps still to Paige, goddess of the second floor.

"Um," Faye says. "Should I be looking away?"

"Why?"

"You're naked, Christine," Paige says, rolling her eyes.

"Underwear means not naked," Christine protests, twanging a bra strap.

"What were you saying in the kitchen? About bombarding these poor girls with new experiences too quickly?"

"Oh. Sorry, Faye. You're not used to this?"

"Only when we're, uh…" Faye starts, but then she looks at Paige and clams up.

"Only when you're with someone you're about to be intimate with?" Christine asks, choosing the most tiresomely appropriate words. Must be a latent sponsor gene activating.

Faye nods vigorously.

"Sorry," Christine says, "I'm too used to just doing whatever around other girls."

"But we're not g—"

"Don't say it," Paige says quickly.

"I'm sorry!" Faye blurts out, looking at the floor, her demeanour almost instantly regressing.

"Come here," Christine says, standing and stepping forward, beckoning the girl into her embrace and feeling her breasts compressed against her chest by Faye's; still a slightly novel feeling after all this time. "It's okay, Faye. But you need to watch out for that. I know I let it go downstairs when it was just us, but Paige and me? We're women. So's Vicky, so's Abby, so's Indira. So're most people around here."

"I know," Faye says, slightly muffled. "It's just hard to get used to."

"Then stop letting your brain override your eyes," Paige suggests, and poses. "You see a man here?"

Christine glances behind her, to see what made Faye's eyes widen. "Put those away, Paige," she says, "you'll have someone's eye out."

Paige pulls the bust of her dress back into place and sticks her tongue out at Christine. "Says the girl running around in her bra."

"Ignore Paige. She's a monster."

"Rude."

"This is something Aunt Bea will want you to get used to," Christine says, stepping out of the hug. Paige, modesty restored, unpacks one of the dresses. "It doesn't come easily to begin with, but she'll want you to feel comfortable around women. And just so you know—" she wags a finger, "—three girls can change clothes in the same room without anything erotic happening." Paige snorts. "Now, go see the tall lady. She has a dress for you."

"I do," Paige says, holding out something in red and black.

While Paige dresses Faye, Christine carefully removes her makeup and starts reapplying the basics, which after a week of practice is something she can manage well enough.

"How did you know?" Faye says, in a tone of voice that suggests she's remaining very still while Paige works on something sensitive, somewhere on her face.

"Know what?" Christine says, rubbing primer into her jawline and idly remembering when, in another life, it felt scratchy under her fingers.

"That you're a woman?"

"Remember I said it was a choice? I chose. It was either that or fight Dorley. And that meant fighting Indira, who I already loved, even back then. She was pretty much the first person ever to show me kindness, after all." Christine dabs under her eyes, grateful that the dark circles from last week have receded. "And what would I be fighting her for? The chance to remain that stupid kid? Nah. Screw that guy."

"Womanhood is both an identity and a social position," Paige says, more slowly than usual; she's concentrating on Faye's eyes. "I discovered quite quickly that I enjoyed occupying the social position of womanhood. Actually *being* a woman, in my head, is a little more conditional. But one day, out on campus, chatting with someone after class, I realised that he was responding to me as a man would to a woman, and that I was fine with that." She shrugs. "Sometimes you don't need to actively *choose* a gender. You can just be you, and accessorise."

"Ask her again next week," Christine suggests, "and she'll have changed her answer."

"And then there's Vicky," Paige continues. "She's simply a girl."

"You mean," Faye says, "she was already trans when she got here?"

"She says she wasn't," Christine says. "And I believe her. I've shown her every egg meme I can find, and she said none of them were relatable."

"If you're looking for a big moment," Paige says, "when you suddenly realise, 'Oh, I'm a girl,' you may be disappointed. For some of us, it never happens. For others, it happens gradually."

"And some of us make it happen," Christine says firmly. "Paige, I think I've done all I can without making my face actively worse."

"Okay," she says. "Good timing. Stand for me, please, Faye."

Faye obliges, and looks like she would be biting her lip if it wouldn't spoil her lipstick. Paige has her in a knee-length black dress with red trim around the bust and the hemline, and has done her face to match.

"Bex is going to *love* that dress," Christine says, and enjoys the burn on Faye's cheeks as Paige guides her away from the vanity and over to the wardrobe, which opens out into two full-length mirrors. Paige, prescient, is supporting Faye by a shoulder, so when the girl staggers a little, knocked off her balance by her own reflection, she doesn't fall.

"Is that…me?" Faye says, waving experimentally at herself.

"What do you think?" Christine says, as Paige grins the smug but enchanting grin she always does when she has successfully inflicted fashion on a fresh victim.

"Incredible," Faye says slowly, unable to keep a smile from spreading across her face.

"I think we have another girl on our hands, Christine," Paige says, watching Faye smooth her elegant dress down around her hips.

Christine steps up from the desk chair, grabs Paige's free hand and pulls her away from Faye. "Now, make *me* beautiful," she says.

"Your wish," Paige says, gripping Christine's hand right back and yanking her over to the sofa. Grinning, she presses Christine down into the cushion. "My command."

Faye says something muffled about needing to pee and shuts herself in the bathroom, leaving Paige and Christine alone. Christine wants to make a smart comment, but Paige is already frowning, clearly daunted by the sheer quantity of work ahead of her. Paige, taller already than Christine and sitting at a higher elevation, leans down over her such that Christine has to look up, and the angle puts their faces rather closer than Christine's been used to recently. Paige's slow, steady breath warms her face.

The woman's skin has no flaws. Not even a pimple. Unfair.

She does have a long strand of hair falling down across her face, though, and no amount of blowing upwards will tame it, so Christine reaches carefully past Paige's busy hands and tucks it back behind her ear where it belongs.

"Thank you," Paige says, as she paints.

"It was in your way."

Paige's mouth twitches. "Not for that."

"What for, then?"

"For Nell. For making sure I was okay. For helping get Pippa under control."

Christine tries to smile but Paige presses a warning finger against her mouth: don't mess with art. "That was mainly Abby and Vicky, though."

Paige stops brushing. "They wouldn't have been there if not for you."

"They would have!" Christine says, confused.

"They're my friends because they're your friends, Christine. Abby would barely know my name without you. People coalesce around you; you must have noticed."

"Paige? Are you really okay?"

"Yes," she says, nodding to herself and fetching another palette. "Just feeling like maybe I concentrated on the wrong thing."

"Paige—"

"It's okay. Maybe…maybe you have to learn *this* from *me*, and I have to learn something from you."

"I can give you lessons in fucking everything up, if you like."

"Quiet," Paige scolds, and leans in to quickly kiss her above her hairline. "I'm working."

"Yes, boss," Christine whispers. Why the kiss?

The makeup doesn't take long, and while Christine inspects her painted face—she'd almost forgotten how good Paige is when she really goes at it—Paige retrieves the new dress from the bed and lifts off the protective bag.

"Shit," Christine says, finally witnessing the dress in all its glory. "No, Paige, I can't." The dress is not only more elaborate than Christine's old one, it's a near-copy of Paige's: the same cut and butterfly pattern, but in contrasting colours. A robe for a goddess, presented to a commoner. "You want me to wear the same thing as *you?* Paige, please. Seriously. There's no way I can pull it off."

Paige hangs the dress up on the hook by the bathroom door and carefully cups Christine's cheek in her hand. A forefinger on her jaw, a thumb tucked gently under her chin. Christine's skin glows hot under the contact.

"You are beautiful," Paige says, smiling. "How many times must I tell you before you believe me?"

"Maybe a couple of hundred more," Christine says, eyeing the dress. It's incredible, she has to admit.

"I'm not taking no for an answer," Paige says, smiling. "Arms up."

Christine knows she's lost. Any real resistance would be token, anyway; no Indira to save her today. She complies, and Paige drops the dress over her head, carefully guides it past her face, smooths the fabric across Christine's bust and belly, and billows the skirt around her thighs. Wordlessly she hands Christine a pack of jewelled stockings, and when Christine sits on the stool and starts rolling one of them up her left leg, Paige starts work on her right, hooking them in place, pulling out the creases in the nylon, resting a hand for a moment on the inside of Christine's thigh, but moving it before Christine can comment. Shoes are next—a low heel, thank God—and Christine slips them on and stands up, her heart already in her chest at the thought of seeing herself in the mirrors, an imitation Paige, next to the real thing.

"Sorry I took so long," Faye says, ducking around the bathroom door, back into the room. "I'm still not used to redoing my— *oh.*" She pauses part-way through miming the action of tucking when she sees Christine standing uncertain by the sofa, Paige's steadying hand on the small of her back.

"Faye?" Paige says. "What do you think?" But Faye's only response is a sharp breath and a high-pitched noise, and Paige giggles, proud once again.

Maybe Christine *can* get that reaction out of people. With help.

***

"Hey," Faye whispers, as they descend the main staircase, "when we see Bex, you should call her Rebecca."

"Oh?" Christine says, managing to tear her eyes away from her reflection in the windows; Paige did a really good job.

"Bex is…it's *my* name for her."

"Does she have a name for you?" Paige asks, exchanging looks with Christine.

Faye blushes and says, looking down into the bust of her borrowed dress, "She calls me Effie."

"That," Christine says, "is ridiculously adorable."

They round the corner at the bottom of the stairs into the main foyer, shoes *tap-tap-tapping* on the tile, catching glimpses of themselves in the night-dark windows and, in Christine's case, resisting the urge to pose.

The kitchen comes up all too soon, and while Paige fiddles with the notoriously twitchy biometric lock on the door—it gets weird when it's had a lot of fingerprints to process, and there are a lot of people in the hall tonight—Christine takes Faye gently aside.

"How are you feeling, Faye?"

"Good, I think."

"Confident?"

"Definitely not."

"Ready to see your sponsor again?"

"*Definitely* not."

"Let me text Abby, then, and ask her to ask *her* to keep away from you for a little bit."

"All right."

Christine texts with one hand and with the other turns Faye towards her reflection in the large glass doors that lead out to campus. Faye is smiling at herself, again.

"Feeling like a girl yet?" Christine whispers.

Faye twists, examining herself in the glass. "Maybe."

"Good enough."

"Was it…Paige?" Faye asks.

"Was it Paige what?"

"Who you used to…"

"Oh. I understand. And I'm not telling you."

"You seem so close."

"We are. But we're also pretty different."

"But—"

"Ready to go?" Paige says, forcing Faye into silence. Christine nods.

By unspoken agreement, Christine and Paige bracket Faye protectively as they pass through the kitchen and into the brightly lit dining hall. Feeling quite good about herself for once, a part of Christine wants everyone instantly to fall silent and gaze upon the three of them with awe and wonder, but the desire dissipates the moment she feels eyes on her. Suddenly she feels clownishly unfeminine next to Paige—back to normal, then. She wants nothing more than to scuttle over to their table and hide from everyone, bury her nerves in wine. Butterflies in her belly, butterflies on her back.

But Indira, bless her and curse her equally, wolf whistles and triggers a wave of imitations from the room.

Aunt Bea stands up from her chair at the central table, silencing the hubbub without having to say a word, and approaches. Christine's heart ceases its embarrassed bounce and switches to a nervous one.

"Christine," she says quietly. "A quick chat?"

"Yeah," Christine says. "Oh, give me a second." She points as subtly as she can to Paige and Faye, who are heading for a group of girls at a table on the other side of the room, sitting with a few sponsors Christine recognises—and no Nell. A girl who must be Rebecca greets Faye with a hug and a gentle kiss on the cheek. They release each other and Rebecca talks excitedly with Paige while Faye turns brighter and brighter shades of red and glances around the room. She finds Christine, who gives her a small wave and then nods to Aunt Bea that she's ready for whatever she has to say.

"Sit down, please," Aunt Bea says, walking Christine into the kitchen and pulling a chair out from the table. Wordlessly, Christine complies. "You took a second year out of the permitted area without consulting her sponsor. And you involved Paige. Why?"

There are several baskets of breadsticks on the table, ready to be delivered to the dining hall. Christine takes a breadstick from the nearest one, turns it over in her fingers, bites off a small piece and chews it. She needs something to do with her hands while she thinks, and she can't have a cigarette.

"Remember how Francesca was, with Paige?" she says. Francesca, Paige's sponsor, had remained hostile to her charge through most of their second year for reasons none of them could understand. It took Paige petitioning Aunt Bea directly to get her removed from duty. Paige hasn't had an official sponsor for months. "Nell's worse."

"The other sponsors *have* noted that Nell's approach is somewhat antagonistic," Aunt Bea says.

"More than somewhat," Christine says flatly. "She's triggering Faye. Whether on purpose or by accident, I don't know, but that makes her either cruel or incompetent. Take your pick as to which is worse."

"Triggering her how?"

"May I be blunt?"

"For the moment."

"We fucked up," Christine says, and breaks her breadstick in half. "And I know I'm not trained in stuff like this, but I know my own life, and I see some of it in Faye. I think she comes from an abusive family, Aunt Bea. Assuming she needed to come here at all—which is a decision out of my hands *and* over my head—she needed a completely different sponsor. Someone capable of dealing with those kinds of triggers. She needed an Indira, someone able to redirect her anger without turning irritation into outburst; she got Nell, who seems like another Francesca. Faye told me stories about Nell, how she 'helped' her early on, and yeah, sure, while *she* conceptualises it that way, I don't. What she described to me…. Look, I *know* we have to do what we have to do, but there are ways to do it without…" She stumbles over her words, struggling to express her thoughts without implicating the foundations of the programme, something to which Aunt Bea is rather attached; and so, if she's honest, is she.

"I thought you were being blunt? Say what you need to say, Christine."

Fuck it. "I think we took a traumatised girl—or boy, or whoever—and recreated the circumstances of her abuse. Her sponsor shouts and yells and locks her up and even knocks her down, seemingly at random! That's not reform; that's just…changing the colour of the wallpaper in purgatory. I'm amazed— No, I'm *dumbfounded* she made it through the first year without washing out. Or worse! And that would have been a tragedy because, Aunt Bea, she is *such* a sweet kid."

"Hmm. A degree of hostility, even outright aggression, can be warranted during the early stages of the programme."

"*Can* be. Case-by-case assessment, right? You don't get a Christine out of my, uh, raw material by using the same methods that got you an Edy, yeah? I think Nell went in angry, took it out on Faye, and never stopped. Or maybe she saw something in Faye that made her think acting like that was somehow the right move. Like I said: cruel or incompetent. And, I shouldn't need to point out, Faye isn't *in* the early stages of the programme. She's two months into her second year and her sponsor, who is supposed to be her friend at this point, is *still triggering her.* You know what? I think she reformed *despite* us. Not because of us. Maybe her friendship with Rebecca saved her; maybe Rebecca's sponsor, too. But not Nell." Christine throws both halves of her breadstick down on the table. "Look: Paige and I both come from homes that were emotionally abusive. Occasionally physically so. We both responded very poorly to raised voices when we came here, and I think it's no surprise that of the two of us, it's me who doesn't flinch anymore when somebody shouts, and Paige who does. Because I got Indira and she got Francesca. And Faye got Nell."

Bea picks up one of the scattered halves of breadstick and regards it. "Are you done?"

I might well be. "Yes."

She smiles. "Thank you, Christine," she says.

Christine, realising she's stood halfway out of her chair with both palms planted on the table, sits down sharply and says, "Uh?"

"A good sponsor must know how to tailor her approach to her charge," Aunt Bea says, almost absently. "At the very least, she must know when to withdraw. I will talk to Nell. I'm not sure I agree with your assessments regarding her conduct during the first year—although I will look into it—but she does seem overdue for a re-evaluation of her methods." She sighs. "We're having staffing problems. Were you aware?"

"Um, no. Not really."

"It's hard to assign appropriate sponsors at the best of times, and normally Maria would be taking a more active monitoring role, but with the large intake this year and the amicable departure of several of our more experienced sponsors, *and* with her research commitments to the university, she simply hasn't had the time. I can't solve the latter problem, but I'm going to solve the former." Aunt Bea nods to herself. "I'm going to assign Indira as monitor."

"Indira?" Christine says. "My Indira? I mean, obviously, she's great, but—"

"Do you believe in the programme, Christine?"

Christine, taken aback, says, "Yes," automatically.

"And you are making progress in the areas we discussed?"

"Yes. Every morning."

"Then I think you, like Paige, have evolved beyond the need for a sponsor. Don't you?"

"Oh. Um. Yes?"

"Don't get ahead of yourself," Bea says, "you haven't graduated yet. But you have a strong support network, and you will, I imagine, continue to see Indira socially."

"Yes. Definitely. She's my sister," Christine adds defensively. She hates that she's fallen into exactly the sort of relationship she was supposed to have with her sponsor, that her friend group is composed entirely of people inside Dorley; that she is, as Stef said, a true believer. But she is what they made her. The other choices were always worse. "She's my family."

"Of course," Aunt Bea says, and Christine could swear there's genuine pride in her voice. It still doesn't always feel good to please Aunt Bea, but it's probably better than the alternative.

"Indira's new role will, of course, come with a pay raise."

"Good for Dira," Christine mutters, still coming to terms with the concept: no sponsor. Very nearly free.

"I do hope so," Bea says, placing a breadstick half carefully on the table. "I'd be interested in your read on Faye. How is she progressing?"

"She's a sweet kid," Christine says again, distracted.

"I mean, how do you think her gender is developing? Out of everyone, bar perhaps her friend, Rebecca, you've had the most intimate conversation with her."

Christine clears her head. Pictures Faye trying to kiss her, talking nervously about Bex, dumbfounded by her reflection. "I think she's warming to womanhood."

Aunt Bea nods. "You have an instinct for sponsorship, it seems. You proved quite adept at gaining that girl's trust."

"Hey," Christine says, raising a hand, "I wasn't trying to gain her trust—"

"I know."

"I just…She was hurting. I needed to help her."

Bea smiles. "How much you've changed, Christine."

***

Christine doesn't get to sit down straight away. Indira, not content with announcing her presence by wolf whistle when they first came down, makes Christine stand at the side of the room with Paige, so she can document their matching dresses and makeup. Positioning them under one of the more dramatic landscape paintings, Dira busies herself, conveniently too distracted to notice Christine's nonverbal but increasingly desperate pleas to let her out of this obligation. Christine acquiesces, but when she and Paige pose with each other—Paige gracefully, Christine awkwardly—it's not just Indira's flash that goes off.

"Make sure you edit the pictures before posting," Aunt Bea calls out.

Christine catches Hasan asking Dira why that would be necessary, and she starts rattling off a practised line about Dorley Hall's draconian privacy policies. Christine misses the end of it because Vicky starts yelling out suggestions for more elaborate poses and Paige, clearly having enormous fun, shamelessly abuses the leverage granted by her extra height to manoeuvre Christine into position for each one, waiting for everyone to get their photos before moving on to the next.

"Did you plan this?" Christine whispers to Paige, as the taller girl leans down to kiss her on the cheek. Thanks, Vicky, for that idea.

"No," Paige says, her breath flowing lightly across Christine's face and down her neck, igniting a warmth in Christine's chest that is only part memory. "But it's exciting, isn't it? Being the centre of attention."

"I want to die."

"You big baby," Paige says, and nips her once more on the cheek before straightening up.

Christine's fingers twitch. She wants to rub her face where Paige kissed her, but almost everyone looking on knows they have a history together and she doesn't want to give them the satisfaction. There's almost definitely a betting pool on whether or not they'll get back together—not that they were ever necessarily *together* in the way, say, Vicky and Lorna are—because the sponsors are just like that.

"Now do *Charlie's Angels!*" Maria shouts from the next table. Her face is already a little red and she's being lightly supported by Adam's sponsor Edy; with her nightly obligations to Aaron discharged, she's been at the wine.

"What's that?" Christine yells back, mostly to be annoying. Maria, the oldest sponsor, can be prickly about her age.

Paige says loudly, "We need a third!" and before Christine can protest that a) she genuinely doesn't know what a *Charlie's Angels* pose is and b) she would quite like to sit down, Vicky's joined them, pointing finger-guns out into the room. Christine follows her lead, but when the flashes of phone cameras die down she breaks formation and slumps into an open chair before anyone can make her do anything even more embarrassing, although she struggles to imagine what they could possibly pick that would be worse.

You okay? Abby mouths at her from across the table, and Christine nods that, yes, despite everything, she's fine, or she will be, once her heart retreats from her throat. *You look amazing,* Abby mouths. Christine smiles and, too overwhelmed to lean forward and talk normally, forms a heart with her fingers, earning a delighted smile from Abby.

She permits herself a moment to close her eyes. She doesn't know what to conclude about her conversation with Aunt Bea. Sure, Nell's going to be re-evaluated, whatever that means, and Indira's going to be assigned to watch over the sponsors, but Christine's come away with the uncomfortable impression that she's being recruited. Was this how it was for Pippa? Did she, one day, show concern for someone and suddenly find Aunt Bea, congratulating her and implying that she may have a productive future in boy acquisition and torture?

Christine's ahead of the game there: she's managed to put someone in the basement before she even graduates the programme. Granted, not a boy, but still; Christine is already, unofficially, recruiting for Dorley.

A buzz against her hip: her phone. She extracts it from her purse and finds a text from Abby, who is waving hers at Christine with what she probably thinks is an extremely clandestine look on her face.

Abby Meyer: Delete these messages after you've read them, please.

Christine Hale: Duh

Abby Meyer: Stef is okay. I mean, he's struggling. He briefly asked me not to call him ANYTHING, before relenting and reverting to Stef. Dysphoria's kicking him in the arse. I felt pretty bad about being all dressed up in front of him, I don't think he knew which he wanted to look at less, me or my dress! We talked about Melissa, a bit more about Dorley -- he still has ethical concerns -- and we agreed what to tell Pippa: that he's totally and completely cowed by her threats to tell his sister he's dead. As long as she has that to hold over him, he'll do whatever she says.

Christine Hale: Right, good

There's still Pippa to think about though

She's clearly having a hard time

Abby Meyer: You want to help her, too? Chrissy! You're so kind!

I'm proud of you 😘

Christine Hale: Please don't

Kind of don't want to be praised right now

Just the act of being nice to the kid, Faye, made Aunt Bea's eyes light up with little cartoon hearts in them

Now she wants to recruit me to be a sponsor

No good deed goes unpunished around here

Abby Meyer: You shouldn't worry about that. When you're out of the programme, you're free to choose. She might put some pressure on you to accept a sponsoring position if she really does want you, but you can say no and she'll (mostly) back off. Postgrad benefits, freedoms, etc. aren't conditional on doing what she asks.

Don't forget our stated goals. When you leave, you're genuinely free, with restrictions only for your own safety and the continued secrecy of the programme.

Christine Hale: To quote Stef, I forget you're a true believer

Abby Meyer: Oh shush. You are, too.

Christine Hale: I like to think I maintain a healthy dose of scepticism

Abby Meyer: LOL!!! 😂

Christine Hale: Now you're just being mean

Abby Meyer: Oh, before I forget. Stef's cohort have their first medical exams tomorrow.

Christine Hale: Oh shit

Isn't that kind of early?

Abby Meyer: It's not out of spec, but it's earlier than usual by a couple of weeks, yes. The sponsors, as a group, have some concerns about the wilder elements of this cohort, and have switched to the faster track.

Christine Hale: I'm worried about Stef again now, screw Pippa

Abby Meyer: Maybe you should find a way to go see him soon.

Christine Hale: I don't know Abs

It's way scarier to visit the bedrooms than the cells, and there are no hiding spots

And the locks in the emergency exit take forever to turn over

Abby Meyer: You really do know a lot about the security system here.

Christine Hale: The point is

If I get stuck

It's game over

I'll try and hit him up on Consensus tho

Abby Meyer: Okay. He likes you, you know. Goes a bit pink when he says your name 😍

Christine Hale: I mean, I AM a vision.

Abby Meyer: I mean it when I say you look gorgeous tonight, by the way. Have confidence in yourself.

Christine Hale: I refuse.

Abby Meyer: Christine, how many more times do we need to tell you you're beautiful before you believe us?

Christine Hale: A couple of hundred more

Across the table, Abby grins at her and taps exaggeratedly at her phone, erasing the conversation. Christine resolves to check it later, to make sure she did it properly. Can't trust anyone's opsec but her own.

"Christine," Hasan says, shifting his chair closer. She gives him her attention; he gives her his broad smile, the one she's willing to bet Indira fell in love with long before she came to Dorley. "How have you been? Cruel and unusual punishment aside, of course."

It takes Christine a second to realise he's talking about the ridiculous poses Indira, Paige and Vicky made her pull and not the cruel and unusual punishments that are inflicted with some regularity under the dining hall. "I'm doing pretty good, actually," she says, and nods gratefully at Indira, who is pouring her a large glass of white wine. "First year Linguistics is going well. Early days, I know, but so far it's everything I hoped."

"I'm glad," he says. "This one—" he intercepts Indira on her way back to her chair and hefts her onto his lap; she squeals with delight and kisses him, "—said you were doing a lot better this year."

The fiction, as far as Hasan is concerned, is that Christine's first year as a student at Saints—her second at Dorley; first above ground—was a foundation year. Hasan thinks Indira discovered Christine at a support group on campus, struggling with her transition, and took her under her wing. Dira argued for and got Christine a room in Dorley Hall, the residence for women from disadvantaged backgrounds, and essentially adopted her. There she could study for her foundation year in peace, surrounded by supportive friends, away from the abusive family life and dysphoric depression that afflicted her during her A-levels.

It's not a million miles from the truth. Christine was a mess when Dira first picked her up, and she got through her last couple of years of schooling only by being, according to an exasperated teacher, "too clever by half". But the deception makes her uncomfortable, as does their choice of story. Christine feels unworthy of it.

"You look fantastic, by the way," Hasan's saying. "Really stunning. That dress is amazing! And I know this isn't something you're supposed to say, but you were so worried about it when we met, so I'm just going to say it." He switches to a stage-whisper. "I'd never know."

"Really?"

She doesn't disguise how much she needs to hear such things. Her Sisters can call her beautiful until the sun goes down, but Hasan's clumsy reassurance is far more valuable; or, at least, easier for her to believe.

That she'd been struggling with her womanhood when she first met Hasan is not part of the lie, although she wishes it was. It had been her first time off-campus as a woman, and her already shaky confidence took a fatal knock when a drunk man on the train clocked her, shouted at her and pursued her through two carriages before Indira could find a member of staff to officially encourage him to please, sir, sit the fuck down and shut the fuck up. Christine arrived in London in tears, and will forever feel guilty that the first time Indira's mother got to see her daughter, she was busy comforting a crying, insecure little thing who wasn't even sure, back then, if she was a woman at all.

Sad girl on her dress.

"Really." He says it sincerely, kindly, like he knows exactly how much it means to her.

"Thank you!" Christine says, pushing warmth into the words by pitching down and expending a little effort to move her voice from its usual slightly lazy top-of-the-throat position to the front of her mouth. The sort of intonation that can, with enough breath behind it, fill a cathedral (or the large bathrooms attached to the dining hall, where Christine did a lot of her voice training). "And you do, too," she continues. "Look great, I mean. Like, really, really good." He's dressed semi-formal, but the shirt is fitted and he has a great figure underneath. He's tall, taller than Indira—who, like most Dorley women, is taller than average—and the way he casually embraces his girlfriend makes Christine's throat tighten whenever she thinks about it. He probably makes Indira feel so safe.

Hasan gives her a mock bow, the deepest he can manage without dislodging Dira, who is absorbing their conversation with obvious and slightly tipsy pleasure. Indira considers Christine family, and has suggested that if she ever wants to consider the Chetry name *officially* her own, all she has to do is ask. Aasha, Indira's mother, asks after Christine weekly, and occasionally shyly forwards memes to her newest daughter's Sister on WhatsApp, along with local gossip and sincere encouragement.

Christine, who never wants to see her own family again, who doesn't bother checking the info packs on them anymore, has considered asking, several times.

After a few minutes of small talk, Dira excuses herself to the bathroom and Hasan leans forward, close enough to Christine to touch her, and says quietly, "Thank you for being there for her. I think she really needed someone like you. Getting to be your big sister, having you be hers—" he glances towards the bathrooms, smiling, "—it's been healing for her. She never had that, growing up; just a lot of heartache none of us could ever seem to resolve. Siji loves her, of course, but didn't even know she was still alive, let alone that she was her sister and not her brother, until last year. So, Christine, thank you."

He holds open his arms, inviting Christine to move into his embrace. She does so, grateful for the excuse not to look at his beautiful, kind face. She hates the lies so much. Can't imagine ever feeling comfortable about them, for all that they are necessary and, for Indira, freeing. Indira can be with her childhood crush, she can be a sister to Siji and a daughter to her mother and father. She can be *alive,* and all it takes is a handful of falsehoods. *Indira was always a girl. She ran away out of fear. She chose this.* The smallest price to pay for so much happiness.

Christine hugs him more tightly. A silent apology.

"I was lucky she found me," Christine says, taking refuge in absolute honesty. "She changed my life. Saved it, probably. And you!" she adds, as they separate. "Look at you! Last time I saw you in the flesh, you were wearing that huge coat and making shy eyes at her across the garden, asking me to ask her if she possibly maybe happens to remember Hasan, the boy from three doors down, who thinks she looks just gorgeous."

He laughs. "I was lucky, too," he says. "Lucky she remembered me, lucky she was interested in me. Lucky I didn't take the overseas job and stayed home, when I heard she was alive, when I heard she was…her." His smile deepens as, on cue, Indira returns from the bathroom and perches herself on Hasan's knee again, encircling him in her arms.

"What are you two talking about?" she says.

Hasan kisses her. "You. And I really hate to do this—" he places his hands on Dira's hips and lifts her off his lap; Christine's throat tightens again, "—but now *I* have to visit the little *boys'* room."

They watch him go.

"Goodness, I love that boy," Indira says.

"He's absolutely smitten with you," Christine says.

Dira can't stop the giggle from bubbling up. "I know! I'm so lucky."

"Yeah. We talked about luck. You seem to bring it with you."

"Glad to be of service," she says, taking Christine's first two fingers, the ones that twitch, and gently massaging them. "He's always been kind, you know," she continues, looking away, living somewhere in the part of her past Christine carefully doesn't ask about, "even when we were kids. Even when I wasn't always so kind in return." She shakes her head. "Of course, these days he says he must always have known I was a girl, deep down, and that's why he was so drawn to me."

"Why do *you* think he was drawn to you?"

"He's a lot like you, Christine. He can't bear to see someone in pain."

"God. Dira, I hate *lying* to him."

Indira reaches for her glass, refilled by Hasan while she was away. "If, knowing everything, I'd go back and do it all again, then are they really lies?"

"I, uh, I'm not sure."

"I know you're the same. I know your regrets are all from before you came here."

"Mostly," Christine says. Dira applies gentle pressure to the tips of her fingers, rolls them in her own, draws out from Christine something that's been lurking inside her since she talked to Faye. "I'd be less of a bitch if I got to do it all again. Yell at you less. Cooperate a bit more, a bit earlier. I made life so difficult for you for a while."

Indira laughs quietly. "That would have been nice. You called me such terrible things."

Christine leans forward, balls her hand into a fist, gathering Dira's fingers inside it and squeezing. "I'm really sorry. I was awful to you."

"I love all the things that make you *you,* Teenie. Even the things you'd rather forget. I've never once been anything other than glad I became your sponsor."

"Actually," Christine says, "you might want to chat with Aunt Bea soon."

"Oh?"

"You're getting new responsibilities. You're officially relieved of the burden of Christine Hale."

"Oh, sweetie!" Indira squeals. "I'm so proud of you!" She hooks her free hand around Christine's shoulder and pulls on the fingers Christine's still grasping, drawing her up and into her arms. "You've become an amazing woman," she whispers.

"I wouldn't be here without you," Christine replies, not knowing if she means *I wouldn't be a girl without you,* or *I wouldn't be alive without you.* Both are Indira's gifts to her, and she cherishes them.

"And you were *never* a burden, Christine. Never ever."

That's something Christine could stand to hear more often.

Dira gives her a final squeeze. "I'm going to go talk to Aunt Bea before Hasan gets back," she says. "If they come round with the starters, make sure we both get one. You know what I like; he likes the same." She pecks Christine lightly, on the back of her jaw. "Kisskiss."

"Kiss," Christine whispers back, pressing her cheek hard against her sister's, blinking her eyes clear.

* * *

"So, Hasan seems like a nice guy," Paige says quietly to Christine.

"Hmm?" Christine says, mouth full. Unlike Paige, who's been on a diet since the start of the second year, Christine maintains her usual weight by forgetting to eat some days, so when something gets put in front of her that's actually pretty good, she'll generally eat and keep eating until every plate in the local area is clear. She picked the curry for her main course—given the choice, Christine will always pick the curry—and it's a lot better than she could have made with the same ingredients. Definitely better than her cohort managed last year. "Oh, yeah, he's sweet, right?"

"He likes *you* a lot," Paige continues, elbowing her gently in the ribs.

"Hey!" Christine says. "Be careful with the bits of me that have food in! They might burst!"

"Pig," Paige says with a grin. Christine replies by leaning close and doing her best porcine impression, which causes Paige to respond in kind and the rest of the table to give them an interesting selection of looks.

When eventually she finds her dinner straining against the fabric of her fairly snug dress she sits back and surveys the room. They aren't the only friend group who've staked out one of the smaller tables in the corners. On the far side, Jodie from down the hall—who spots Christine looking at her and exchanges waves—sits in a surprisingly colourful dress with her sponsor, Donna, and some of their friends. At least one of them isn't a Dorley girl, and thus is probably a vampire enthusiast. Looking harder, Christine recognises xem from Jodie's *World of Darkness* streams, and catches Jodie leaning over and pointing her out. Another wave. She probably should go say hi, later; ask where xe got xyr vampire teeth.

Most of the other small tables host people Christine doesn't know, or knows only by face. Graduates, probably, who live upstairs, off-campus, or away from Almsworth, having moved on from Saints as well as Dorley. People who live in the real world. Scary.

Faye and Rebecca notice her sweeping the room, and Christine waves again.

In the middle, at the largest table, with Aunt Bea at its head, are most of the sponsors whose charges are unable to participate in the birthday event due to being locked up in the basement. There's also a scattering of women and nonbinary people who Christine mostly knows, or knows of: the terminally Dorleyed, the ones who haven't left, can't bring themselves to leave, or return every chance they get. It's like Lorna said once: when all your friends are queer, you forget how to relate to cishets. What if all your friends were resocialised in a secret underground facility?

Pippa, sitting near Maria and looking somewhat overwhelmed, catches her eye and makes *please come over* hand gestures. Paige is busy discussing her plans to start learning self-defence with Abby so Christine just pokes her until she moves her chair out of the way, and gets up to see what Pippa needs her for. As she walks away, Christine makes a mental promise to herself to spectate those self-defence lessons, both to show her support and to enjoy watching the svelte, delicate-seeming Paige kick a succession of unsuspecting men in the face

At the central table, Maria is holding court, gesturing with a fork and complaining about her research supervisor. "Every time he pulls me up on something stupid or for being five minutes late, I get a little bit tempted to maybe, kinda, possibly, uh, bop him on the head and drag him here."

"Maria," Edy says, leaning with both elbows on the table and looking at least as full as Christine feels, "are you saying you want to force-feminise your supervisor just because he's pissing you off?"

"A little bit, yeah."

"Maria thinks forced feminisation is the solution to *all* her problems," Harmony says.

Maria shrugs sheepishly. "When all you have is a hammer…"

"Hi, Christine!" Pippa says brightly, before another of the assembled sponsors can say something disturbing. "You wanted a word, yeah?" She cocks an eyebrow.

"Yeah," Christine says, recognising someone who needs a break, "you want to come over? We have room, and I don't think Dira and Hasan are going to stick around for dessert, anyway."

"Oh, Christine?" Aunt Bea says, while Pippa rounds up her wine glass and purse. "Could you ask Indira to bring Hasan over, before they retire? I would very much like to meet him."

"Warn him!" at least three sponsors say, almost in unison, and collapse into giggles at their shared hilarity.

"Hey," Christine says, pointing at the table, taking advantage of her light drunkenness to be mildly rude to people who could still, technically, order her around and expect to be obeyed, "don't be rude when he comes over. He's a lovely man. Don't scare him."

Maria sits up from her slouch and drags Edy back up with her. "Best behaviour," she promises.

"Best behaviour," Christine repeats, and escorts Pippa back to their significantly less raucous table. "Jesus," she mutters, when they're out of earshot, "they're all so drunk."

Pippa snorts, and nods. She drops into a spare chair at Christine's table. "It's like Christmas with the extended family," she says, "and that's the table where all the embarrassing aunts get quarantined. And all they talk about when they're not being rude is work! Work, work, work." She glances at Hasan, who is watching with polite interest. "Schoolwork, I mean. I thought tonight was going to be about getting away from all that."

"I think they're all a bit institutionalised," Christine says, sitting back down next to Paige, who immediately leans her head on Christine's shoulder. Christine playfully pushes her off; Paige pretends to take offence and goes back to talking to Abby.

"They're the ones who should be able to leave, but don't," Vicky says, looking up from her phone. She smirks and adds, "The living failures."

Paige turns around. "Vick, I know for a *fact* that that's a *Bloodborne* reference. Stop it."

"Paige—"

"I know you miss your girlfriend."

"I—"

"But you're seeing her tomorrow night, so stop texting her and be sociable."

"Don't wanna. Oh," Vicky adds, consenting to lay her phone on the table but not actually turn off the screen, "you're still coming, right, Tina?"

"Tomorrow?" Christine asks. "Lorna's thing? Yes. I remember. And, yes, I'm coming." Pippa, who is suddenly directing all her attention towards playing with her bracelet, prompts Christine to give Vicky a meaningful look.

"Pippa?" Vicky says, picking up on it. "Wanna come? Tomorrow night. Clubbing. Just us Dorley girls. And my girlfriend."

"Really?" Pippa says. "I'd love to!"

"Come to Vicky's room on the second floor," Christine says. "We'll all be getting ready there. Except Vicky, because she doesn't actually live in her room anymore."

Pippa nods vigorously, which helps to hide her startled reaction when Hasan leans across the table to talk to her.

"I'm Hasan," he says. "I'm hers." He points to the side, where Indira, Paige and Abby are having an animated discussion.

"Pippa," she says. "I'm a friend of— I know Christine."

Christine elbows her. "She's my *friend*," she says, and throws in a glare for good measure. Pippa flushes, and Christine wonders how close she is with the others from her intake. Probably not very; most of them fled the nest, choosing to finish their degrees away from the hall that made them. Hints dropped by one of the others who stayed, and who pops down to the kitchen every so often, suggest to Christine that Pippa's cohort had a rather tense time of it in general. Three washouts; scary stuff.

Exactly how lonely has she been all this time? Christine's barely seen Pippa talk to anyone who wasn't Aunt Bea or another sponsor, now that she comes to think about it. And then there's her bracelet, the one she always wears, the one she's still wearing tonight even though it clashes with her dress, the one she's slowly turning around her wrist as she talks to Hasan. Very much like the bracelets she and Indira share, only the owner of the twin to Pippa's doesn't know if she's alive or dead.

God fucking damn it, Christine; why did you have to go and dump a problem like Stef in this girl's lap?

"I'm studying Philosophy," Pippa's saying to Hasan. "It's not been so bad up until now, but this year, all of a sudden, it's been confusing, difficult, and I don't know how to respond to it." Hasan leans farther forward, bringing Indira's hand, enmeshed in his own, with him. Dira laughs and disentangles herself, kissing her boyfriend on the cheek as she does so. Pippa, looking inward, doesn't notice, just continues talking almost to herself. "I wasn't going to do it this year. Third year uni is hard enough as it is, you know? But she asked me to be on standby, just in case, and when it looked like it wasn't going to happen I was *so* relieved. And then, suddenly, all this responsibility just *drops* in my lap and I'm running around with no idea what I'm doing except that I know I'm doing it *all* wrong."

"That sounds rough," Hasan says. "Which module is this for?"

"It's a group project," Abby says, switching chairs to sit next to Pippa and taking her by the hand. "And it's a hard one. Why don't you let me help you, Pip? Like I did earlier. All you have to do is ask, and I can talk to…your supervisor. Make it official."

Pippa closes her eyes, exhausted, and leans gratefully against Abby's shoulder. "I'm asking," she whispers.

Yeah. Well fucking done, Christine.

***

As predicted, Indira and Hasan make their excuses before dessert, as do several others. The second years are permitted to stay and enjoy their own cakes—no less delicious for being, probably, quite violently made—but are gently encouraged to leave by some of the more sober sponsors before Aunt Bea's speciality coffees come out. Faye and Rebecca excuse themselves from the frankly adorable procession of new girls and trot over to where Christine and Paige have been roped into the effort to drag all the remaining tables into the middle of the room.

"I wanted to say hi," Rebecca says, in a clear, high-pitched voice. More developed than Faye's. Either her sponsor okayed the voice surgery that Dorley very occasionally hands out, or she's been training her voice longer than the rest of her cohort. "And thank you. To you, Paige, for making Effie look *so* beautiful."

"You're quite welcome," Paige says, strangely formal.

"And to you, Christine, for helping her. She told me all about you."

Lost for platitudes in the face of someone so genuine, Christine resorts to a curtsey. She's been relying on these too much lately, but Aunt Bea seems to like them, and Paige's bloody butterfly dress is so tight around the hips it's almost the only manoeuvre she can reliably perform.

"Thanks, Christine," Faye says. "For everything. Um, is it okay if I contact you sometime?"

"Anytime," Christine says, more at home with Faye's nervous stammer than Rebecca's sincerity. She rattles off her Consensus ID, and starts reciting her phone number until Paige reminds her that second-year girls don't yet have fully enabled phones. "Aw. I was going to forward you all the terrible memes Dira's mum sends me."

"Dira's…mum?" Faye asks. "She's allowed to talk to her family?"

"That," Christine says firmly, "is a *long* conversation for another day. Ask me on Consensus."

"Okay. Oh, Paige: when should I give the dress back?"

"Do you like it?" Paige says.

Faye glances shyly at Rebecca before answering. "Yes."

"Then it's yours."

Paige's reply prompts an excited hug from Faye and a small amount of commotion from Rebecca, which continues until Bella, Rebecca's sponsor, arrives to drag them up to bed. Bella shoots a smile at Christine and mouths, *Thank you*. Christine, unaccustomed to so much gratitude in one night, replies with a hesitant nod.

"They're so cute, aren't they?" Paige says, as they take their seats around the newly enlarged central table, between Pippa on Christine's left and Abby on Paige's right.

Christine avoids Aunt Bea's knowing grin, and replies, "Yeah. They kind of are. Hard to believe we were ever like that."

"That was only a year ago, for you," Maria points out, sounding a little more sober now.

"Seems like longer," Christine says.

"I don't know why we bother with the basement at all," Abby says. "Just give them to Paige for an hour and they'll walk out the door the most enthusiastic women you ever saw."

"Well—" Maria starts, but she's cut off by Aunt Bea, tapping a coffee spoon on the side of her mug, calling for attention.

"Good evening, ladies," she says, and smoothly adds, when someone at the other end of the table coughs, "and nonbinary individuals. Thank you all for coming, and thank you all for staying with me to ride out this long evening to its end. I know *some* of you had no choice—" she smiles at Maria, sitting at her side, who rolls her eyes and noisily slurps on her coffee, undercutting whatever gravitas Bea is trying to impart to the moment, "—but the rest of you did, and stayed anyway. My special thanks go to those who have returned from far afield—" several people, including the one who coughed, raise glasses and coffee cups, "—and to those who are yet to graduate from our programme." Surprised murmurs from the far end. Bea points her spoon at Christine. "Christine Hale and Paige Adams. Thank you both for indulging an ageing woman on her birthday."

Shit. They really are the only non-graduates at the table, aren't they? "Hey," she says, pointing around Paige to Abby, "I just go where she goes."

Polite laughter ripples across the table. "And you, Miss Adams?" Aunt Bea says.

Paige points at Christine. "I go where *she* goes."

Christine slaps her ankle against Paige's, lightly enough to keep from hurting her but hard enough to say, *Hey!* Paige responds by hooking her ankle around Christine's. Unexpected. When Christine looks at her, Paige looks back with a somewhat intense and only slightly unsteady expression.

"And an honourable mention, of course," Aunt Bea says, "to Victoria Robinson, our first two-year graduate in quite some time."

There are one or two gasps this time. Vicky, much more accustomed to attention than Christine, accepts the smattering of applause and says, "Well, the sales pitch was just *so* good."

Has everyone been taking public speaking lessons except Christine? Or is this something else she's expected to be good at by now? She covers her embarrassment by diverting her attention to the coffee in front of her, which is definitely better than the stuff out of the coffeemaker in the kitchen.

Aunt Bea draws all attention back to herself when she continues, "As many of you know, this is an important year for me. Not only is it my fifty-fifth birthday, but this year also marks fifteen years since I officially took control of the hall. I know not many of you were raised under Grandmother's hand—"

"Under her fucking *whip*," Maria mutters.

"—but I like to think that, under *my* hand, the programme here at Dorley Hall has benefited *every* girl it has embraced."

Maria looks like she wants to throw up, but before she can say anything, someone at the other end of the table coughs politely.

"And every nonbinary individual, too," Aunt Bea continues smoothly, as Edy takes Maria's hand. "Thank you, Amethyst, again, for the welcome reminder."

Amethyst, dressed for their name in a dark tuxedo with a purple bowtie, says, "You are quite welcome, Beatrice."

Christine almost inhales her coffee. She's never heard Aunt Bea addressed by her full forename before; she wasn't even sure she *had* one. Clearly, when one has been away from Dorley for many years, one becomes cheeky.

"And what *are* your pronouns, my dear?"

"Quite mundane, I promise you: they/them."

"Wonderful!" Aunt Bea says. "Do we have anyone else here tonight with, shall we say, pronouns other than the traditional?"

Another of Amethyst's group holds up a hand. "I'm a she/they now, actually."

"Oh? And how does that work?"

Whether from alcohol, tiredness, or whatever's in the coffee she can't stop drinking, Christine's completely lost the ability to tell whether or not Aunt Bea is being genuine—she's *definitely* encountered that pronoun set before—but Amethyst's friend continues as if she's been asked a serious question. "Some days I feel more like a *she*, other days, a *they*. If on a particular day I have a strong preference, I'll tell my friends, but otherwise I'm happy with either." She pauses to listen to Amethyst whisper something in her ear. "That's just how it works for me, by the way. I know a few she/theys who take a different approach."

"How fascinating!"

"I know! Gender's fun, isn't it?"

"That is not," Aunt Bea says gravely, "the official position of Dorley Hall."

"You know what? Back when I lived here, that serious face of yours used to scare me. But I'm worldly now. I can see the grin you're holding back."

"I don't know what you're talking about."

"You're just a big shitposter, aren't you?"

"Margaret," Aunt Bea says, dropping into a more severe tone, "please remember there are girls here who are still supposed to be intimidated by me."

Christine, entirely genuinely, says, "Don't worry. I definitely still am."

"Bless you, child. And you, Margaret: are you feeling *she* or *they* today?"

Standing up to reveal a flowing red dress with crystalline details, Margaret twirls, raising the hem above her knees and says, "Today, I'm emphatically a *she.*"

This prompts a conversation amongst the half-dozen people at Margaret and Amethyst's end of the table and Aunt Bea, wisely, decides that her speech has thus concluded. She exchanges a few murmurs with Maria, who nods, smiling and seemingly mollified, before addressing Christine and Paige as one. "How about you two?" she says. "Will either of you be adopting new pronouns when you graduate?"

"No," Paige says. "I've examined myself thoroughly—" she's definitely had more alcohol than Christine; she's stumbling over the multisyllabic words, "—and determined myself to be, socially, rather binary. I won't be changing pronouns any time soon." She frowns. "I don't like the way I have to have strangers think I'm a cis woman, but there's nothing I can do about that. I've already established myself that way; I'm stuck with it."

"Just say you're AFAB," Maria says. "You don't have to tell them the B stands for 'basement'."

Edy stops holding Maria's hand and delivers a mild tap to the side of her head. Deserved. Apparently the studious and sensible senior sponsor develops a bit of a mouth and a tendency towards mood swings when she's had a drink.

"And you, Christine?" Aunt Bea asks.

Christine shrugs. This, at least, is easy. "I'm a girl," she says. "Sometimes I'm a tomboy; sometimes I'm a girly girl. Always a girl, though. A she/her."

In Aunt Bea's widening smile Christine reads pleasure, possibly relief; not quite as tolerant as you try to be, are you? Paige, perhaps seeing the same thing, nudges Christine's foot again, as if to say, *At least she's trying.* Christine suddenly has to hold back laughter, imagining the headline: DIVERSITY WIN! KIDNAPPER RESPECTS YOUR PRONOUNS!

Aunt Bea moves on to Pippa next, and Christine feels the girl tense when the questions start. Pippa gives a rough rundown of Stef's stay in the basement up to this point, and repeats some of her frustrations. She admits to Aunt Bea and the table, as she had obliquely to Hasan, that she's feeling overwhelmed. Towards the end of her summary, Aunt Bea reaches over to take her hand, and Christine feels Pippa go from tense to completely immobile.

"We are so grateful that you stepped up, Pippa," Aunt Bea says, "and I'm aware that your plate is…rather full, what with your final year studies as well as your duties as sponsor." She takes a sip of coffee. "We'll have Maria assist you, when needed. She is the most experienced, and many of her overall responsibilities have been shifted, as of now, onto Indira."

"Oh," Pippa says, "um—"

Abby pipes up. "Actually, Aunt Bea, I was going to offer my support. I'm available to spend a lot more time here, and—"

"Nonsense!" Aunt Bea says. "Your offer is *greatly* appreciated, Abigail, but you have your career to think of. Maria's, happily, is based on campus."

"But—"

"And, might I remind you, your sponsorship methods are… singular. Should young Stefan require a firm hand, could we trust you to administer one? Maria has much more experience in tailoring her approach."

"She's saying I'm a bitch," Maria stage-whispers from behind her hand.

Aunt Bea rolls her eyes. "You young people do persist in putting the most awful words in my mouth."

"Yeah," Maria says, pretending misery, "I'm a bitch." Edy comforts her.

"Pippa, my dear?" Aunt Bea says. "Are you happy with this arrangement?"

"I am," she says. "Thank you, Aunt Bea." It can't only be Christine who hears the tension in her voice, can it? She's bringing the conversation to the quickest close she can manage. She wants to reach out, reassure Pippa, but she doesn't know her well enough to predict her reactions.

When conversation resumes around the table, Christine feels Pippa relax, and engages her on a deliberately light-hearted topic.

"Hey," Abby says a little while later, leaning around to speak to Pippa, "where's Monica? I wanted to talk to her."

"Oh, uh, it's her boy, Declan," Pippa says. "He got to three strikes today, so she left after the main course."

"Three strikes? Already?"

"A sponsor's work is never done," Paige says, and finishes her coffee.

***

"My house is your house," Christine says, pushing open her bedroom door with her bare foot and throwing her shoes in the rough direction of the wardrobe.

"Are you *sure* this isn't a bother?" Vicky says.

"You can still sleep in your room, Vick," Paige says, closing the door behind them and immediately stepping out of her dress, "if you don't want to impose."

"No," Christine says, leaning against the wall and declining to undress until the room consents to stop slowly rotating. "Her room is cold, it's lonely, and it's full of *your* clothes, Paige."

Vicky, by the time coffees were polished off and a third round of sherries politely refused, declined from morose to depressed, all but outright asked if she could stay in Christine's room rather than sleep alone. Paige made an acid comment about how she ought to be able to cope for just one more night before Lorna returns from her dad's place, but Christine insisted; Vicky gets scared sometimes, more so when she's alone, and the last thing she wants is the girl having a crisis born of alcohol and loneliness, with no-one there to help her. So they agreed: Christine's room tonight.

When the three of them left the dining hall, arm in arm, Christine glanced back and took in with one glance Aunt Bea's satisfied expression and Pippa, surrounded by empty chairs, watching them walk away.

"Reminds me," Christine mutters, and pulls out her phone.

Christine Hale: Hey can you check on Pippa for me?

It's dawning on me that she has like no friends and I'd look after her myself but my room is absolutely CHOCK FULL of girls

Abby Meyer: Will do.

And chock full of girls, eh? Don't do anything I wouldn't do!

Christine Hale: You mean sleep?

Maybe drool a bit?

That's the extent of my plans

Abby Meyer: That sounds so hot.

Christine Hale: Horny jail, population: you

Thanks tho

You do too much for me

Abby Meyer: I think you'll find I'm doing this for Pippa.

Say goodnight to the girls for me.

"Abby says g'night," Christine says, throwing her phone back in her bag and her bag onto the desk.

Paige, unsteadily crossing the room in her underwear, leans down and says, "Good night, Abby," to the phone, before placing a hand on each side of Christine's waist, turning her round, and unzipping her dress.

“Thanks, Paige,” Christine says. “Oh, Vick,” she adds, as Vicky finishes dropping the component parts of her two-piece outfit onto hangers, “spare toothbrushes are in the cupboard under the sink.”

Vicky flashes her a thumbs up and makes it through the door to the ensuite on her second go. Paige makes impatient motions with her hands that Christine eventually interprets as a request to step out of her unzipped dress. They manage to get both of their dresses back into the garment bags and hung on the wardrobe door before the alcohol in Paige’s bloodstream gets the better of her and she staggers, almost falling.

“Woah, there,” Christine says, looping an arm around her and positioning one of Paige’s around her shoulders. “Let’s get your teeth brushed and then we can all sleep this off. Vick? A little help?”

Between the three of them they manage to pilot Paige from bathroom to bed, and they both fall in next to her, Christine in the middle.

“Thanks, Tina,” Vicky whispers, blowing her a kiss and turning over to face the window. Almost immediately her breathing turns heavy and regular.

“And she’s out like a light,” Christine says. “You okay, Paige?”

“’m fine,” she mutters, shuffling over under the covers and looping one of her legs over Christine’s. They’re both still wearing their sparkly stockings, and the sensation is strange.

“Um,” Christine says, “Paige?”

“Sleep,” Paige suggests, and folds an arm under Christine’s bosom. It’s not long before her grip goes slack and she starts to snore, the same soft growl Christine remembers.

It takes her a while to fall asleep, but the curtains are open and the stars are out, so Christine counts the lights in the sky and considers, with Paige’s arm around her and Vicky’s cold foot occasionally lightly kicking her in the knee, how little she deserves the bounty she’s been handed, and how lucky she is to be here to receive it.

II

Friction Burns

26 OCTOBER 2019 — SATURDAY

"Up! Up! Up! No fucking dawdling! Mummy's got a hangover and the sooner you little shits climb into your hamster wheels and start running, the sooner I can go back to bed!"

Maria's voice, hoarse and echoing in the concrete corridor, drags Stefan out of his nightmare, and he's already halfway out of bed when the door opens and Pippa enters, looking very much the worse for wear. Tactfully she looks away, giving him time to climb back under the covers before she settles against the wall and leans her head against the brick.

"Good morning," she says. Sounds like an effort.

"Good morning." Stefan keeps his voice low, mirroring her mood in the manner that's become habit. He tightens the sheets around his chest, gathers his knees under his chin. "You have a hangover, too?"

"No," Pippa says. Her denial is undercut by her wince. Aunt Bea's birthday last night, Stefan remembers. Kidnappers getting together for a nice meal and a bit of a drink. Bizarre to imagine them having such normal things in their lives as birthday parties and hangovers. "I'm fine," she insists, more loudly, and he looks away. His scepticism must have shown on his face.

Pippa's hard to predict. Sometimes she seems like someone he can get on his side. Other times she's as perfunctory as Maria usually is with Aaron. Occasionally she seems so angry she might ignite. Which is the real Pippa? No way to know.

He's learning what to watch for. This morning, headache aside, she's all business, hands folded over her chest.

"Medical examinations today, right?" he says. Keep it factual.

"Yes. Don't bother dressing; you'll be showering in twos this morning. Supervised. We're re-examining some of our security procedures after Declan's little episode. For now, your unmonitored shower privileges are revoked."

Stefan nods. Locks his jaw so he doesn't give away his reaction. Just what he doesn't need right now: more eyes on him. "Can you turn around, so I can put on my robe?"

"I'll see it all in a minute, anyway," Pippa says. She's still inserting that sneer into her voice, but it's even less convincing than usual today. "Why bother?"

"Please?"

"Fine. I'll wait outside. If you're not out in two minutes—" she yanks on the door, "—we're coming in and *dragging* you out, whether you're fully clothed or buck naked."

She slams the door on her way out. He hopes it makes her headache worse.

Quickly he throws on his dressing gown and assembles his wash kit. He uses the rest of the time to buzz his chin with the electric razor. Being watched is one thing; being seen shaving, quite another. He's never been able to put his finger on exactly why, but he doesn't have the luxury of questioning his neuroses. His composure is fragile enough right now.

His shower buddy waits in the corridor, under guard. "Morning, Mother Theresa," Aaron says. "How are the healing hands?" He's got a plaster over the cut near his eye; Maria must have got it for him. Stefan tears it off—it'll come off in the shower, anyway—and ignores Aaron's whimper as he inspects the wound: almost healed.

"Looks good."

"Hey!" Aaron squeals. "Personal space! Personal space!"

"Like that matters here," Stefan says. Pippa glances his way; he pretends not to notice.

"I mean, yeah, okay, sure." Aaron folds twitchy arms in on themselves and looks up at him. "You okay, Stefan? You seem kind of tense."

When did Aaron ever ask him *that* before?

Stefan weighs the pros and cons of telling the truth, finds the whole exercise exhausting, and shrugs. He dreamed over and over of Declan attacking him and Aaron in the shower, and no matter how often he woke and forced himself to think of other things, Declan was waiting for him when he fell asleep again. He even watched a movie, in pieces, between dreams. Didn't help; just got *Happy Working Song* stuck in his head.

He's probably had less sleep than Pippa or Maria.

"Hey," he asks Pippa, "what are we waiting for?" The question earns him a prod in the small of his back from one of the women standing guard behind him. The impertinence of asking questions.

Maria, leaning lazily against the wall by the open double doors, replies for Pippa, who has her eyes closed. "We're waiting for *that*," she says, and nods at the door to the bathroom, which bursts open a few seconds later, heralded by some troublingly masculine shouting.

It's Declan, and he looks like he's fallen down a flight of stairs, been taken back up to the top and thrown down a couple more times, for fun. He's naked, and barely a square centimetre of skin is unbruised. His hands, cuffed behind him, shake, and he drips water on the floor as he staggers past the end of the residential corridor, trailed by Monica and three other sponsors, all armed with tasers and batons.

"Hey!" he yells. "Why don't you fucking poofs *fight?* They wouldn't be able to keep us here if we all—!"

Monica interrupts him with a baton strike to his chest, and for a second he looks like he might retaliate, start a brawl right there in the hallway, but he backs down when the other sponsors level their tasers at him. Slowly, reluctantly, he faces front and hobbles back down the main corridor to the cells, followed by his escort.

Aaron breaks the silence. "He has a point. We should definitely fight. What do you think, Maria?" He balls his fists, raises them like a newsreel pugilist. "You want to go a few rounds?"

Maria, massaging the bridge of her nose, says, "No."

"You sure? Best two out of three?"

"Go. Shower. Now. Before I put you and your friend in the cell next to Declan just for annoying the piss out of me when I've got a hangover."

Pippa and the others escort them in, but Maria stays behind, to coordinate with the other sponsors or possibly just to indulge in her headache. Stefan's always been perversely irritated that the guards don't have any kind of uniform to distinguish them from the sponsors. According to Abby, they mostly *are* sponsors, but to second- and third-year women who don't need constant supervision any more, filling out the numbers so not every first-year sponsor has to be on the job all the time; Stefan's been waiting to see Christine's sponsor, Indira, amongst them, but so far few have been South Asian and none have matched his hazy memory of the picture Abby showed him over Consensus. Today one of them is wearing particularly nice clothes, and it's all he can do to keep his eyes away, to stop comparing himself to her. Pippa's habitual dresses are bad enough; this girl's outfit makes his chest hurt.

He needs a distraction, so he asks Pippa what happened to Declan.

"He got three strikes."

"I heard. But what *happened* to him? He looks like he lost a fight with a brick wall."

"What happened to him is what happens *after* three strikes. Privileges taken away. Supervision increased. Carrot removed, stick emplaced." She nudges at Stefan with an elbow, and the contact makes him flinch. "Now go join your little friend in the shower before I push you back out the doors and let Maria use you for headache relief."

Stefan nods. Stops halfway into the shower annexe. "Do you really have to watch us shower? Can't you just leave the room? Or look away?"

"No," one of the women he doesn't know says. The other one, scrolling on her phone, rolls her eyes.

"Sorry," Pippa says, sounding almost like she means it. "I'm just as unhappy about this as you."

"I really doubt that," Stefan says, and Pippa gives him another of those searching looks—moderated by her hangover—that suggests she's still trying to figure him out, so he turns away quickly.

He needs to stop just *saying* shit.

Aaron—his "little friend"; great, they're inextricably linked!—is already washing, facing away from both of them, for once not taking advantage of the situation to waggle his dick around. Maybe he feels the gaze of all three women, too.

Stefan takes the shower at the far end, putting as much distance between him and the sponsors as possible. Maybe they all need glasses and won't be able to see him clearly? Wouldn't that be a lovely thought?

His skin prickles anyway.

"You didn't answer me before," Aaron says. Stefan risks a glance: the boy's facing the wall, angling himself away from Stefan and sponsors both. Shy, all of a sudden. "Are you okay? You really did seem tense out there. And then there's Declan—"

"Why do you care?" Stefan asks. There's no hostility in the question—he really, truly does not have the energy to spare—but he's curious. He turns the tap to its hottest setting and ducks under.

Only lukewarm, but getting warmer.

"Why do I *care?* Because we're buddies! Compadres! Fucking… friends, man. Aren't we?"

Water's getting hotter.

"Aren't we?" Aaron repeats.

"You shouldn't antagonise Maria like that."

"What? Man, you're really—"

"You want to end up like Declan? Back in a cell? Bruised and limping? Three strikes, Aaron. How many do you have?"

"One." Aaron's usually lively voice, already somewhat depleted out of apparent concern for Stefan—what a joke!—flattens completely. "You weren't here yet when it happened."

"Oh yeah?" Stefan starts rubbing in the shampoo, leaning away from the flow of water, which is starting to make his skin throb when it strikes. "What did you do?"

He leans against the tile to rinse his hair. Fingers are already pink.

"Uh," Aaron says. "You don't want to know that."

There's a feeling Stefan gets sometimes, when he's being watched. It's a heat in the back of his neck. More a rash than a blush, it stings like an insect bite, itches like a burn. At his job, about a week before he came here, the feeling hit him so powerfully he had to abandon his till and excuse himself to the staff toilets and lock himself in a cubicle so he could slam the back of his head (where bruises don't show) into the stall wall over and over, until pain overrode discomfort.

No such privacy here, but there are other ways to cause pain. How hot can the water here get? Time to find out, before it becomes overwhelming.

Pippa and the other two women, standing at the other end of the annexe, watching him. Witnessing him. He knows how he looks in their eyes: pathetic; broken. Their nonchalance amplifying their contempt. Another man, brought here to be corrected. Another *boy*.

"If you don't tell me what you did," he says to Aaron, "I'll assume the worst."

"Yeah, well, you'd probably be right."

Stefan laughs and water floods his mouth. He spits. "You showed her your dick, didn't you?"

"Only a little."

"Jesus fucking Christ, Aaron."

"That's why she hates me. I mean, it's not the *only* reason, but it's, y'know, enough."

Stefan threads conditioner through his hair, leaning his head against the wall. He could do it right here: slam his head into the wall over and over. Scatter himself across the tiled floor.

Yeah. Until the sponsors come to stop him. Until they *put their hands on him*—

Hot water scalds his bare back.

"She probably *should* hate you, Aaron," he says. Whatever filter he usually tries to apply to his thoughts is long gone. "Hell, I should hate you, too. Don't know why I don't. Don't know why I'm even a little bit happy to see your stupid face every morning."

"Aww. You're happy to see me?"

"Don't get too excited. Who else am I going to talk to? Fucking Declan? I hated you, Aaron. And now, for some reason, I don't."

"Well, I'm flattered, but—"

"I hated you," Stefan continues, because the only way to stay in control is to keep talking, to keep spitting out everything in his head, to keep his mouth too full of bile to scream, the way he wants to, "because you're a prick. A misogynist prick who harasses women." Shower water flows into his mouth again, and little roots of pain burrow into his gums and teeth. Hands on the tile again. Steady. "You sent pictures of your dick to women who did *not* ask to see them. Pictures fucking plural!" Water sears his back, burns through his skin, exposes muscle and fat and warped, fragile bones, all of them the wrong shape, too big, too clumsy. He can feel his body's weight, pressing him down, holding him in place. "Did you find the best light, Aaron? Did you find the right angle? Did you trim your fucking pubes to make your cock look bigger?"

"What? No. That'd be weird, dude."

"Oh! *That* would be weird, would it?"

Stefan can't hold himself still. A body reacts to pain, tries to save itself, and he fights to stay under. Locks his limbs to keep from shaking. He needs this. Deserves it. Can't live without it. He straightens, slicks back his hair, raises his face to the boiling water. Stretches up on his toes, elevates his whole body, feels it like acid rain on his shoulders, his neck, his cheeks, his chin—

"Stefan!" Aaron's seen the colour of Stefan's skin and he's running over, almost strobed by the film of water obscuring Stefan's vision, steadying himself on the taps of the showers in between. "Stef! You're hurting yourself!"

"Fuck *off,* Aaron!" He tries to push Aaron away, but the boy is pulling at his arm, wincing as the hot water sprays over him, dragging them both away from the shower and into the clear space in the middle of the annexe. Stefan tries to get rid of him, but Aaron holds on. "What the fuck are you even doing here, anyway?"

"What do you *mean?*" Aaron practically screams.

Finally Aaron has to let go, for the sake of his own balance. Stefan, relieved of the weight, slips on the wet floor and falls, lands on his rear. Barely even registers the pain. Fuck it; embrace it. He rearranges himself on the tile, legs crossed, leaning back. Exposed.

You all want to see this wreck? Want to witness it? Then here it is. Look at it. Fucking look at it.

"I *mean,*" he says, "that you're a fucking idiot, Aaron. Don't you see how stupid all the shit you keep doing is? How unnecessary? It's not a part of *you.* You're just fucking around. It's not in-trin-sic!" He strips the word apart, hits the floor with closed knuckles on every syllable. "You didn't have to do any of it. You could have just been a regular guy. You didn't *need* all that shit!" He looks up, fixes the confused Aaron with a sneer. "Why'd you do it? Were you bored? Lonely? Did you just fancy her *that* much?"

Aaron flails his arms as he replies. "I don't know, all right? I just do things sometimes!"

Stefan laughs. The water, still running, pools around him. There's a little red mixed in, and he inspects his knuckles. Bleeding.

"You're a likeable enough guy, you know, Aaron?" he says. "You're nice looking, you can be fun. You even have money! You could have just been you. Got along fine. You didn't need to be a fucking prick. But you were, anyway, and it got you dragged down here, under all this… fucking concrete."

Aaron crouches. His eyes quickly cover Stefan's body. Looking for what? "I didn't get along," he says quietly. "Nobody liked me, okay? Nobody. For a million reasons. I *know* what I'm like, but what the fuck else am I going to do?"

"Oh, boo fucking hoo, Aaron. 'Nobody likes me so I harass women.' That's *sad.*"

"Fuck you, Stefan," Aaron says, straightening up.

"No, fuck *you,* Aaron, you little perv."

Aaron throws his wet towel on the floor of the shower room, wraps himself in his robe, and leaves the annexe as quickly as the slippery floor will allow. Stefan, uncaring, hangs his head back and stares at the concrete ceiling.

"What are you doing, Stefan?"

It's Pippa, advancing on him, leather boots kicking up spray. Frowning. Great, he's a puzzle again. She holds out a hand to help him up. He ignores it, pushes up from the floor on his own, returns to his shower. But it's not helping any more. It's just really fucking hot water. He closes the tap.

"You're red," Pippa says, with a gasp in her voice. "You're *so* red! All over! Doesn't it hurt?"

He smooths his hair up and out of his eyes and slips his robe back on. The rough fabric scratches as it drags over his scalded skin, and he bites the inside of his cheek to keep from crying out. As soon as he's covered, as soon as he's hidden again, he follows Aaron out of the bathroom.

Of course it hurts. That's the point.

* * *

It's not that the lock on her door wakes her, it's that Christine's been slipping in and out of consciousness for perhaps five minutes, perhaps thirty, and the electric hum of the biometric sensor, followed by the creak as the lock turns over, is an unwelcome reminder that the world outside her door still exists, and probably doesn't have as much of a headache as she does.

"Oh, Teenie!" Indira calls, entering the room with all the joie de vivre of a cartoon princess. "And, ah! Hi Vicky, hi Paige!" She's dressed for a day out, in the light colours she prefers, sunglasses atop her head, knee-length skirt billowing in the breeze from the open window. "Remember when I used to bring you your brekkie?" She cocks her head behind her at Hasan. "I have a helper now!"

In the second year, it was a common occurrence for Indira to wake Christine with a tray of breakfast, some good cheer, and the details of whatever aspect of her feminine bearing she had to attend to that day; usually Dira would reminisce about how good Christine had it, because in *her* day they'd yet to phase out the archaic mannerism training—hours of learning how to stand gracefully from a chair while wearing a short skirt—whereas Christine and her cohort were lucky enough simply to be handed a pair of high heels each, given access to the dress-up box, and left more or less to their own devices. If it hadn't been for Paige and Vicky competing with each other to put together something beautiful or fun and encouraging the others, Christine would probably still have trouble walking in heels. Even if sometimes Paige did have to take the phone out of her hand and physically drag her over to the shoe tree. The internet can't be *that* fascinating, Paige would say, prior to handing her a shoe with a platform or an open toe or a lacy bit that needed tying around her calf.

She raises two fingers to her lips in memory. They are, with the possible exception of Vicky, different people now. And yet still always together.

"Beatrice said you might need fluids," Hasan says, following Indira through the door with a tray laden with drinks and cereal bars, which he hefts to illustrate his point. "So: fluids."

"This is very nice of you, Indira, Hasan," Christine says, pushing up in bed and making sure to take the sheets with her; there's discarded underwear on the floor and she's not about to assume it's not hers without a visual inspection, "but we're in kind of a compromised position, here."

Indira refuses to be scolded. "Aunt Bea said you all ended up in here." No need to ask how she knows: the corridor cams. A reminder to hop into the system later and make sure she and Faye weren't caught on video using the back stairs; there are no cameras around those doors that she knows of, but it's possible they might show up in the corner of a video frame somewhere, accessing an area they shouldn't.

"And we thought," Hasan continues, "that at least one of you could use some hangover care."

Paige, the guiltiest party, shuffles up onto her elbows. She curls a section of sheet around her chest with one hand and fetches from Hasan's tray a glass of orange juice with the other. She smiles her gratitude, passes the glass to Christine, and retrieves another for herself.

"I don't mean to be rude," Vicky says, not yet sitting up, "but could we have a little privacy now? We're all rather, uh—"

"We're naked," Paige says, and takes a deep drink from her juice.

"And I'm pretty sure we *all* have headaches," Christine adds.

"Say no more," Hasan says, and takes Indira's hand. After some minor negotiations—yes, Christine will come down to the kitchen within the next hour to see her off; yes, Vicky can give them a lift because she's going that way anyway—they leave the three girls alone.

Vicky rubs her face and groans. "Why do embarrassing things always happen around you, Tina?" Vicky says. "No-one's boyfriend sees me in my underwear at home."

"Because I'm cursed," Christine says. "Do you even allow men in your house, anyway?"

"It's not like a rule. It's just coincidence."

" 'No men except by appointment'." Christine mimes nailing a plaque to a wall. "What do you do if a stray wanders in by accident? Do you even *have* a basement?"

"Bad taste, Tina," Vicky says, throwing off the covers and revealing herself to be, out of all of them, possibly the most clothed; she must have dug through Christine's drawers at some point and borrowed a cami. A process of elimination, which Christine participates in by rolling her chest and feeling her breasts move inside last night's bra, establishes Paige as probably the most naked one. "We have an actual trans girl in *my* house. No feminisation jokes allowed."

Christine bites her lip against the temptation to retort that they have one here, too, and her throat tightens momentarily. Medical exams this morning, right? She'll have to check on Stef later. "That's literally my entire repertoire," she says. "I *run* on gallows humour. And estradiol. Actually, Paige, can you pass me my pills? They're in the drawer."

Paige complies, popping one out for herself. "Exactly how much did I drink last night?" she says, mostly unimpeded by the pill; they've all had considerable practice at talking normally while estradiol dissolves under their tongues. "I feel worse than I did after the Christmas bash."

"Too much," Vicky says.

"There were sherries," Christine says.

"And those little alcoholic chocolates."

"And you had, I'm pretty sure, more wine than me and Vick combined."

"I hate myself," Paige mutters.

"Consider it a valuable life lesson," Vicky says. "Tina, can I borrow some clothes?"

Christine waves her permission and Vicky starts digging, eventually pulling out a pair of white shorts and pairing them with a sky-blue top, a combination that reliably makes Christine look like she's off to play sandcastles at the beach and so, obviously, looks incredible on Vicky.

Wordlessly Christine drains her orange juice and then drops an estradiol into her mouth, trying not to think about how much work she still has ahead of her if she wants to be as effortlessly and consistently feminine as Vicky. Step one might be to become an entirely different person, but she's done that once already and isn't keen to repeat the experience.

"I," she announces, "need a shower."

She's not all that surprised when Paige follows her into the bathroom and sits heavily on the toilet. As Christine finishes pulling off underwear, throwing bra and knickers at the small hamper in the corner and hanging the beautiful borrowed stockings carefully over the towel rack, she marvels once again that Paige, with her elegant figure and torrent of dark blonde hair, can make naked look like high fashion. As usual, Christine is the clumsy, unfeminine Hobbit amongst serene, pristine Elves.

The frosted shower door saves her from any further unflattering comparisons.

"When, exactly, did I take off all my underwear?" Paige asks eventually.

"I have no idea. You were still wearing your stockings when I fell asleep." Christine doesn't add that she knows this because Paige trapped her with her leg for at least half the night. "If you need clean stuff, you can borrow some of mine. I'm dying to see how much better my bras look on you."

"They'll look worse," Paige says. "You're bigger than me, there." She doesn't sound quite like herself. The hangover?

"Sports bras, then."

"Okay, thanks," Paige says, and falls silent for a while. It's not until Christine gets done shaving her legs that she says anything else. "Christine, what are you going to do when you leave the programme? Aunt Bea is very close to giving you your freedom, I think."

Christine's reply bubbles in her throat as she rinses out the conditioner, so she doesn't answer until she steps out of the shower to see Paige still sitting on the toilet, knees together, uncharacteristically pensive.

"I don't know," Christine says, carefully. "I'll probably keep living here until I graduate Saints; maybe longer. Paige, is something up?"

"I'm not sure," she says. "After Nell…I've been thinking. About the last couple of years. About the way I've been. About *who* I've been. And about us. As friends, I mean. *All* of us. Remember what I said last night? About how our friends are actually just *your* friends?"

"I remember disagreeing," Christine says, wrapping herself in a towel and wincing slightly. Her nipples are still a little sensitive.

"I feel like I'm about to lose everything," Paige says. "Vicky's already drifting away. She spends more time with Lorna and her other friends than with us. And now you're not being actively sponsored any more, you're a step closer to leaving, and then will I even see Indira or Abby again? I just— I don't want to be alone, Christine."

Christine holds out her hand and waits patiently until Paige takes it. She tugs gently, encouraging her to stand, to accept the hug. "You won't be alone," she says into Paige's shoulder.

"I feel so pathetic," Paige says. "Everyone else is moving on, and even though I have these plans and I can step through them, point by point, I can talk to brands and do photoshoots and put myself out there, but all I can think is, what's the point? If I come back home and I'm the only one here, what's the point?"

"Hey! One, you have a plan and you're actually executing it, which is…*beyond* amazing, Paige. *I* don't have plans; I have vague intentions. And, two—" Christine pulls away a little so she can look up at her, "—you're not the only one who doesn't have anyone outside these walls, okay?"

"That's not all I am, though, right? Just someone you live with? Someone you know, someone you…went through some stuff with." Paige hiccups. "Someone you experimented with."

"No." Christine keeps looking up, into beautiful amber eyes that don't look back. "You're one of my best friends, Paige. I never, ever thought, when I was— when I was how I was before, that I would have someone like you in my life. That I would ever be so *lucky*. You're incredible, okay? I'll *always* choose to have you in my life."

Paige leans into the hug, drawing Christine back in, pressing whole-body against her. "Okay. It's just…I realised that my plan, the one you're so impressed by, it doesn't have *people* in it. Just me. And I couldn't stand it. I can do it, I can go out there, be the cis girl I'm supposed to be, but I need a *life*, not just a career. And I need people in it who are real. Who belong to me, not to the— the *persona*. I want to stay close to them. I want to stay close to you."

"Are you saying you want to be one of those women who leaves uni and moves straight into a flatshare with her dorm girlfriends?"

"More or less."

"Let's do it, then. Let's add that to the plan. You and me. Abby if she wants to come. We'll live near Vicky and Lorna." Christine draws distracted circles on Paige's back. "You know what?" she says. "I might be at least as scared of the future as you are. Making a life? As Christine? I want it, but it's *terrifying*. I know how to be me, sure, but mainly I know how to be me *in here*. And I don't want to be like Maria and Aunt Bea, calcifying in here. I want to get out there. And Paige, if I can do that with you, with Abby, with Vicky, with Indira, that's, like, *half* the terror factor gone, instantly."

"Good," Paige says, muffled—she's buried her face in Christine's wet hair.

"You know what I've never been scared of, though? Being alone. Not really. I've never doubted we'll stay together, all of us, in some way. I'm fully expecting to be ninety and still have you in my life. You, Dira, Abby, Vicky. We're family, Paige. We always will be."

"You mean that?"

Christine stands on her toes and whispers into Paige's ear, "Let's be crotchety old ladies together." She's instantly hugged tighter, lifted almost off the floor and held there until Vicky bangs on the bathroom door, breaking the spell.

"I'm going downstairs!" Vicky yells. "I need *medicinal* amounts of coffee."

Paige puts her down and steps back, smiling. "I'm incredibly naked, aren't I?"

Christine lifts the hand she's still holding, brings it to her lips, and kisses Paige gently on the knuckles. "Babe, you are *so* fucking naked."

***

"You're an idiot, *Stefan.* What are you? A fucking idiot. Why do you—*schhh!*—do these things to yourself? These people—*gchhh!*—are going to see every inch of you by the end of the day! So why—*fuck!*—can't you just *cope?*"

Taking off his robe dragged a layer of skin off with it, or felt like it did, and now Stefan sits gingerly on the chair in his room, dabbing carefully at himself with a towel, trying to dry himself without making anything worse. There's a tube of moisturiser by the computer and every time he gets a new patch halfway dry, he rubs a handful into his pink, stinging flesh.

"Had to mouth off at Aaron, too, didn't you? Idiot. You have *one* friend down here, and just because you're too stupid to compartmentalise, you might have alienated him for good. Keep—*fucking piece of shit!*—your mouth *shut!*"

He didn't get a chance to collect himself. That's what it was. Straight from bed to the shower, from alone to naked and surrounded by people, and faced with Pippa and Aaron and Maria and a couple of random upstairs girls and fucking *Declan* in quick succession. No time to prepare himself. No wonder he got caught in his worst attack yet of…

Stefan's never known what to call it. He's looked it up online but nothing's ever felt adequate. It's being witnessed, known, understood; reduced. As if he exists in a quantum state, balanced equally between the things he is and the things he is not, and the act of observation collapses him into only the things he is not. Unmakes him.

Best prepare, then. Because diving into the shower on its hottest setting and waiting for his skin to sluice away from his body is not a coping strategy he can use long term.

By the time his door opens and three women file in—Pippa, Maria, and another, older woman he's never seen before—Stefan's dried, dressed, slightly less pink, and marginally more prepared for what's about to happen. Abby described it: there'll be a full-body examination, although she was light on the details, and then he'll have some blood drawn and provide some sperm.

The sperm thing is a worry.

Pippa leans against the wall and Maria, the door. No getting out except through her. The nurse shoos him off the chair so she can sit down.

"Strip," she says, as he perches on the end of the bed.

"Hi," he says, running through his prepared script. "I'm Stefan. Would it be okay if it was just you and me in the room, please? I'm uncomfortable being naked around so many people, and I promise I won't give you any trouble."

"Ah-ha!" the nurse says, half-turning to grin at Maria. "This one's polite, isn't he?" She turns back. "They stay. Now *strip.* The third time I have to ask for anything, I do so with this." She pulls a taser out of a pocket; it has the same touch-sensitive strip as the ones the sponsors have, although it's a bulkier unit. A heavier charge? And still usable only by sponsors and, evidently, nurses.

Stefan nods, and turns away from them to undress. He's not wearing much—less weight on his sore skin—and it takes only seconds to drop the t-shirt and trousers onto the bed.

"Underwear too," the nurse says, waving her taser. As Stefan complies, she turns back to Maria. "Wow. What happened to him? Some new protocol? He looks like he's got five sunburns."

Stefan can't help twitching at the question.

"The shower water was too hot," Pippa says.

"That's it?"

Out of the corner of his eye, he sees Pippa shrug. "I think he was distracted. Didn't notice until it was too late. One of the other boys was needling him. You know how it is."

"Hmm. There's scabs on his knuckles, too."

"Y—yes," Pippa says. Apparently she hadn't seen those. "He fell."

"He fell? You're sure?"

"Yes."

"Fine. All right, boy. Turn around. *All* the way round. To face us." The nurse sighs. "And move your hands!" She strikes the back of Stefan's wrist with a biro.

Stefan complies, forcing stiff hands behind his back, exposing himself, keeping his mind as blank as he can. He's a robot, following instructions. He's a mannequin, a poseable doll. He's not *here.* He finds a spot of wall near the door to look at, but can't stop his gaze flickering every so often to Pippa. She looks…concerned? And either she really hadn't understood what happened in the shower annexe, or she just lied for him. Why?

"Okay," the nurse says. "Let's go. Tasers up, please."

Maria and, a second later, Pippa raise their weapons and keep them raised, pointing right at him, as if he might suddenly become dangerous, and Stefan understands why when the nurse leans down and cups his genitals in her hand.

He forces his teeth together. Balls his hands into fists behind his back.

"What's this, Karen?" Pippa says.

"It's just procedure," the nurse says, rolling Stefan's testicles around in her fingers.

"This wasn't how it was done with m—"

"—with your last boy?" Karen finishes. Stefan's almost too occupied keeping himself frozen to notice Pippa's slip-up. "No, I imagine not. But I heard your girl up and left you all. So, now you have me. And this is how I do things."

"This is too—"

"Maria, do we need to have this girl removed?"

Maria moves her steady, practised gaze to Pippa, though her taser remains focused on Stefan. "No," she says. "Pippa's fine."

"Yeah," Pippa says, and locks eyes with Stefan for a moment. He doesn't know what he reads there, and she looks away quickly. "I'm fine."

"Good!" the nurse says, and rummages in her bag for an iPhone and a measuring tape. Stefan manages not to react when she pulls his penis out to its maximum length and holds the cold tape up against it. "I must say," she adds, tapping a number into her phone, "he's a credit to you. Very docile. Normally we'd have had to knock them down at least once by now. About half these exams are on boys who are unconscious. I'm sure *you* remember." The nurse cocks her head when she says it, and Stefan can't tell which of Pippa and Maria that little barb was aimed at. "Well done, Pippa."

"Thanks," Pippa says.

Stefan closes his eyes. No-one comments on it, as far as he's aware. He stops listening to the nurse, tries to listen to the sound of his own heart instead, and by feeling for his pulse in his wrist he's able to do so, or so he imagines. He lets his body be guided into whatever positions are required, he breathes slowly and carefully, and he concentrates on being nothing but a functional automaton.

A machine made of meat, he remembers.

Muffled, the nurse goes about her inspection, has him stand on a scale, notes down his height and weight with a comment that both are "very suitable", and pushes him down into a sitting position on the edge of the bed so she can examine his head and neck.

The sharp rap of a biro on his forehead forces him back into the room.

"Boy! Hold out your arm and make a fist! If I have to ask again, I'll shock you first!"

God, it's bright in the room. Stefan, still naked, still being watched, takes a moment to pick something new to look at—the computer, fine—then unlinks his fingers and holds out his arm, fist still clenched. The nurse gives him a strange look, and starts pinching at his forearm until she finds a vein.

Five vials.

Another rap on the forehead. "Hey! Brain-dead boy! Put your clothes back on. None of us enjoy looking at all that." He controls his flinch. At least this time he can turn away while he dresses. Puts on a clean hoodie this time, no matter the weight on his skin; the more armour, the better. When he's done, the nurse drops a collection cup and an iPad onto his bed. "I imagine that's his first porn in weeks," she says. "Make sure he doesn't blow his load before he can get it in the cup."

He doesn't look up as they leave, just sits down carefully on the bed again and slowly leans back, keeping his feet on the floor, resting his head against the duvet. He's aware of a mild commotion outside, but occupies himself counting the cracks in the concrete ceiling.

At least he has some time while they talk. How long will it take to become properly human again? To reassemble his imitation of a functional person?

But then the lock cycles again and Pippa quietly re-enters, closing and locking the door behind her. Stefan, barely limber, finds himself locking up again.

Whatever. At least he's dressed.

Pippa sits delicately on the end of the bed, moving the cup and the tablet onto the desk. "You can fill that later," she says. "Or whenever. Look, I'm sorry about her. They didn't do the…the crotch stuff before. That's new. I would have warned you."

"Why?" Stefan's voice is dry, and difficult.

"Because!" Pippa says, indignant. She makes a fist, like he did, but releases it. Starts messing with her bracelet instead. "I know I haven't given you much reason to trust me. And I feel like…this…might have put us back where we started. Worse, even." Stefan snorts. "But I'm here to help you, Stefan. I really am. I'm here to make you better. This place works, if you let it. I've…I've seen it."

He has nothing to say to that. He knows too much, and isn't in a frame of mind to edit. And her suddenly earnest face reminds him of Christine. He's surrounded by true believers, and all of them, even the nice ones, want to tell him the good news about Dorley fucking Hall.

"Why won't you *talk* to me, Stefan?" Pippa says, kicking the bedframe.

"Because," he croaks. He doesn't mean to antagonise her, but her mood has swung around to *conversational*—or possibly *confessional*—at exactly the wrong time. He's in no position to be the man he's supposed to be right now. Surely it's obvious that he needs time to recover? How can she not see he's been freaking out all morning? Is he that good at hiding it?

He knows he's not.

Pippa looks at him. He feels it on his skin, like boiling water. "Breakfast time," she says.

"I'm staying here."

"You won't eat?"

Eating means Aaron. It means Will and Adam and all the other fuckers out there. It means sponsors looking at him the way Maria and the nurse looked at him. "No."

"I could count this as a strike."

Stefan pulls the covers over his head, would keep pulling if he could, more and more layers. He'd bury himself; anything to be even more comprehensively hidden from the world than he already is, here in this concrete dungeon.

"Do what you have to do, Pippa," he says.

He can only guess at her reaction. After a minute or so the mattress shifts as Pippa's weight leaves it. The door opens and closes quietly and, finally, grants Stefan peace.

* * *

The mug tree's been emptied of all the joke ones. For security purposes, obviously; when there are outsiders in Dorley Hall's main kitchen and dining hall you don't want them discovering anything that even hints at the place's true purpose, like a mug that says, *Don't feminise me until I've had my coffee,* or Maria when she's had too much to drink. So Christine sips from something disappointingly plain, with koalas on it—"Smoothest brain of all mammals," she was informed by a revitalised Paige when she picked it—and smiles indulgently at Indira and Hasan, who are failing horribly at their stated goal of leaving to visit some of Hasan's extended family in the next county, because they're perched on the end of the kitchen table, kissing again.

"You're going to be late," Christine says.

"You're going to make *me* late," says Vicky, who is driving them to the station.

"Fine," Indira says, between kisses, "fine, fine. Look! We're done."

"She says that," Hasan says, pecking Dira on the cheek, "but just wait until we're in the car."

"No!" Vicky says, wagging a finger. "No canoodling on my back seat."

Canoodling? Christine mouths to Paige, who's mostly been ignoring the commotion while she absorbs caffeine. She shrugs and smiles, with the little one-sided grin she used to throw Christine's way all the time.

Dira tugs on the strap of Christine's tank top—she couldn't be bothered to dress femme, not before she's finished waking up, and if Aunt Bea has any complaints, then she knows where the appropriate retort is printed on the side of a mug—and drags her up and out of her seat, into a hug. Indira's going away again, and when she comes back their relationship will have changed forever, so Christine squeezes her former sponsor as hard as she can, coaxing a surprised squeak out of her.

"Sorry."

Indira draws back, and kisses the end of Christine's nose. "I'll be back in a few days," she whispers.

"I know. It seems like you're always away, though."

"I know."

"And when you get back…things will be different."

"I'll always make time for you, Teenie. You know that."

"I know. Sorry for being clingy."

"Shush. And welcome to your first day as a free woman."

A final squeeze and Christine releases her. "Have a good trip," she says, and kisses Indira on the cheek. Another change. Another inflection point. Too many of those in too short a time. She knows how Paige feels: everything's suddenly moving fast. You're not panicking about being girls anymore, so get out and make room for the next lot!

Not actually how it works—the programme couldn't function if dozens of programme graduates didn't stay on, and it would probably actually be healthier for some of them if they took a year away from Dorley and found themselves a new hobby—but it's hard to remember sometimes. Christine rebuilt her whole life on a foundation that now feels unstable.

When she cries, watching Indira step out of the front door, blowing kisses and waving, it's entirely natural that Paige embraces her, rubs the back of her neck, sits her carefully back down, and refills her coffee. They share wordless smiles and keep fingers entwined on the table as they drink, listening to the sizzle of the coffee machine, the mechanical mutterings of the dishwasher through the open door to the utility room, and birdsong from somewhere outside the high, barred windows.

Old ladies together.

A few minutes later, after a pair of haggard-looking sponsors pass through the kitchen on their way downstairs, Pippa barges her way through the doors, deposits herself at the table and buries her face in her folded arms.

Christine exchanges glances with Paige, who puts a tentative hand on Pippa's shoulder.

"You okay, Pippa?" Christine says.

She breathes heavily through her teeth. "I'm not cut out for this," she says.

"You want to talk about it?"

"No." She sighs with her whole body, lifting her shoulders and letting the tension ripple down her spine. "But I should. It's Stefan. I'm just completely lost."

"Is he okay?"

"Right now? *Absolutely* not."

"What happened?" Paige asks.

"He was just…different today. The whole time up to now he's been no trouble. At all. The worst he's ever given me is, I don't know, flipping *sarcasm.*" She lifts her head, props it on her wrist, and accepts with her free hand a fresh cup of coffee from Christine, who sits back down on her other side. "And that should be exactly what I want, yeah? But he keeps, I don't know, short-circuiting me, because I remember what I was like when I was in his position, and he's just completely different. And I remember what everyone else in my intake was like, and he's not like *them,* either. He's not like anyone I've seen in the files, and I've read *everyone's* files while I tried to work him out. You two included; sorry."

"It's fine," Paige says, and smiles at Christine over Pippa's head. "We're not those people anymore."

"He's not even like Melissa! Even she was a *little* trouble, at the start. Not combative, not if you believe Abby, but she argued. Or at least sulked, I guess. I don't know; Abby's redacted *a lot.* But Stefan! He just sits there and takes it. We get them up early, and he just goes along with it. We send them to their rooms, and he just goes along with it."

Christine relaxes a little. She's been tense since Pippa mentioned Melissa: there are too many things that link her and Stef, and only the routine redaction of biographical information from the daily files seems so far to have kept them from being obvious. But Pippa merely mentioned her as an example, and moved on instantly. *Paranoid, Christine,* she scolds herself.

"But that's good, isn't it?" she says. "His sister—"

"Yeah, yeah," Pippa says. "His sister who he loves so much he'll suffer any indignity for her. Feels a bit unlikely, but I get it." Turning her bracelet around on her wrist again. "It didn't really feel like it matters that I'm always messing up with him, because he never actually makes trouble. But I've still been worrying about it because, when push comes to shove, I *need* to know how he works to help him through the steps; but I've not been *too* worried because, you know, I've got time. They only start on the estradiol tonight, and it's going to take a while for that to bear fruit. And he's so steady, you know? Just keeps going and going, watching his movies and reading his books. He's even been a moderating force on the three boys he hangs out with. Kind of." She laughs for a moment. "I think it'll take a hundred-mile-an-hour wrench to the head to change Aaron. Just knock out the chunk of brain that compels him to— uh, never mind." She coughs, and Christine rubs her shoulder: *It's okay.* "I've felt a little, in just the last day or two, like I've been establishing a rapport with him, but this morning, everything came crashing down."

"How so?" Paige asks. Christine's biting her lip, looking away to mask her concern for Stef.

"When he woke up this morning—when we woke him up, earlier than usual—it was like whatever gets him through the day just didn't wake up with him. He yelled at Aaron, and it might have been bad enough to seriously screw up the fragile friendship they've been building. He scalded himself badly in the shower, deliberately, I'm sure. It was some kind of self-harm thing, like he really, really just wanted to hurt himself—"

"Hey," Christine says gently. "Slow down. Take your time." Pippa's been tensing, raising her voice. Especially with Aunt Bea in the next room, calm is preferable.

"Thanks. Sorry. He wouldn't talk to me, after the shower thing, just marched back to his room. And for the physical, it was me and Maria, she's helping me out, now, I don't know if you remember her getting the assignment—" a pair of nods reassures her that they do, "—but the new *nurse*…She's horrid. She gave him the physical and he *completely* shut down. It was like, you know how some people get after the, uh, after the, um, you know, down there—"

"Pippa," Paige says, "neither of us are sensitive about our orchis any more. You can say the word."

Christine wants to argue—she reserves the right still to be pissed off about it, even if she'd definitely get it done voluntarily if she happened to need one and was asked, say, today—but she keeps quiet.

"Well, the, uh, the orchi," Pippa says, apparently at least as sensitive about hers as Christine is, "hits some of us like an invasion, right? Like, no matter all the changes that have happened up to that point, it's the first big one, the first real, total disruption of bodily integrity, yes?"

"It's mutilation," Paige says. "If you don't ask for it, it's mutilation."

"Right. Yes. Well, Stefan behaved just like that. Like he was being… invaded. And the only way he could get through it was just to switch off. To wait it out. Like he was being, um…"

Christine can guess what Pippa wants to say. She's not going to say it. But Christine's thinking it, and she's wondering if there's still a way she can get Stef out, because this is far from the last time someone is going to do something like that, and punish him if he makes even the slightest fuss about it.

"Who's this new nurse?" she asks.

"Barbara retired. We were expecting it, but not quite so soon, I think? The new one, Karen, I don't know her. I assume she's, you know, one of us, but she's old, older than Aunt Bea, I think, and I've never seen her before. And she talked about Stefan like he wasn't even *there*, like, like she was a vet and he was a dog, and she—" she lowers her voice, "—handled his genitalia. Inspected it. Measured it."

"Oh," Christine says.

"That's new," Paige says.

"Afterwards, he barely said a word. Wouldn't go to breakfast. I apologised to him for…how it was, said I would have warned him if I knew, and he said, 'Why?' and I was really *angry* with him because why *wouldn't* I be? But then I saw myself through his eyes and it just made me feel so flipping *wrong*. But it was like I couldn't keep a lid on it. I even—and I don't know why—threatened him with a strike if he didn't go to breakfast, and he didn't seem to care."

"What did you do?" Christine asks.

"Left him in his room. Couldn't think of anything else to do."

"Did you give him a strike?"

"No!"

"You know what I think?" Paige says. "I think you need to forget about him for a while."

"Paige!" Christine says.

"I'm serious! He's not going anywhere, and if he's in his room, he's safe. Hungry, maybe, but you can ask one of the duty girls to send a couple of cereal bars down in the dumbwaiter. He might be miserable right now, but you know what always helped me when something happened that I just couldn't deal with?"

"What?" Pippa says.

"Time. Give him time. Don't bother him while he's recovering. And come out to Almsworth with us instead of sitting around, worrying about him."

No. Not this. Christine's willing to go along with Paige's assertions and not bother Stef for the moment, but this is beyond the pale. "I said I didn't want to go *shopping*, Paige. I said I wanted a nice, sleepy day where absolutely nothing happens. Until tonight, when we go out, I guess."

"That was before. Now we have two reasons to go: to get you some clothes, *which you need,* and to give Pippa a chance to de-stress and get away from all this." Paige catches Christine's eye when Pippa looks away, and there's a request there.

"Fine," Christine says. "But I still don't see why I need clothes; I have all of yours."

"First: presumptuous. Second: I'm two inches taller than you, Christine, and smaller in the bust. You need clothes that *fit,* and your selection of nice things is pitiful. Besides, this is—" she makes quotes with her forefingers, "—a 'fun bonding activity for girls'. It's in the manual. Back me up, Pippa."

Pippa blinks and takes a second to gather herself before answering, and Christine's forced to agree with Paige: the girl really needs some relief. From the situation that Christine put her in.

"Yes," Pippa says. "Not exactly that wording, but yes. Group bonding while engaged in traditionally girly activities. Rerunning being a teenager, but in your early twenties. And with more money."

Christine holds up her hands. "Fine. I'm beaten. We're going shopping."

"Good," Paige says. "You don't know how long I've been looking forward to putting you in something cute, taking you into town and buying you something nice, and this might be one of the last sunny days of the year. Go ask Aunt Bea for the card."

"Why me?"

"You're the one who's been put on the accounts."

Christine drains her coffee and pushes away from the table. The other two follow her into the dining hall, flanking her as she heads to the central table, where Aunt Bea is eating breakfast with the second years and some of their sponsors.

No Nell. An enforced break? Or is she downstairs, applying her signature brand of unpleasantness to the boys running around down there?

Faye and Rebecca beckon her over, so she joins them at their end of the table, and accepts quick hugs from the pair. Most of the second years are still wearing exercise clothes with hoodies and shirts thrown over the top, in order to be presentable for breakfast. Christine grimaces; she doesn't miss being rounded up with all the other second years, four times a week, at various times of day, to run on the treadmills and lift hilariously small, pink weights in the upstairs exercise room. It might have been necessary—a year underground with no easily-weaponisable gym equipment leaves you quite out of shape—but it's a chore she's grateful to be free of, even if her own exercise regime has degraded to the occasional jog around campus.

Paige quietly explains their plans to Aunt Bea, whose eyes flicker to Pippa and then to Christine, with a smile. "You'll be well-behaved, I trust?" she says.

Christine straightens up and draws a cross on her chest. "Like saints, Aunt Bea."

"And this evening? Your plans?"

"We're meeting up with Vicky and Lorna," Paige says, "and going out."

"Exact destination TBD," Christine adds.

Aunt Bea nods, reaches into her bag and, after a little rooting around, passes a credit card across the table. Six pairs of second-year eyes follow it into Christine's hand. "Don't go mad with it."

Christine squeezes Faye's shoulder and steps away from the table, linking back up with Pippa and Paige. "No promises!" she calls. On her left, Pippa laughs.

* * *

There's a selection of white noise files on the phones they hand out, and Stefan's been plugged into one—rain_valley_3hrs.mp3—since shortly after Pippa left. Eyes closed, lying on his back under the covers, clenching and unclenching his fists, calming himself down.

Despite the duvet he'd still felt exposed, so after a little while he added a long-sleeved top over the t-shirt and put the hoodie back on over it all. He lies there now, layers over layers, too warm but safe. Even if they spy on him through the cameras, there's nothing to see but his face.

Stefan wants badly to berate himself, but there's no reason and no point: there's no version of him that could have borne the examination gracefully. He tries instead to blank his mind and listen to the rain.

I'm not here.

Ninety minutes of rain sounds later, Aaron knocks. Yells through the door that he just wants to see what's up. Stefan struggles out of bed—he got more wrapped up in the duvet than he realised—and lets him in. Doesn't cover up again when he sits back down, though. Aaron looking at him isn't so bad; he doesn't make judgements.

At least, he didn't before.

Aaron kicks the door shut behind him and sits on the chair. Like Stefan, he's wearing more layers than usual. Maybe the examination got to him, too?

"Soooooo," Aaron says. "How're you doing? You wank yet? Ah—" Aaron spins on the chair and picks up the sample cup from the desk, "—evidently not. Me neither. Something about having an evil old hag digitally masticate my meat-and-two-veg just doesn't put me in the mood, and no amount of heavily curated iPad porn is going to change that." He balances the cup on his finger, spins it like a plate, and catches it when it threatens to escape. "I don't know why they even need the cup. I have this patch on my wall I got pretty good at hitting. It's like a sport—making your own entertainment the way our ancestors did. If I hit the spunk spot, it's a good wank; if I don't, I have to keep going until I do, or until the blood from the friction burns gets too distracting. Anyway, they have whole gallons of my precious, precious baby batter soaking into the paint that they could come for at any time." He starts flipping through the iPad. "Huh. Yeah. They gave you the same shit they gave me. I was hoping you got better stuff, but this is just, like, swimsuit models, blowjobs, blah blah fucking blah. Would it kill them to have given us some sexy aunts or rubber maids or girls using toys on each other or trans girls sucking each other off? This is all so fucking vanilla; no wonder the women here all act like they've had no fun in years. And no wonder I couldn't get it up. Look at this one! It's just a chick, sitting on a rock, hair all billowy in the wind. Like a shampoo ad. I can feel myself getting softer just looking at it. Hell, I'm practically inverting."

He throws the iPad onto the bed next to Stefan.

"So, quick question, not really very important at all, don't worry about it if not, but have you been finding it hard to get hard, lately? Trickier than usual, I mean? Because I feel like I've got no petrol in my tank and nowhere around here is selling premium unleaded. Talk to me, Stefan. You dismissed my very real, valid concerns about my pecs getting flabby, and I don't want you to dismiss my incredibly tragic erectile dysfunction with the same nonchalance. Seriously: quality of wanks, better, worse, about the same…?"

"I, uh, haven't tried yet," Stefan says.

"Not at all? Not since you came here?" Stefan shakes his head and Aaron coughs nervously. "God, if I'd known I was masturbating for two I wouldn't have wasted all that time sleeping. No wanks? Not even a quick toss after waking up with a boner? You really haven't put on one of those lame-ass movies they loaded us up with, found the part that's most suggestive and just gone to town? No dick flick to a chick flick? Shit, man, I know this place is hell on the libido but that's something else. You know it's not November for another week, yeah?"

"Um. What?"

Aaron launches into an explanation of No Nut November; Aaron strongly disapproves, because suppressing the natural urges is how you get serial killers and electro swing bands, man. Stefan just listens, inserting the occasional syllable where it seems to be required to keep the flow going but otherwise letting the stream of consciousness flow over him. It's calming; way better than forest sounds.

"So," Aaron says, bouncing himself onto the mattress at the other end of the bed from Stefan, "that medical exam was weird, huh?"

Fuck it. Might as well come to terms with it: he's friends with the little bastard. And talking to him is better than the alternative. "Right?" he says. "The nurse was even freaking Pippa out. And I don't know why I had to be naked the whole time. You don't need to be naked to have your blood drawn."

"It's a power play. Maria's been giving me these books to read about, like, toxic masculinity and stuff, expanding my vocabulary, so now I can say with confidence that the whole thing was carefully planned to disempower us—" he says the word like he just learned it in junior school, with a grin, "—to make us feel vulnerable and completely at their mercy. And also kinda cold."

"I'm amazed you read *any* books Maria gave you."

"Yeah, well, she temporarily deleted all my movies and all the books on my phone. No choice. What's Pippa been making you read?"

"Um. Nothing?"

"Really? What *is* she doing, then?"

"Literally nothing. I just watch movies and read books when I'm alone. I don't have any homework or anything like that."

"God. Swap?"

"Yeah, like they'd let us. Maybe the lesson I have to learn is about dealing with extreme boredom."

"Yeah," Aaron says, and shifts a little closer. "Missed you at breakfast, man. Weetabix and oat milk isn't the same with just Will and Adam to stare at. And Raph is still lurking like a big fucking weirdo. He walks past, looking at me, and the music from *Jaws* plays. So, what do you think? Come to lunch?"

Stefan stretches, keeps the sleeves wrapped around his fingers, feels the fabric grow taut across his back, scratching at the sensitive skin. It's energising; he's still here, still alive, and here's the pain to prove it.

He'll be ready for the next thing. He won't get caught out like that again.

"Yeah," he says.

"Okay!" Aaron jumps up from the bed. "Good."

"I'm sorry about this morning."

"Hey," Aaron says, standing by the door, waiting for Stefan to open it with his thumbprint, "it does me good to look my demons in the face sometimes, even if they are naked, damp and strangely earnest. Besides, this place gets to all of us, eventually. Some of us have a freakout in the privacy of our own rooms, others of us try and give ourselves second-degree burns in the shower. You still sore?"

Stefan prods the biometric reader and hauls on the door. "Little bit, yeah."

"Here?" Aaron says, poking at Stefan's shoulder as they head out into the corridor.

"Ow! Yes, I'm still sore there."

"What about here?"

"Ow!"

"How about…?"

"Hah! Missed!"

"Hey! Come back! You were mean to me and I need to punish you! It's the only way I can get personal satisfaction! It might be the only way I can cum in the cup!"

"Leave me alone, you psycho!"

Stefan evades him, dodging away from Aaron's fingers and rounding the corner into the main corridor, almost tripping over Maria. The perplexed look on her face only makes him laugh harder.

12
Queen of Hearts

26 OCTOBER 2019 — SATURDAY

"We're really not going to talk about it?"

"We're *really* not going to talk about it."

"Really? Because I feel like a little group therapy session, a lot of sharing of our feelings, maybe a group hug—"

"Discussion over! Go snuggle with your boyfriend if you want to talk about it so much but right here, right now, over my tomato soup, we are not. Fucking. Talking about it."

"Hey, Stef; you hear what Will just called you?"

Stefan regards his spoonful of tomato soup. Regards Will, who seems more full of compressed rage than usual; Adam, quieter than usual; Aaron, even more talkative, but with his usual level of tact.

"He doesn't necessarily mean me," he says.

"Oh, babe!" Aaron says. "You wound me!" Stefan kicks him under the table for his trouble. If it's harder than it might otherwise have been, well, that's just revenge for poking Stefan on his scalded shoulder.

"He definitely means you," Adam says, almost too quiet to hear. "There's no-one else who'll put up with him."

Stefan laughs. Important to show he appreciates the joke. Of all of them, Adam has the hardest shell, reveals the least of himself, but he's been opening up little by little over the last few days, and as soon as Stefan saw it was happening, he decided to encourage it, if only to find out what he did. A smile, nervously returned, is Stefan's reward.

"No-one at this table has any appreciation for the therapeutic process," Aaron says. "I'm trying to open up, people! To live in my moment!" He's been trying to get Will to respond to his theories about Karen the nurse, but Will is uncharacteristically reluctant to engage, and every time the topic is raised, Adam becomes more withdrawn.

Stefan, sensing another round of argument, puts a cautionary hand on his arm. Aaron flinches only a little.

The four of them sit at the lunch table in their usual places: Stefan and Aaron near the door to the main corridor but with their backs to the wall, Will and Adam a few places down, facing the door to the common room. Two pairs of eyes on both entrances. They've maintained this habit for almost a week, the better to warn each other should something unpleasant seem about to happen. Declan, Raph and Ollie, their oppositional group, take their lunch at the tables in the common room, and for the last several days have declined to cause any trouble at mealtimes, apparently acknowledging that four beats first three—now two, with Declan out of the picture. Adam might be quiet and Stefan might be scrawny and Aaron scrawnier, but Will is the opposite of all of them and easily the physical equal of anyone in the basement.

He also calls himself "a man of words", an appellation Stefan finds annoyingly smug and which has prompted Aaron privately to comment, "He's a rare breed: a dude capable of calling himself 'a man of words' both without irony and without being forced by his own sense of self-satisfaction to immediately bend over and blow himself to orgasm over just how thoroughly intellectual he is," but putting up with his pomposity and the occasional homophobic remark is a small price to pay for the protection he represents.

Stefan senses a moment of tension from all of them when the door from the corridor opens, but it's only Martin Holloway, clutching a tray and hovering in the entrance like a schoolchild searching for the safest seat in the canteen. Martin normally eats alone in his room. More out-of-character behaviour from one of the boys; there's probably a reason for that.

"Moody!" Aaron says. "We've missed you, buddy! I was trying to figure out what was missing from the lunch room. At first I thought it was ketchup but then I realised it was your intense aura of crippling depression. Please, come, sit; engulf us."

"Hello, Aaron," Martin says, monotone, and with a nod to the table picks a chair and dumps his tray in front of it. "Hello, everyone."

Stefan's grateful that Martin sits closer to Will than anyone else. He still can't stand the man. Maybe it's just a lack of exposure. Maybe if he'd been subjected to a little bit of Martin every day, he might have built up a tolerance, like with Aaron, but maybe not; all Stefan can think of when he looks at him is that the sad bastard's left a dead man and a grieving widow in his wake. Of every sin under Dorley Hall, his seems like the worst.

So he does his best to ignore him.

"Uh, Stef?" Aaron says quietly. "Aren't you being incredibly rude?"

Stefan nods and dips some bread in his soup. "Yep."

"Oh. Good. Okay. Just checking. FYI, I'm calibrating my morality off of yours, so you'd better not steer me wrong. I don't want to blink and end up a serial killer or a member of the Conservative Party or something."

"Says Captain Dick Pic."

"Hey! You can't kill with those."

"No, but you can hurt someone badly."

Aaron drops his plastic spoon in the bowl, splashing his hoodie with soup. "When are you going to stop going on at me about that? Seriously, Stefan. It's getting old."

Stefan shrugs. "When you show some remorse."

It's a risk: Stefan's already made Aaron mad at him once today, and it was Aaron who extended the olive branch, not him. But he's still going to keep at it, keep pressing on the sore spot and keep making Aaron be the one to make peace, until he gets the result he wants. He's not sure exactly why this is so important to him—beyond the fact that it bothers him to be friends with someone who would do something like that—but it would definitely be satisfying to reform Aaron before Dorley gets to him. Two fingers to the whole bizarre programme.

"Why are you always so self-righteous?" Aaron mutters.

"I thought you were calibrating your morality off me?" Stefan says innocently.

Aaron snorts. "You shit. I'll find out what you did, eventually. You're a bastard, too, somehow."

Stefan nudges him with his elbow. "Now *you're* being rude. Eat your soup."

Aaron blows him a kiss and starts dismembering his bread roll.

"Hey, uh," Martin says, "Stefan?"

"Yes?" Stefan says, not bothering to hide his irritation. Across the table, Will looks annoyed and Adam upset, and Stefan realises he probably should have paid attention to their conversation instead of testing Aaron's malformed conscience.

"I, uh, just wanted to ask: how many times did they tase you?"

"I've never been tased, Martin."

"Not even this morning, with the nurse?" Martin says, turning his plastic spoon over and over in his hands. It's clean; he hasn't touched his soup.

"No."

"Not even when she—?"

"*No,* Martin."

"I don't believe this," Will says, standing up out of his seat and ignoring Adam pulling on his sleeve, trying to sit him back down. "You didn't fight back *at all?*"

Declan, bruised, walks past in Stefan's memory. *Why don't you fucking poofs fight?* "Of course I didn't," Stefan says.

Will bangs the flat of his palm on the table, making Adam jump. "Why the fuck not?"

"Calm *down,* Will," Stefan says.

"What the fuck did you say, you little fa—?"

"Jesus, Will." Stefan points past him. "Look at Adam!"

Will twists, finally seeing it: Adam, withdrawing, pulling his hands away from the table, pulling his legs up under him. Reducing the amount of space he takes up. "Fuck," Will says, instantly dropping the attitude. "Adam. I'm sorry."

Adam whispers something too quiet for Stefan to hear.

"No," Will says, sitting down, moving his chair away from Adam, giving him some space, "I said I'd do better."

"What's happening?" Martin says, but Will silences him with a glare.

"What's happening," Stefan says quietly, as Adam slowly uncurls, "is we all got assaulted." He's talking not for Martin's sake but for Adam's, Aaron's, even Will's. Perhaps for his own sake, too; or for the persona he performs down here, among these men. "Just because I didn't fight back doesn't mean— Look. I had a bad morning. Aaron knows how bad. And on top of that, we saw Declan being taken back to the cells, looking like he'd been beaten. Badly. He got his third strike when he came at Aaron and me yesterday, and apparently *that's* what happens *after* three strikes. No more comfy bed. No more movies. No more lunches at the table where we bicker about whatever stupid shit is bothering us that day. No more afternoon telly. You just get the living shit beaten out of you, and then you get escorted to the showers, washed, and escorted right back to your cell, where presumably they carry on beating you."

"But that's Declan," Will says. "You don't care about Declan."

"No. But I care about me and, God help me, I even care about you lot. Declan's our canary: he gets violent with the metal cutlery, they take it away; he misbehaves too much, they beat him up until he stops. He's a message to the rest of us: don't fuck around or you'll end up like him. And so that's what I'm thinking when the nurse strips me naked and starts fondling me: put up with this or you'll get the Declan treatment." A lie, but a believable one, and probably more useful than the truth. "So I take it. I don't fight back."

"That's the point of this place," Aaron says, gesticulating with his hunk of bread and spraying the table with droplets of tomato soup. "To make us not *want* to fight back. To train us to put up with whatever shit they feed us. And I admit, man, I was sceptical at first. Plush bedrooms and free food? What, they're going to bore us until we submit? No. Turns out, being bored is the reward. The punishment is being made to look like a mouldy orange that can't walk straight. So, yeah. Some old bitch of a nurse wants to feel me up? I'm going to lie back and think of England. Hell, it wasn't my *worst* wank."

"I pushed her," Will says. "Got my first strike and got tased. When I stood up, Tabitha hit me, and warned me I'd get another strike if I tried again." He pulls his t-shirt back, revealing a raised welt on his right pectoral.

"I tried to get away," Martin says. "Tased."

"I didn't," Adam says, and all heads at the table turn to him again. He's got his hands locked together, arms touching at the elbows. Like he's in prayer. "I didn't try to stop her." He sounds almost like Martin in his monotone. "I didn't try to get away. Even though I wanted to, I couldn't. I froze up. It's what's best. I froze."

"Adam," Stefan says, standing slowly, "it's okay." He shoots a look at the others at the table. "You guys want to go watch some TV?"

Aaron takes the hint first, dragging Martin with him into the common room.

"I'm not leaving," Will says. His fingers are twitching as if he wants to comfort his friend but can't bring himself to display even a small amount of physical intimacy.

"I'll bring him through," Stefan says. "I promise. Just, please, give us a minute?"

Will glares at him. "Fine," he says eventually.

As Will reluctantly joins Aaron and Martin in the common room—Aaron's already turned on the TV—Stefan sits carefully in the empty seat next to Adam. Gently, he cups Adam's shoulder in his right hand and rests his left hand on the table, open and available.

Adam, with some hesitation, takes it.

"Do you need to talk about it?" Stefan asks.

Over the next twenty or so minutes, Adam hesitantly tells Stefan a story. It's unclear, incoherent, and ultimately doesn't leave Stefan with significantly more information about Adam's past than he already had, but it makes one thing certain: Adam is the person in the basement least able to deal with someone like Nurse Karen. Stefan, at least has ways to compartmentalise, and Aaron already has a hundred theories with which to comfort himself, but Adam has nothing to buffer the trauma. He's almost a blank slate, albeit one on which his church has scrawled a lot of nonsense about demons and subservient women and the requirement to procreate and the primacy of the unadulterated human form.

It's not hard to imagine how a man like Adam, inculcated with such bigotry his whole life, might say or do something that would put him on Dorley's radar, but it's impossible for Stefan to believe that he deserves it. And while escape from this place, for Adam, is impossible, Stefan can at least do his part to make the next year or so a little less pointlessly traumatic for him. For all of them.

He returns Adam to the common area and sits him down next to a compliant Will, and then Stefan returns to the lunch room. He checks the light on the biometric lock on the door to the corridor: still green. Outside, two sponsors are leaning against the wall, keeping watch on the basement residents as usual. Tabitha, Will's sponsor, is lazily messing with her phone, obviously bored, but Edy, Adam's, anxiously meets Stefan's eyes as soon as he steps out into the corridor.

"I'm Stefan," he says, stopping a safe distance away from them and folding his arms around his waist, to seem as nonthreatening as possible. "I'm Pippa's— um, I'm her responsibility, I guess."

Tabitha rolls her eyes. "We know."

"Good. I want to speak to someone in charge, please."

***

Almsworth town centre is concentrated around a hill even more shallow than the one graced by the university, with a small cathedral at its apex and a cluster of smaller, church-aligned buildings giving way, halfway down, to a shopping district that connects directly to the old townhouses by the river. The large bus station is the newest building, having emerged recently from the shell of a department store. It's become a minor social hub, extending towards the railway station on one side and the cinema on the other, with chain restaurants and small shops on its upper level and a covered walkway on the ground floor that crosses three side streets and provides shelter to people queueing for the town's most popular nightclub. It's one of only two truly modern sprawls in the town centre, which otherwise comprises mostly brick buildings abutting each other, three streets thick along the river, separated by the occasional cramped alleyway. Smaller chain stores and an ever-increasing number of estate agents inhabit the antique buildings in the manner of hermit crabs, their flashy fasciae protruding from shabby, crumbling brickwork.

The other modern building is the main shopping centre itself, which climbs the street closest to the station and embraces the angle of the hill like a collapsed layer cake: each level is roughly equal in size and juts out from under the floor above, a giant's staircase leading up to the cathedral, against which the shopping centre's top-floor semi-open-air café squats as closely as is legally permitted. The cathedral fights back against the noise of shoppers and diners with a skirt of trees and bushes, voluminous and several layers thick on the graveyard side and trimmed back almost to the bare branch where they intersect with the shopping centre property line.

Paige takes Christine and Pippa straight from the bus station to the café, insisting on a real coffee—meaning one with two shots of sugar-free caramel and a swirl of something fluffy on top—before serious shopping can feasibly commence.

Christine doesn't enjoy being away from the university grounds, a whole bus ride away from her bolthole at Dorley Hall, but it's nice up here, with the rain shutters pulled back and a light wind rippling through the surrounding greenery, lending the café a lush, earthy smell and providing occasional glimpses of the magnificent cathedral grounds. She drinks daintily from her caramel coffee, trying not to get too much lipstick on the straw—Paige insisted she make herself beautiful—and concentrates on her friends and not, for example, the roomful of strangers who might at any moment make unfavourable judgements about her.

Pippa, who chose a plain black coffee and seems not to be regretting it, leans back in her chair and stretches. "I *really* needed this," she says. "My world's contracted to just the library, the Philosophy buildings, and Dorley flipping Hall. I was starting to forget what civilisation looks like."

"I'm not sure I needed this at all," Christine says, trying to keep her tone light. A pair of younger men sat at the table behind them a few minutes ago, and their presence is inhibiting in more ways than one. She remembers when that was her, although she'd be alone; hoodie up, headphones on, innocently circling the food court and the surrounding shops with an exploit app running on her phone, waiting for—

No. She was different then. She wasn't herself; she was still *him.* She closes her eyes, edits the memory. Inserts her old self in her place. Funny; she's starting to forget what he looked like. Even though it feels like everyone out here who gives her so much as a passing glance can see him perfectly.

"It's okay," Paige whispers, stroking her thumb gently on the back of Christine's hand. "You're safe with us." Christine concentrates on the sensation, skin against skin, forces herself to inhabit the present, to remember the face in the mirror. The boy is dead; let him stay buried.

I know who I am now, she tells herself. Another little litany from Indira's repertoire. "Am I that obvious?" she says aloud.

"To me, you are."

"I hate this, Paige. I feel…conspicuous."

"No-one thinks there's anything strange about you. You're just another girl."

"Easy for you to say."

"Only because I've had the practice. You need to get out more."

"I should be better at this by now," Christine says, and slurps some more coffee to give her free hand something to do.

"Paige is right," Pippa says, offering a tentative smile. "None of us was instantly good at any of this."

"Except Vicky," Christine says.

"Even her," Paige says. "She was the most immediately natural of all of us, but she still had to learn how to…" She trails off, considering her words, and Christine resents yet again the entire outside world, a place where none of them can truly drop their guard. She imagines a life spent that way, always careful, and understands why people like Maria and Aunt Bea retreat to Dorley, to a world that gets them. That's not going to be her, though. Even if she forgot quite what it's like to be out here. "Vicky had to learn how to leave the hall," Paige continues, still reassuring Christine's stiff fingers, caressing her from nail to knuckle. "She had to learn how to be *Vicky* out here. Lorna did, too, when she transitioned. It's jarring for all of us."

"That's not the same," Christine whispers. "Lorna's trans. *Actually* trans."

"It's close enough. I know you believe there's a huge difference between you and her—"

"Yeah, because she's authentic and I'm not."

"—but there *isn't.*" Paige leans closer. "You may have come by your genders differently, but the material effect is still the same. You *know* she'd tell you that if she knew your history."

"She doesn't," Christine says. "And she can't, ever. So she won't."

"It gets easier, you know," Pippa says. "I went out once a month to start with. Into town. I'd go to random places, like a coffee shop or Waterstones or that place by the river that sells paintings of cats, and I wouldn't let myself leave until I'd talked to at least one person. About anything." She grins into her coffee mug. "I learned a lot about cats."

"How do you stop feeling like a fake?"

"It fades." She takes a sip and spends a moment in thought. "I don't know you all that well, Christine, but I think you've said before that you see yourself as a girl, right?"

"At Dorley, yes, I'm a girl," Christine says. "Even at Saints. If it gets bad in a lecture, I can just leave. Go straight home and curl up under a blanket. But out here, I feel trapped. Here, I'm a girl only as long as no-one asks me any difficult follow-up questions. I hate this, Pip." She's too visible; she imagines herself easily disassembled, breasts and pretty face torn away as messily as they were once applied, reduced to a thin, scared boy in girls' clothes. Obvious to everyone.

Behind her, the men finish their drinks and stand up, startling her and causing the tooth biting her lip to break the skin. She wipes away the blood and inspects it: pleasingly real. An anchor.

"I forgot it could be like this," she whispers. "I think I want to go home, Paige."

"No," Paige says, moving her chair close and making contact with Christine, shoulder to shoulder. "You're staying here. As long as it takes. You need to."

"Because Aunt Bea wants me to?"

"Because *I* want you to. And because it'll help."

"Are you sure about this, Paige?" Pippa says.

"Yes. She's my— my best friend, and she *fades* as soon as she steps out of our front door. It kills me to watch it happen."

"Did you know it would be like this?"

Paige nods; Christine feels her weight shift. "It's easy to forget at home," Paige says, and resumes gently stroking Christine, a finger along the length of her bare forearm, "but she's as new at this as the rest of us. In some ways, she's as advanced as anyone, and when she's somewhere she knows she's safe, she's confident, sweet…fully herself. But Indira wasn't great at pushing her to do difficult things, especially after they grew close. A lot of the time she forgot to act like a sponsor. I remember being jealous: when Francesca was making me walk the grounds of Saints, still swollen from surgery, Christine and Indira were watching movies together in Indira's room. But, as awful as she was, Francesca prepared me for life out here. Practically rubbed my face in it. But Christine…Everyone loves her too much." There's a smile in Paige's voice. "No-one wants her to hurt."

Christine leans her head against Paige's shoulder. The gentle soprano of Paige's near-whisper is as effective a balm as anything else she can think of. Nevertheless: "You're talking about me like I'm not here, Paige," she says.

Paige squeezes her forearm. "Sorry."

"How are you doing?" Pippa says.

"I'm…riding it," Christine says. "The longer I'm here, in one place, and nothing happens, the easier it gets. Maybe I'll try talking to someone in a minute. About cats."

"Would you like to know *my* method?" Paige says. "None of these people matter."

"That's your method? No-one matters?"

"Some people do." Paige lets Christine go and lays her hands out on the table. "I sort people into two groups: those who matter—" she curls one hand into a ball, "—and those who don't." With her other hand she describes a huge volume. "And I choose who matters to me. Right now? Here? That's you two. Christine and Pippa. The rest of them might as well be cardboard. And *no-one* cares what cardboard thinks, do they?"

Christine nods slowly. Enjoys the sensation of her hair rolling across Paige's shoulder and tickling her cheek as it falls. "I think I'll try the cat thing first," she says.

They sit that way for a while, slowly drinking their coffee, Pippa filling Christine's silence with complaints about her Philosophy dissertation and her millennial supervisor—"He made a 'can has cheeseburger' joke last week. I had to Google it."—and Paige contributing chatter about her History with Human Rights modules and the professor who keeps trying to look down her top. Eventually Christine feels able to join in. Later, when she leaves to use the women's bathroom and realises she forgot to feel at all anxious about it until after she gets done washing her hands, she announces to Paige and Pippa that she's ready to get on with things.

"You're a star, Christine," Paige says, rising to embrace her and punctuating her praise with a kiss to the temple. "Now," she adds, gathering up her bag and her phone and dragging Christine along by the wrist as she strides towards the exit to the rest of the mall, "who wants to *shop?*"

* * *

They put him in the cells. It's not punishment—though he can hear Declan's moans from the other end of the corridor, which is unpleasant enough—but it's best none of the boys know where he is or what he's doing, and the cells are the only place down here where that can be accomplished without locking down the whole basement. They left the door open for him so he can stretch his legs, even go look at Declan if he wants. Edy told him he has a reputation as the one who's no trouble.

Stefan doesn't go look at Declan. Remembering his first days under Dorley, he does a little yoga instead. He's been neglecting it.

He's been running through the encounter with the nurse, over and over, and still finds no sense in it. Granted, today's been Stefan's first actual encounter with the methods they use to reform and transform their patients; it's possible they're all like this, one invasion after another, that they have nothing in their future from here on out but constant violation. That doesn't ring true, though. They can't possibly induct their charges into womanhood with an assault.

Pippa said it was new. That she hadn't expected it. And—although the nurse interrupted her before she could finish her sentence—that it hadn't been done to her. And she spent the whole time shaking, Stefan remembers. Two hands on the taser to keep it steady. Like she was scared. Or angry.

He lies back on the cot, hoping someone cleaned it after the previous inhabitant of this cell moved on, and thinks through what he wants to say to whoever comes down.

He hears her before he sees her: echoing footsteps in the corridor, the twin-tone *click-clack* of heels on a hard surface. Something about her gait suggests an older adult, and images of severe schoolmarms and society proprietresses merge in his mind. It's a surprise, then, when a friendly looking woman, aged somewhere above the mid-forties, raps gently on the side of the open door and smiles when he meets her eyes.

She wears a light dress, low heels and no tan on her pale skin, she cuts her blonde hair to the shoulder, and she stands like she owns the place. Aunt Bea, he presumes.

"Knock knock," she says. "I'm Beatrice. I run this establishment."

He looks at her outstretched hand for a moment before taking it. "Stefan," he says.

"I'm aware," she says, and her smile falters as she looks around. In his cell, down the hall, Declan yells a string of particularly potent expletives. "I do hate this place," she adds, and pulls on his hand, encourages him to stand. "And there's nowhere to sit, unless we're to share that horrid little cot. Why don't you come with me?"

Her suggestion startles one of the girls waiting outside, someone Stefan doesn't recognise. The girl immediately starts to protest.

"Oh, we will be quite safe," Beatrice says. "Won't we, Stefan Riley?"

Stefan Riley, full-named for the first time in a while and temporarily lost for words, crosses his heart instead, a gesture which unaccountably makes her chuckle.

He follows Beatrice out of the cell corridor, through the doors at the end and up a winding flight of concrete stairs. He'd expected her to lead him into a room in the upper basement, the one Christine said functions mostly as admin and security, but she keeps going. Soon they emerge into a dining hall of the sort one might find in a National Trust property.

Stefan unconsciously ducks away from the high ceiling. Agoraphobia, that's new! Too much time underground. Beatrice notices his reaction and takes his hand again, pulls gently until he moves of his own accord, and eventually sits him down at a rustic, wooden table in a bright, airy, lived-in kitchen. There's a small pile of dirty dishes on the table, which includes a mug that says, *Once a Princess, Always a Princess,* though the first double-s has been mostly scratched off. The mug is quickly cleared away by the other occupant, who turns out to be Abby, wearing rubber washing-up gloves.

She's standing at the sink, behind Beatrice, and is thus safe to mouth the obvious question: *Does she know?* Stefan shakes his head, both to answer Abby and to pretend amazement at the opulence of his surroundings. “This is so much nicer than the basement,” he says to Beatrice, who smirks.

Abby rinses the incriminating mug, stacks it on the drying rack with several others, and drops her rubber gloves over the edge of the sink. “I expect you’ll want the room,” she says to Beatrice.

“Thank you, Abigail. This is Stefan; he’s our guest from downstairs.”

“Actually,” Abby says, “we’ve met. Pippa asked me to check on him. Hello again, Stefan.”

“Hi, Abby,” Stefan says. “How was the birthday dinner?”

“Alcoholic. Would you like some coffee, before I go?”

Beatrice shows her a professional smile and, as Abby pours coffee into two plain mugs, turns it on Stefan. It shouldn’t be a surprise, particularly, but Stefan nonetheless is a little perturbed that the woman in charge of the place that took eight boys against their will—and immediately subjected them to unwanted hormone suppression—is able to meet his gaze steadily and without apparent difficulty. Is her conscience really so clear? Or is she just that confident in the results she gets?

Abby—living, breathing exemplar of the results Beatrice gets—nods at them and scurries from the room, no doubt texting Christine as soon as she gets out of sight. A part of Stefan has to admit that Beatrice might have a point: no matter her origin, Abby is graceful and gorgeous, even in a hurry and a battered *GO SAINTS!* t-shirt. She’s had nothing but time for him, and she’s never seemed anything other than happy.

If all monstrous men could become like her…

“First things first,” Beatrice says, clasping her hands together on the table; terribly sincere. “I would like to welcome you to Dorley Hall. Officially.”

How should he reply? He was expecting, despite the fondness with which Abby speaks of her, a tyrant. Not this affable and attractive older woman, with her coffee and her light and airy kitchen and her novelty mugs. How might one of the boys respond? How might Aaron?

He quickly decides against the idea of attempting to channel Aaron. “I don’t know if I can thank you for that,” he says, with precision: he can thank Christine for it.

“In time,” Beatrice says, smiling, “you will. Our programme can be quite transformative.”

Ah, they’ve reached the stage of the conversation where the vampire starts talking suggestively about “wine”. Earlier than he expected. “I suppose I’ll have to see it to believe it,” Stefan says, hoping his performance of ignorance is adequate.

"I'm sure you will."

Stefan gets the feeling Beatrice isn't done with her little routine quite yet, so he sips his coffee and rehearses the points he wants to raise. Her gaze is uncomfortable, and he tries not to squirm under it; angry he may be, but that doesn't mean he's any happier meeting yet another new person while still his unmodified, unsatisfied self.

"You intrigue me, Stefan," Beatrice says, narrowing her eyes a fraction. "Your record suggests that you are, frankly, dangerous to be around, but in the two weeks since you arrived, you have calmly followed all instructions and made no trouble for anyone. You claim to love your sister so much that the thought of her believing you dead is enough to guarantee your submission, but you frequently go beyond what is asked of you. I hear you've been pushing particularly firmly against the Holt boy's unpleasant habits."

"Um," Stefan says, "the Holt boy?"

"Aaron."

"Oh. Yes, well. He shouldn't have done what he did, and if I'm going to be friends with him, I need him to acknowledge that."

"And what precisely will that achieve?" Beatrice asks, tapping lightly on her mug.

"I'll feel a bit less gross when I laugh at one of his jokes."

"Why, Stefan? Why are you so pliable? Why do you try to do your friend's sponsor's job for her? And why, after your only incident of aberrant behaviour to date, did you ask immediately to see me?"

He sips his coffee again, playing at savouring the flavour. It's an obvious ploy for time, but he wants to seem intimidated by her, a cover for his mounting discomfort. The back of his neck itches again, and he scratches at it distractedly.

"I don't see what other choice I have," he says. "The doors are locked; the girls are armed. There's nowhere for me to go. Besides, you provide food, a bed, washing facilities; as long as I'm safe, I have no reason to push back." Beatrice nods. Doesn't give anything away by her expression. "As for why I'm here right now…"

"Do enlighten me."

"Your nurse sexually assaulted us this morning."

"Is that how you would describe it?"

Stefan dumps his mug heavily on the table. "Yes. She came to each of our rooms, had us strip naked, and groped us. We were given no option to refuse, and we had weapons pointed at us the whole time."

"Karen Turner is a medical professional."

"Medical professionals ask for permission," Stefan says, looping both hands around the mug and pressing hard. The heat is a useful reminder. "*She* didn't. Not only that, but she enjoyed herself. Treated me like an animal. And Pippa, a woman I've trusted up to now, *let her do it.* You say this programme is transformative? If this is an example, I have to wonder what you're transforming us into. Perhaps," he adds sweetly, expending much to maintain a steady voice, pressing his fingers harder into the hot mug, "you intend to teach us to submit quietly and without complaint when we are touched intimately under threat of violence?"

Beatrice looks him directly in the eye. "We most definitely do not."

"Then help me understand. Pippa came to me afterwards and told me that this nurse's methods are new. I didn't want to listen to her at the time because it was all so fresh, but if she's right, then I'm even more confused." Is he playing this too innocent? Hard to say; Beatrice is difficult for him to read. She stays silent, inviting him to continue. "Can I be blunt?" he asks.

"I am suffering from an overabundance of bluntness of late," Beatrice says. "Oh, go on," she adds, waving a hand at his confusion, "say your piece."

Controlled breaths. He closes his eyes, to block out as many senses as possible; better for remembering the second half of his prepared thoughts, better for managing the itch at the nape of his neck. It doesn't matter that she gets to see him struggling. It probably pleases her. "I think this was unintentional. The nurse, Karen, she said the old nurse left, and I bet it's hard to get replacement staff here. Most nurses would report you immediately. So my guess is, you take whoever you can get. And that's Karen: a vindictive old pervert who gets off on exerting power over people less than half her age. Who likes to traumatise people. Boys. Men."

"You would consider yourself traumatised by your experience?"

"Wouldn't you be?"

"My emotional responses are not a consideration," Beatrice says, and then snaps her head around. "*Yes,* Abigail?"

Abby stands in the doorway connecting the kitchen to the vast dining hall, nervously shifting from foot to foot. "He's right, Aunt Bea," she says. "It's wrong."

"Thank you, Abigail."

"You never did anything like that to *me.*"

Stefan and Beatrice realise at the same time that there's only one possible conclusion to be drawn from Abby's statement: that she was once under Beatrice's control, just as Stefan is. A little gift from Abby: another thing he doesn't have to pretend ignorance about. He wants desperately to thank her, and hopes she doesn't get in trouble for helping him.

"Times were different," Beatrice says.

Abby shrugs. "*We* weren't." She doesn't wait to be dismissed, but turns and marches back into the dining hall.

Stefan picks up the cue he's been given. "Abby was in the programme?" he says, with just the right amount of incredulity. He keeps looking at the door into the dining hall, trying to give the impression that he's wondering if the handful of other women he saw in there were in the programme, too.

Beatrice maintains a creditable poker face. "She was unruly. Girls can be too, you know."

"That's hard to believe. Last night, she was very kind to me."

"That's the whole *point*," Beatrice says, her composure briefly faltering. She sighs and picks up her drink with both hands. "Since you were so generously blunt with me," she continues, "I will be blunt with you. You are correct: we don't have a lot of choice when it comes to nursing staff. Our previous nurse was a graduate from this house, but she chose eventually to move on. She informed us ahead of time, of course, but I'm now given to understand that an absolutely *perfect* home came on the market, and she left the country early." Beatrice sighs. "Not her fault. Usually the examinations are done a few weeks from now; likely she thought she would have time temporarily to return. But with the accelerated timetable, one of my sponsors was forced to turn to…an *old* contact. One who happens to live nearby. I was *not* informed until the examinations were already under way."

She probably wasn't even awake. Maria especially had seemed extraordinarily disgruntled to have to be walking around so early. As the custodian of an underground forced feminisation facility, Beatrice probably has privileges her staff lacks, such as getting to sleep through her hangovers.

"What would you have done if you'd known?" he asks.

"Postpone the examinations," Beatrice replies instantly. "Stefan, I assure you, I do *not* condone the actions of nurse Karen Turner. She will be contacted and disciplined." She sips from her coffee, carefully places her mug back on the table, and pinches the bridge of her nose.

"What a day," she says, her voice losing some of its pitch and accent. "I'm having my authority undermined by a twenty-one-year-old *child.*"

"Don't worry," Stefan says. "I'm still extremely intimidated by you."

Beatrice goes still for a moment, looks placidly at Stefan, and then bursts out laughing. "Good!" she says. "Good. Although," she adds, almost to herself, "it's likely not the best sign that several people have told me that lately."

Abby's briefly visible in the dining hall, checking up on Beatrice's laughter from a safe distance. "And," Stefan says, realising there actually is something he can do to reduce the likelihood that Abby gets censured, "knowing Abby went through the programme…It really helps."

"Does it now?" Beatrice is still smiling, still coming down from her mirth, but something of her edge is returning.

He nods. "It's proof I'm not going to be down there forever. Proof that there's a light at the end of the tunnel." And the light's coming from a kitchen right out of an AGA brochure. "And she's sweet. Kind. A role model."

"I will be sure to let her know," Beatrice says. She finishes her coffee. "Pippa's agreement with you, to guarantee your good behaviour: I'm invoking it."

"Okay," Stefan says, thanking Christine once again. Whatever feat of manipulation she pulled off to get Pippa and Beatrice to agree to those letters is going to be hard to repay. When he's done, when he's finally a girl just like her, he's going to find out what she likes and buy her a hundred of it.

"You did *not* meet with me," Beatrice says. "You do not know that some of the residents of Dorley Hall are programme graduates. And whatever you might have inferred about the duration of your stay, you will keep to yourself. Say you understand and agree."

"I understand and agree."

Beatrice stands briskly. Holds out her hand for Stefan's empty mug, places it upside down in the sink next to hers. She leans against the sideboard with both hands. "You met with Abigail, not me. You discussed this morning's events. She passed on to you the message that the nurse will be disciplined. And you are all to have a vitamin jab tonight; it will be administered by someone else. That is the information you will take back down with you. This and nothing more. Say you understand and agree."

"I do. I mean, I understand and agree."

"Good. You really are an interesting boy, Stefan," Beatrice says, before raising her voice and calling, "Abigail!" While they wait, she turns a smile on him and adds, "I find it particularly fascinating that, in your whole time here, you haven't so much as glanced at the way out." She points to the other exit from the kitchen, through which a pair of external doors and the Saints campus are visible. Before he can respond—before he can even decide what she means—Abby's returned. "Abigail, please return young Stefan to the facility."

"Of course," Abby says. "This way, Stefan."

Beatrice watches as they leave the room, but Stefan doesn't relax until they've passed through the double biometrics and started heading down towards the first-floor basement. He holds up a hand, asking for a moment, and leans bodily against the wall, closing his eyes.

It's something about how Beatrice looked at him. It was like the way Pippa and Maria looked at him, back when they thought he was going to be just like the others—as opposed to whatever they think of him now—but more intense and more impersonal. It makes sense: this place has been rehabilitating men, by its own curious methods, for a long time. Beatrice will have seen dozens of boys go through the programme. Dozens of boys just like him.

Awful to be counted among their number.

"You okay, Stef?" Abby says, not quite in a whisper. "We're mostly out of camera view here, so we can stop for a while if you'd like. Everyone will understand you needing a moment to get yourself together after your first encounter with Aunt Bea."

"She really wasn't all *that* bad," he says. "This is mostly me stuff."

Abby touches him gently on the forearm, almost as a request. He covers her hand with his, and she firms her grip. "Like last night?" she says.

"Like last night. Like this morning. I kind of thought I'd be stronger than this, that I'd be better prepared." He scratches at his neck again. "I picked the wrong time to crack."

"May I hug you, Stef?" Abby says, and when he nods she embraces him. It's a while before they release each other, and Stefan wonders, with his face buried in her shoulder, how many times she's done this for Christine.

***

Context is everything. No matter how much your world changes, no matter how much you change with it, when it consists only of Dorley

Hall, the mini-supermarket on campus and the well-trodden paths to the Anthill, the Student Union bar and the Linguistics department, you can adjust to anything, given time. Christine became a girl there, and draws comfort from familiarity and routine.

The fitting rooms in the upscale section of the largest department store in Almsworth Mall are a very different context in which to be a girl. Christine clings to Paige's arm as she looks at herself in triplicate, stuffed into a mid-thigh dress which makes only the barest contact with several important parts of her upper body. It's beautiful, and causes the small part of her that still remembers what it was like to be a (nominally) straight man to want to wolf whistle, but the prospect of wearing it out tonight is not one that sits well with her.

"Paige!" she hisses. "This dress is missing large chunks of dress!"

"So?" Paige says.

Paige spent an hour patiently guiding Christine through the racks and watched her pick out calf-length skirts, low-heeled shoes and other disappointingly ordinary attire until she just couldn't take it anymore, irritably snatched Christine's bag away from her, pinned her against the wall, and told her quietly but firmly that if she doesn't select something stunning and sexy to go with the sensible skirts and Sunday-lunch sandals then she's going to start a bonfire right there on the border between lingerie and the designer dress department, throw all of Christine's modest purchases on top, and use the smoke to call Vicky for aid.

"So," Christine explains, "usually those parts of me are covered up?"

"We're going clubbing," Paige says, untangling herself from Christine's grip and pushing her closer to the triple mirrors, "not to church."

"But—"

"All the stuff you picked out is really nice," Paige says, standing behind her and holding her by the shoulders, "but none of it really makes a statement. Except 'I work the front desk at a funeral home', perhaps."

"It's not *that* bad."

"Oh, it'll please Aunt Bea, I'm sure. But it doesn't please *me.*"

Christine decides to get to the heart of the matter. "I look *stupid.*"

Paige's fingers stiffen on her shoulders for a second, and then she turns Christine around to face her. "You *don't.* You look sexy. You look gorgeous. And you're also not going to be alone. I'm going to be wearing something at least as immodest, and earlier I heard Pippa making appreciative noises over something *highly* revealing."

Christine tries very hard to let that sink in. What's the most vital thing about becoming a girl at Dorley? You don't have to do it alone. And tonight she's going out with Paige and Vicky, the two girls who helped her through some of her darkest moments. So what if she has to show off an alarmingly large section of hip?

Besides, she has to get good at this. Step one, stop panicking that random people can see a boy in you: in progress, and currently going pretty well, because she keeps not getting found out, and even Christine can't maintain a consistently high level of anxiety over something that continuously fails to become a problem. Step two: be confident!

Trickier.

Be kind to yourself, Christine, she tells herself, and appends, *but don't be a bloody wimp.*

"Okay," she says, prying Paige's fingers off her shoulders and turning around; the reflections help, and she's never seen her bottom from quite this angle before, or in quite so perky an outfit, "I'm done wussing out. I'm good. I'm buying this."

Paige does not exhibit the delight Christine expected. Instead she holds up another net basket. "Not *just* that one, I hope. I have more for you to try!"

"Paige—"

"Come on, Christine. For me?"

It's generally easiest to let Paige have her way, so after a cursory argument, Christine agrees to step in and out of anything Paige hands her. Eventually they narrow it down to three dresses, Christine's selections, and a few other things Paige picked up while Christine wasn't looking. She needs variety in her wardrobe, Paige told her very seriously.

Christine's shrugging off the last dress when Pippa joins them, twitching aside the curtain to make sure no-one is too much on show, and then entering with a giddy smile, smoothing down something in an attractive blue-green and requesting critique. She has a few other options, of course, but this—

Paige stops her. It's perfect. She doesn't need to change a thing.

Christine holds a couple of her chosen dresses up against her body so Pippa can enthuse about colours and patterns while she gets changed, but then Paige hands Christine her phone: it's buzzing.

She unlocks it and scrolls through her messages. There are *a lot.* "It's Abby," she says, flicking through. "Holy shit."

"What?" Pippa says, re-clasping her bra.

"Stefan asked to see Aunt Bea."

"*What?*"

Pippa drops the rest of her clothes on the floor and races over to where Christine's sat. She makes insistent gestures with her finger until Christine scrolls back up and they both read through everything together. "Oh, sweet baby Jesus," she says.

"Anyone want to explain?" Paige asks. She's dividing their purchases from the clothes to be returned to the rack and looks about five seconds away from complaining that no-one's helping her.

Christine explains quietly as Pippa swipes up and down through Abby's texts, and then, when her own phone starts buzzing, reads through her own messages from Abby, as though they could possibly provide any additional information. "Oh, Jesus, God in heaven," she mutters. "Oh, Jesus, Mary and *flipping* Joseph." She shrugs off Christine's comforting hand on her shoulder. "I shouldn't be here. I shouldn't have come. This is a flipping *disaster*…"

"It seems like it was actually okay," Christine says, re-reading the texts. "Abby was there, and it sounds like Aunt Bea agrees about the nurse. No harm."

Pippa throws her phone back in her bag and buries her face in her hands. "Aunt Bea's going to think I'm a terrible sponsor."

"So? Screw Aunt Bea. You're not a sponsor for life, are you?"

"God, no. It's just a one-time thing until I'm done with Saints."

"Then why care? Be like Abby: do it once, produce an amazingly girly girl who annoys everyone around her with how effortlessly feminine she is, and quit while you're ahead."

Paige, with a basket hanging off each elbow, passes Pippa the dress she wore out this morning. "She's right, you know," she says. "You don't have to be a 'good sponsor' for him. You don't have to follow the scripts. I'm not convinced everyone needs that kind of constant pressure, anyway. Besides, you're not Maria and this isn't your career. This is just pocket money, right?"

Pippa stands and drops her dress over her head. "It was *supposed* to be paying it forward," she says. "And how come Abby texted you first, Christine?"

"She texts me about everything!" Christine says, covering. At least Abby remembered to be circumspect. "Sometimes I know what she's having for breakfast before her stomach does. And I know Stefan, remember? I asked her to keep me in the loop. I want him to get through this okay."

"Okay," Pippa says. "Good. I do, too."

"You think he will?"

Pippa sits back down on the bench, turns her bracelet around on her wrist a few times. "Last night I would have said yes, guaranteed. But this nurse situation…It hit him *hard,* Christine."

"It does seem like he calmed down, though," Paige says. "He asked to see Aunt Bea, and they took him up to the kitchen. You don't do that with someone who's falling apart; you don't put him in a room full of sharp knives."

"Sharp knives and novelty mugs," Christine says.

"I think he's okay," Paige says, warming to her theory. "Remember what I said this morning? That he just needed time? I think he got it. And now he's up and advocating for himself? He's fine."

"Coping, anyway," Christine says.

"Come on," Paige says. "Let's go abuse Christine's credit card privileges. The sooner we get out of here, the sooner we can get home and the sooner Pippa can check up on Stefan. Christine: you're still nearly naked."

"Shit; so I am."

***

"Sit still!"

"This is why I need to practise doing my own makeup," Christine says, "so you'll stop torturing me with all your brushes and sponges and things."

Paige swats her on the shoulder. "Sit still means no talking," she says. "And they're *your* brushes and sponges and things; hygiene, Christine."

Christine frowns at herself in the vanity as Paige leans away to find a better brush or sponge or something. "This is a lot heavier than last night's foundation, Paige," she says, resisting the urge to poke at her cheek.

"Of course," Paige says, painting a careful line along Christine's nose. "Different looks for different nights."

"*This* heavy, though?"

"It's a simple equation. Last night was an elegant dress plus refined company—don't laugh; *some* of them count as refined—plus warm, dim lighting. I enhanced your natural features and chose colours to suit your outfit. Tonight is a sexy dress plus dancing plus club lighting. I'm not going for elegant, I'm going for *hot.*"

Christine eyes the dress. They bought the one with the cutouts in the end, but it's not the one Paige wants her to wear tonight. Paige's choice is *worse:* strikingly red, shorter than the other dress and even more attention-grabbing. Something to do with the colour looking just right with Christine's deep brown hair, although that's probably just an excuse.

She decides to deflect from one source of anxiety to another. "Natural features, Paige?" she says. "I don't *have* any natural features. I was *made.*"

"No, Christine," Paige says, frowning as she works, "I was there, remember? I know what you looked like before and after. Estrogen changed you enough that when you went under the knife they took only *millimetres* off you, made changes so subtle it took until the swelling went down to see what was different. They didn't 'make' you; they just...brought you out."

Christine taps the spot on her neck where her Adam's apple used to be, marked now by the faintest scar. "They took much more than millimetres off of here," she says, unsure why she's stuck on the subject but needing to follow it to its end.

"True," Paige admits. "But it *was* big."

"It was. I kind of hated it."

Paige puts down the brush and traces Christine's frown along her brow with the back of her finger. "I'll get you to believe you're beautiful if it's the last thing I do, Christine," she says. "Besides," she adds with a businesslike air, turning back to her tools, "if anyone here is artificial, it's me."

Shit. Well done, Christine. "Paige, no."

"I had a *lot* more work done than you. I think that's how you found it so easy to sleep with me, early on; I was like a completely different person. Rebuilt from scratch."

"No, that's not it. Paige, you were my—"

"I wonder sometimes if that's why I had an easier time adjusting," Paige continues distantly, still rummaging in Christine's motley makeup pile. "When *you* looked in the mirror you saw you, but different; someone who might have been your sister. When I looked in the mirror, I saw a stranger."

"Paige—"

"It took me a long time to come to terms with it," Paige says. "Hours looking at myself, feeling almost like my thoughts were coming from someone else. A monster in my own labyrinth."

"Paige, please— Oh, you fucker."

Paige turns back to Christine with a grin. "Got you," she says, and sticks out her tongue.

"You cow!" Christine says, nudging her with a foot. "I knew 'monster in my own labyrinth' was too melodramatic for you."

"Here endeth the lesson," Paige says, once she's put her tongue away. "Be careful who you complain about your extremely minor alterations in front of. I made peace with my plastic long ago; others haven't."

"Yeah. Okay. You got me. And you're right. Sorry."

"Don't apologise," Paige says, returning to her work. "Just rein it in when you're around Pippa, okay? She's coming by soon."

"Is she…sensitive about the work she had done?"

"Very. I was talking to Willow, and she said—"

"Willow?"

"Yes. She graduated with Pippa. She does outreach now for one of the brands I work with. I've mentioned her, I'm sure?"

"I don't think you have," Christine says.

"I've mentioned her."

"If you say so."

"Willow said she's glad Pippa's making friends at last." Paige worries at her lip for a moment. "She was—is—kind of a loner. And she said she has a real thing about her facial surgery. She wants to see her cousin again someday, and she's terrified she won't be recognisable."

"God," Christine says, glaring at herself in the vanity mirror, "I'm an idiot."

"No," Paige says, swatting her again. "Idiots don't know when to *stop*."

When Pippa arrives with Abby several minutes later, they find Christine sitting very carefully on the end of her bed in full make-up, dress and sandals, with her largest and puffiest coat—Paige's only concession to the late October chill—folded up on her knees, and Paige prettying herself at the vanity with the staggering efficiency of someone who absorbs new makeup techniques the way other people absorb oxygen. It takes Christine a second to notice them come in because Paige, consumed by concentration and sitting with crossed ankles in a dress at least as daring as Christine's, is a sight so arresting she has difficulty looking away. Abby has to cough, politely and knowingly, for Christine to recover herself sufficiently to greet them.

Pippa's wearing the blue-green dress she tried on earlier, and she's gone light on the accessories, with the exception of her ever-present bracelet. She's done a lot of work on her face, especially around the eyes, where an iridescent swipe of eyeshadow connects her eyelids to her temples. She returns Christine's wave and perches nearby on the edge of the bed, radiating nerves. Abby, however, is still inhabiting one of her favourite ratty old t-shirts, and plants herself on the sofa behind Paige, decently positioned to look suggestively from Paige to Christine and back again, a gesture packed with significance that Christine deliberately ignores.

"Hey girls," Abby says. "Guess what?"

"You're not coming tonight?" Christine says.

"Yes, but—"

"Abbyyyy," Christine whines, abusing the final syllable and feeling gloriously childish. Something about Paige's scolding has left her energised, and while she can't claim to be feeling confident, she is, for once, excited to leave campus and shake what Paige and three carefully aligned mirrors all insist is a very nice booty. "You have to come! You said you'd come!"

"No, *you* sent me eight—sorry, nine—texts informing me that I *am* coming. I was never consulted."

Christine pouts. "Fine," she says. "But at least stay with us until we go."

"Actually," Abby says, and grins at Christine's exasperated expression, "I'm here because Maria's coming up. We have news."

"News about what?" Paige says.

"The nurse. Maria'll be up in a few minutes."

Rumours of the nurse, her actions, and their subsequent consequences spread through the hall enough that five sponsors dived on Pippa when they got home from their shopping spree and had pestered her with questions. Did she *know* her boy had come up to see Aunt Bea? After being here only *two weeks?*

It didn't take long for the three of them to discover that the rumour mill held little information they didn't already have. Abby promised to find out what she could from a *reliable* source, and had helpfully corralled the curious sponsors, allowing Christine, Paige and Pippa to make their escape. So the girls had got to work, reasoning that they might as well be putting on their faces while they waited for Abby to come up with the goods. The goods being, apparently, Maria.

"Pippa," Christine says, to break the nervous silence, "I thought you were going to go see Stefan?"

"I was. But I need to know what Maria has to say and, anyway, Stefan seems fine. I checked the feed and he's watching TV in the common room, sitting with the usual people, chatting away. Edy and Tabitha and a couple of others have an eye on them. I kind of didn't feel like intruding."

Christine nods, and goes back to watching Paige put the finishing touches to her makeup.

A few minutes later and they're all arranged in varying states of comfort around the room while Maria paces.

"First off," she says, "this goes nowhere. I know, I know, everyone will know by tomorrow morning, but I'd like to at least pretend we have some semblance of opsec around here. Christine, I can see you trying not to smirk."

"Sorry."

"So, the nurse. Karen Turner. She's not one of us." Maria pauses for reactions, and gets them: everyone at Dorley is a graduate; that's how it *works.* "Barb, the old nurse—who you remember, if not fondly—she was one of us. Older than me, actually. Which means that, like me, she came up under Grandmother, an experience which instilled in her a profound sense of empathy and a strong desire to rescue the next generations of girls from the people who hurt her here. People like *her* nurse. And her nurse—and mine—was Karen Turner."

"Shit," Christine says. "She's one of Grandmother's people?"

"Yes."

To the best of Christine's knowledge, the only people still knocking around Dorley Hall who came up under Grandmother's regime are Maria and Aunt Bea herself, neither of whom are habitually loose lipped about prior operational procedures. But enough older graduates have come back now and then, whether for events like Aunt Bea's birthday dinners or to serve as nurses, electrolysis technicians and the like, that bits and pieces of information about the old programme have trickled out.

By all accounts, it was a bloodbath.

Grandmother, Christine has inferred, had the tendency to view womanhood as inherently degrading, at least when applied to those who'd been assigned male. To her, Dorley Hall was a place to enact punishment and indulge her desire to humiliate men, and she surrounded herself with people whose proclivities matched her own. It was only when Aunt Bea—a young graduate who, in her years away had developed enough contacts and honed enough skills to create for herself an entirely new identity—returned to the fold and started to make reforms that graduates like Maria were allowed to stay on and attend Saints as ordinary women. Christine suspects Aunt Bea has something on Grandmother, some leverage that made her hand over control, but what, she can't hope to guess. Reportedly, the few years when Bea and Grandmother ran the place together were turbulent.

Christine's also aware that there are probably holes in the data she's acquired and the theories she's come up with that you could drop the entire hall through.

"She worked for Grandmother?" Pippa says urgently. "She's cis, then?" Maria nods. "Jesus. She's cis and she knows about us. About *me.*"

"Yes," Maria says.

"No wonder she looked at me like that."

"I promise you, briefing and debriefing her in the security room was just as little fun."

"Why did we allow her back?" Pippa says.

Maria finally stops pacing and sits on the arm of Christine's sofa, and starts speaking in a tone so rote Christine suspects she's already gone through this a half-dozen times this afternoon. "Barb's out of the country for a couple of weeks. And *we* moved the examinations up without, apparently, informing her. So Monica woke up this morning, hours before the rest of us, texted Barb to ask when she was due to come in, and then had to reach out via other methods when she didn't get an answer. Meanwhile, Beatrice and I and everyone else were still asleep, so after Monica got done talking to Barb, she looked in the directory and found a nurse. One who's local and who used to work here. And though Bea kicked her out immediately, Karen wasn't *officially* taken off the books until Grandmother was, two years after the switchover, so…" She waves a tired hand.

"Ah," Paige says.

"Monica didn't know she was a Grandmother hire," Christine fills in.

"Precisely," Maria says. "The usual shitstorm. Lack of communication, lack of documentation, lack of preparation. If Bea or I had been up and available to consult—or even Edy, actually—we would have put the examinations on hold. But then Karen was here, inside the bloody building, and she promised to cooperate." She rolls her eyes. "More fool us. She knew once she was down there, she could do whatever she wanted. We couldn't stop her without making the whole place look weak. Imagine the boys seeing us squabble amongst ourselves!"

"Is that why you bottled it?" Christine asks. "Why you let her assault Stefan and the others?"

"I didn't 'bottle it,'" Maria says, glaring at Christine. "I made a decision."

"We can't get Barb back?" Pippa says, as Paige puts a hand on Christine to calm her.

Maria leans against the wardrobe. She looks tired. "Barbara's husband got a job in Canada and she's going with him. Fifteen-odd years helping out? She's done her bit. Besides, she's in escrow now."

"Wait," Christine says, "our identities can survive international travel?"

"Of course. We're understaffed, not incompetent."

"Um," Paige says.

"Not *completely* incompetent," Maria corrects, irritated. "Regardless, the point is, Barb is never coming back except to visit. Karen is simply never coming back."

"So," Paige says, "what are we doing for a nurse, then, if we can't have Barb and we don't want this Karen woman?"

"I don't know," Maria says, "not yet. Pippa, you're comfortable with doing a basic injection, yes?" Pippa nods. "You'll be doing Stefan's jab tonight. All of us will be doing it for our boys. And unless we have any unexpected problems, we have a while to secure a new nurse. One of our graduates is in nursing; she might be willing to transfer to a hospital nearby."

"This is such a fucking disaster," Christine says, leaning back on the bed. "You know how fucked up what she did is, right?"

"I was there."

"This is a delicate time for those…boys."

"I know. I was *there.* And unless you want to volunteer, Christine, your input is strictly advisory."

"I'm just saying, I would have turned my taser on the bitch if I'd been in charge down there."

Maria offers her a brittle smile. "Yes, well, perhaps one day you will be."

***

Christine spends most of the bus ride back to town silent. Paige, in the seat next to her, knows when she needs to be left alone and merely offers her hand.

She'd been all set to go after Maria, to confront her alone about the nurse, to demand to know why she hadn't done more to protect Stef, but Abby had taken her aside, shut them both in Christine's bathroom, and asked her to give Maria time.

"She's probably not dealing very well with this," Abby had said, sitting on the toilet lid.

"She definitely isn't," Christine said, feeling awkward.

"Don't be too angry with Maria."

"I really, really want to be, Abs."

"What I mean," Abby said, "is that we don't know what it was like back then, under Grandmother, and she does. I heard she was the only Dorley woman to have spent time in the cells after graduation!"

"She— what?"

Abby leaned forward on her knees. "Lisa told me the story. Maria was celebrating some milestone or other, went out drinking in Almsworth with friends—other girls from the programme, some of whom she helped sponsor. They were very close. They still keep in touch. Some of them are…pretty conveniently placed for us. Anyway, on their way home they stole a sign from outside an employment agency. Wrenched it off the wall and brought it back here, intending to put it up in the security room downstairs. They thought it was hilarious. Grandmother didn't."

"I thought she wasn't in charge after Maria graduated?"

"She wasn't, but she hung around like a bad smell. Had some kind of leverage. But she insisted to Bea that Maria be punished and, for whatever reason, Bea relented. Maybe Grandmother threatened a spot of mutually assured destruction; I don't know. Maria said she'll always remember being marched down to the cells, still drunk, and locked in. 'As an example to the other boys,' Grandmother told her. She was down there two weeks."

"Shit."

"Yeah. Power-tripping old cow."

"What was the sign? Is it still around?"

Abby smiled. "It said, 'Transition Services' and, it's still in one of the storerooms somewhere."

Christine snorted. She'd had to admit, in Maria's position, she might have stolen that.

The conversation—and the image of Maria, already a woman, confined once again to the cells—stays with Christine even after they disembark, and she shakes it only when they finally get where they're going. They've arranged to meet up with Vicky and Lorna at the bar at the back of the station complex, a cheap place that gets rowdy later in the evening but which, for now, is host mainly to shoppers knocking back a quick drink before their train arrives. While they wait, sitting carefully in their stunning dresses and idly playing with their drinks, Christine fills Paige and Pippa in on everything Abby said.

"I think the whole thing was a twisted power play," Christine says. "Karen was a nurse under Grandmother from before the reforms. That makes her a sick bitch who gets her kicks humiliating men, just like Grandmother. She comes back, 'just to help out', makes promises about being on her best behaviour and then immediately reverts to type as soon as she gets her hands on someone."

"And she was flipping smug about it, too," Pippa says. "Complimenting me on making Stefan 'docile', when anyone could tell the poor boy'd practically left his body by that point. Jesus, actually, she said something like, 'Half the boys are unconscious for this. I'm sure you remember.' I thought that was directed at me, which was confusing because I *wasn't*, but…"

Paige picks up the sentence where Pippa dropped it. "It was obviously aimed at Maria. A reminder: 'I know who you were.' "

"Maria said the debriefing in the security room was no fun," Pippa says. "I wonder if Karen deadnamed her?"

"From what I've heard about Grandmother's Dorley, I wouldn't be surprised," Christine says. "The whole performance, it wasn't just about her power over the— over the boys, it was about her power over *us*. All the unworthies of Dorley, from Aunt Bea on down. All the unreal women. Shit." She pulls out her phone. "I'm going to find her Facebook. Fiver says she's a TERF."

"You know," Pippa says, stirring her drink and looking into the middle distance, "you get locked up for a year, you have your sex changed against your will, you get a new name and a new face and you can't ever see your family again, but it's not until after you graduate, after you turn around and start doing all that to someone else, that you finally find out what a flipping snake pit Dorley *really* is."

"Was," Paige says.

"Is," Pippa insists. "As long as people like Karen can still come back, I'm sticking with the present tense."

"Yeah," Christine says, putting her phone down on the table, "about that. Abby said she's going to talk to Aunt Bea. She's worried that someone like Karen, who's still bitter after two decades that we're no longer an evil little playroom where she gets to take the toys apart, might make things difficult for us."

"You think Aunt Bea might try to shut her up?" Pippa says.

"She thinks Aunt Bea might have her killed," Paige says. "Right?"

"Yeah." Christine nods, as Pippa gasps. "She knows *everything,* Pip, and she's kept quiet up until now for some reason. Loyalty to Grandmother, maybe. But whatever it is, her incentive to keep quiet, especially after all these years, has to be *way* weaker than ours. We have no choice but to stay silent, but Karen might throw caution to the wind, especially if she sees Aunt Bea ending her contract as a snub. It might call for drastic measures."

"What do you mean," Pippa says, "about us having an incentive to keep quiet?"

"It's the cold logic of Dorley," Paige says, having finished her drink. "Whatever we—" she indicates the three of them with her glass, "—think of what happens there, what was done to us, what we're currently doing to a whole new batch of people, we all have attachments there, right? That's part of the sponsor bond, or it's probably supposed to be. Christine's never going to go to the police, or the media, or dump all our secrets on Pastebin, because even though she and I are arguably victims of Dorley, she doesn't want anything to happen to Indira or Abby."

"Or you," Christine says to Pippa.

"Me?"

"You're part of it, now," Paige says. "Another reason for us to never blow a whistle."

"That's…cynical."

"It might just be a happy accident," Christine says. "A lucky side-effect that just happens to benefit Aunt Bea. But the fact remains that even when we leave the programme, our whole world is Dorley. Our friends." She glances at Paige. "Our family. The freedom of everyone we love is reliant on the wellbeing of Dorley Hall. Even Indira, who has her family back, who's dating a nice cis guy who's probably never even heard of forced feminisation, she's tied to the place. To me. I might not like Maria that much right now, but I don't want her *arrested.*"

"We all have a reason to stay silent," Paige says. "To keep the place going, year after year. If you discount wherever Aunt Bea gets her money from then we're effectively self-sufficient at this point. Aside from the major surgeries, and this Karen woman, all the roles that keep the programme going are filled by Dorley graduates." She twirls a finger in the air. "We're an endless loop: girls femming girls femming girls. A snake biting its own tail."

Christine can't resist. "Not its own *tail*." She snorts into her drink.

Paige hits her lightly. Christine's about to respond with some mild violence of her own when Pippa points towards the door: Vicky and Lorna, looking stunning as usual, are waving and grinning wildly. Christine's happy to drop the subject. She's found nurse Karen's Facebook and discovered that she's a member of an organisation called Women Run The World, who has some worrying content on its social media posts. Quickly she forwards a few screenshots to Abby, bags her phone, and does her best to put the whole thing out of her mind, because Lorna is striding towards her, arms out, and it's time to be a cis girl for the rest of the evening.

* * *

Legend—still popularly considered the worst nightclub in Almsworth; also still the cheapest, which is important because Christine's access to Dorley's accounts isn't supposed to cover nights out—is packed, and Christine can't decide whether she finds the crowds reassuring or intimidating. And being bundled along with Pippa and Lorna to the women's bathroom swiftly becomes an education on the subject of how many women can fit in front of one mirror. She feels a little childish when Lorna deals with attention from excited and complimentary cis girls with grace and humour while Christine hides in a stall, controlling her breathing.

Better at this doesn't mean good at it, not yet.

"The secret is to have really good eyeliner," Lorna says to her as they make their way back to the tiny table Paige and Vicky are guarding. "Cis people love it when you have good eyeliner."

"Do they?" Christine says, and mentally kicks herself for saying 'they' and not 'we'. Fortunately, Lorna doesn't seem to notice, and Christine successfully delivers her back into the arms of her girlfriend without making any more mistakes.

Lorna and Paige dole out the drinks and Christine takes a long swig to steady her nerves.

"How did your chat go?" Lorna says, over the music, which is quietest in this corner but still loud enough to inhibit conversation.

"My chat?"

"With the trans group. About your friend?"

"Oh! Good. They were really helpful."

"How is your friend? Do I get to know her name yet?"

Stef's name hasn't been decided on; "Stefanie" isn't a foregone conclusion. Few of them take names so derivative of their given names. "She's, um, really private," Christine says. "I don't have permission to share anything much."

Lorna nudges her with an elbow. "Don't break any confidences on my account. I'm just— I wanted to thank you."

"Oh? What for?"

"For taking an interest. For wanting to help. And for not assuming you already know best just because you're cis."

"Um," Christine says, looking away, "it's– I just– I hate seeing her be miserable." She congratulates herself on hitting the right pronoun. Bloody Stef and her– *his* insistence on valuing self-loathing over identity. "Oh," she remembers, "congratulations on the surgery date. That's what we're celebrating, right?"

"Right."

"Is it okay to ask what you're having done?"

She laughs. "It's probably not okay? I don't mind, though. Here, here, here and here." She points at a few spots on her face: hairline, brows, nose, jaw. Christine notes that it's essentially the same work she had done. "They're just making tiny changes, but it's enough."

Christine nods. "I'm looking forward to seeing you get even more gorgeous," she says, and Lorna giggles and bites her lip. Vicky, Christine reflects, is *lucky*.

"I was asked to ask," Lorna says, "are you with someone?"

"With someone? Like, a girlfriend? No."

Lorna grins. "You like girls, then?"

"I don't actually know!" Too much alcohol—two drinks; lightweight—making her too honest. "My last relationship was with a woman. But I'm still figuring myself out. I want to be better at being *me* before I inflict myself on someone else again."

"Oh, I'm sorry. Did it end badly?"

"Kind of," Christine says. Paige took the break-up calmly, kindly, and didn't talk to her for two weeks.

"Anyone I know?" Lorna asks. Christine leans closer so she can point to Paige, currently dancing with some guy, without anyone seeing. Lorna's eyes round out and she giggles. "Paige?" she whispers. "Wow."

Christine nods. "I started getting messed up about who I was, what we were doing together, what it 'meant'—" she air quotes viciously, "—that we were together. And she didn't have any of those problems herself. She knew *exactly* who she was. Which made me a little bitter for a while. I dealt with it badly. I didn't exactly take it out on her, but it didn't help, either. She can do better than me, anyway."

"Tina," Lorna says, borrowing Vicky's nickname for her, "I've seen the way she looks at you. *You* might think that. I don't think she does."

"Who asked you to ask, by the way?"

"Oh, it was— Oop!" Lorna's interrupted by Vicky swooping in behind her, looping her arms around her and dragging her laughing away from the table, allowing her back only briefly to put down her drink, and then they're gone, dancing, leaving Pippa and Christine alone to guard their rickety little outpost.

"They have so much energy!" Christine says to Pippa, who's been looking thoughtful. "I can't stand it."

"I know!"

"What's up?"

Pippa shrugs. "Just thinking about Stefan," she says.

"I thought you said he was fine?"

"Yeah, no thanks to me. I just stood there, Christine. I watched that— that *bitch* hurt him, and I did nothing. Said nothing. I should have helped him, but I was too busy being his stupid sponsor."

Christine takes her hand, squeezes it. "Remember what Paige said?" she says. "Earlier on, in the changing rooms? You don't *have* to be a good sponsor for him. You don't have to be like Maria. I think he probably needs a friend more than he needs someone to point out all his masculine failings."

"Yeah, well," Pippa says, "I flipping suck at that. I go too hard or I don't go at all."

"So don't try! I bet you'll make more progress talking to him than lecturing him or doing all that shit where you're supposed to make him hyper-aware of the way his body's changing."

Pippa slumps a little on the hand that's holding her head up. "I wasn't looking forward to that. You really think I can just drop all the sponsor stuff?"

"I think so. But more importantly, Paige thinks so, and Paige is always right."

"Paige *is* always right," Paige says, descending on them. She's got her hand around a handsome guy, slightly taller than her, clearly already and understandably besotted, and she's dragged him back to their table. "What am I right about this time?"

"Pippa and Stefan," Christine says.

"Oh," Paige says. "Yeah. Just hang out with him, Pippa. Now, come on; I've got us a couch! This is Nadeem, by the way."

It doesn't take much of Paige's persuasion to get them to abandon their tiny table and decamp to one of the couches in the bar area, where Nadeem and his friends—mostly men, with a couple of girls—are gathered. Paige immediately claims an empty space at one end, pushes Nadeem down into it and perches on the cushioned arm of the sofa, knees hooked over his legs. Christine and Pippa take stools by the nearby table, and one of the girls greets them. They're Saints students, most of them at the start of their third year, pissing away their student loans.

"You should warn your friend," one of the girls, Rani, says to Christine as they return to the couch with a new round of drinks, "Nadeem isn't the relationship type."

"It's okay," Christine says, "Paige isn't, either. Not with boys, anyway."

"Oh?" Rani says, grinning widely. "She likes girls, too?" Something in Christine's face gives her away. "You?" Rani squeaks.

"Yeah. For a while."

Two of the men vacate the couch, giving Rani and Christine a place to sit and relieve themselves of their armfuls of drinks. "Is it hard, seeing her with someone else?" Rani says.

"I wouldn't say I *like* it," Christine says, necking half her bottle, "but it was me who ended it, so I don't really have a leg to stand on."

"What are you two talking about?" Nadeem says, leaning around Paige to collect their drinks.

"You!" Rani says. "I was telling Christine here that you're not into commitment."

"Nope!" he says. "Too young, too gorgeous." He kisses Paige on the cheek, and Paige leans into it, laughing.

"Me neither," she says, as Pippa, Vicky and Lorna cluster in to retrieve their own drink orders. "Besides, boys are for fun!" She takes Nadeem's jaw in her hand and twists it so she can kiss him on the mouth. "And that's all!"

"That's kind of cold, isn't it?" Pippa says.

Paige stops kissing Nadeem long enough to grin at her. She reaches her free hand down into Nadeem's trousers. "Nope!" she says. "Pretty warm." He laughs and nudges Paige on the cheek until she resumes kissing him.

Christine rolls her eyes, ignores Pippa's concerned look, and goes back to talking to Rani; she's taking Electrical Engineering, which Christine knows just enough about to be able to understand her. It's an interesting enough topic that it distracts from Christine's incipient fear that Rani—beautiful, confident, and almost definitely cis—will see right through her.

When Rani playfully pushes her in response to a terrible computer science joke she couldn't resist telling, it takes almost a full second for Christine to start panicking that she will somehow turn out to have male bones, detectable by the slightest touch, by which time it's already obvious that Rani thinks nothing is amiss. *I know who I am, and I'm definitely getting better at this*, she tells herself.

Behind her, Paige and Nadeem finish their drinks and Paige drags him back out to dance, allowing Vicky and Lorna to claim their spot on the couch and resume kissing.

"Being single sucks, right?" Rani says.

Paige is dancing with her back to Nadeem, pressing herself against him, exuding confidence and sexuality and inspiring in Christine the usual mixture of envy and interest. "Yeah," she says, "it really fucking sucks."

Later, when a few more of Rani's friends have arrived and monopolised her time, and Vicky and Lorna are off dancing again, Christine and Pippa sit together on the end of the couch, having fended off two random men each.

"This is the club where Melissa got taken from, you know!" Pippa says, to break up an awkward pause in the conversation.

"Can we talk about something other than Dorley, for once?" Christine snaps. "Sorry," she adds quickly, and puts an apologetic hand on Pippa's knee. "I'm just trying really, really hard to be a normal girl. It doesn't necessarily come easily, especially somewhere like this."

"You don't need to apologise," Pippa says. "I'm kind of running out of things to say, anyway."

"How about," Christine says, glancing back at Rani and her friends, who look to have the couch under their protective custody for the foreseeable future, "we go dance, instead?"

"Um," Pippa says. "Okay?"

"You don't want to?"

"I'm no good at it."

Christine stands and holds out her hand, inviting Pippa up as if she's a debutante. "If there's one thing I've learned from looking out there—" with a flourish she directs her free hand towards the dancefloor, "—it's that if you're pretty, you don't have to be good at dancing. Just move around a bit, and the boys won't be able to keep their eyes off you."

Pippa allows herself to be lifted off the couch. "Girls," she says, following Christine, still holding her hand.

"What?" Christine yells, over the music.

"Girls! I want the girls to look at me!"

Christine manoeuvres them through the throng and finds Vicky and Lorna, enraptured by each other near the middle of the dancefloor. "I think we can arrange that!"

***

Three trips up and down from the dancefloor and Christine, exhausted, falls into the middle of the couch between Vicky, who looks like she wants to fall asleep, and Pippa, who is talking animatedly with Rani, who has one hand on her thigh. She meets Christine's eye and smiles, looking happier than Christine's yet seen her, so Christine winks and starts to lift herself back up off the couch, intending to give her some space. She's intercepted by Paige, alone.

"Hi, Christine," Paige says.

"Hey. You having a good time?"

Paige takes her hand, pulls her along with her, back towards the dancefloor, but slowly, keeping them for the moment in the quieter bar area. "Yes," Paige says with a smile.

"How was he?" Christine asks with, she hopes, good humour.

"Fun!" Paige says, leaning down so she can talk at a normal volume. Her breath tickles the fine hairs on Christine's neck. "And that's all. How about you? You okay?"

"I'm fine. It's not as scary as I thought it would be."

"Of course it's not," Paige says, wrapping an arm around Christine's waist and closing her fingers around her hip. "You're beautiful. No-one is ever going to think otherwise."

"Paige—"

"Come with me," she says. She unwinds Christine from her arm, a dance in miniature, and catches Christine's hand again, leads her through the thinning crowds.

"Paige, I don't—"

"*Come with me.*" It's like a spell. It carries Christine to the middle of the dancefloor with her.

Their spot claimed, Paige holds Christine in place and dances slowly, in half-time with the music. Wickedly smiling, she runs her free hand around Christine's jaw, down her neck, eventually rests it on her back, and pulls her gradually forwards, one heartbeat at a time.

"What's happening?" Christine says.

Paige presses her lips against Christine's ear. "We're not the way we used to be," she says. "We're not confused, we're not finding ourselves, and we're not scared all the time. We know who we are now. Both of us. Don't we?"

Christine moves with her, her hands finding tentative spots on Paige's hips. Paige is still leaning down, her face buried in Christine's hair. "Yeah," Christine says. "We do."

"This doesn't have to be any specific thing," Paige says. "It can be whatever you want. But I miss you. And, just for one night, I want to feel like you miss me, too."

"I do, Paige. I do."

"Then be my girl, Christine. Just for tonight. Please?" Paige's voice is shaking, and she breathes carefully between each sentence. "Let me have you. Just for one night. Will you do that for me? Will you let me have you?"

Christine looks up and Paige steps away, and suddenly she loathes the instincts screaming at her that this is too soon, that it's not right, that she's not ready. She digs her fingers into Paige's hips, refusing to let her retreat, pulling her back in, stepping into her and kissing her on the collarbone, once, twice, then moving up, warming Paige's neck and allowing herself to be pushed away, just a little, just enough, so Paige can kiss her back, first on the jaw, then on the chin and then, finally, their lips meet and Christine is, for the first time in a long while, and maybe just for tonight, Paige's again.

"Good girl," Paige whispers as they part, but it's only for a moment, enough time to look into each other's eyes, enough time for Paige to raise her hands to the back of Christine's neck, enough time for Christine to think, *Yes, I know exactly who I am,* and then they're kissing, once more, once again, and it's nothing like it used to be.

***

The door closes behind him. The biometric lock engages. Perhaps the most welcome sound Stefan's heard all day.

Abby dropped him off in the common room and he told Aaron, Will and Adam exactly what Beatrice asked him to. The news that the nurse would not be the one to administer the promised vitamin injection released a tension from the room that Aaron had been covering with nervous babble and Adam with wary silence. Even Will seemed relieved, relaxing his neck and sitting back on the sofa, and when Adam joined him and leaned his shoulder against Will's, he didn't move away, accepting the other boy into his space without comment or fuss.

It was easy to hang out with them all afternoon. To talk about nothing. To watch a cooking show, a makeover show, a dating show, a couple of light comedies. To laugh at the bad jokes and at Raph and Ollie sulkily stalking out of the common area, lost without Declan's chest-thumping idiot bravado. Even Martin, sitting on a beanbag chair a safe distance from all of them, didn't seem so bad, offering some commentary on the TV shows that, while not actually especially interesting to Stefan, showed more of a commitment to participating than he'd shown at any other point.

But that was then, and this is now, and he's alone, with nothing but the memory of the nurse and the look on her face when she touched him.

The advantage of the thick concrete walls: you don't need to muffle yourself when you cry. Stefan lets it all out. Everything from Mark's disappearance to his own growing masculinisation to meeting Christine to waking up in the cell, and everything since. Eventually his stinging skin, still pink from the hot water, drags him somewhat out of it. He's drying his face and applying another layer of moisturiser when there's a knock on his door.

He gets up, opens it, but it's not Aaron. It's Pippa.

"Hi," she says. Quiet. She's wearing a lovely blue-green dress with eye makeup to match, although her lipstick is a little smeared. When his eyes flicker to her lips she covers them shyly with her fingers. But only for a second. "Can I come in?"

Stefan opens the door the rest of the way, returns to his bed and slips his hoodie back on. His upper body is not something he particularly wants her to see under any circumstances, but especially not after this morning. His skin is peeling in a few places, uglier than usual.

"Does that hurt?" she says.

"Yeah," he says.

"How are you treating it?"

"Moisturiser. It's all I've got."

"I'll get you something better in the morning."

"Thanks."

Pippa sits delicately on the chair and shuffles it closer to the bed. She puts her bag down by the computer desk, and deposits a little plastic container by the keyboard.

"Is that the vitamin jab?" Stefan asks. If Abby's right, that's his first shot of estradiol. He can barely take his eyes off it.

Pippa nods. "Are you ready for it?"

"I am."

It doesn't take long, and for all that Pippa has obviously had a little to drink, she has a steady hand. She settles awkwardly back on the chair and looks away while Stefan pulls his trousers back up and retreats to the corner of the bed. He imagines the estradiol spreading through him, curing him, fixing him. Sternly he reminds himself not to expect quick results. Everyone responds at their own pace, he remembers. It would be foolish to imagine his body will change at anything but the slowest possible rate, given its track record.

"Once per week, for the foreseeable future," Pippa says, boxing up the needle and putting away the swabs. "Are you okay with me being the one to administer it from now on?"

"I understand and agree," Stefan says, to be annoying.

"Don't— You don't need to say that."

"Oh?"

Pippa shifts on the chair, like she wants to sit more comfortably but is restricted by her dress. Normally she wears things with a little more room. "Damn," she says to herself. "Should've got changed."

Stefan smiles, waves a hand at his wardrobe. "I have more hoodies than I can wear in a week, if you want to borrow something."

She blinks at him, surprised. "You wouldn't mind?"

He laughs. "It's your stuff, anyway. Take what you need. You can lock all the doors and change in the corridor."

"I'll, um, change in here, if that's okay," Pippa says, pulling a hoodie out of the wardrobe and draping it over herself so she can drop her dress under cover.

"Oh," Stefan says, "uh, shit. Just a second." He pulls his knees up and turns to face the wall, and stays that way until the sounds of Pippa struggling with fabric have ceased.

"Thanks," she says, now wearing more modest clothes that don't go nearly as well with her makeup. "I didn't want to change outside." She folds the dress a few times and drops it into the main compartment of her bag, then crosses her legs under herself and leans back in the chair. She stares at him for a few moments, and he has time to wonder what exactly it is she sees, before she says, suddenly, quickly, "My apology was crap."

"What?"

"Earlier. After the nurse. I didn't give you time to breathe, I just came at you, and when you didn't immediately accept my apology, I got mad. I'm sorry. Sorry for the crappy apology, sorry for the nurse, sorry for…me."

"For you?"

She breathes through her nose for a second, thinking. "What you need from me, down here, is consistency," she says. "Like Maria, with Aaron. She's been a sponsor for a long time, and she's good at it. I, on the other hand, am terrible at it. I hate being strict—unless I get angry, and then I'm a complete and total cow—and it makes me… unpredictable. And that's the worst thing for you, when you're already trying to cope with everything else down here."

"No," Stefan says, allowing himself to smile, "the *worst* thing is what Monica's doing to Declan."

"You know what I mean."

"Yeah. Sorry. Too much time around Will. I'm getting pedantic."

She matches his smile. "The least of your worries, surely."

"True."

"That was brave of you, by the way, talking to Aunt Bea."

"She wasn't so bad. Bit of a softie, really."

Pippa snorts. "Don't let her hear you say that."

"Actually," Stefan says, grinning, "I get the impression she'd find it kind of funny."

"Yes, she probably would. Look, Stefan; are you okay?"

He shrugs. "I'm not. But I've been not okay for a long time."

"This morning—"

"Can we not talk about that?"

"Of course," Pippa says. "I just— Can we start again?"

"What do you mean?"

"Do you like hot chocolate?"

"Um. Yes?"

Pippa pulls her phone out of her bag and taps away at it for a few moments, texting someone. "Wait for it," she says with a smile, putting her phone away and stretching. "I asked for marshmallows, too, if that's okay."

A few minutes later—time they fill with awkward small talk about the TV shows he watched that day—the light on the little dumbwaiter by the door goes green, and Pippa extracts a pair of hot chocolates, in plain mugs, piled high with marshmallows. He takes his. It's hot enough that he has to put it on the bedside table for the moment.

"So," Pippa says, blowing on hers, "I was saying, I want to start again. From the top." She takes a sip, winces at the heat, and sets it down by the computer. "I'm Pippa. I'll be your sponsor. Hi." She holds out a nervous hand, and Stefan resolves to talk to Abby and ask if anything's up, because she seems anxious for Stefan's approval, which when previously offered tended to be thrown back in his face.

What the hell.

"I'm Stefan," he says, taking her hand. He adds, "Stef, actually."

"Hi, Stef," Pippa says. "Hey, do you want to watch a movie?"

She doesn't give him a chance to reply, just passes him her hot chocolate—he puts it down next to his—and practically leaps onto the bed next to him, stretching her legs out so her feet dangle off the side. She leans forward, fetches the mouse and hands it over, silently offering him the choice of what to watch.

"You're serious, aren't you?" Stefan says, giving her back her hot chocolate as *A Christmas Prince* starts playing. "You really want to start again?"

"I do. I got some advice from some friends of mine and I've decided, sod being a bad sponsor. I'm just not going to be a real sponsor at all."

"That's, uh—"

"You don't need to know how to feel about it right away," Pippa says. "Take your time. And we'll still do all the stuff, I suppose. I just… won't be as weird with you as I've been. Now shush! I haven't seen this one."

Stefan shrugs, and settles back into his small pile of pillows, pulling one out and handing it over before he gets too comfortable. Pippa stuffs it behind her head, smiles her thanks and starts working on her hot chocolate, and the smell of it is too much to bear. He sips gingerly at his, expecting it to scald his tongue, but he's not at all prepared for the marshmallow that gets stuck to his nose.

He leaves it there until Pippa notices and laughs long enough and loud enough that they have to rewind the movie.

13
Driftwood

27 OCTOBER 2019 — SUNDAY

Day 1.

No boobs yet.

28 OCTOBER 2019 — MONDAY

Day 2.

No boobs yet.

29 OCTOBER 2019 — TUESDAY

Day 3

No boobs yet!

30 OCTOBER 2019 — WEDNESDAY

Day 4

No boobs yet.

31 OCTOBER 2019 — THURSDAY

Day 5

No boobs yet.

Aaron knocked on my door this morning and asked if my nipples were sensitive, but I think he was just trying to get me to look at his chest again. He's DEFINITELY not developing faster than I am. It's only been five days!

1 NOVEMBER 2019 — FRIDAY

Day 6

No boobs yet.

Maybe Aaron IS developing faster than I am? It'd be just my luck.

Christine's notes: Don't do this to yourself, Stef.

Stefan's notes: Stop reading my diary entries and stop hogging all the double-strength estrogen.

Christine's notes: Maybe you can gaslight Pippa into injecting you twice on Saturday? Once in the morning, once in the evening? Just make sure to present the other thigh.

Stefan's notes: Were you born unhelpful or is it a skill you developed in some kind of torture basement?

Christine's notes: I cultivated it entirely on my own. You have to be a little bit of a douche every day. It's a whole regimen.

Stefan's notes: You're doing really, really well.

Christine's notes: You know, we could have this conversation over Consensus like normal people.

Stefan's notes: We're not normal people. Besides, I'm enjoying how passive-aggressive this is.

Christine's notes: I have to admit, your punctuation is better in this format, for some reason.

Stefan's notes: How's my punctuation now?

```
............................./´¯/)
..........................,/¯./
......................../..../
.............../´¯/'..'/´¯¯`·¸
........../'/.../..../......./¨¯\
.........('(....´...´... ¯~/'....')
..........\..............'........./
............\....\.........._.·´
..............\.............(
................\............\
```

Christine's notes: I'm viewing this on my phone and it messes with the line structure so I'm going to assume you're breaking out the ASCII art solely to express your undying love for me.

Stefan's notes: It's a middle finger. In a way, it DOES express my undying love for you.

Christine's notes: How sweet. I'm impressed, though. You couldn't have Googled that; does that mean you know how to type it in from memory?

Stefan's notes: It's literally the only transferable skill I retain from my junior school computer classes.

2 NOVEMBER 2019 — SATURDAY

Day 7

One week on estradiol. I'm due my second injection today sometime. Probably this morning; I know Pippa's seeing Rani tonight and she won't want to be weighed down with sponsor stuff in the evening. It's their first real date since they met a week ago. I hope it goes well, but I admit to being a bit jealous. It's lonely down here. Yes, I have Aaron and the others, and that's fine, in its way, but I have to be the same edited version of myself that I was with Russ. The same version of myself that I am with Pippa, even. I hate that I never see anyone who KNOWS me. The last time was with Abby, and I freaked out at her, so maybe it's better I keep myself in check.

It hurts to see other people getting on with their lives while I'm…stuck. Oh well. At least I'm dot dot dot stuck with bloody estradiol and goserelin swimming around inside me. Even if their effects on my body thus far have been underwhelming.

I can feel it in my head, though. Starting goserelin was a bit like turning off a pair of speakers that had been blaring awful music into my head, all my life. And I was in silence for a little while there. Now, estradiol's starting up new music, music I like and fuck, this metaphor sucks ASS.

I hope Rani's good enough for Pippa. She deserves some happiness. Sometimes she seems so sad and I really want to hug her, but we're not there yet. I think sometimes she still sees the Bad Guy when she looks at me, like she remembers who I'm supposed to be. Not often, but enough to keep a little bit of distance between us.

Still, she held my hand when she found me crying that one time. Okay, those two times. I'm doing that a lot more, now. Before it was like a, I don't know, a storm, a really bad one, one of the ones they have to name, the ones that come once a year and knock down buildings. Now it's like normal, boring rain showers. I still get wet, but it's not the end of the world.

I am terrible at metaphors. I'm discovering this about myself. Glad I took Linguistics and not Creative Writing.

Christine, if you read this, you nosy, nosy cow, I'll come at you with my morning Weetabix. You won't stand a chance: it's hard as a rock and barely qualifies as food.

Christine's notes: Ah, the many cruelties of Dorley.

9 NOVEMBER 2019 — SATURDAY

Alarm at seven. It's loud, and mindlessly musical, like an orchestra warming up. He has no control over the time it goes off, nor the music, nor the volume, but he refused Pippa's offer to ask permission to change it. Keeping the same schedule as everyone else is good for the role he's playing, and for his stability. Because when he rolls out of bed and checks himself over in the mirror and sees no progress, no changes, it's hard to swallow it all and prepare for another day of doing, essentially, nothing. Routine keeps him in check where optimism fails him.

He came here, he stayed here, he gave up years of his life for this: to break this body, strip its flesh, burn it back to the bone and start again. To become new. And so he waits.

Stefan covers himself. He wears joggers and a robe to the showers so he doesn't have to be naked until the last possible moment and he pulls them on, stretching the sleeves to the knuckles, closing the robe to the neck. He buzzes his face with the electric razor, picks up his wash kit and heads to the bathroom. They still have designated time slots to wash up in the morning. Thanks to Declan, supposedly, but he's rarely allowed out of the cell and never when anyone else is around. Showering in shifts is, like the plastic cutlery, just another step in a gradual tightening of restrictions that was always, one way or another, going to happen. Christine said something about that: that Dorley is like a checkers board. There are only so many moves it's possible to make and, sooner or later, as a group, you'll make all of them.

At least the sponsors wait outside while they wash now. Pippa's doing.

Aaron, late as usual, takes the shower next to his and starts running through his routine at double speed, making up for lost time. Stefan, hair and body already washed, conditioner soaking in, enjoys the hot water—below scalding this time—and laughs as the shampoo bottle slips out of Aaron's soapy hands.

"I'm going to have to bend over to get this," Aaron says, "and before I do—" he presents a cautionary finger, "—I want you to know that there is no unsexy way for me to do this. I'm just going to have to bend down, and you, somehow, are going to have to cope."

Stefan nonetheless retreats to a safe distance. "You could bend at the knees instead. Very unsexy."

"What?" Aaron says, his rear end elevated. "I can't hear you down here!" He wiggles his bottom for emphasis; Stefan resists the temptation to step forward smartly and slap it. It'd be funny, probably, but the message it would send is not one Stefan wants to endorse.

Because over the last couple of weeks, Aaron's gotten even more physically demonstrative—a lot more forward with his backside—and Stefan can't decide if the boy is just teasing him or if he is trying, perish the thought, to *flirt*.

The idea is distracting enough that he almost swallows shower water, and he coughs it up with the help of a few slaps to the back. He decides, when Aaron's hand doesn't linger, when the little perv behaves exactly as one ought in such a situation, that he's imagining things.

Besides, Aaron likes girls. That's what all those dick pics were about. Life down here is strange enough without convincing himself that Aaron, of all people, is coming on to him.

"So," Aaron says, starting work with the shampoo, "did you hear we're due our next round of dick deflation?"

"Um. What?"

"The Goserelin. You know, the implant? The thing they stuck in our bellies when we got here that suppresses all our snips and snails and severely limits the function of our puppy-dog tails. It's been a month—longer for me, actually—and I don't know about you, but I'm itching for a new belly bump." He finishes rinsing out the shampoo and then puffs out his stomach, cradling it in his hands like an expectant mother.

"I didn't know." Stefan pretends to think about it. "But it makes sense."

"Yeah." Aaron holds out the conditioner bottle. "Rub it in for me?"

"What? Why?"

He makes a show of stretching. "I slept funny. My shoulder's sore. My World War One injury is acting up. I have a fear of reaching above my head. My wrists only move counterclockwise. A bottle of conditioner killed my father. I'm very weak and don't think I can rub hard enough, and you have those long fingers—"

"Aaron."

"Just help me out, would you? I'm tired—" he interrupts himself with a huge yawn that doesn't inspire one in Stefan; faked, "—and I kind of want to do nothing more than sit down and stare at something interesting until it does the magic eye thing. Like you; I bet you'd look like a Picasso."

"Fine." Stefan snatches the conditioner bottle out of Aaron's hand and, with a firm grasp on the shoulder, turns him away. When he starts spreading the conditioner through Aaron's hair, the boy makes moaning noises. "Aaron, what are you doing?"

"Relax," Aaron says, twisting his head as far as he can to grin at Stefan, "I'm just teasing."

Stefan turns Aaron's head back towards the front. "Don't."

"Aww. But you seem so secure in your masculinity. I can't help but give it a little prod."

"What does masculinity have to do with anything?"

"Stef," Aaron says, trying to turn around again and failing; Stefan's palms lie flat against the sides of his head, holding him in place, "it has *everything* to do with *everything* in this place. Like with the second shot of Goserelin: what are the chances, do you think, that we're in for another round of very manly rebellion from Will and Raph and all the others who fought back before?"

Stefan shrugs, rinses his hands, turns his own shower to cold and starts finger-combing his hair under the water until it runs clear. He's almost pleased to have to give a moment's thought to a sensible question, for once. "After the nurse? Low. Unless the mean girls try something."

"Mean girls": Aaron's nickname for Raph, Ollie and Declan. Not one Stefan would have chosen; too obvious, although if it has a saving grace it's that none of the boys appear to have seen the movie.

Maria smirks every time Aaron says it.

"Exactly my point!" Aaron says, whirling around, finger-first. "That nurse was softening us up. We had weapons pointed at us and were borderline sexually assaulted—"

"—no 'borderline' about it—"

"—and now we're all just going to calmly submit to the next indignity! We've been manipulated into suppressing our natural masculine responses for fear of reprisal."

Stefan can't help it. "You have 'natural masculine responses'? Where?"

"Maria!" Aaron shouts. "Stef's being mean to me again!"

Maria, waiting around the corner, just out of sight, yells back, "Good!"

"Everyone's a critic." Aaron rinses his conditioner—too soon, in Stefan's opinion, but he always times it so they finish their showers together, and Stefan just got done with his—and shuts off the water. "Anyway, Stef, we're all kind of…softening up. In more ways than one. I know you've noticed. And you don't seem to be particularly bothered by the prospect of another month on the floppy dick juice. Less bothered than I am, even, and all it's done for me is made my wanks more challenging."

Stefan's bad at remembering to dislike the implant. Principal among its many beneficial effects is that he hasn't had an unwanted erection for weeks, although the downside was that it took him four days to fill the sperm cup, given his reluctance to "coax the old boy into life with a bit of soft music and gentle yanking" as per Aaron's suggestion. Pippa, for reasons she hasn't yet explained, covered for him with Maria, claiming to have dropped his first sample.

"What would be the point in caring?" he says. "I feel like I say this over and over again, but they have the tasers, Aaron. And the batons. And the keys to the many, many locks."

"You don't think we should fight even a little?"

"No."

Aaron claps him on the back. "Good! Hah! Shit, Stef, that's all the excuse I needed to just sit down and take it. Fighting's for idiots, you know?" He quickly wraps his robe around himself. "Maria! I'm ready for my emasculation now!"

Pippa, waiting with Maria, intercepts Stefan as they leave. "Hey," she says, touching him gently on the shoulder, "I heard you talking about the new Goserelin shot. Are you ready for it? I know it's not a *good* thing—" she looks sideways at Maria, who is preoccupied with Aaron, "—but it's the rules. We can do the, um, the vitamin jab at the same time. Get it all over with at once, you know? That way, you won't be waiting around for—"

She's starting to babble. "Yeah," Stefan says, cutting in. "Sure."

Her eyes are everywhere but on him, and he has to remind himself: she doesn't know. She thinks she's deceiving him. The "vitamin" shot! Maybe that's the barrier between them? Not her perception of him, but her perception of herself.

Her fingers stiffen on his shoulder. "I can get one of the others to do it, if you'd rather."

"It's fine," Stefan says. The smile is easy to make genuine, and he reaches up to cover Pippa's hand with his own. "I'm not going to make a fuss."

"Maybe you should," she whispers, and bites her lip.

"Hey, Pip," he says. "I won't."

She looks at him at last and brightens. She matches his smile, comes back to life, and pushes him away with a laugh, shaking water off her hand. "Ew, Stef! You're all wet!"

He squeezes out a few more drops from his hair and flicks them at her—she evades, giggling—as he leaves with Aaron.

"So," Aaron says, out in the corridor, nominally alone together, "are you two kissing, or what?"

"Who? Me and Pippa? No! She's just…We're friends. Besides, she's dating someone."

"How do you even *know* that?" Aaron shoves him gently. "You really do have the Stockholm Syndrome, don't you?"

Stefan plasters on his toothiest grin. "What, you don't hug Maria?"

"No. I think if I tried, I'd set off a bunch of booby traps hidden in her clothes. And, hey, speaking of boobies—"

"Nope," Stefan cuts him off, and turns away to unlock his door before Aaron can get his nipples out again, "I don't know why I have to keep telling you this, but reducing your testosterone is very unlikely to make you grow breasts. You're still just as flat-chested as I am. Now go and, for the love of *God*, put some clothes on."

"Yeah, yeah."

"Maybe several extra layers, to be safe!" Stefan yells, as Aaron's door closes behind him.

He can't help checking himself in the mirror again. Aaron *definitely* isn't swelling up on the chest—he had ample opportunity to check in the showers—but, unfortunately, neither is he.

A few minutes later, when he's dried and dressed, Pippa enters, carrying the "vitamin" injection kit and the slightly more intimidating Goserelin implant needle. Smiling apologetically, still remorseful about the lies. He keeps up the chatter with her, tries to make it feel as normal and routine as possible.

One in the thigh, another in the belly, and he's out the door again, waving Pippa goodbye and heading to the dining room for his rock-hard Weetabix.

Aaron doesn't waste any time getting to the point. Ever since Will and Adam seemed finally to resolve their ideological differences—Adam doesn't mention demons anymore, and Will hasn't called him a "religidiot" for weeks—it's generally Aaron who cuts through everyone's morning haze. The boy's mouth has no brakes.

"It's come to my attention," he says, "that my 'sponsor'—" he air quotes with a Weetabix, for emphasis, "—is aloof, highly critical, and physically undemonstrative, and I consider myself discriminated against in this regard. Thoughts?"

"No thoughts," Stefan says. "Eating."

Aaron uses his Weetabix as a pointer. "Stef has movie nights with his. Meanwhile, Maria treats me like a disobedient child."

"Perhaps if you didn't behave like a disobedient child," Will says, "she might upgrade you to deeply unpleasant adult?"

"You're one to talk. I've seen how Tabitha treats you. If she could get you behind a big sheet of glass and only touch you with those big rubber gloves they use to manipulate nuclear material, she would."

"That's called professional detachment, Aaron. She's got a job to do and, no matter how much I don't like it, no matter how much I don't particularly like *her,* she's doing it."

There's a whistle as the speakers set into the ceiling activate and Tabitha, amid a small amount of microphone whine, says, "William, that's the most sensible thing you've said this week."

Will nods, satisfied.

"Hey!" Aaron yells, looking up. "Tell Maria I want hugs from now on!"

The circuit clicks off with a loud thump and a spit of feedback. Stefan imagines Maria, in the security room, hitting a rocker switch slightly too hard.

"No hugs for you," Adam says, and Will grins, nudges him with his elbow.

"I'm getting it from all sides today," Aaron says. "Martin, what about you? You best buds with Pamela? Does she tuck you in at night?"

"She hates me," Martin mumbles.

"Yeah, well. You did kill a guy. Adam? How's Edy?"

"She combs my hair," Adam says. He's not eating, just drinking a glass of oat milk and resting his chin on his hand.

"It's true," Will says. "She combs his hair. I've seen it."

"That's it," Aaron says, throwing down his plastic spoon. "Maria!"

The speakers remain stubbornly silent for the rest of breakfast, denying Aaron his catharsis, and when Maria arrives to escort them into the common area she doesn't respond to Aaron's outstretched hands and pleas to "just hug it out".

It's a little concerning that she's there; for the last week or so they've largely been watched over remotely and left to their own devices, except when one of the sponsors has something they want to say in person. Abby says security room detail is preferable to standing around in the corridor or sitting on the sofas at the back of the common area, because they don't have to expend the extra effort to appear menacing and can just talk, catch up on schoolwork or, more likely, as long as at least one girl stays alert to the screens, nap.

Maria ushers the five of them over to the sofas by the television, the area Stefan's group has essentially colonised. Stefan is alarmed to realise that a lot of the other sponsors are back: Edy, Adam's sponsor, leans against the wall by the TV; Tabitha, Will's sponsor, sits on top of the cabinets by the storeroom; Jane and Harmony, attached to Raph and Ollie, are positioned at one of the central tables, watching over their charges; and a handful of faces Stefan doesn't have names for—sponsors to second- and third-year girls, most likely—are lounging around near the entrance to the room.

All of them are armed.

What the hell is going on?

Stefan's not the only one to notice it, and conversation around the television is subdued. Adam and Will huddle slightly closer than usual, and Aaron's complicated arrangement of legs is reduced simply to hugging his knees. Stefan, looking around, catches Maria's eye and mouths, *What's going on?* but her only response is to shake her head.

"I don't like this," Adam whispers, leaning back against Will's shoulder. "It's too tense."

Stefan nods. He's been waiting for the other shoe to drop ever since their first estradiol injection. When one of the boys finally realises he's growing breasts, it's all going to kick off, and that's presumably where the slow development of trust with the sponsor comes in, but how anyone who doesn't want it can be talked through it is still a mystery. Although Christine did warn him, weeks ago, that part of the process of rehabilitation was— how did she put it? Prying their fingers off the driftwood of masculinity and forcing them to learn how to swim?

He knows he's been living in the calm before the storm, but he's not ready for everything to go to shit just yet.

Eventually, the reason for the amped-up security becomes clear: Declan, escorted by Monica and two others, saunters back into the common room like he never left. He's wearing his hoodie open, with no shirt underneath, and while he looks perhaps a little leaner, he's no less intimidating a figure than he was when he attacked Stefan and Aaron in the showers and started all this.

"I thought you said he was so bruised he looked like a mouldy orange!" Will whispers, edging away from Adam and causing the other boy to have to shift his balance. Stefan couldn't have missed the dismayed look on Adam's face if he'd been a hundred metres away.

"That was two weeks ago, Will!" Aaron whispers back. "I assume they eventually stopped beating him when they found out you can't cure dickhead with a baton."

"Hi, Aa-ron," Declan says, sauntering over and leaning on the back of Stefan and Aaron's sofa. "Hi Stef-an. Nice to see you both again."

"Hi, Declan," Aaron says, angling himself out of Declan's reach. "How was life in the cell? Read any good books?"

"You're so *funny*, Aa-ron!"

"Well, you know, I try."

"It won't help you."

"All right," Monica says, tapping Declan on the shoulder with her baton, "come on. Let's get you settled back in your room."

"I'm coming back for you," Declan says. "You too, Stef-an."

"No, you're not," Monica says, hooking an arm around Declan's elbow and pulling. He steps back, shrugs her off and raises his hand, and for a second it looks like the shitshow is about to start, right here in the common room, but every sponsor in the room points their taser at him and he smiles, flattens his palms in surrender, and allows himself to be walked out of the room. He throws Aaron and Stefan a grin as the door closes behind him.

"You really had to let him out?" Stefan says to Maria. "Couldn't have kept him in there another couple of months?"

"That's not how things work here, Stef," Maria says, and she follows Monica, Declan, and half the other sponsors out into the corridor, leaving them almost alone.

"Fuck," Aaron says.

***

The rooms on the second floor and up are arranged in twos, so their bathrooms can share plumbing. One of the consequences is that, for Christine, waking up in Paige's bed can be disorientating: the room is laid out in perfect mirror image to her own.

Once upon a time it would also have been the room with the most clothes in by far, but since their first shopping trip together two weeks ago Christine and Paige have been into town twice more, to look through the smaller shops down by the river, and once down to London, to poke around the massive cathedrals of commerce on

Oxford Street. All in the name of acclimating Christine to being seen as a normal girl—and a pretty girl, Paige insists—by a variety of cisgender strangers, and accelerating her through six months of feminine development in a fortnight. Christine's room bulges with bags, boxes and piles of clothes, cluttering to the point where Paige cleared her a small space in Vicky's room, now also almost consumed.

Clothes, it turns out, are *fun.*

"What time is it?" Paige moans, rolling over in bed and flopping her hand over Christine's chest.

"Ouch!" Christine pushes Paige off for just long enough to pull her arm tightly around her waist, where it can do useful things, such as embrace her and not, for example, brush roughly against her sore nipples. "I'm aching again. Be careful," she scolds.

"Sorry," Paige says with a grin, and uses her advantageous new position to kiss Christine on the cheek. "If this is another growth spurt, I'm going to be so mad at you."

Christine waits for Paige to pull back a little and then she turns over, kissing her on the lips. "Stay mad," she whispers.

It's warm in the room despite the November chill—Dorley Hall's centrally controlled heating is too miserly for Paige, who feels the cold, so she runs an electric heater on a timer and probably wipes out a reasonable percentage of the money saved in the process. Christine kicks off the blankets, enjoying the sensation of the high thread count sheets (another influencer bonus) gliding smoothly over her legs and suppresses a giggle: her old self would never have got to discover how *good* that feels. He never tried shaving his legs even *once.*

Paige rolls over again, onto her back, causing her teardrop breasts to flatten against her chest, and it's too tempting not to ambush her, to push up with an elbow and let the momentum carry her onto Paige's side of the bed, squashing one of her own breasts against Paige's ribs, slipping a cheeky hand into her underwear, searching.

Thin scars buried under pubic hair; new since the last time they were together. Christine's discovered them, kissed them, run her fingers over them, blessed them in every way she knows how, added a third finger in the middle and coaxed from Paige sounds Christine never wants anyone else to hear. Those moans, those squeaks of delight, are hers.

Christine has scars to match, and because Paige treasures everything about her, she calls them beautiful.

"Scars are powerful," Paige said a few nights ago, when they lay next to each other out on the green, soaking in the starlight. "Scars mean survival."

Christine doesn't like to think of herself as someone who *survived*—she prefers *reborn*—but Paige is all about the redefinition of self, so she hugged and kissed her, and took her back to her room. She had to run back out the next morning before class, to retrieve the dewy picnic blanket before the heavens opened.

Today she contents herself with a quick and playful caress before dropping a kiss on Paige's nose and skipping off to steal her shower.

A minute later, Paige joins her, opening the frosted glass door with a shyness Christine feels she's the only one ever to have seen, and whispers, "Tease."

They take their time getting ready.

Together they head downstairs for breakfast, on the way exchanging greetings and smiles with Julia and Yasmin, who they catch returning to Yasmin's room. Their rekindled relationship is apparently melting the hearts of even the second floor's most dedicated loners.

"Christine!" Aunt Bea says, as they flop into chairs at the packed kitchen table and accept coffees in plain mugs from a second-year girl Christine only sort of recognises. "You look wonderful. Paige must be rubbing off on you."

At the other end of the table, Jodie hiccups and inhales her orange juice. Christine, probably visibly bright red under her light foundation, doesn't believe for a second Aunt Bea doesn't know exactly what she's implying.

That Aunt Bea! What a jokester! Christine can almost ignore the many disturbing things she knows or suspects about her—to which she's recently added the discovery that Nurse Karen Turner's entire electronic profile has vanished. Facebook: gone. LinkedIn: gone. Her staff page at the local hospital: gone. She's not even on the electoral roll and, when Christine used a random (and, miraculously, still functional) London payphone to call the council, she turned out to not be on their records, either. The woman's just gone. The suggestion that Aunt Bea, or someone she's close to, is able to perform such a feat is more than a little disturbing. Christine spent a whole afternoon last week making triple-sure her unauthorised escapades around Dorley Hall have had their digital footprints wiped clean.

Whatever. Aunt Bea could be a mafia don and there'd still be nothing Christine can do about it. And if she did have the nurse killed and her presence scrubbed from the internet, that means there's one less devil in the world. She tries to put it out of her head.

She's surprised to see Jodie downstairs, though. It's not that she's unsociable, like Julia and Yasmin; she just has other friends. She also looks considerably less goth than usual. Is someone at Dorley attempting a teen movie glow-up on her? Is Aunt Bea? Christine hopes it backfires, and that she returns to her usual all-black-with-frills by next week. Jodie, patting her chin clean of orange juice with a kitchen towel, notices Christine's attention and rolls her eyes in good humour.

Pippa wiggles her fingers at them. She's sitting next to Jodie with a bowl of porridge and a mug that reads, *It's all fun and games until someone loses their*— and Christine would ask what the last word is, but she can guess; to describe Dorley's institutional sense of humour as monomaniacal would be appropriate but leave you with no words to describe Dorley's institutional approach to the male gender. Pippa's not normally one for the novelty mugs—she takes a more reserved view of the whole process than most of them—and Christine regrets missing the look on her face when it was handed to her.

Aunt Bea meets her eyes. Raises her eyebrows, expectant. Oh yeah; Christine's been spoken to by the custodian of Dorley Hall. Whoops.

"Thank you, Aunt Bea!" Christine says, belatedly. "That's very kind of you to say." She takes a deep sip of coffee. Aunt Bea's right, though: she does look good. Paige suggested a skirt-and-top combo that is in practical terms equivalent to her habitual shorts-and-t-shirt, especially with a pair of bike shorts underneath, but that makes her look—and still she struggles sometimes to say the word even in her own head—*cute.* She likes the feeling, especially when Paige takes her in with a smile. "How'd the new Goserelin injection go?" she says to Pippa. "That was this morning, right?"

Pippa swallows her porridge. "Easy as pie," she says.

Aunt Bea drums her fingers on the table for a moment. "He's still cooperating?"

"He told me he wouldn't make a fuss, and he didn't. And I overheard him talking to Aaron." She blushes into her novelty mug, gives up fighting the pleasure straining at the edges of her mouth. "He said we're friends."

"Excellent work, Pippa!" Aunt Bea says, causing a frown to flicker across Pippa's brow. No happy moment unsullied: Aunt Bea has a way of making any friendship between sponsor and subject unpleasantly transactional. "How do you believe he will respond when the physical changes become apparent?"

"I'm, um, still not sure. He didn't seem comfortable when Aaron challenged his masculinity this morning. It might be a problem."

Aunt Bea finishes her coffee. "Then your priority is to continue to deepen your rapport. If you're his friend, become his *best* friend. And when the changes start, don't forget: they are mandated by *us*, not you. You are there simply to help him through an ordeal you are powerless to prevent. *We* are his enemy; *you* are his ally."

That's not the way it's usually done. Bea must have discussed this strategy with Pippa, though, because she nods calmly. Whether or not she follows through with it doesn't especially matter, but it does at least have the benefit of not putting Pippa at odds with a Stef who glares at his chest morning and evening, willing it to swell. Christine's more concerned about Stef's acting skills, which haven't exactly been stellar thus far. It's going to be hard for him to coast on fake apathy when everyone around him is panicking.

She feels bad about reading the diary entries he vouchsafes to her care, but after the showers, after the nurse, she was worried about him, and it's now become another of the games they play, another forum on which to bicker. Christine smiles, remembering a three-page tirade on the subject of Will's tiresome Reddit atheism which, if you took out all of the insulting asides directed specifically at her, would read like a first-draft essay for the blogging website of Stef's choice.

God, she hopes it's a game they're playing. She likes him a lot, but has no real idea how he feels about her. For all she knows, he could hate her, and his little jokes might be his only way of expressing that. She needs to find a way to see him in person again, to recalibrate. Text-only friendships—if that's even what this is—suck.

His "true believer" jabs are the only ones that really hit home. They remind her of the awful things they're in the process of doing to everyone down there with him, things she could put a stop to at a stroke if she were willing to pay the price. She's not. "Dorleypilled", he calls her, and the worst thing is, he's right: she looks around the table, at Pippa, at Jodie, at Bea, and most especially at Paige, and can't imagine any of them any other way.

Fine, she can imagine Jodie a little more goth. She's wearing light blue and it's *weird*.

"No! Maria! It's fine!"

The shout echoes in the dining hall but probably comes from the basement stairs. It sounds like Monica, and it's accompanied by the staccato steps of someone wearing medium-high heels and a seriously bad mood.

"I just need *ten minutes* away from that odious piece of shit! Ten minutes where I don't have to breathe his stink! Ten fucking minutes of peace and *fucking* quiet!"

Monica, charging into a full kitchen, flushes when she realises how many people—including Aunt Bea—witnessed her outburst. She stands almost to attention for a moment and Christine wonders if she was ever a soldier, or just an overexcited boy scout. "Sorry," she says. "Won't happen again, Aunt Bea."

"See that it doesn't. Now, are you okay, Monica dear?"

"I'm okay," Monica says, dropping heavily onto the rickety wooden chair by the door. "It's Declan. He's back among the boys as of a half-hour ago and he's learned *nothing* from his time in the cell."

"Declan's out?" Pippa says, dropping her spoon in her porridge and getting halfway out of her chair before Aunt Bea stops her with a hand to her shoulder.

"Don't worry, Pippa," Aunt Bea says. "It's all under control."

"Yeah," Monica says, leaning her head back against the wall and closing her eyes, "not exactly. First thing he did was threaten Aaron and Stef."

"Stef". Even the other sponsors call him that now. Pippa started it and now everyone does it, including half the boys downstairs. On the day he finally extracts his head from his arse and starts thinking of himself as a girl, he's going to have the easiest name transition ever. Unless he decides to go by something completely different. Some people have strong opinions about their names. Christine didn't; she had Indira pick it, with her only specification being that it share no syllables and no initials with her deadname, deeply buried and quickly forgotten.

Pippa shakes off Aunt Bea's restraining hand. "He threatened Stef? What did he do?"

Monica's still got her eyes closed. "He said, 'I'm coming back for you.' Don't worry; Maria's still down there and so are, like, ten more of us, and the PMC guys have been told to stop napping and watch their phones. Stef's safe, Pip."

"All the same," Pippa says, "I'm not going to the library today. I'm staying here."

"So, if he's under control," Paige says, innocently sipping her coffee, "what's got you so upset?" Aunt Bea directs a frown at her that Paige ignores.

"I'm *upset* because I have no control, Paige," Monica says, leaning forward on her knees and clenching and unclenching her fists. "I'm upset because I shut my eyes and helped turn a man into a bag of bruises and he just fucking grinned at me while I did it. I mortgaged my conscience for that piece of shit and he doesn't even have the decency to care. And now he's wandering around down there, knowing full well that we just threw everything we had at him and he didn't break."

"That's not *everything* we have," Christine says. "Has he been getting the shots?" Monica nods. "Then he's going to have a fun surprise soon enough."

"He's not going to make it that long," Monica says. "He's going to revert right back to his old behaviour—except worse, because we've made it clear that he's a block of concrete and we're a rubber fucking hammer—and create ten times as much work for the rest of us trying to keep him under control. That place is a shitpit of tension, now that he's out. The other boys are all on edge, except for Raph and Ollie, who have their big, tough role model back, and that means we need to be on active duty again, twice as many of us, at all times, just when things were starting to feel nice and calm down there."

"Yes, well," Aunt Bea says, "it doesn't do for our subjects to get *too* comfortable." Pippa bites her lip. "Besides, the reintroduction of an undesirable element can be a catalyst."

"He's a fucking catalyst all right," Monica says, standing heavily. "I'm going upstairs to get some proper shitkicking boots on, and then I'm going back down there to spend the next six hours looking very much like I'm ready to kick some shit. Pray for me, girls."

"I still don't understand why we don't just wash him out," Pippa mutters, angrily re-engaging with her breakfast. "I mean, I know that's the last resort and everything, but still."

"Everyone deserves a fair chance," Aunt Bea says. "Four or five, even. If we washed people out as soon as they became difficult to handle, this house would be empty."

Monica yanks open the door to the entrance hall. "Not quite," she says, pausing on the threshold. "It'd just be Melissa, sitting alone at the kitchen table like the bloody *Twilight Zone*."

***

The bedrooms in the basement can comfortably seat two—one on the bed, one on the chair—three perhaps, if two people don't mind sitting together on the bed.

At four, they get cramped.

Stefan's taken the head end of the bed, after stuffing his pillows into the wardrobe to protect them from Aaron's roaming feet, which unfortunately are still attached to Aaron, camped out at the other end of the bed and twitching nervously. Adam's perched on the roller chair and Will's sitting with his back against the door, long legs almost interfering with the computer desk. Martin, to Stefan's relief, didn't follow Stefan and Aaron the way Will and Adam did, and is presumably locked in his own room, doing whatever he normally does in the eighteen hours a day he spends in there, only perhaps with added Declan-related anxiety.

None of them seems to want to start the conversation. Not even Aaron, who stops fidgeting after a little while, draws his feet up under himself and starts quietly drumming on his knees. Stefan puts some music on—one of Pippa's playlists; it's mostly Taylor Swift—and decides that if no-one else will break the silence, it's up to him.

"So. Declan."

"Declan," Aaron says quietly. "Again."

"What do we do about him?"

"We go back to the old system," Will says. "We've been getting slack, anyway. Getting soft. We stay in our group." He whirls his finger around the room. "This group. Fuck Moody Martin; he's useless. He can fend for himself."

Adam reaches out towards Will, but Will ignores him. "What if Martin needs our help?" he says.

"He doesn't deserve our help," Aaron says into his chest. "Hands up everyone here who's killed a guy." No-one raises their hand. "Exactly. I'm a bastard, Will's a bastard, and it's anyone's guess about Adam and Stef, but none of us are killers. So Declan can have him, if he wants him."

"He doesn't," Stefan says, and then frowns when they all look at him. He said it quickly and without thought, but it feels right. He continues, "Declan never went for him. None of them did. Because he wouldn't fight back."

"Exactly," Will says.

"Yeah," Aaron says. "Martin'd take a punch and beg for another." He raises his hands in pretend plea, but drops them again almost immediately. Doesn't even have it in him to shit-talk Martin properly, which is almost heartbreaking.

"Why did they let him out, anyway?" Adam says. "I've been thinking about it, and it doesn't make any sense." He leans forward on his chair. "People, when they get taken like that, they don't come back."

"I don't know, but it's fucked their authority right up," Will says. "Maybe not with any of us—I don't know about you, but I have a healthy respect for those tasers and I especially don't want to spend two weeks getting the shit kicked out of me in a cell—but Declan's got them beaten. They've spent a fortnight repeatedly fucking him up, and now he's back."

"What about washing out?" Stefan says.

Will waves a dismissive hand. "That's the bogeyman. Always lurking, never seen. The big threat they never deploy."

Not true, unless Abby and Christine both lied, which seems unlikely at this point. The washouts leave and they don't come back, and given that anyone who went through what Declan did and subsequently got released would go straight to the police, it's not likely they go anywhere good.

"I'm choosing to take the threat of washing out seriously," Stefan says.

"Suit yourself."

"No, but seriously," Aaron says, "what *is* their plan with Declan? With all of us? I mean, we all got our new Goserelin implant, right? So we're here another month. And then another. And another. What's the endgame here? Unless we all wash out in the end, some of us are walking out. And then we, what, *don't* go to the cops? Or the papers? Out of the goodness of our hearts? And are they even going to stop with the Goserelin? Are we going to start getting psychotropic shit next, or something?"

"What are you saying?" Will says. "That we're here forever? You said you thought this was an experiment or something, that we'd all been gotten drunk and made to sign a consent form. Eight weeks max, you said."

"Yeah, and *you* thought it was 'woke jail' and *you* thought it was demons—"

"I never thought it was *demons,*" Adam whispers.

"—and I have no idea what Stef thought it was because he never opens his fucking mouth unless it's to needle me about my fucking dick pics and for Christ's sake, Stef, *I know* it's a messed up thing to do, of course I do, and I've had more than a month in a concrete hole to think very very hard about how absolutely and comprehensively I've fucked my life up and you know what I realised? You know what makes me hate myself in a very very special way? I'm exactly like Martin the fucking murderer. His family leaned on the court; my family leaned on the uni. He ran off from rehab; I carried on right where I left off. I'm exactly as pathetic as he is and I have to live with that and, to be brutally fucking honest, I'm almost pleased to be facing some kind of real consequence for it, if only because it'll piss off my family, but I still go to bed every night thinking about it, so *will you please stop bothering me about it every single fucking day?*"

"Yeah," Stefan says. "I'm sorry. I just—"

"I get it. You don't want to hang out with a little freak pervert."

"No! You're— Shit, Aaron, you're my *friend.*" No pretending like he's not, not anymore. What's that saying? *There are no atheists in foxholes?* Well, maybe there are no truly healthy friendships in the Dorley basement. No ethical fraternity in late-stage feminisation.

Anyway, his moral high ground is a lie. All of them here fucked up and hurt people. Including Stefan. He barely knows his parents anymore, and his sister is a near-stranger because he decided closing himself off completely after Melissa left was a better option than facing up to his shit. Sure, it felt safer at the time, to burn away quietly over years and years rather than take a risk, but there's no such thing as self-immolation without collateral damage. No son/daughter for his parents. No older brother/sister for Petra. No best friend for Russ, when he needed one the most. All his fault.

He hurt people. It almost feels good to realise it.

"That's a joke," Aaron says. "We're not friends. We're just…here at the same time."

"No," Stefan says, reaching forward. Aaron doesn't flinch at the hand on his arm. "I mean it. Look, I've been alone for a long time. I wrecked *everything* in my life. Lost everyone. Was barely even talking to my housemates by the time I got dragged down here. And meeting you—all of you—has been…I don't know, healing? I used to have two best friends; one left me, the other one I abandoned, and I've been missing them ever since. In you, I have something I haven't had since I had them."

"Uh—"

"I'm being serious, Aaron. You're my friend. I fucking like you, okay? Don't give me that look, Will, unless you think the emotion we call friendship is queer or something. I've not been as close to anyone since Russ or Melissa."

"Oh, shit," Aaron says, "are we finally getting *your* tragic backstory?"

"No," Stefan says, and then remembers: "You're not even close to unlocking it."

"Hey! No callbacks."

"Anyway, I'm sorry. I won't bug you about it again."

"Good," Aaron says. "Thanks. Fuck. And, hey, sorry about the feelings, William."

By the door, Will throws up his hands in exasperated surrender. "You're all gay," he says.

Fuck it. Stefan takes Aaron's hand, meets his eye and cocks an eyebrow. Together they look over at Will. Stefan makes a kissy face and says, "And that's why you love us," and is relieved when, after a moment's conflicted hesitation, Will laughs.

***

Stef's screwed. He has to be. He's down there, under pressure, he's already cracked at least once, he's tried to hurt himself in the shower, he was made practically catatonic by that nurse's assault, and now Declan is back, throwing his weight around, making insinuations and threats. Amping up the stress levels. Monica called it a "shitpit of tension" down there. How long until Stef, trying to adjust to yet another new normal, fucks up and exposes his true self? To a man who already attacked him once before? Will Maria and Monica's twenty-four-hour attention be enough to protect him?

God, and if Stef *does* accidentally out himself, and it gets back to Aunt Bea…that's everything Christine wanted to prevent in the first place. There's no telling what Bea would do. If anything, the ambiguous fate of the nurse has left Christine more scared of her than she used to be.

Shit.

Shit!

Christine's well aware that she's spiralling. She excused herself from the kitchen table and practically ran upstairs, shut herself in her room, faked a forgotten assignment when Paige messaged her, and now she's lying on her bed, drumming her fingers on the frame, wishing for a cigarette.

She needs to situate herself when she gets like this. She needs context, needs *information.* But she's already messaged Stef and got no reply. She's messaged Abby for moral support; no reply there, either. And with that, she's got nowhere to turn to except the security feeds. She's out of confidantes.

No. *Almost* out of confidantes.

She yanks her laptop open, loads the Consensus app, and starts thinking through how to translate Stef's situation onto that of the anonymous "friend" she invented, weeks ago.

> **WELCOME TO TRANS YOUTH UK! (Not affiliated with the Egg Society of Great Britain.)**
> All the usual Consensus rules apply. Click **>here<** for server rules. Obey them or begone!
> There are no stupid questions. Only stupid answers! Please refrain from giving stupid answers.
> Message **Ralph Ride** for moderation. Message **GAYBOT IV: THE VOYAGE HOME** for automated server functions.

Christine
Hi everyone
Me again
Oh hey Lorna

cicada
oh my god, Tina, hi!

distilled
her name's christine not tina

cicada
I call her Tina

distilled
but it says christine

cicada
and I call her Tina

> **Christine** has changed her name to **Tina**.

cicada
ha!

Girl Alex
Please stop owning Penny. They're very delicate about how easily owned they are.

distilled
god dammit

Tina
Lorna, how's Vicky?
Tell her to visit, we miss her

cicada
she misses you too!! she just hasn't been by because she doesn't want to get in the way of you two LOVEBIRDS!!

distilled
wait there are lovebirds
where
are there pictures

Girl Alex
What have we said about horny jail, Penny?

distilled
that it's a real place you will personally escort me to if I'm inappropriate in front of anyone else
I believe there was a shiba inu involved too

Tina
Okay this is weird, I'm changing it back

> **Tina** has changed her name to **Christine**.

distilled
does this mean I'm still owned

Girl Alex
Obviously.

Christine
Do you all just dunk on Penny all day on here?

distilled
they do tina and they're so mean to me
every day I get up and I'm subjected to so many awful things

Christine
That's terrible!
Bad Lorna!

cicada
hey it's mostly Alex tbh

Girl Alex
It's true. I came out only a few months ago and the universe saw fit to grant me a horrible little gremlin to message me weird internet porn in the small hours, and make fun of my boyfriend.

distilled
but your boyfriend's so rubbish, he makes it so easy

Girl Alex
I'm screenshotting everything you say about him.
He owns a technology company.
He can make your phone explode.

distilled
bitch motorola already made my phone explode, your boyfriend sucks

Christine
Hey, so actually I came online for a reason
I kind of have a problem, like last time I was on here
Sorry I swear I'll come on socially at least once before the end of the year
Is it okay if I just get straight into it even if it's really depressing?

cicada
oh no, Tina, is something wrong???

Christine
I'm fine Lorna
But I'm really worried about my friend, the one I talked about last time
She's still in a bad environment, surrounded by guys who are mostly not actively unfriendly, but almost entirely unknown as to how they respond to trans girls
And she's just started hormones

Girl Alex
How "just"? Yesterday? A week ago?

Christine
Two weeks ago
And blockers for about a month
I've been doing my best to support her
But I guess I've been a bit wrapped up in my own thing lately
Not as much help as I should have been
Kind of distracted

cicada
distracted by Paige???? ♡

Christine
Not just Paige but yeah mostly
The thing is
Things have been kind of calm for her lately
False sense of security for her and for me
But now a guy has come back from holiday
And he's the worst of all of them
He already tried to hurt her once and I don't think it was because he figured her out, he's just an awful guy
I'm scared he's going to try again
And I'm even more scared that with her starting to change, physically, that he'll work it out what/who she is and make it ten times worse for her

cicada
ok so that's bad, definitely, but I think you can take a breath here, Tina because apart from the dangerous guy being back, nothing's really changed

Christine
What about when she starts to show?

cicada
what about it?
I don't get the impression she's going to start running around saying, I love my new breasts, right?

Christine
That's unlikely

cicada
so this is the thing
cis people DO NOT see this kind of thing, like EVER
I know that sounds fake but it's true, almost none of them ever look at a "boy", even one who is visibly gender variant, and ask them if they're trans, it just doesn't happen
yes ok maybe it happens in like, queer circles, where everyone's a little bit gender, but "ordinary" men and women, the cishets, they don't see ANYTHING
if the guys who live with your friend see nothing but an amab kid with, I'm guessing, a personality closed up tighter than her hoodie, none of them are going to ask, hey, kid, are you by any chance an egg??? it doesn't happen
we're the last resort of cis people's imaginations
they'll ask if we're two sheep in a trench coat before they ask if we're trans

Christine
You really think they won't see anything?
That she can just keep going as she is?

cicada
I mean, it depends on if she starts doing voice work or wearing affirming clothes or something, but from what it sounds like, she's just trying to

stop the testosterone in its tracks and start her body on fixing itself, right?
she's going to wait until it's safer to actually socially transition?

Christine
Probably, yes

cicada
I think she'll be ok then
I hope so anyway, obviously there can always be variables, but I don't think her situation just got significantly WORSE
I don't think you need to start panicking yet

Girl Alex
I don't know about this.
I'm not so sure that cis people won't ever guess.

cicada
Alex, no
your experience does not apply, I know your boss was wondering if you were trans even before you were, but you were LITERALLY in a dress and puckering your lips at him for DAYS on end

Girl Alex
I didn't pucker!
Mostly I panicked.

distilled
you panicked in a dress though
you can't deny it we've all seen the pictures
you were on boothbabes.co.uk
lorna's right you don't exactly have a typical transition story

Christine
Oh?

Girl Alex
Technically, I was force femmed.

Christine
What

Girl Alex
It was a whole thing.

cicada
she learned about forced fem stuff like a week ago and won't shut up about it, she thinks it's terribly funny

Christine
You mean, forced fem in stories, right? Fiction?

cicada
what else?

Christine
Okay good just checking

cicada
are you all right?

Christine's halfway through her reply when the door slowly opens and Paige steps carefully through. She smiles, but it's a nervous smile, one that causes Christine's heart to lurch, so she quickly types out a grateful goodbye, closes her laptop, and stands up from the bed. Paige takes a step back, leans against the door, and Christine, limbs going cold, doesn't move any closer. She doesn't know what's going on, but Paige hasn't seemed this brittle since the end of their second year, when Aunt Bea locked her in her room for a week.

"Paige—" Christine says.

"You don't have an assignment due, do you?" Paige says. She's hugging herself, balling her fists in the fabric of her long dress, drawing it up almost to her knees.

Shit. "No," Christine says.

"You seemed so scared when you left the table. More than you would be just for schoolwork. It was more like the way you used to get, years ago, when you thought you'd done something wrong. When you were just waiting for the consequences to find you. And when you—"

Paige sniffs, and Christine aches, "—when you lied, and told me you had some assignment to do—"

"It's not anything bad," Christine says, wanting desperately to move towards her but anchoring herself with the fear that if she does, and Paige bolts, this might all end. Paige, the girl who has endless confidence and boundless grace, until suddenly, sometimes, she doesn't.

"Are you seeing someone else?" Paige says.

Christine's reply is instant. "No." They never agreed to be exclusive, never even really talked about whether they're girlfriends or not, and yet they both know they are. They fell in deep with each other, almost too quickly for Christine to really think about what she was doing.

Almost too quickly. Because the lies, like the guilt, have been weighing on her.

Paige nods. "Okay," she says. "Would you like a cup of tea?"

Christine nods, confused. "Yes."

"Good. Because there's something going on that I don't know about. Something that makes you really scared sometimes, something that makes you close your laptop when I look over, something that is *really* important to you, but which excludes me. And I need to know what it is, Christine. So I'm going to go around the corner to the kitchen and make us both a cup of tea, and when I come back, I want you to have decided whether or not you want to tell me. Okay?"

Christine sits down on the bed, slowly, moving every limb with care so as not to overbalance. She looks up at Paige, sees the tear tracks on her face, and knows at that moment that she will never keep anything from her ever again.

"Okay," Christine says.

* * *

Will predicted that Declan, Raph and Ollie would have taken over the sofas by the TV and, sure enough, when the four of them returned to the common room, there they were, slouching across as much space as possible, marking their new territory. It didn't take a lot of four-versus-three intimidation to get them to shift back to their usual spot on the metal tables. Between the numbers disadvantage and the roomful of women with weapons, Will's gamble worked. Declan might not be intimidated by the worst Dorley can dish out—as far as he understands it, anyway—but he doesn't seem to want to go straight back to the cell before he's had the chance to enjoy a single night in a soft bed.

"They've never actually properly thrown down with any of us, right?" Will had said, back in Stefan's room. "Yes, they've chucked the odd plate, they've made threats, but correct me if I'm wrong: the only time any of them came at any of us was Declan, with you two in the showers, right? And all he really managed then was knocking you on the floor, Aaron."

"And then Stef made him look like an idiot," Aaron said, grinning.

"Not the point. With anyone else, I'd expect them to respect you for outsmarting them, but Declan's thicker than a pig's knuckle: that won't even have occurred to him. But what he does know is, we're all basically unknown prospects, yes? I'm about his height and at least as built, and Adam's slim but not at all weak."

"We arm-wrestled," Adam said.

"And I only just won. And you two, you're both kinda small, but anyone who's been in a real fight knows you can't discount the skinny guys. It's the skinny guys who're quick. It's the skinny guys who'll break a bottle over your face."

"Or shove a plastic fork up your nose," Aaron muttered.

"So," Will had continued, ignoring Aaron, "we're a united front. Like before, only more so. We do *everything* together. No exceptions. If one of us has to piss, we *all* have to piss. I don't care if it makes us look like a bunch of girls. You'll have to learn to make sacrifices if you don't want to get your face split open. Declan and his cheerleaders are going to want to get us alone and we just don't let them. We stick together and we intimidate them right back. Agreed?"

Stefan, sitting in his usual spot on the sofas and filtering out the vast majority of the baking show on the TV, is still a little surprised that Will turned out to be right, and reluctantly gives him a few points on his internal scoreboard. He's not able entirely to relax, though, not just yet, not with his back to the room and Declan undoubtedly irritated. So he keeps his ears open, half to Aaron's prattle—reassuringly resumed after an unsettling period of keeping his thoughts mostly inside his head—and half to Declan, Raph and Ollie's conversation, in case there's anything of value to be found there.

He's never listened to them before, not really. And mostly they talk about what he would have guessed: a mishmash of sexist and racist jokes, some bravado about a time in their life they kicked a particularly large amount of arse, that sort of thing. Declan dominates the conversation, spending much of the time telling Raph and Ollie how he showed that bitch Monica by never backing down, and Stefan's ready to tune him out completely when he changes the subject and Stefan's mouth goes dry.

Declan had a girlfriend, his last before being snatched by Dorley. And she was pathetic and she said she loved him, and even when she stormed out, she came back. Even when he hit her, she came back.

Even after everything, she came back.

Declan's talking about one night, towards but not at the end of their relationship. She walked out again, determined to make it stick, to not think of him, to not come back. And part of making it stick was coming back for her things, taking them with her to her mum's place. And Declan had had a lot to drink that night, and she had her usual smart mouth on her, and he was feeling—

Oh. Oh God.

Declan is describing a rape.

And he thinks it's *funny*.

Raph and Ollie are barely saying anything and *why don't they?* Why don't they challenge this shit? Because Declan's describing in detail the things he did to her and Stefan can't listen to another fucking word of it.

It's over in less than five seconds. Almost before he knows what he's doing, Stefan's vaulted over the back of the sofa and launched himself at Declan, catching him hard enough in the face to knock him off his seat and onto the floor. And as Declan stares up at him, confused, clutching his nose, as Stefan cradles his fist in his other hand, as the room around him slowly starts to react, Stefan realises that he doesn't regret hitting Declan at all.

Not even if he gets back up.

Not even if he balls his fists.

Not even if he shouts Stefan's name with venom and spittle.

The man towers over him and outmasses him by an amount Stefan doesn't want to contemplate. He squares up, not like a boxer, but like someone who doesn't fight by the rules, and Stefan finds himself glancing from Declan's hands to his feet, wondering which will strike first.

Wondering how much it will hurt.

Stefan checks quickly around, looking for something he could use as a weapon, but then Declan's coming for him and he's out of time and he ought to regret this, but the thing is—

The thing is: *fuck* Declan.

He wants a fight?

He can have one.

14
The Sense God Gave Her

9 NOVEMBER 2019 — SATURDAY

Declan gets tased. Stefan doesn't, but that doesn't stop Declan's spasming body from colliding with him, momentum carrying him past the point of physical sensibility right into Stefan's stomach. The impact jolts him, knocks him off balance, and ruins Stefan's chances of absorbing the weight of them both and falling with grace.

At least he remembers to go limp at the last moment, so hitting the floor is merely extremely painful and not actually injurious. But that leaves him with Declan's moaning, drooling body, deliriously bear-hugging him on the concrete, too heavy for Stefan to shift on his own, and tasers don't *keep* you down, right? They just *put* you down.

He's trapped, and unless someone does something, Declan's going to be mobile again, really fucking soon.

The seconds tick by, and still Declan remains. How are the sponsors going to let this play out? Are they going to help him? They've intervened in confrontations before, haven't they? Though not, it occurs to Stefan, in such tight quarters. Perhaps they consider the situation contained for the moment; with Declan on the floor, there's nothing he can possibly do to anyone except Stefan, who is after all just another of the abusive, violent boys they stash down here.

God, he wants to scream it: he's not like them! Do the sponsors even know Declan's a rapist? None of the other boys seemed to until he bragged about it, so maybe the sponsors don't, either. To them, he and Stefan are the same.

Situation contained.

Then Declan rolls off him, and as the man starts to get his control back, he's lifted away from Stefan into the arms of several sponsors, who bundle him quickly out of the room, leaving Stefan lying there, breathing heavily, bruises most definitely blooming on his elbows, his arse, and all across his back.

Fucking Declan. As Stefan watches the sponsors drag him away, batons at the ready, he can't get it out of his head: this fucker *revelled* in the power he had over that woman. Not just his physical power, either; she kept coming back to him, again and again, caught in a cycle of leaving when he abused her and coming back when he put on sufficient charm. When he persuaded her that, this time, he'd changed.

Repulsive.

Stefan's never wanted so much to hurt someone, even now, after the consequences of trying knocked him on his arse.

He doesn't really pay attention as Aaron helps him up, nor as Maria leads him to a cell. It takes him several minutes, minutes he spends getting his heartbeat under control, breathing slowly until his pulse stops thumping against his temples, gripping the edge of the awful little cot so tight he thinks his fingers might bruise, to realise she left the door open.

Pippa's there. Watching him. For how long?

"You okay?" she says, and her tone suggests she's asked him once already. She's flushed all the way up to her bleached hair, like she's been crying. Her voice has that delicate lilt some people get when they're trying not to strain it after pushing it too hard; Stefan wonders if that still applies for someone who's had as much voice training as Pippa's obviously had. Maybe it goes double.

He remembers hearing shouting, now that he thinks about it. From down the corridor.

"Maybe," he says. "I thought you were going to leave him on me."

"We're not stupid."

"I thought—"

Pippa's voice softens. "Stef, we wouldn't let him hurt you." And then she has to cover her mouth, but she can't hide the amusement in her voice. "Any more than you already hurt yourself."

He lets go of the edge of the cot, flexes his fingers, arches his back. Winces as pain from all over his upper body, but most particularly from the base of his right hand, reminds him of his mistake. Stupid, impulsive Stefan.

"I think I broke my thumb," he says, sheepishly holding it aloft.

"Did you hit him with your thumb inside your fist?"

"Yeah."

"That's not how you throw a punch."

"First time."

Pippa holds out a hand; her left to take his left, to pull him up off the cot without hurting him more than his inexperience and stupidity already has. He accepts it, and wobbles a little as he finds his feet again. Never had an adrenaline rush so intense; never had a comedown so draining.

"Come on," Pippa says, tugging on his wrist. "Let's get you back to your room."

"No punishment?"

"Just the bruises," she says, yanking on him again. This time, he follows. "He deserved that and ten times more."

He looks to the right as they walk down the main corridor. In the common room—locked; red LEDs on the biometrics—Aaron, loitering by the door, grins and gives him a thumbs up, pressing his hand against the glass. Stefan reaches out and touches the glass as he passes, returns Aaron's smile.

You okay? Aaron mouths, comically over-enunciating.

Stefan nods. He doesn't know if he is or not, but there's no sense in having Aaron worry. At least Declan's back in a cell. No more danger.

Aaron mouths something else, but it's too complex a sentence and Stefan is no lipreader, so he just shrugs. They can catch up later.

In his room, he staggers the last few steps and collapses onto the bed. Pippa closes the door behind them, pulls up the chair and drops onto it, slumping forward immediately, elbows on her knees, hands supporting her chin.

"What a day," she says.

"Are *you* okay?" Stefan asks. She's still red, although it's faded a bit. She's so pale-skinned that even the slightest hint of colour dominates her face.

"I'm supposed to be. I'm your sponsor. Your authority figure."

"Pippa—"

"Yes. I know. It's just…We ran the video for him. In the cell. Playing what he said, before you hit him. And I had to listen to it. Brought back a lot of memories, you know?"

Stefan shoves himself up painfully. Now the adrenaline's spent he feels sore and overworked, a machine without oil. It's worth the effort, though, to move closer to Pippa. To offer comfort, if she wants it.

"You can talk about it," he says, "if it would help."

Pippa sniffs grotesquely and reaches out to grip his fingers. She hooks hers into his, not so much holding hands as reinforcing the bridge between them, the one they've slowly been building over the past two weeks.

"I have a cousin," she says. Quiet, steady, talking almost to herself. "Three years older than me. We were always close; she made this, actually. It's one of a pair." She reaches over with a finger and spins her bracelet. "She always took care of me. Even when things got bad, she'd be there for me, to calm me down and talk me through it. But it all ended when she met a man a bit too much like Declan."

She pauses for a while. Chews on her lip, flexes the fingers connected to Stefan, testing their link. He waits. She doesn't need his contributions, just his presence.

"Some men have a way of making themselves a woman's whole world. And some women are vulnerable to it. My cousin, Sarah, she was definitely vulnerable to it. He was her first, and he used that to control her, to make her think that if he left she'd never find someone else. He hit her, and she didn't leave. Wouldn't leave." She shifts on the chair, moving her weight around. "He took her away from us a little at a time. Away from *me.* First, I got to see her only at the weekends. Then, once a month, maybe. And when I did see her, she was different. Reduced. Less and less and less of her every time. And she would have…bruises."

"I'm so sorry, Pip," Stefan whispers, and she tightens her fingers in his.

"It was all so stupidly predictable," she says. "We all saw him coming. Even me. He got angry at the slightest thing. A horrifying mirror, sort of, for me, although I didn't truly realise that until *much* later. But we all tried to tell her: me, my dad, her mum. We all tried. And Sarah, she'd say, 'It's only when he's had too much to drink,' or, 'He wants to change for me,' or, 'You don't understand him, but I do, because I love him.'" Pippa clenches her fingers and Stefan feels her nails dig into his skin. "One day," she continues, "she texted me. Said she was going to leave. But she didn't. It took us almost a week to find out why. Dad found out, in the end. Her boyfriend, he had raped her. He found her trying to leave. Trapped her. Hurt her. And when my dad beat him into the hospital, Sarah took *his* side. Testified against my dad. Prison for six months." She rubs at her eyes with her free hand. Her makeup is a wreck. "All for a monster who took advantage of her kindness and her naïveté and her terror of being alone. A monster who hurt her and hurt her and hurt her, because he never cared enough to stop."

"Is she okay now?" Stefan asks.

She sniffs again. "I don't know!" she says. Too loud. Too raw. "She moved away with him. Left me all alone. Left me with no-one. Left me to find out I was seventeen and had no real friends. You know how lonely you get when someone you're that close to just leaves? You find out that you don't know how to function without them. You don't know how to talk to people. You barely know how to live. And if you're like me, and you get angry a lot, without her there, it gets out…" She shakes her head, and continues, rather more brightly, "So I came here. Started fresh. And now I sponsor. Terribly, apparently."

"You're doing great. Really."

She looks at him, smiles. "I still don't understand you, Stef," she says, freezing his heart for a moment before she continues, "but it doesn't matter. I know you're not like him. At this point, I think that's all I need to know."

She keeps smiling at him, looking for someone in him that he hopes he can be for her. He leans forward, using their entwined fingers to pull her closer, slowly, making a request out of it. She answers by matching him, stepping off the chair and onto the mattress next to him. As they embrace, as he holds her, as she leans on his shoulder and cries gently, he thinks he can see her whole life:

A troubled girl, closer with her cousin than anyone else, suddenly alone. She seeks a new start, leaves home for Saints, and loses control of the anger her cousin and maybe her father helped her manage. She takes out her misery on people or things she shouldn't, and gets picked up by Dorley. And wears around her wrist every day the remembrance of her cousin, of her grief.

Stefan grieves, too, for the person she might have been had she been given the chance to heal at her own pace.

Pippa pulls away, borrows a tissue, dabs at her eyes and grimaces at the dark makeup left behind. Stefan has to make himself remember that his imagined younger Pippa is not, in fact, a girl. Because she wasn't always like this: that younger, broken, angry Pippa was a boy, a boy whose name he'll never know, and whose path to redemption was decided for him by someone else. Baffling, because she seems so complete. But fragile, today. The cracks showing on traumas that, whatever else happened to her here, never quite healed.

Fuck Declan for triggering her memories. When he washes out, which he probably will, Stefan hopes it fucking *hurts.*

"Stef?" Pippa says.

"Oh," he says, "sorry. Got caught up in my head for a second there."

"I know." She taps him on the forehead with her free hand. "I know what that looks like on you. If you're back in the land of the living…?" She pauses and he nods. "I asked if it's okay if I stay here a little while."

"Sure," he says, and they separate. Pippa finishes wiping her face, using some of his moisturiser as makeshift makeup remover. Stefan distributes pillows around so they can sit in their usual position, propped up against the wall, facing the computer. "What was that movie you were talking about?"

"*Legally Blonde?*" Pippa says. Without her makeup she looks strangely young; that might be why she wears it so heavily.

"That's the one."

"It's a classic."

"So, show me!"

She finds some energy for the first time since she came in, grabbing his phone off the bedside table before swinging back onto the mattress next to him. She sits closer than usual, shifting her pillow along, and scrolls through the PC's media library on the phone. When she starts the movie, she folds her arms around her belly. Her elbow touches Stefan's, and he maintains the contact.

The movie is ridiculous. Fun, though. And clearly something they both needed.

About an hour in she pauses it for a toilet break, locking down all the other doors so she can use the basement bathroom without one of the boys walking in on her.

"Come with me?" she says.

"Are you sure?"

"I feel kind of antsy being down here alone. Even with all the doors locked."

"I know the feeling."

She takes his hand and leads him out of his room, down the corridor. Stefan has the strangest feeling that he's being conspired with, like they're two kids in a vintage comic strip, sneaking down to steal cookies from the kitchen.

In the bathroom, he leans against the wall that backs onto the shower annexe while she closes herself in a cubicle and sits down.

"Thanks for this, Stef," she says, echoing a little.

"No problem."

"I feel stupid for letting him get to me like that. Declan, I mean."

"I get it," Stefan says. "I mean, not in the same way. But he set something off in me. Like I said, I've never hit anyone before."

She laughs. "You are the least toxic person we've ever had down here, I swear."

"Hey," he says, "what's going to happen to him?"

"I actually don't know. At the very least he'll be kept in the cell for the time being. He's been nothing but trouble since he got here, and your safety will be valued considerably higher than his freedom." She coughs delicately. "His relative freedom, anyway."

"That's a relief. We were making these ridiculous plans to stay together all the time, in case he followed up on his threats. We were even going to piss as a group! I wasn't looking forward to getting up every forty-five minutes so Will could drain the snake. For such a big boy he has a really small bladder."

Pippa flushes the toilet. "When did you make this plan?" she asks, emerging from the stall.

"Earlier on in my room, after Declan made his entrance. We all crammed in there like sardines to strategise. And, uh, get yelled at by Aaron."

"Who did? Will?"

"Me. Apparently I've been pushing him too hard about his dick pics."

Pippa doesn't say anything else until she's finished washing and drying her hands. "Listen, Stef," she says, "can we finish the movie another time? I need to, um, check in with Maria and Aunt Bea. Get the whole post-debacle debrief."

"Oh. Yeah. Sure."

She steps forward, takes his hand again. "Thanks again, Stef, for helping me. I really needed it. I know I should have been helping *you*, but—"

"No problem," he repeats with a smile, and squeezes her hand.

She returns both gestures, then turns and skips out of the bathroom, in an obvious hurry.

Back in his room, Stefan closes down the movie player, puts on some quiet music, and lies down, closing his eyes and letting his mind go blank.

He's okay. Pippa's okay. Declan's in the cell again. Stefan's bruises will heal. It's all over; normality, or what passes for normality down here, can return at its own pace.

***

It takes three cups of tea. Christine goes with Paige to make the second and third, unable to stomach the thought of leaving her side, and stands on the other side of the second-floor kitchen, looking out at the woods while the kettle boils. The November cold has set in, and the trees are brittle. By the third cup, they're standing closer together.

There's a lot of ground to cover. A lot of explaining to do. Paige wouldn't initially move from her position by the door, a place from which she could bolt if she needed to, and cradled that first mug of tea as if it was her only source of heat. As Christine's story continued, Paige moved to the sofa, to sit next to her.

For a moment, Christine remembers Paige before she was Paige: scared, angry, far too thin, and ready to batter down any obstacle she couldn't run from.

"I'm sorry, sweetheart," she whispers. Paige takes both hands in hers, shows her a smile that might shatter, and that's all the reply Christine needs. She cries. Falls into Paige, forces her to catch her. She knows it's her fault, that it's Paige who deserves comfort, but the weight of her mistakes has fallen upon her and it's impossible not to collapse under it.

In Paige's arms, she shakes.

After a while, fingers tangle in her hair. Paige carefully and slowly runs her hands from Christine's temple to the back of her neck, smoothing out the locks. Every stroke thaws the fear that's kept Christine frozen in place. Eventually her tears dry, but when Paige hooks her fingers back around Christine's neck so she can draw back, meet her eyes, and kiss her forehead once, twice, Christine weeps anew.

She hasn't lost her.

"Paige?" she says, her voice unsteady and wet.

"Christine," Paige says, "it's okay."

"It is?"

"I won't say I'm not hurt. But if there's one thing in the world I don't want, it's to lose you again."

Christine squeaks Paige's name and dives back into her. She makes the only promise she can under the circumstances: she'll never again be so stupid.

And Paige will never lose her again. Old ladies together.

Their third mugs are still warm when they retreat from their embrace. Paige takes a heavy drink from hers, deliberately puncturing the gravity of the moment with appalling slurping sounds and making Christine laugh.

"God," Christine says, "I feel like this is the first chance I've had in a month to catch my breath. Between Stef, Aunt Bea, makeup practice, schoolwork, shopping, clubbing…it's been non-stop. And that's not an excuse for not telling you," she adds quickly. "It's just—"

"I know. Don't forget how well I know you." Paige grins, her slightly elongated canines cheekily resting on her lower lip. "You don't plan; you react. And with Abby barely around and Indira out of the loop, you've been reacting on your own, every time." She tucks a finger under Christine's chin. "But you're not on your own anymore. No more rash decisions, okay?"

"Okay," Christine says, feeling the pressure of Paige's finger against her jaw.

"And no more lies."

"No more lies."

Paige nods, sets down her empty mug, and draws Christine into her, wrapping long, lithe arms around her shoulders. "I love you, Christine," Paige says, and Christine has a moment to realise that this is the first time either of them has said it before she answers in kind, instinctively, finding it obvious, putting all her apologies and all her love into every little prayer she whispers into Paige's hair.

Eventually Paige releases Christine, each of them stealing kisses before they fall out of reach, collapsing into the cushions on opposite ends of the sofa, tired. Still holding hands.

They sit together for a while, reconnecting, Christine mostly stays quiet, not wanting to intrude on Paige's thoughts: she'll be sifting through the emotions raised in her today for a while yet. Paige isn't good with feeling abandoned or isolated, not after her parents, not after Aunt Bea locked her in her room for a week. Not after Christine left her last year for stupid reasons. Another wound on a girl more delicate than she makes herself seem.

So she lets her set the pace, gives her the time she needs, and holds in the voice that scolds her over and over for hurting Paige again. For almost ruining the best thing ever to happen to her, again. She's almost succumbed to her exhaustion and fallen asleep when Paige stirs.

"Just when I think this place can't get any weirder…"

Christine takes the cue. "Rule one: this place will always get weirder. That's why I don't bother adjusting to new normals anymore."

"Wise." Paige sits forward. "Show me."

"Hmm?"

"I want to see what you can do! Show me how you break into our systems. The cameras and everything."

"Oh," Christine says, "yeah. Definitely."

She sets the laptop up on top of the beanbag chair, drags it in front of the sofa so they can both see the screen without contorting themselves, and walks Paige through the software she cobbled together. As she goes through the basement cameras she drops in on Stef, who looks to be napping and thus taking Declan's return with more aplomb than Christine expected.

"I can't believe we finally hooked a girl," Paige says, peering at Stef. "That is, someone who knows she's a girl already," she adds, grinning. "A real-life, self-aware trans girl! What's she going to think of *us* when she moves upstairs?"

"Actually," Christine says with a shrug, "she already told me." She preens. "I'm 'surprisingly normal'."

"She must not know you that well, then." Paige leans over, kisses Christine delicately on the temple. "You're the furthest thing from normal. That's your appeal."

"I have an appeal?"

"Don't push it," Paige says, nudging Christine with her elbow. "You're cute, but you're not *that* cute."

Christine pushes it. "I'm not that cute?"

Paige giggles, pulls her in, kisses her again. "Fine. You're adorable."

Christine nuzzles her back, then remembers: "Oh, it's *he,* by the way. For Stef, I mean. *She* prefers *he,* for now. Just in case you ever meet her. Him! Fuck."

"That's odd."

"Right?"

"Shoe's on the other foot at last," Paige says. "Remember all your pronoun confusion back then? This is the universe getting you back for all those times you misgendered Vicky."

Christine snorts. "At least she stopped kicking me. I was worried I'd have a permanent limp before we even got out of the basement."

"I asked her to."

"Oh?"

"I knew you weren't being malicious. Just slow."

"Thanks, Paige."

On the screen, Stef sleeps. It's good to see him calm and untroubled, even if only when he's unconscious.

"I'm glad we're getting to do this," Paige says. "We should help more trans people."

"Preaching to the choir," Christine says, taking control again and flipping through the rest of the basement cameras, trying to get up to speed. Wait, that's weird… "Huh. Declan's back in a cell. He was out, right? Monica made a big fuss, Pippa panicked. He was definitely out."

Paige hovers her fingers over the trackpad. "Mind if I—?" Christine nods and gets out of the way, and Paige starts flipping through cameras with far more expertise than someone who's been exposed for only a few minutes to Christine's janky, home-built software should be able to manage. "Where's Pippa…?" Paige mutters to herself, and goes through the cameras above ground until she finds her.

Pippa's in the office, which is, apart from her, as empty as Christine would expect on a random Saturday afternoon. She's cross-legged on the floor next to an open filing cabinet, referencing something on her phone against a file she has open on her knees. She's running a finger down the printed text and whispering to herself, too quietly for the microphone to pick up.

"That's not good," Christine says, fighting against sudden shortness of breath for the third time today. The archives contain the original, largely non-redacted records on all Dorley graduates: the information considered important to have on file somewhere, but best not left lying around on an easily accessible server. Aunt Bea decided, long ago, that she didn't want the sponsors to be easily able to look up each other's pre-Dorley histories every time one of them irritated another at the breakfast table. But it's archival; there's nothing in there on Stef that Pippa doesn't already have access to from the comfort of her own bed. Which means she's looking for information on a graduate.

She's got to be looking into Melissa. Stef must have slipped up somehow, revealed too much on one of their cosy movie nights.

Shit!

"Is there a way to zoom in?" Paige says, looking over the controls.

"It's an optical zoom," Christine explains, balling her hand into a fist, "and an old camera. She'd hear the motor and know someone's watching her."

"Maybe we should— wait," Paige interrupts herself. "She's getting up."

They watch on the screen as Pippa lays out a few sheets of paper from the file, takes pictures with her phone, puts everything back in its proper place, and marches out of the room. Paige follows Pippa around the building with the cameras and Christine leans against her, borrowing some of her body heat and forcing breath into her lungs, one heave at a time.

Why can't things be normal for just one day?

***

Pippa wakes him from a dreamless sleep by sitting down heavily on the end of his bed and startling him back to consciousness. She throws her phone, unlocked and showing a paused video file, onto the mattress next to him. He blinks a few times, wishing for coffee or possibly something to hide behind—Pippa's face is absolutely still—until he starts getting his focus back.

"Who are you really, Stefan?" she says. He shakes his head, pretending not to understand the question, buying himself a little more time. He picks up the phone, squints at the screen, and drops it back onto the bed as he pushes up on his elbows, discards the sheets, and disentangles himself, ready to run, should he need to.

The question of *where* enters his head, but he ignores it. One problem at a time.

"You said you made a plan with the other boys," Pippa says, "and I might not be much of a sponsor but if *four* of you are doing things like meeting in a bedroom and making plans, then it felt like something someone might need to know about, and I figured it was better that I look into it first rather than have someone who doesn't know you and doesn't care about you stumble over the footage in the archive review. So I looked. And I heard that."

She nods at the phone. Stefan looks at it properly for the first time: the video is frozen on a top-down view of his room, earlier that day, with the four of them packed in. There he is, paused in the act of saying something, as difficult to look at as ever.

He looks at Aaron, instead. Fear clogs his throat: what could any of them have possibly said to upset Pippa so?

She reaches out and taps the screen.

"—the emotion we call friendship is queer or something. I've not been as close to anyone since Russ or Melissa."

"Oh, shit, are we finally getting your tragic backstory?"

"No. You're not—"

Another couple of taps to rewind the footage and show it again. Three times, before she scoops up her phone and drops it into her bag.

"Russ and Melissa," she says. "*Russ and Melissa, Stef!*"

"I know!" he says, making sure his arms are free in front of him, in case he needs to defend himself. Her shoulders are rising and falling too fast as she takes short, quick breaths. "I heard!"

"You have thirty seconds to tell me how you know Melissa, or I'm taking this straight to Aunt Bea." She's speaking levelly but every so often her control wobbles and a word hisses out through clenched teeth. He's never seen her like this.

He swings his legs out of bed, rests his hands in his lap. "I followed her here," he says, telling as little of the truth as he thinks he can get away with. It's not just his future on the line but Christine's, too. "To Saint Almsworth, not to Dorley. We were close. She disappeared when I was young, but I never believed she was dead, the way everyone else did. I was convinced if I came here, if I attended Saints, I might be able to find out what happened to her. But I never did, and I— I got depressed, started behaving badly—"

"Stef," Pippa says, looking right through him; hearing him but not seeing him, "stop lying."

"I'm not—!"

Pippa punches the mattress, making Stefan jump. "Her name wasn't always Melissa and you *fucking* know it!" She whips her head around. "I know you knew her before she was Melissa, from her file. Your name shows up in there as much as her brother's. But she—*he*—vanished from your life. So. How. Do. You. Know. Her?" She emphasises the pronoun by slapping the mattress again.

He works his mouth uselessly, silently, swallowing down the rushing in his ears. That was probably the worst mistake he could have made. He's too damn used to thinking of Melissa as Melissa! A favourite phrase of his mother's drops into his head: *Engage brain before opening mouth.* And of his father's: *Stupid boy!*

"I know," he says, editing his story again. "I'm sorry. It's just that I got used to thinking of her that way. Years ago, I saw her, out near the supermarket. She seemed to recognise me and I recognised her.

She dropped her debit card and when I picked it up, I saw her name. I was never completely sure she was the same person as Mark, but it was better than believing he was dead."

"What are you saying?" Pippa says, her eyes focusing on him again at last.

"When I saw Aunt Bea upstairs, Abby was there. She said she was in the programme herself, and that's when I finally put it together. That Melissa was Mark, that she had a difficult transition, that she was brought here for the same reason as Abby, and—"

"Shut! Up!" Pippa yells, throwing her bag across the room, switching so quickly from stillness to violence that Stefan hiccups in surprise. She stands, fists clenched by her sides, quivering with rage, a wire of uncoiled energy with nowhere to strike. "You keep *lying!* I can see it in your *eyes!* You're panicking, trying to find a version of the story that will make me *go away!* Jesus, Stef!" She kicks out at the chair, knocks it over, starts pacing in the tiny area of floor between the door and the bed. "I thought we were close, Stef! I thought we were friends!"

It comes out before he can stop it. "Then why do you keep lying to *me* about the injections?" he shouts.

Pippa freezes. Stefan, too.

Stupid boy.

"What do you mean?" Pippa says, quietly, slowly. Almost inaudibly.

Stefan reaches up with a stiff hand and presses hard on his chest, massaging movement back into his body. It's obvious there's no point in continuing the charade any longer: she has more than enough information, one way or another, to get to the truth, or something close to it, with or without him. And if he tells her now, himself, in his own words, he has at least a chance at regaining some of her trust.

"I know about the estradiol, Pippa," he says.

She doesn't say anything. Doesn't move.

"It's what you say— what you've been *told* to say is a vitamin injection. Once a week. It works with the implant in the stomach, which you'll move us off before too long."

"What else do you know?" she whispers.

"I know *how* you move us off the implant."

Pippa, a marionette with her strings cut, trips towards the bed. Stefan intercepts her and helps her sit, piles cushions behind her, gently lowers her until her head and neck are supported.

"You know everything?" she whispers.

"More or less."

"And when you say you know what comes after the implant, you mean the orchi." It's not a question.

"Yes."

"I didn't know how I was going to deal with that," Pippa says, glassy-eyed. "I didn't know how I was going to send you into that room, knowing what's going to happen to you."

Stefan takes a risk: he holds her hand. She grips it like a life preserver.

"It's okay," he says.

"It's not okay. It's barbaric."

"You survived it."

She sits halfway up, stares at him, and then her energy leaves her and she slumps again. "Jesus," she says. "You really do know everything."

"Look," he says, "Pippa, you don't have to worry about that." He finds himself smiling. It's different, coming out to her; he's had weeks to think about it, weeks to be certain that, finally, he knows himself. And Pippa's not a near-stranger like Christine was, in those early days. She's his friend. "The truth is, I really did seek this place out because of what happened to my childhood best friend. She became Melissa; I wanted that for myself. I needed it. I'm transgender, Pippa. I'm a girl. Or I'm supposed to be."

It's like she forgets how to breathe for a moment. She can't take her eyes off him, stills completely, her only movement in her knuckles as her grip on him tightens. "This isn't a joke, is it?" she whispers.

"No."

There's a horrible silence, and then laughter bursts out of her like a firecracker. She rolls over, wraps herself suddenly around him, encloses him with her whole body. All her energy directed into holding him tight, the way Abby did. The way no-one else has for a long time. "Stef!" she says, pulling away, cheeks flushed, hysterical. "You're a girl! My goodness, Stef. Wow. God. Stef. What the hell? You're a— you're a flipping *girl*."

"Yep," he says, shrugging.

"You could have told me."

"I'm sorry about that."

"No," she says, "it's okay. I understand why you didn't." She rolls onto her back again and empties her lungs with a long, coarse, descending whistle. "Wait; you didn't tell anyone about this place, did you?"

"No. No-one."

"Good. Because *that* was a scary thought." She chews on her lip for a second. "I had sudden visions of police showing up, all of us being dragged away in cuffs..."

"I wouldn't do that to you. Even if I, uh, don't exactly agree with everything that happens here."

"It's worth it in the end."

"Clearly."

"I still don't understand, though," Pippa says slowly, cracking her knuckles and resting her hands on her stomach, looking for a moment like a corpse prepared for a funeral; she's still too pale. "How did you find out about this place? I mean, I guess you staged that thing outside, with the girl screaming, and you passing out in the flower bed, but who was she? Stef, if you have an accomplice, we need to know, before—"

He's saved from having to think of a new lie, a new way to keep Christine out of it, by the whistling of the speaker set into the strip above the door.

"What—?" Pippa has time to say.

Christine's voice, a whisper loud enough to fill the room, says, "Pippa, it was me."

***

Christine hasn't been back up to the roof since the night she met Naila and Ren, who are now staples of Vicky and Lorna's social group and joining the clamour for Christine one day to play *Bloodborne,* if only because Naila thinks Eileen the Crow is hot. It was much warmer then. She shivers inside her jacket and wishes for the wisdom of Paige, who pulled on a calf-length cardigan and a sleek, double-breasted coat and looks amazing, despite her layers; Christine, in her huge, puffy jacket, looks like an M&M's mascot, and is still cold.

She did little talking in the end. Her intervention gave Stef permission to tell the whole of the truth, so he did, in detail, holding Pippa's hand and laughing with her about some of the sillier parts. When he was done, Pippa thanked him, nodded up at the camera, and left. They tracked her through the building on the cameras and when it became clear she was headed for the roof, they followed, at speed.

Pippa's not leaning dramatically over the railing, as Christine had feared. She's not even near the edge; a week ago the fifth floor had a party up here and left behind a tarp hung over the central gravel garden and an assortment of old couches. Pippa's pulled the clear plastic off one of them and she's idly playing with a loose thread on its arm, staring at nothing.

Paige gives Christine's hand a final squeeze and passes Pippa the spare coat she brought. Wordlessly Pippa accepts it, struggles into it without getting up, and slumps back into the cushions. Paige sits next to her. Christine, not wanting to crowd her, sits cross-legged on the couch opposite, not bothering to remove the plastic cover. The roof is both empty and lacks microphones, so they have more privacy here than almost anywhere else in the hall.

"Hi," Christine says.

Pippa turns red eyes on her. "You know," she says, "I'm almost too relieved about Stef to be angry at you. Almost." She laughs, hoarse. "She's not going to be mutilated. She's going to be saved. And," she adds, rolling her eyes, "I know, that's the point—all of us were saved—but she wants it. She *needs* it. This might—" she coughs, her voice straining against a dry throat, "—be a good year for me after all. I get to do something unequivocally good, not just good-with-an-asterisk, like I expected."

"Good-with-an-asterisk is still good," Paige says.

"Pretty flipping big asterisk, though," Pippa says.

"True."

"Pippa—" Christine starts.

"No. I still want to say my bit. You lied to me, Christine. All that stuff with the letters, the manipulation, the whole, 'Oh, I just had a great idea about how to deal with Stef!' thing…And that's not even why I'm angry at you, really. You made me think I was your friend, Christine."

"You *are* my friend!"

"Maybe that's how it turned out. Maybe that's how it *will* turn out, again. But you need to give me some time, okay?"

Christine nods. "Okay."

"I get it," Pippa says. "Stef is…I don't know. She makes me want to help her. Always did, ever since I stopped screwing my eyes shut to yell at her, trying my hardest not to see who was really there. I understand why you did what you did. But just…time."

"Time. Of course." A much more generous reaction than Christine deserves, probably.

Paige says, "Stef likes to be called *he*."

"I know," Pippa says. "I'm not doing that. I haven't told her, not yet, but it's my price: no self-pitying denial of your own gender, or I'll get *really* annoying." She smiles, rubs at the corner of her mouth where the skin on her lip has split. "Without the guilt, without worrying I'm going to hurt her in a way she can't handle, I'm free! She has *no* idea what she's unleashed."

"A force of pure meddling," Paige says.

"When we're alone together, she's going to be a *she*, and I'm going to make sure she knows it."

"That's probably exactly what Stef needs," Christine says.

"Damn right. And at least it all makes sense now," Pippa adds, rolling her head around in the couch cushion and messing up her hair. "Even the way she's been bugging Aaron about his crap."

"I think Stef's trying to beat us to it," Christine says. "Win a moral victory. Reform Aaron before we can turn him into a girl."

"No. I mean, that might be a tiny part of it, but I've seen them together. In person, not just over the cameras. She *likes* him. And she can't stand having a friend with such a glaring moral blind spot. So she's been working on him, bit by bit. There might even have been a bit of a breakthrough, earlier today."

"Wow. Go Stef."

"We need a plan," Paige says, leaning forward on her knees and interposing herself between Christine and Pippa. "There are four of us who know now, including Abby, so we need to decide how to move forward."

"Uh," Christine says, nodding towards the door down to the dorms, behind Paige and Pippa, "that might be a moot point." The door's swung open and spat out Maria, who frowns and hugs her belly as the cold air hits her.

"Girls," Maria says as she approaches, and Pippa and Paige twist in their seats to look at her, "can you give me a few moments alone with Christine, please?"

***

Stefan's put some quiet music on—another of Pippa's playlists—and is tapping at his phone, starting and restarting another diary entry to send up to Christine. He wonders how she's doing, now that her part in all this has been laid completely bare to Pippa, warts and all, rather than the edited, sanitised form they supplied to Abby. Pippa, for all that she was happy not to have to lie to him anymore, seemed pretty angry with her.

He shrugs. Nothing he can do about it, except perhaps to ask Pippa to give Christine a chance. She didn't ask for him to come barrelling into her life, and he's demanded an awful lot of her.

The music is suddenly obliterated by the noise of the lock cycling. Stefan wastes a whole second panicking. Quickly he pauses the song and throws his phone under the pillow while he wonders who it could be. Even Maria knocks before she comes in these days; perhaps it's Monica or one of Adam or Will's sponsors?

No. It's much worse.

It's Beatrice, custodian of Dorley Hall and the woman with, ultimately, the power of life and death over him and almost everyone else he knows. She takes up position between the door and the bed, arms folded over her chest. Blocking the exit. She lets the silence roll out until it threatens to suffocate him and then says, with a pleasant but deliberately neutral tone, "Hello again, Stefan. Or would you, perhaps, prefer Stefanie?"

Yeah. Okay. *Now* it's over. Her voice reminds him of Pippa's, when she's angry. It's too level. Too controlled.

"Just Stef is fine," he says, struggling to speak through a throat suddenly thickened by fear.

Beatrice hooks the chair with a foot and drags it over, sits daintily on it, still positioned such that Stefan, should he wish to leave, would have to go straight through her, would not be able to open the door without first shoving her out of the way. "Well then! *Stef.*" She says his preferred name in the manner of a waiter suggesting the best and most expensive item on the menu. "I've had the most intriguing evening. Maria came to me with a problem: we've been used." She smiles. "What do you think we should do about that?"

His breath freezes in his throat, and when he tries to speak he manages only a strangled, undignified noise.

"A short while ago, Pippa—wonderful girl; very loyal—left your room and headed straight to the roof. Didn't even stop at her room to pick up a coat, and it is *such* a cold evening. Unusual behaviour, to say the least. So, naturally, she looked into it, and do you know what we discovered? One might term it a conspiracy! Between you and Christine. To hide from—"

"Please," Stefan says, pushing the words out, "this isn't Christine's fault. I forced this on her. Don't punish her."

"*Relax,* child. Christine may well have been running around right under my nose for the past month, lying and scheming and making an enormous mess that she will, I guarantee, be required to clean up, but she appears to have acted entirely out of compassion and concern. She protected this house, she protected this programme; she even tried to protect *you* from yourself. Her most major mistake was that she didn't come to me immediately, but I can understand that. I am, I've been told, rather intimidating. Frankly, I'm quite proud of her. So don't worry about Christine." She smiles her quick, predatory smile again. "Worry about yourself."

He coughs when he tries to speak, and Beatrice rolls her eyes.

"For goodness' sake," she mutters, and pulls a bottle of water out of her bag, throwing it onto the mattress next to Stefan. "I'm not *that* scary. Drink. I haven't come here to punish *you,* either." She rolls her eyes at his confusion. "Yes, yes, I'm upset with you, Stef, *obviously.* But we can help each other, as long as you abide by some new rules. Drink!"

Stefan obeys, almost unable to feel the lukewarm water in his throat. What new rules?

"Now," Beatrice says, settling back on the chair, making herself look comfortable somehow on the horrible, rattly thing, "before we get to the point, you need to understand something of how the programme works." She pauses for a reaction; Stefan nods. "It works because we, all of us, believe in it. We get up every morning and we go to bed every night secure in the knowledge that the suffering we inflict is temporary, that it is for a purpose; that, ultimately, we are *helping* those we appear, superficially, to be hurting. If we didn't believe in the work, we could not continue. Nevertheless, it is *work,* and it is *difficult,* especially for thoughtful young women like Pippa, who do not relish the hardships we must inflict on the young people in our care. I understand you are au fait with our methods? Then you are aware that, not too far in the future, you and the boys will undergo orchiectomies? Good. I would like you to imagine how Pippa, sweet, kind Pippa, would have felt, escorting you into that room."

"I didn't—"

"I am *not* finished!" She's suddenly a teacher scolding a disruptive child, and Stefan instinctively retreats farther into the pillows stacked up at the end of the bed. "Every hour she has spent in your company has been coloured by the knowledge that she has had to lie to you, to maintain your ignorance so that your reform can proceed in the manner that it should! And that means sleepless nights! Stressful days! Endless worry about how you will respond to the treatments! It is a *considerable* burden, and she took it up *for you!* You understand this, yes? So *how dare you* inflict that suffering upon her for *no purpose!*"

"I didn't want to!" Stefan yells, finding the tiniest crack between sentences. "And I was trying to be her friend!"

"For your own sake! You offloaded all the responsibility for your life, your transition, onto her, and you didn't even marshal the sense God gave you to tell her the truth." She leans forward, glares at him. "That is *supremely* selfish."

Screw it. "I'm selfish?" Stefan says, gathering himself, pushing up out of the pillows. "*I'm* selfish? You're sitting on the mother lode of boutique transition services and you're— you're *hoarding* them for your little pet project! Do you know how many trans women would kill for this? How many have died for the *lack* of it?"

"*Yes!*" she yells, and pauses, finger raised, reconsidering, the anger vanishing from her face. "Yes," she repeats, and sits delicately back on the chair. "Of course I do, Stef. I'm…I apologise for shouting."

"Um," Stefan says, unable to keep up with Beatrice's mood, "what's happening here?"

"I'm sure we do look selfish," Beatrice says, sounding almost wistful. "But there are reasons. I expected you to have intuited them," she adds, with a little of her former sharpness. "Dorley Hall has a history, and an awful lot of graduates. For the most part, they've melted seamlessly back into the world from which they were taken, but they all share a common point of origin: this house. Our shared vulnerable point. And while I would deeply love to provide our care to those who would request it as well as require it, I inherited a responsibility when I took over this house, a responsibility to everyone who passes through our doors, to protect their new lives and keep their old secrets. And it is an unfortunate reality of transgender medical care in this country that *any* facility which falls outside the jurisdiction of the NHS comes under sustained and hostile investigation."

"That can't be true."

"Ask Pippa to look it up for you. Or do it yourself when we remove the restrictions on your computer. We can give you lists of names: providers of private transgender medical care who have been *hounded*. It is an inevitability for those who would follow that calling. If one of the cockroaches who scurry around this country's inhumane mental health system doesn't report you, then one of the professional busybodies who comprise most of our national press will run a piece on you for pennies, and before you know it, you're under investigation. I've seen it happen every time—" she slaps her fist into her open palm to emphasise each word, "—a new practice starts. Five years, they last. Ten, if they're extraordinarily clever or taking advantage of some loophole. And we *can't* withstand that kind of scrutiny. Every one of us would be exposed. Many would go to prison."

"I don't understand how you're even still here," Stefan says, "if you're so vulnerable."

"Because we are a family, Stef. We take care of each other. We are reliant upon each other, even those of us who leave and never return. We provide stipends, references, documentation. A *complete* new life, but one that has its foundations here, at Dorley Hall. If the hall falls, everyone falls with it. We are, I admit, a house of cards, but thus far we are a resilient one."

Of course. It makes a kind of sense: an interdependent group, all complicit. And all made to start their lives again from scratch, at Dorley, to find new family and friends here and only here; if you get it into your head to turn on the others, who do you have left?

Forced feminisation on the honour system.

Stefan's still certain they could find ways to treat trans people at Dorley without risking the safety of the existing graduates, if they applied the same effort and enthusiasm to the process that they currently reserve solely for growing breasts on unwilling men, but Beatrice is clearly unreceptive. She's had years—decades—to stew in her own bullshit; the chances of him arguing her around are slim.

But it's slowly sinking that he's not actually doomed. She talked about "new rules" he'll have to follow, and this conversation has gone on far longer than it would have if she planned simply to wash him out. The realisation is almost calming. And it means he'll have time to work on her. To work on the others. Make some suggestions, here and there. Improve things, maybe.

There's something he has to know, though: "Why? Why do this to men in the first place?"

She smiles. "I admit, it's unorthodox. And the series of events by which we came to it, even more so. But it works. You've met countless examples of that. And it's necessary."

"No," he says, "I don't accept that. Look at Pippa, right? She was just this lonely kid, struggling with loss and grief and immense family turmoil, but she makes *one* mistake and she gets kidnapped, gets slung down here. I can't bring myself to believe she deserved it."

"You know her so well, after a month?"

"I think so."

"You don't even know what she did."

"It doesn't matter. You never gave her a chance to change!"

"This *was* her chance. And she took it. Struggled with it, yes, for a while—" a smile flickers across her face, and Stefan almost doesn't want to think about what she might be remembering, "—but she prevailed."

"But—"

"Christine," Beatrice says, counting on her fingers. "Abigail. Monica. Edith. Tabitha. Every other sponsor you've met down here. All of them, at one time, were like Adam, William, or your Aaron. Some of them were like Oliver or Raphael or Martin. All of them reformed. All of them happy."

"They couldn't have been happy as men?"

"I don't see how that matters."

Stefan laughs, bitter. "I think it matters a lot!"

"You think William's happiness mattered when he found out his younger brother was gay, and beat him? When subsequently he took out his guilt on other students? You want to send him back out there, to spiral, to hurt people, to find his *happiness* on the bodies of those weaker than him?"

"But—"

"Or what about your Aaron? Did *his* happiness matter, when he inflicted himself on women who barely even knew him?"

"He *does* regret that," Stefan protests.

"Right now, he regrets it, but purely because you require it of him, and you are his only friend, and he's stuck down here with you. Do you think your…tinkering will last, out there?"

"It might."

Beatrice laughs. She pulls another water bottle from her bag and takes a long drink from it, making a show of looking around the room. "It won't," she says. "Are you familiar with Charlotte Church?"

"No. One of yours?"

"Not one of ours, no. She is a singer, one from, I now realise, considerably before your time. Goodness, but you all get younger every year." She sighs, and blows a strand of hair out of her face. "Charlotte Church was—is—a Christian singer. She became famous in the nineties for her angelic voice and sweet manner. Famous enough that it was, for a time, quite difficult to relax in front of the television on a Sunday evening without encountering mention of her." Beatrice grins. "That's something we used to do, by the way: switch on the television and watch whatever was put in front of us. I know that's hard for someone your age to understand."

"Yeah, actually."

"Charlotte Church was eleven when she made her debut," Beatrice continues, "and she became a constant presence in the media. A mascot for chaste, Christian—and very, very white—innocence. And then, four years later, when she was just fifteen, our largest national newspaper published a huge photograph of her, taken from an angle that emphasised her chest, above the headline, 'She's a big girl now'."

"That's…disgusting."

"Precisely! Here was a girl, fifteen years old, known to us all since she was eleven, and the publishers of our largest newspaper were so eager to post pictures of her developing bosom that they were unable to make themselves wait until she was an adult. That is the environment in which we all have to live, Stef; the sea in which we swim."

Driftwood, Stefan remembers. Driftwood in the ocean. "What are you getting at?"

"In this country we prioritise—celebrate—the objectification of women while simultaneously condemning and even legally punishing women who have the nerve to take their lives or their sexuality into their own hands. Women speak out about the abuse they've received and are pilloried on television. Sex workers are forced to operate at great personal risk to themselves while the men and women who run our media salivate over *children.* At every level the message is the same: *women's bodies are not women's property.* How do you expect a young man who has become like the men we induct into our programme to reform in the outside world, when it is run by and for those exactly like him? Men like your Aaron *infest* our culture, and at every level they grant permission to themselves and those around them to be as repulsive as they please. It is easy to be an abusive man in Great Britain, Stef. Horrifyingly easy. And it escalates with privilege. I believe Aaron himself sidestepped responsibility for his repeated exposures, did he not? Excused consequences on account of being wealthy, white, and male?"

Stefan nods. He's been searching for a counterargument, but all he has is *torture is wrong, actually.* Nothing in his education prepared him to have to support that statement, and in the face of the reminder that Will, his supposed ally against Declan, beat up his younger brother—and others besides, it sounds like—he's less sure than ever that he even wants to.

"Imagine returning Aaron, as he is now, to the world," Beatrice says. "Can you really guarantee that he wouldn't backslide? Renege on his meagre progress? In a country that elevates behaviour like his, excuses it, rewards it?"

"Okay," Stefan says, "maybe not. But not all men are like that—" He groans as Beatrice interrupts him; did he really just pull a *not all men?*

"And that would be a good point if we had *all men* in our basement, Stef. We do not. We are selective." She leans forward, smiling gently, adopting the air of a concerned guidance counsellor. "Stef, if I may be blunt—and everyone around me is, so I believe I shall indulge—you are a woman. You have always been a woman, whatever your external appearance might suggest. You have, therefore, experienced masculinity, and particularly the kind of grasping, possessive, abusive masculinity that we as a society have decided is appropriate to teach our young men, as nothing but a curse, correct? An unpleasant and often entirely irrational system of behaviour to which you have been expected to conform, and uphold in others."

"Um," Stefan says, trying to control his reaction to being called a woman, to having his womanhood recognised so casually, acknowledged so completely. "Yes, I suppose."

"Would you agree that your compliance with masculinity has been, shall we say, coerced? Not something you would have chosen for yourself?"

Stefan nods, and carefully avoids getting lost in memories.

"Then I suspect you will find it hard to believe how…seductive it can be," Beatrice says. "Imagine that you are a boy. Masculinity, as expressed by the patriarchy, all the way from the repulsive man who currently occupies the office of the prime minister down to your peers at school, your family, the men you see on the television and online, it tells you what you are. It dictates your behaviour, lays out the rules around which you must structure your life. But in return it offers *power.* Power over other men, should you make yourself strong enough; power over women, by default. 'You are strong,' it whispers to you, as you grow taller than the girls at your school. 'You are powerful,' it tells you, as you get into your first fight. 'You deserve her,' it insists, as you look at a pretty woman at a bar or in the street. And, to those who will listen, it says, 'Even if she refuses you, she is nonetheless yours. Take her!'" Stefan jumps a little when she raises her voice. "'Take her and do with her what you will, for it is your right.'"

"Most men, of course, are not so ruled by their desires that they will act on every impulse. And many men are capable of ignoring these messages entirely, filtering them, discovering a healthy masculinity inside the radioactive dust that infests our social atmosphere. But, as you have seen, there are men who are overwhelmed. Who are shaped by their masculinity so completely that there is practically no room inside them for anything else. They are…broken people. Excellent vessels for the—oh, what did that absurd scientist with the honey fixation call it?—the *meme* of masculinity. The infectious idea that burrows into the brain and takes over.

"The problem for these men is that masculinity—toxic masculinity, if you will; violent, virulent masculinity—is a seductive lover but an abusive husband. Once you are in its grip, you can never be strong enough, never exercise enough power, never hurt enough people. You find yourself trapped between two destinies.

"Some of these broken men, they despise themselves. They victimise others because they are too weak not to, and they loathe their weakness. Many of them manage to put up a front—brusqueness; belligerence; humour—but the self-hatred eats away at them, and eventually they will be destroyed by it, consumed by the parasite.

"Others become nothing but the violence. They have contempt for their victims. They admire only strength and cruelty. They are, essentially, monsters.

"The one who hates himself, who lives with the weakness and the guilt and the shame, even if he takes them out on others, he can be fixed, but only if he is willing properly to purge his masculinity. To confront his abuser. Extract his parasite. The monsters, however, are irredeemable, and must be dealt with accordingly." She rests her chin on her hand and drums her fingers against her lips. "The programme, in its early stage, is designed to tell us who among the boys we have taken in is a monster and who is a victim. Who is lost and who can be saved. And, to a lesser extent, who is malleable enough to accept the transformation and who is not. A difficult task at the best of times."

"One that I'm currently…complicating," Stefan says.

Beatrice laughs. "Your amateur meddling thus far has had little to no effect. But you can, I believe, be of use to us in the coming months."

Stefan coughs. "Of use to you?"

"Yes. And please don't let my pleasant manner deceive you into thinking you have room to decline. As I said: you used us. You used Pippa, particularly; made her into an accomplice in your torture. Made her *hurt* you. Made her stand there and watch as the nurse assaulted you. A very difficult weight to hang around the neck of someone as kind as she. That kind of carelessness comes with a price, Stef. You owe us. You owe Pippa. You owe *me*."

Lanced with guilt, Stefan nods.

"It won't be a difficult job," Beatrice assures him, returning to her earlier bright tones. "Mostly you'll carry on as you are now. And except as much as is required to keep up appearances, you'll be exempted from anything unrelated to your biomedical transition, which we will, of course, continue to provide for you, as we would have had your deception remained undiscovered."

"Thank you."

"You're quite welcome. But there will be times that are particularly difficult for the boys. The true onset of their second puberties, for example, and our surgical interventions."

"You mean, the castration."

"The orchiectomy, yes. And it is in those times that a positive example can work wonders. Someone who takes to the changes with, if not pleasure, then without the sense of apocalyptic doom that invades even those who are ultimately saved by our methods. Someone who can talk them through their feelings, help them to grow comfortable with their changing bodies. You'll be our Judas goat."

" 'Judas goat'?"

"It's an archaic term. Put simply, it is an animal, kept in comfort and trained to lead the other animals, with a minimum of panic, into the slaughterhouse."

"That's…startlingly appropriate, actually," Stefan says, prompting a rather less appropriate laugh from Beatrice.

"You are inside the boys' trust," she says, still smiling. "They view you as one of them, and as such they will accept reassurances from you that would sound empty and self-serving from the rest of us. I also suspect it's nothing you weren't planning to do already. Your empathy for these boys is commendable; I doubt you would be able to witness your Aaron, for example, in distress without attempting to help him."

"This is a lot to ask," Stefan says. "Staying quiet is one thing, but helping you mutilate these people…?"

"My dear Stef," Beatrice says, "I am not asking." She spreads out her hands. "These are the new rules. If you comply, you will live in comfort, your transition will be paid for, and you will exit this house with the same rights and privileges afforded to all our young women. If you do not comply, you will leave this place in the same manner as young Declan."

"Declan's washing out?"

"Yes. He is a rapist. An unrepentant and persistent one. By his own testimony he has damned himself. But that is beside the point: this is not a negotiation. You have no hand to play. Do you know how many boys have passed through this basement? Would you care to venture a guess at how many of them have never been seen again, in *any* form? Your disappearance, should it be required, would not present any difficulties at all. I don't like to *waste* people, Stef, but I do require your compliance. You have, ultimately, the same choice all our girls have to make, at one time or another: to accept my methods, or reject them."

Stefan forces a few breaths. Buries shaking hands in the folds of the duvet to keep from giving himself away. "That's no choice at all."

"Exactly," Beatrice says. "And relax! You're getting everything you wanted. So, Stef Riley, do we have your cooperation?"

Stefan, out of options and quite possibly out of his mind, shrugs. "I suppose we do."

There. Now he's complicit. Just like Christine.

"Magnificent." Beatrice brushes some imaginary crumbs off her skirt. "I'm looking forward to seeing how you turn out; you have such pretty features buried under there. And your progress through the programme and your influence on the boys will make for an interesting case study! Oh, and don't worry about the nurse. I'm grateful that you helped bring her to my attention. She won't be bothering anyone again, thanks to you."

"Um, what? What did you do to her?"

Beatrice contorts her mouth, like a smile. "I had her removed."

The implication is clear. Stefan bites the inside of his cheek for a second, and nods. Now he's complicit in that, too.

"Now, if that is all," Beatrice says, "you have a new future to prepare for and I have other tasks to accomplish tonight."

"Oh, yes, fine," Stefan says, hesitant, still imagining a dozen possible final fates for the nurse. "Um," he adds, sheepishly feeling like he should say something more, "thank you for the opportunity."

Beatrice stands, smooths out her clothes, and steps over to the bed. She holds out a hand and smiles a bland, corporate smile.

"Welcome to the team."

15
Simply Irresistible

30 JULY 1988 — SATURDAY

It's a dangerous thrill, being outside, and still rather a novelty. She can't keep doing this forever: they fixed the rusted lock on the conservatory door and they replaced the loose pane in the front hallway. Today she took the back route, slipping out of the window halfway up the rear stairs and dropping onto the water tank, and while she doesn't think anyone saw her, it's very nearly the last escape route she has left, and every one has an expiry date.

Better make tonight count, then.

At least it gets easier every time. When she first struck out on her own, months ago now, she was so scared she could barely meet the gaze of the girl behind the bar in the Student Union, had to keep looking away, hiding her face with her fingers, in case her recent past was somehow obvious, was written on her skin. And it is, in burns and scars and in the very shape of her, but she dresses to hide the obvious marks and, as for the rest of it, she thinks she looks more or less like a girl. Enough to pass. Enough to start learning to get by with smiles and nods and bashful looks. Enough that when she ties up her hair and exposes her slender neck, she's treated like something beautiful; of such experiences a facsimile of confidence is born.

There was a time she thought she could never leave, when she believed her fate lay entirely in the hands of her captors. Now…Now she feels almost ready. Now she can look up at the open sky almost without fear.

She smiles at a couple of girls and they greet her in kind, easing the extant remnants of her anxiety. It's exciting to be normal, and it's all good practice for the day she finally follows through on the promises she makes herself, takes up the handful of stolen coins and paper money she's hidden away, and leaves, never to return.

A light breeze picks up as she passes the old Chemistry building and she laughs, wants to dance with the wind, and so she does: she skips, spins, lets it billow out her sleeves and play with her hair, and when the brief burst of energy it granted her fades, she leans for a moment against the wall, breathes it in, fills herself with it, relishes it, delights in the grassy odour it picked up from the mown college green and the damp edge it skimmed off the lake. The wind feels alive; nothing like the perfume-clogged haze of the dining hall, which primes her for humiliation and degradation and cigarettes stubbed out on her back; nothing like the stale, bitter air of the bedrooms, which invades her dreams and tastes of innumerable nights spent underground, carrying in its stulted grip the bloody remnants of every wound inflicted upon her.

She's supposed to be serving drinks tonight—waiting on those old bitches and trying not to choke on their stink, accepting from them without complaint any vice they might choose to indulge upon her body—but the last time she got out she found a flyer and for the whole week she's thought about nothing but the party by the lake. Music! Dancing! Girls drink for free! She's not invited, she's not a student, she's not even a woman, but for one evening she can play at being all three, for a while.

The lakeside promenade doesn't belong to the university and doesn't share its character. It reminds her instead of the places she grew up, all of which came into her life aged and shabby and growing more decrepit every year, bricks crumbling dusty into the weeds. Iron posts strung together with chain follow the riverbank to an overgrown car park and a squat little building, remnant of a gentlemen's club that closed down in the early seventies and which these days is held together more by dirt than mortar. It is, by virtue of being the last plot of land in the area that hasn't been lavished with money and inflicted with architecture, undeniably the coolest place around.

Music and raised voices drift towards her as she descends.

Someone's rigged up a gadget that broadcasts the signal from a tape deck out through a portable radio, and as she walks, she passes car after car, tuned in and bellowing through their open doors a song she doesn't recognise, surrounding the makeshift dancefloor with music. There's a bar set up against the outside wall of the gentlemen's club, and she pushes through a throng of drinkers to get there, borrowing the swagger and confidence she's seen in the best of the real girls, and waves to catch the attention of one of the men handing out bottles.

So many people!

She wanted to wear a dress for this, but the box of scavenged outfits she's spent the last year carefully assembling had none that fit, so she's doing her best in a denim skirt and a cream top with loose sleeves and a scoop neck that sits wide on her shoulders and makes her breasts look fantastic.

That's what Val used to say, anyway, in the moments they stole together. If she could see her now…

So many men!

Back at the house they regularly throw her at men and she's tried to enjoy it, she really has, and she's gotten pretty good at faking it. But here, where her choice actually matters, she turns away three guys in the first ten minutes, and stops disguising her irritation after the second one. All she wants is to have a drink, listen to music and pretend to be someone she's explicitly forbidden from becoming; how hard is that to understand? So when the fourth guy comes strolling up, she's ready to yell at him, to take out the last four years on him. Before she can, a girl, walking over with a ready-made sneer, takes the sleeve of his shirt between two delicate fingers and tells him in no uncertain terms to piss off.

He protests.

"She's not interested, mate!" the girl says, making shooing motions.

He leaves them alone and she smiles, nervous.

"I'm right, though, aren't I?" the girl says, turning back to her. "You weren't interested, yeah?"

She shakes her head.

"Good. Right. I'm Anita." Anita presents a brusque hand. "Call me Annie, though. Everyone does."

She swallows, tenses up her throat, and hopes like hell that Val's illicit midnight voice lessons aren't about to let her down. "Hi, Annie," she says, and takes the girl's hand.

Annie cocks her head, waiting, grinning. "Isn't this the part where you introduce yourself?"

"Usually!"

"But you're not going to, are you?"

"I shouldn't," she says. There's no way to tell Annie that she has only one name, that it ceased to describe hers long ago, and that she hasn't yet had the courage to claim anything new.

"Hah! A girl with a bit of mystery to her; fantastic!"

They're still holding hands, and Annie does something that causes her to lose her grip, grabs her by the wrist instead, the better to pull her away from her ineffective hiding spot. She tenses, almost tries to shake her off, but all Annie wants to do is drag her out onto the promenade; she follows, revelling in the thrill of granting consent, of not fighting the hand on her. Annie turns halfway, walks backwards, looks her up and down with a half-smile that makes her chest tight, and then laughs as the song ends and a new track thumps against the cobblestones.

"I love this one!" Annie shouts, releasing her hand and toasting her with a beer, lips playfully lingering around the rim of the bottle. "It's so cheesy!"

"I don't know it!" she admits. She doesn't know anything much.

"It's Robert Palmer! It's new!"

She shrugs, laughing, and drains her beer to lyrics which feel extraordinarily apposite. Discarding the bottle on the grass at the edge of the promenade, she skips back to Annie who greets her with a wicked grin and a hand on her skirt.

The song is called *Simply Irresistible,* and she takes the cue, leaning in for the kiss Annie is obviously inviting, and Annie reciprocates, pressing soft against her and nipping lightly at her lip. A group of onlooking men whoop and whistle at them, probably thinking it's a show meant for them, but Annie's tongue in her mouth, Annie's hand on her hip and Annie's low moans confirm to her that it's anything but.

It's the first kiss she's chosen in her life.

The song moves on, and she moves with it, until a repeated line makes her laugh, makes her giggle hysterically against Annie's lips, because if there's one thing that's been made explicit to her it's *exactly* where the money went: when she woke up, almost two years ago, in pain from all corners of her body and with dressings cocooning her face, they told her she was beautiful and they made sure she understood just how much her beauty cost, what each part of her altered body was worth and how much money each donor had contributed.

Where once that knowledge made her feel like a possession, now she throws it to the wind with the glee of someone who is, for tonight, free.

9 NOVEMBER 2019 — SATURDAY

When someone's washing out, they lock all the doors that connect to the cells and they keep it dark. It's tradition, and like many traditions its origins are a little stupid: fifteen years ago, when she was still finding her way, still writing the new rules, a fuse blew on the night of their first failure, blacking out the whole cell wing. And you have to honour traditions in a place like this, no matter how silly, or you'll eventually lose your mind.

These days, they leave one light on for the condemned man.

The cell wing is completely different now: minimally comfortable with a bed and a toilet in each room, and the girls have been instructed, in all cases but the most severe, to escort the residents to the bathroom every two or three days, to shower. It was rebuilt along with the rest of the underground, a process that took far too long, but every ounce of effort expended to wipe Grandmother's scars from the walls was worth it.

She might have done it with her nails, gouged them into illegibility herself, if it could have helped.

The years since have changed the place as much again. The walls have new marks now, new scars, relics from a new regime that is, she hopes, cruel only when it must be.

The shudder of glass reminds her why she's here and she quickens her step, comes face to face with Declan, leaning against the door of his cell, kicking it idly, illuminated ugly by the single light.

"Who the fuck're you?" he says.

"I'm here to tell you how it ends," she says.

8 AUGUST 2004 — SUNDAY

It's difficult, coming back, walking amongst these buildings again, assaulted by memories. But she's older now, more experienced, less easily shaken; and she's come in via the new entrance by the lake, the one that leads her through the parts of the university that have changed the most, the one that backs onto the new lecture theatre complex that students have nicknamed the Anthill, the one that was built over the demolished remnants of an old gentlemen's club and a decaying promenade where she once kissed a beautiful girl.

Like all good things back then, it didn't last.

Her captor caught up with her in the end. Frankie—short for Frances or something; she doesn't actually know, and the one time she asked she got a ringed fist in her mouth for her impertinence—yanked her out of Anita's arms just as the evening was winding down and dragged her away to the edge of the promenade, forcing her to wave Anita away, to act as if Frankie was just a friend saying hi, and not someone likely to lock her underground for a month to teach her a lesson.

"David! Such a surprise to see you away from home." A lie, obviously. At the time, she hadn't understood how they always found her so quickly.

"That's not my name."

"Funny, because I've got your birth certificate, and guess what it says on it?"

"What do you want?"

Frankie leaned in, imitated with impish glee the closeness she'd been enjoying with Annie just moments before, and whispered, "To remind you of what you are, of course!"

"And what am I?"

"You're mine, David. Mine, until I say otherwise."

"I could scream!" she'd hissed back, full of foolish defiance but tired of being touched and used and claimed and never getting to have a body or a moment that was truly her own. "I could shout out for Annie to save me from the pervert molesting me!"

"Oh, David," Frankie whispered. "David, David, *David.*" Frankie's hands tightened around her hips, fingers digging in. "You *don't* want to do that. Because if you do—" Frankie tugs at the fabric, "—I'll pull down your skirt and show all of them, including Annie, which of us is the pervert and which is the innocent girl."

They could have bulldozed the place twice and it wouldn't have been enough.

She takes her time walking the university grounds. She's dressed as she prefers these days: loose trousers, a light jacket over a cami, low heels, hair up. Subtle makeup. When she left, she had to learn how to dress, style her hair and make herself up almost from scratch, like a teen would. It was hard, and humiliating in its own way.

She walks with real confidence now. Of all the things she had to learn, later in her life than most, that was by far the hardest.

But she's still a little shaken by the approach to Dorley Hall.

It's insultingly unchanged, wearing the years in nothing more than a few extra vines, a handful of cracked flagstones, and double-glazing in the entryway. It remains six storeys of brick monstrosity, mostly empty, a fake finishing-school-within-a-school, an aristocratic wart on an already unpleasantly upper-class university. It backs onto the forest behind and wears the tree cover like a cloak, under which it hides its worst excesses.

The entryway is held open, a concession to the August heat, and as she strides up the steps, she carefully doesn't look down, doesn't let her eyes stray to the spot in the corner where she and Val hugged on Val's last night, gripping each other with the fear and the rapture of those who will never meet again.

Grief never quite fades; it lingers in the spaces it was first forged, and she can't afford, today of all days, to be weak. She dismisses the memory. Dismisses them all. All she needs is the hatred.

And the key she's been given.

Deep breath.

The kitchen doors slam open in front of her and a pleasure she thinks she'll never forget blooms in her belly when, toast slipping from hands and glasses spilling their contents across the table, Grandmother and her assorted cronies look up and face the beginning of the end of the easy lives they've enjoyed.

Frankie, at the far end of the table, contorts her face with familiar disgust.

Grandmother recovers first. "David!" she says, gathering all her wizened bonhomie. "Where *have* you been?"

The name doesn't hurt any more, and as a barb it's pathetic: first on the list of things she expected the old woman to say. No originality to her cruelty.

She takes two quick steps over to the table, glares at one of Grandmother's underlings until she gets the hell out of her way, and drops a folder, open at the appropriate page, onto the table. At the top of the facing document her name is spelled out in bold: BEATRICE QUINN.

"I'll thank you to call me *my* name," Bea says, "in *my* house."

9 NOVEMBER 2019 — SATURDAY

Grandmother left scars everywhere, not just on the walls of the hall. Her other legacies have been much harder to live with, impossible to cover with concrete. But even those fade with time: Bea hasn't felt the need to hide her back from her lovers for decades, and Maria, who's always been sensitive, started wearing short-sleeved tops a few years ago.

Scars fade; memories remain, and mingle with the outraged boy she left behind in the cell, screaming her name.

Bea's second gin of the evening finds a home alongside the first.

"If you're going to drink," Maria says, from the doorway, "can't you at least use a glass? It's more dignified."

Bea hadn't noticed the door open. Too absorbed in her own worries; a pattern, lately.

"What's wrong with my mug?" she says. She doesn't pay much attention to the mugs, unless one of them has a particularly good joke on it. She certainly didn't think to look at what was printed on this one when she grabbed it from the kitchen on her way up. She's not even sure who buys them, and in her more fanciful moments might believe that no-one does, that a house this large and this old just acquires them, like spiders.

Maria raises an eyebrow, steps over to the desk and picks it up. Holds it out wordlessly. On it is printed, *Never ask a man his salary, a woman her age, or an aunt what's in her basement.*

Bea laughs, at least partly because of Maria's silent exasperation. Her reward is for her senior sponsor to swipe the bottle off her desk and return it to the liquor cabinet in the corner.

"Hey, I needed that!" Bea says, half-serious.

"Really? How was it helping, exactly?"

"It was telling me that the fate I just promised that boy is justified."

Maria pours herself a single shot of vodka and necks it. "He's not a boy, Auntie. He's a man. And a rapist. And unrepentant." She wipes the glass with a cloth and sets it back on the cabinet. "Cruel, violent, *and* a bad influence on the little squad he assembled down there. The world is better off without him."

"And who are we to decide that, Maria?"

"You'd rather someone else took responsibility for him? I don't see a queue forming. Aaron called them the 'mean girls', by the way. I'm beginning to think everyone in that bloody basement is getting a little too self-aware."

"Mean girls? Like the movie?"

"Yes, but I don't think he or any of them have seen it. Correction: I'm pretty sure Stef has, actually. The kid keeps locking eyes with me every time Aaron says it." She frowns. "I suppose now we get to find out what the other two do without their Regina George."

"Oh, Maria," Bea says, scolding. It's a little early to make jokes about Declan's absence.

"That's me," Maria says, walking back to the desk and gently pushing Bea's chair back on its castors. "Come here, Auntie."

There's little choice but to accept the hug, and so she does, sinking into the girl's arms. No-one here knows her like Maria; no-one else can spot when the responsibility is getting to her. Admittedly, no-one else tends to see her drinking gin out of a novelty mug.

"My beautiful Maria," she says. "Are you okay? Has your supervisor stopped bothering you? Because you know you don't have to bother with his nonsense; we can increase your salary here—"

"Auntie," Maria says sharply, and punctuates her rebuke with a squeeze to Bea's ribs, "I'm fine. Just take the hug? You don't have to be in charge all the time, you know."

"Fine," Bea says, hiding her smile and closing her eyes.

Eventually Maria releases her, sits her down, and relaxes into the chair on the other side of the desk with a stretch and a moan of discharged discomfort. A long day for both of them. Bea glances at her phone and is startled to realise it's not even eight in the evening yet; there's considerably more day still to go. A cereal bar and a bottle of water appear suddenly on the desk in front of her, and when she looks up Maria is dropping her bag onto the floor and swigging from a bottle of her own.

Bea looks at the cereal bar. It has cartoon hazelnuts with faces and full sets of limbs on it.

"Eat," Maria says.

"You're sponsoring me," Bea says. "Stop sponsoring me."

"As soon as you stop wallowing in guilt."

Bea unwraps the cereal bar and takes a bite. "Never," she says, through a mouthful of oats and nuts.

8 AUGUST 2004 — SUNDAY

Grandmother reacts predictably: "What is the meaning of this, David?" But Bea, distracted, can't stop staring at the thick age lines around her mouth, as if the woman spent so long contorting herself with contempt that her sneer etched itself permanently into her face. "David!" Grandmother repeats, banging her mug on the table.

"I told you to use my name."

"Fine, 'Beatrice'. What is the meaning of this?"

Bea taps a finger on the folder, laid open on the table, sheafed papers spilling out. "The meaning, I think you'll find, is spelled out quite clearly on pages one through six of this document."

"You can't take the hall away from me!" Grandmother snaps, but undermines herself by leaning forward and snatching up the folder.

She reads, flips through, and laughs bitterly. “This is signed in a fake name; it can’t be valid.”

“My identity is watertight, I assure you.”

“Nevertheless,” Grandmother says, leafing through the papers, “Dorley Hall is mine.”

“Actually, it’s the property of the Lambert family—or it *was.*”

“David, you can’t—”

“*Beatrice,*” Bea snaps, opening a folder of copies and turning it around so that her name, printed clearly atop the first page, is visible to everyone in the kitchen, including the line of girls standing nervous and confused against the far wall. “My name is Beatrice. It’s right there. You *can* read, can’t you, Grandmother?”

One of the girls snorts and quickly covers her mouth.

“Beatrice,” Grandmother says with poor grace, “I don’t know what you’re trying to pull, but there is no way that *any* of this is legal. This…*stunt* serves nothing more than to deliver you back into our hands. A mistake, by the way, in case you were wondering.” She raises a thumb and middle finger, ready to snap, a gesture that would, sixteen years ago, wordlessly require sponsors to step forward and restrain Bea, to prepare her for punishment, but Bea’s ready for this, and drops a hand into her bag as soon as Frankie stands. Holds it there, just for a second, to make them worry about what kind of weapon she might have, and takes advantage of their hesitation to step back, out of reach.

She pulls out her phone, snaps it open with her little finger, and hits the speed dial. When it picks up, she says two words: “Your turn.”

Frankie, awkward and half out of her chair, looks at Grandmother, waiting for instruction. Grandmother irritably waves a hand, sitting her down again. Wise: if Bea’s bluffing, if she’s alone, then another few minutes indulging her won’t make a difference, and if Bea’s not alone, if she did indeed summon a friend with her brief phone call, then it’s best for Grandmother if she doesn’t start a fight she might lose. The thought of being taken is enough to revive the butterflies in Bea’s belly though. She wonders briefly what the cells look like these days; remembers waking for the first time locked up in one, naked, confused, castrated.

She distracts herself by inspecting the line of girls standing ready against the wall, all but one of them confused and nervous. The one she’s looking for stands at the end, an East Asian girl, trying and failing to hide her smirk. She also keeps her arms folded in an attempt to hide the marks. Some of them look recent and quite deep, and Bea wishes for a moment that she'd come today for a massacre and not a coup.

"Maria," Bea says.

Maria nods, takes a smart step forward, and crosses the room to stand next to Bea. She's as beautiful as Bea imagined she would be—for all her perversions, Grandmother has a good eye and good surgeons—but the malicious, satisfied gleam in her eyes is a welcome surprise. Bea knows a fighter when she sees one.

"Nic!" Grandmother gasps. "How *dare* you step out of line!"

"My name is Maria, you sadistic old hag."

"Fantasies," Grandmother dismisses.

"That's not your *legal* name, though, is it?" Frankie says, sounding confused, as if wondering whether Maria somehow nipped out to file a deed poll without anyone noticing.

"It's at least as legal as anything else under this roof," Maria says, and gives her the finger. Bea mentally gets out the pom poms and starts cheering.

"You'll regret your insubordination, young man," Grandmother says.

"No, she won't," Bea says, and waves her folder. "You don't run this place anymore." Bea turns, dismissing Grandmother, and says to Maria, "It's good to finally put a face to the voice. How have they been treating you?"

"Appallingly," Maria says. One of the girls can't hold in her giggle, wilts for a moment when Frankie glares at her, only to start up again straight away. How quickly authority crumbles when challenged! "But that's nothing new."

"And your friends?"

Maria makes a show of surveying the girls. If Bea's information is accurate, most of them are younger than Maria; they certainly seem less confident. Several bear marks from recent physical punishments. Every one of them looks as if all their holidays have come at once. "They hurt us," Maria says, "over and over. But they don't break us." She looks at Grandmother for the first time: blank, disinterested, as if examining an insect. "And they never will."

"You will have a *month* in the dark for this, Nic!" Grandmother spits.

"I don't think so."

"What have you been doing, Nic?" Frankie says.

"I've been passing information to Beatrice, obviously. That wasn't clear?"

"What kind of information?" Grandmother asks, paling.

Bea extracts another folder from her bag. This one is considerably thicker, and makes a satisfying thump when she drops it on the table.

"Everything we could possibly need," she says.

9 NOVEMBER 2019 — SATURDAY

"How did it go with Declan?" Maria asks. They've settled into something less like an intervention and more like one of their regular briefings, and Maria's leaning back in her chair. She's wheeled it over to the side of the desk, kicked off her boots and put her feet up next to Bea's laptop, daring her to push her off, daring her to make her behave like an employee or a subordinate. But Maria, like Bea, has been at Dorley for more years than either of them care to count, and formality doesn't last. The other girls who stayed on when Bea took over have all gone, one by one—the last being Barbara, the old nurse—but Maria's the most tied to this place: she was, in a sense, born here, she found her family here, and she'll probably die here. Just like Bea.

And so they sit together in Bea's flat, connected by their experiences as much as their long association. They live in the house of their abusers, still flinch occasionally at the ghosts around each corner, still find themselves incapable of leaving.

Bea finishes her bottle of water. "The way it always goes," she says. "He gave me the big *blah blah,* the strong-man-weak-woman speech; I chastised him for throwing away all his last chances; he called me a bitch. I told him when he could expect his last meal under our roof, and I left him to it. Last I heard from him, he was yelling and kicking the glass again."

"When do they come to pick him up?"

"Monday. You'll keep everyone out of the cell corridor until then?"

"Of course."

"He was making a lot of noise," Bea presses. "It could be distressing to the others if they know he's still—"

"I'll look after it, Auntie."

Of course she will. Bea couldn't ask for anyone better in her corner. Even though she's cheeky. Even though she's sometimes almost too practical for her own good. Even though she's the reason everyone calls her 'Aunt Bea', a nickname she found distasteful at first—Grandmother's familial affectations were calculated to manipulate and disgust in equal measure; the last thing Bea wanted to adopt for herself—but eventually grew to tolerate. You accept the name given to you by your family.

It's how she came about all her names.

"How's Pippa?" Bea asks.

"She's fine. More than fine: she's ecstatic. And a little smug, actually. She's been convinced since Stef got here that she'd been assigned a nice boy by mistake—with all of us constantly trying to persuade her otherwise—so she's delighted to find out that she was very nearly right all along. She told me to 'suck it', although she was smiling at the time, so I didn't take too much offence. She's, uh, planning to shout at you, though."

"Oh? And what have I done?"

"You should hear it in her own words. Hold on a second." Maria fumes with her phone for a moment. "I have the recording right here."

"Recording?"

"I suggested that this might not be the best night to pick a fight with you, but she still wanted to say her piece, so." She waggles her recalcitrant phone.

"Because of Declan? Am I so fragile?"

"In the face of Pippa with a bellyful of fire? Ah, here we are. I hate the file system on these things..."

She sets the phone down on the table and taps a button on the screen. Pippa's voice, tinny over the speakers, says, "Aunt Bea. It's Pippa. Hi. Um." The pause is just long enough to spark a smile from them both. "Look. I'm grateful you're letting Stef stay. I don't know what I would have done if you'd, uh, done something drastic, but I'm glad I don't have to find out." Bea raises an eyebrow at Maria, who just grins at her. "But," Pippa's voice continues, "Aunt Bea, stay out of her way, would you?"

"Are you sure you want to say it quite like that?" Maria's voice says, on the recording.

"Absolutely sure, Maria! Aunt Bea, I want you to know, whenever you listen to this: I'm honestly disgusted with you! Stef's had enough to deal with, what with losing Melissa, and coming here, and the nurse, and the thing with the showers, and— and *me,* let's not forget *me* and all the awful things I said to her and all the awful things I let happen to her, and the *last* thing she needed was for you to start implying—no, actually, outright stating that she's somehow responsible for all that stuff! That she should feel *guilty* for giving *me* a bad time! That's not just cruel, Aunt Bea—although it is, it's *really* cruel—that's setting us up against each other, and— and— Why? Why would you—?"

Maria taps the phone again and Pippa goes silent. "That goes on for a while."

"I get the gist," Bea says. "You're frowning at me, Maria."

"The thing with Stef? Not your finest hour, Auntie."

"No," Bea says, pushing back in her chair and examining the ceiling so she doesn't have to face Maria's glare for a moment. "No, probably not." The problem of Stef, which just a few hours ago had seemed so urgent, is now clear to her: the girl wants help with her transition and has a vested interest in keeping the secret of Dorley, for Melissa's sake if no-one else's; they help her, she helps them. An easy equation.

Bea's got too used to manipulating people. Show her someone simple, someone with straightforward and clearly stated needs, and she looks for the lies.

"Sod it," she says, sitting forward. "Pippa gets what she wants. She gets full autonomy and I'll stay out of the way. As long as they both stick to the rules, I won't stick my oar in. Sound good?" Maria nods. "Good. You'll keep an eye on them, yes?"

"Of course."

"We're not going to tell Melissa, I imagine."

"I don't think it would be a good idea," Maria says. "Not yet, anyway. She was always very attached to Stef. Talked about him— about *her* all the time. When we tell her we have the girl who was basically her little brother down in our basement, being coerced into listening to Taylor Swift medleys, I want it to be in a controlled environment. Like defusing a bomb. Maybe with Stef in the room, or at least on the phone or something, so Melissa can see that she's okay, that she wants to be here."

"Strange to have someone using *she* pronouns after a month. I suppose we'll have to get used to a lot of firsts, before the year is out." Bea laughs. "Our first walk-in!"

"You should know," Maria says, "Stef prefers *he* for now. Hence my…pronoun confusion."

"Oh?"

"It's this thing about not wanting to be a *she* until— God, I don't even understand it, and I've seen the video where she explained it to Pippa. Guilt, self-loathing, et cetera. Pippa's already decided she's having none of it: something about showing the girl it's okay to be a girl."

"Good," Bea says. "You've got to nip that sort of silliness in the bud, early."

"Have a lot of experience with trans women, do you?"

"Enough to know that if you give them an inch they'll steal ten years from themselves."

"Well, Pippa's got a real bug up her arse about it, so I think she probably agrees with you." Maria brushes the back of her hand against her forehead, as if warding against a headache. "She had a whole thing, up on the roof. I told her I'd defer to her judgement. It's almost like she's trying to beat Vicky's record for the fastest self-claimed *she* pronoun." She giggles and says, in a voice that suggests Bea should know what on earth she's talking about, "Awesome Girls Done Quick."

"I'm sure that's very funny, but I don't get the reference."

"It's a speedrunning joke."

"Speed-running? As in, exercise?"

Maria sighs. "Where's Christine when you need her?"

The worst thing, for Bea, about surrounding herself with millennials and zoomers is that occasionally they'll be outright incomprehensible and then act as if she's terribly old and out of touch when she surreptitiously has to Google new terminology under the table. "Actually," she says, putting the joke out of her mind, "what about Christine? What did she say?"

"She's thinking about it."

"Do you think she'll accept?"

"She likes the idea of you paying her."

"Did you tell her the money comes from a trust?"

"No," Maria says. "I think it helps her to imagine it being dragged reluctantly from your pockets every month. I think the image will encourage her to accept."

Bea rolls her eyes. "When did I become such an ogre, Maria?"

"Somewhere around 2005, Auntie."

"Brat."

"Harridan," Maria says, and sticks out her tongue.

"Tell me," Bea says, "why didn't we think of the letter thing before?"

"The letter thing?"

"The idea Christine cooked up with Stef, to pretend the boy—the girl, in this case—has run off to soul-search and make a nuisance of themselves in another country."

Maria shrugs. "We can't exactly use it often. Once every few years at most. More men fall drunkenly into freezing lakes than spontaneously go backpacking."

"Still. Put it in the handbook. Save it for the ones with close familial relationships."

"A lever," Maria says, nodding. "It's a risky manoeuvre, though. You've always said, and it's been borne out by my observations, that they have to be completely removed from their old support networks. That the complete isolation is part of what makes it work."

She has a way of repeating Bea's own instructions back to her, phrased to make them both sound like terrible people. "I think," Bea says slowly, "that hope can be similarly powerful. For the right boy. From time to time."

"Fair enough. Oh, I thought we'd do the all-hands tomorrow, at lunch? Get the second-year girls to cook, lure everyone in with the promise of free food and wine, and hit them with the news just as they're getting sleepy."

"You're planning to tell the second years, too?"

"Yes? I wasn't going to send them away from a meal they just cooked."

"You don't think that will erode their trust in us?" Bea says. "We locked up a genuine trans girl, closeted but fully aware and actively exploiting our facilities, and it took us a month to notice."

Maria counts on her fingers. "One, they'll find out sooner or later, and it's better that it comes from us and not rumour. Two, don't forget, the kids come in knowing more gender terminology than had even been coined back in my day; we just tell them she's both an egg and an idiot and they'll understand. And, three, it was Christine who brought her in and who helped her hide from us, and the second years love Christine."

"They do?" Bea laughs. "They beat us to it, then."

"You ever wonder if you're getting old and slow?" Maria says.

"No," Bea says, with such certainty that she forces a smirk out of Maria; admittedly not a terribly difficult thing to do. "I'm as canny and alert as I ever was."

"Of course."

"Why do the second years love Christine so much?"

"Remember the thing with Faye's sponsor and her inappropriate rage-outs?" Maria prompts. "How she calmed down seemingly overnight? That was Christine, too."

"Of course," Bea remembers. "Maybe I *am* getting old."

"Hell, Christine even roped Paige into getting Faye all dressed up. Arguably she helped actualise Faye's gender."

"Why isn't she a sponsor already?"

Maria snorts. "She'd *never* do it. Getting her to run our tech is a hard enough sell."

"True. And it's been good to see her becoming close with Paige again. Roping her into things, sitting together at breakfast."

"Close? Auntie, they're *together.*"

"Really?"

"Yes," Maria says, sounding wistful. "Paige has been besotted with her since, I don't know, their first year, maybe. The difference this time is that Paige has learned how to ask for what she needs, and Christine's learned how to listen."

Year by year, the girls become new. Find themselves and find love. It makes it all worth it. "That's genuinely wonderful," Bea says.

"It's disgustingly sweet, is what it is," Maria says, and Bea is reminded that Maria's been stepping out in the evenings herself. Discreetly, but not so quietly that an old busybody like Bea wouldn't notice, eventually.

"And what about you?" Bea asks. "I've seen you with Edy lately; how is she?"

Maria, as always, deflects: "Disgustingly sweet."

8 AUGUST 2004 — SUNDAY

Bea's had a long time to perfect her womanhood, to understand it, to claim it and inhabit it, but Elle Lambert has a way of making her feel like an ingenue. Her heels announce her presence, crisply clicking on the flagstones outside, and by the time she reaches the kitchen doors, Barb—another one of Maria's circle, who adopted the rather old-fashioned name Barbara with an enthusiasm entirely familiar to Bea—has already stepped smartly forward to let her in as if she's royalty, and the abused girls of Dorley her retinue. Elle steps elegantly through the door and smiles at the girl, inspiring in Barb a blush that could probably cook an egg, and hands her a shopping bag.

"Gifts for the girls," Elle says to her, and Barb rushes back to the women standing by the wall, who look equal parts delighted and scandalised.

"Thank you, ma'am," Barb says, as the other girls rifle through and pull out dresses, tops, skirts, shoes. She performs an exaggerated curtsey, which earns her a glare from Frankie that no-one bar Bea seems to notice.

"Please call me Elle."

Elle steps forward and deposits a portable hard drive on the kitchen table. She's short—shorter than Bea and the younger Dorley graduates; shorter even than Grandmother and most of her people, too—but she commands the room effortlessly, with a manner that belies her twenty-five years and which Bea, despite being over a decade her senior, has been trying to emulate since the day they met. She's pale, subtly made-up, and her rich, thick waves of dark hair break on the shoulders of a suit worth enough, by Bea's judgement, to feed a family of four for a year. The only woman in the room who doesn't look dowdy in comparison is Maria, who today has assembled with unexpected skill an elegant outfit from the meagre scraps allowed the girls. Grandmother's coterie, already given to a particularly English variety of rural tweed anti-fashion, look positively antique.

"Elle Lambert," she continues, addressing the room. "My grandmother is—was—guardian of the family holdings and, with her death, that responsibility has passed to me. My first action upon reviewing the portfolio was to note that this house, Dorley Hall, has been *severely* underutilised, and the decision was taken to transfer the deeds to the newly formed Dorley Hall Foundation, of which Beatrice Quinn is sole trustee and administrator; though she will, naturally, be free to hire her own staff."

"Maria, Barbara," Bea says, on cue, "welcome aboard."

"Thank you, Beatrice," Maria says.

"Um, yes, thank you, Beatrice," Barb says, after a nudge from Maria.

"I'm not leaving," Grandmother says. "I have assurances from—"

Elle forces Grandmother back into silence by clearing her throat. "Yes, yes," she says, "we know all about your *assurances.* Only one of them remains; insufficient for you to retain control, but enough to permit you to retire with…dignity."

"That's not—"

"I represent sixty-four percent of your current—excuse me; my mistake—your *former* funding, which as of this morning is no longer available to you. And the majority of your other benefactors were most displeased upon reviewing portions of the information vouchsafed to us by our contacts." Elle leans on the table, palms flat. "You've been very selective with the truth, haven't you, Dorothy?"

Grandmother shrugs. "Say what you came here to say."

"Only the Smyth-Farrow grant is still available to you," Elle says, standing upright again, "for the time being. Per Mr Smyth-Farrow's request, you will be allowed to retain your flat on the premises and act as consultant during the…administrative transfer. Your influence over day-to-day operations will be limited, but your *valuable* experience may, of course, prove useful to the new custodian."

Elle's dismissive hand-wave is intended to suggest that this constitutes a triviality of business that she, the money, does not care about. In fact, the Smyth-Farrow grant represents their one failure. Had they convinced the old bastard to withdraw his support then Grandmother would be out on her ear tomorrow, but their intelligence going in had been incomplete: they'd thought him another clueless aristocrat, but the man knew of everything that went on under Dorley; he even played them videos of his favourite cruelties, and looked upon Bea with a hunger that made her want to climb out of her skin. He dismissed their legal threats—"I'm too old to care; by the time you scale the mountains my lawyers erect in front of you, I'll already be in the ground."—and he's too well-protected for Elle's other measures to stand a chance. In the end, the best they could do was to tie up his grant renewal with red tape, and thus restrict his lease of the flat on the first floor to the two years remaining. He still complained, and vowed to fight them: Grandmother has shipped him many playthings over the decades, and much gratitude is owed.

Bea wondered aloud to Elle, when they were safely away from his manor, how many of her sisters were buried there.

Elle brushes her palms together, as if removing a few specks of bothersome dust. "The Lambert family and our considerable holdings will be providing the Dorley Hall Foundation with a yearly grant, to be administered by Beatrice Quinn and her staff. Dorley Hall will be operated as a dormitory for exceptional but disadvantaged young women who might otherwise miss their chance at an education at this first-rate college. Your people will leave; ours will replace them. You will be free, Dorothy, to sulk in your flat for the two years left on its lease. And that—" she smiles pleasantly at Grandmother, "—is that."

Grandmother glares back, fists stiffening on the table, and for a moment Bea wonders if she's going to go for it, to throw everyone she has at them—which would be interesting considering the armed men from Elle's organisation who've been waiting discreetly outside for such an eventuality. Instead she stretches her fingers, unclenches her jaw, and says with a growl, "You can't do this. I don't care how much money you control. I *know* people."

"I *am* people," Elle says. "Not only do I know everyone *you* know, I'm *one of them*. You're just a wannabe. A tweed torturer carrying out petty brutality in your sad little castle. They respect me, whereas even the few who accept your tawdry products laugh at you behind your back. I also—" she points at the hard drive, which has been sitting on the table like an unexploded bomb, "—have that. Review it, and the paper summary provided by Beatrice, at your leisure. We don't just have your names and your financial records, Dorothy; we have photographs, we have video, we have your phone conversations and your text messages and your emails. We even have some of the *bones,* Dorothy. We have enough evidence to put you away for life. To splash your face across the front page of every newspaper *worldwide.* And we know some well-connected families who are grieving mysterious disappearances and who would likely be minded to ensure your stay in prison, after your international humiliation, is a short one. And that goes for all of you." She sweeps a hand around the kitchen, taking in the rapt glares of a half-dozen sponsors. "There's not a one of you whose life we cannot comprehensively destroy."

"Then why don't you?" one of them snaps. Bea recognises the nurse, Karen, from Maria's files, and forces herself not to shudder: she's read all about that woman's proclivities; she seems a worthy successor to the sadistic medical examiner from Bea's time.

"Because that is our bargain," Elle says. "You're free to leave, to return to your lives—or to squat in your flat on the premises until the lease expires, if that is what you prefer—and if you never breathe a word about Dorley Hall to anyone outside these walls you will all die old and free. But if just one of you makes a move against us..." She taps a nail on the hard drive.

"You still haven't explained *why,*" Grandmother says.

Elle steps back, places herself by Bea's side. Brushes the back of her hand against Bea's: encouragement.

"Because we're reforming Dorley," Bea says. "Under your hand, it's a charnel house. You torture men because you find it erotically appealing. You change them, humiliate them, exercise your vile pleasures on their bodies and then, when you're done, you spit them out."

"You *deserved* it!" Grandmother hisses. "You were a criminal!"

"I was a *shoplifter.* And the criminality was just an excuse. An excuse to *waste* people. But we have a different idea. You hurt men for fun."

She looks from Elle to Maria and then back to Grandmother. "We're going to *save* them."

9 NOVEMBER 2019 — SATURDAY

They never meet in Almsworth. A deliberate choice: Elle wants to keep the circle small, wants as few people as possible to know that she and Beatrice are still in such intimate contact. In Elle's organisation, only her closest assistants are aware of her activities on these nights; at Dorley, only the senior sponsors. And, Beatrice realises with a sigh, since the girl's apparently been running around their secure network, turning over every rock and uprooting every tree, probably Christine.

So it's always a hotel, in a different city every time, and because Elle is Elle, it's always an expensive hotel.

Dorley Hall is, more than anything else, comfortable, wearing its relative wealth in fittings and fixtures that have become worn and scuffed but never actually broken, despite years and years of often tempestuous new girls using, abusing, and sometimes colliding with them; stepping into Elle's life for a night is an amusing reminder that other people—a select few other people, granted—are never far from someone who will call them "ma'am" without smirking.

There's a Lambert family estate somewhere in the country, and various apartments in various cities worldwide, but Elle lives mostly out of hotels, which means that Bea, when she wants to see her, has to call for a car, and be delivered. At least it's relatively close tonight; sometimes plane travel is involved.

"Beatrice!" Elle calls, standing up from her seat at the bar and beckoning her over. She's wearing a loose jacket over something dark and layered, which billows interestingly around her body when she moves and reveals itself to be two pieces when she raises her arms for a hug, exposing her taut belly. "It's been *too* long!"

Bea accepts the embrace when it comes, breathes in her scent and the memories it provokes, and leans back for a kiss, cheek-to-cheek. "Elle," she says. "I've missed you."

"What you missed," Elle says, sitting back down and making hand gestures at the bartender which result almost immediately in fresh drinks being deposited, "is my fortieth. I'm *certain* I invited you."

"Apologies. There's been so much going on—"

"Relax." Elle places a calming hand on Bea's, and leaves it there, fingers knotting carefully around fingers. "I'm teasing. It was boring.

So many people, all of them frightfully posh. You would have hated it. I did."

"You're probably right," Bea says, sampling her drink with the hand Elle hasn't trapped. "I would quite like to make it up to you, anyway, if you'll let me."

"I look forward to it," Elle says, releasing her. "Have you eaten?"

"Nothing especially satisfying."

"After dinner, then."

A few minutes later and they're being seated in what is undoubtedly the hotel's costliest and most exclusive restaurant. Elle orders a bottle of wine for the table with the detached but knowledgeable air of someone who does this all the time, and Bea looks over the menu for something light, preferably with mushrooms.

"So," Elle says, when they are alone in their candlelit corner, "how's life in Almsworth, tall girl capital of Great Britain?"

"Quiet, until recently."

"And how are the girls?"

"Unruly, as always. How's *your* girl?"

"Self-denying, as always."

Bea smiles. "God," she says, "look at you."

Elle places a manicured hand on her chest. "Look at me? What did I do?"

"Aged better than I have."

"Ridiculous. Those little lines around your eyes rather suit you."

"That's very kind of you to say. How's the world of high finance and international intrigue?"

"Dreadfully dull. And rather annoying. At least in your line of work, when someone gets a smart mouth on them you can, you know…" Elle makes a *snip-snip* gesture.

"We usually reserve that for those whose attitude problems go somewhat beyond rudeness," Bea says.

The waiter returns, pours wine, takes orders, collects menus, and glides away, leaving them alone once more and giving Bea the opportunity to drink in both wine and moment. Elle really has aged magnificently: if Bea didn't know better, she'd swear she looks the same at forty as she did at twenty-five, and she's retained her aptitude for rendering Bea fumbling and adolescent in her presence.

"Tell me about this girl," Elle says. "The one who just showed up one day and got your whole house in a tizzy."

"Oh, yes," Bea says, "Stef. The subject of my every other conversation." She gives her the short version, which takes long enough for her stuffed mushrooms to arrive and partially disappear. Elle looks on, fascinated, offering a comment here and there but content, for the most part, to let Bea talk. She asks to see a picture; Bea has one from Stef's first lunch downstairs. The girl is enduring Aaron Holt and looking sceptically at a veggie burger, eyebrows raised on a forehead that will require, despite her insistence otherwise, minimal alteration. Even in such unflattering lighting, her potential is clear.

"They're friends now, actually," Bea says, when Elle hands the phone back. "Her and the little flasher boy."

"I can see why. He's rather cute. Like a puppy."

"She's trying to reform him."

"You think she'll succeed?"

"No," Bea says, and rolls her eyes at the face Elle pulls. "I have to say that, don't I? If she manages it, it calls our whole operation into question."

"Not from just *one* boy," Elle says.

"As long as she stops at one," Bea mutters.

Elle chews thoughtfully on the last bite of her omelette. "I'd like to meet her. Not now, of course. I'm sure she's got enough on her plate without me barging in on her just to satisfy my…professional curiosity. But later, when she's ready, I'd like to meet her. And do send me a photo every so often, won't you? You know how I love seeing them bloom."

They revert to small talk: upkeep of the hall, Saints gossip, complaints about some Duke or Lord or something—Elle doesn't know which and doesn't care—who thinks Elle can cure him of bachelorhood. Neither of them raise the elephant in the room until dessert:

"I'm concerned about Dorothy," Bea says. "I think she's going to try something."

Elle nods. "I concur."

"Thank you for dealing with the nurse, by the way."

"*Beyond* my pleasure," Elle says. "People like her give me indigestion."

"I think she was a shot across the bows," Bea says. Elle raises her eyebrows, so Bea continues, "One of my sponsors reached out for assistance, unaware of the exact nature of her history with the hall, and I suspect the nurse's first act was to call Dorothy. Who then immediately persuaded her to disregard her obligations. A little reminder: *I'm still out here and I'm still watching you.* I imagine Karen was only too eager to agree; I bet she jumped at the chance to have a bit of old-time fun with the residents. Dorothy will have either downplayed the potential consequences for her, or overestimated her own hand."

"Do you think Dorothy will leave it at this? Disposing of Ms Turner ought to be quite the lesson, but I don't recall her being a quick study. I'd love to believe she'll go gentle into that good night, but you know her better than I."

"Honestly? I don't know." Bea chews thoughtfully on her cheesecake; it is distractingly excellent. "If she's dying, we can't rule out her pulling the ripcord and taking us down with her. Flooding the internet with information or sending it to the papers. And you *know* the situation in this country right now. Having our operation exposed would be TERF Christmas, and she knows it. That bloody Frost woman will burst a blood vessel from excitement. Going to prison would be traumatic enough without having to see her smugly pontificating on breakfast TV."

"Exposing you—us—exposes all of her associates, too," Elle says.

"She can't care for them that much, judging by the stunt with the nurse. I think she'd happily see them all jailed or dead or bloodily dismembered if it meant seeing us suffer, too."

Elle nods. "I'll put someone on it. A full investigation. She's got to be reaching the end of her funds by now, and all her old patrons are long dead. We might even be able to— *Magnificent,* thank you!"

Bea manages not to be startled by the sudden waiter, and mumbles something to support Elle's effusive praise of the food, the service, the decor and the ambience. Elle gives her a significant look and another nod, which Bea reads as confirmation that she'll have one of her mysterious people, the ones who made the nurse disappear, attempt a similar magic trick on Dorothy, and the subject does not come up again.

At Elle's door—the elevator leading to the penthouse suite, naturally—Bea fights temptation and, as always, loses. So when the doors open and Bea doesn't step away, Elle nods, drags her by the lapel of her blouse into the lift, and presses the appropriate button with an elbow because as soon as the doors close she needs all hands available to start removing Bea's clothes.

Backwards they stagger into Elle's room, Bea's top layer already discarded, her bra already unclasped. She intercepts Elle as she reaches for her skirt, splays their fingers together and redirects her hands, using her considerable extra height to her advantage, controlling her with one hand and reaching out with the other to knock Elle's jacket off her other shoulder, trapping her awkwardly in the fabric. Elle grins and rolls her shoulders, freeing herself from Bea's grip and shrugging off the jacket, letting it fall where it may as they keep stepping backwards together.

The lamps are automatically lighting themselves as they move around the suite, illuminating Elle from below, sharpening her features and making her grin seem almost demonic as she takes control again, slipping hands inside Bea's skirt and pulling it down, causing them both to trip, laughing, landing shoulder-to-shoulder on the bed in the middle of the suite.

Floor-to-ceiling windows surround them on three sides and a skylight spans half the ceiling above them, and for a moment Bea feels the old terror of being seen, of being discovered compromised and near-naked and deserving of punishment, before she realises that the building is the tallest one around and that the only things watching them are the stars.

Elle, still mostly clothed, lunges for her, and Bea grabs her instead, runs her fingers up her arms and into her top, lifts it up and over her head in one movement, and then, finally, they're almost equal. Elle relents, kisses her quickly on the lips, and stands to drop her skirt to the ground and step out of her boots.

Bea rolls onto her back. Looks up at her, resplendent, half in lamplight and half in moonlight, and Elle matches her appreciative smile and steps back once more, the better to give Bea a view as she reaches behind herself and unhooks her bra.

The bed is in a small, stepped depression, the centrepiece of the room, so when Bea stands up from the bed and reaches forward to embrace her, their faces are near-level, a novelty and clearly a delight to Elle, who laughs and throws arms around Bea's neck, leaning forward across the space between them as Bea puts one leg up on the bottom step, to steady Elle and to anchor herself.

Elle's fingers dance across Bea's back, around her waist and across her belly, and then she pulls closer, dives her fingers into Bea's underwear and begins slowly to massage her, assaulting her equilibrium with every slow pulse until she falls again, back onto the mattress, and Elle falls with her.

"You're glorious, Beatrice," Elle breathes, twitching her fingers, coaxing from Bea a moan that ends only when she kisses her.

Bea, caught in the rhythm, begins moving her hips in time, until the pressure that starts at Elle's fingers and ends at the tip of every nerve is provided by both of them, as one, a single organism with a single purpose.

Elle kisses her again, finding her collarbone, her neck, her jaw, her chin and her mouth, and when Bea opens her eyes a memory returns of her first kiss, back before she was free, under a different night sky, in a place that no longer exists, as a person who no longer exists, and she revels in it, exults in it, and laughs against Elle's lips.

"Simply irresistible," Beatrice whispers, a thirty-year echo, and kisses her harder still.

Acknowledgements

Thank you to Benjanun Sriduangkaew for her help with cover design and general encouragement. Thank you to my friends, for coping with my unfathomable enthusiasm for writing this story. Thank you to my readers, who have supported me and this story since its inception as a rant about the state of the NHS. And thank you to my wife, for all her terrible, terrible ideas.

List of Characters

The Sisters of Dorley Hall

Graduates:

Abby (Abigail)
Amethyst
Bella
Donna
Edy
Francesca
Harmony
Indira
Aunt Bea (Beatrice)
Jane
Margaret
Maria
Melissa
Monica
Nell
Pamela
Pippa (Philippa)
Tabitha

Current Programme Members:

Above Ground:

Name	**Sponsor**
Aisha	*Unknown*
Christine	Indira
Faye (Effie)	Nell
Jodie	Donna
Julia	Lisa
Mia	*Unknown*
Paige	Francesca
Rebecca (Bex)	Bella
Vicky (Victoria)	*Unknown*
Yasmin	*Unknown*

Basement:

Name	**Sponsor**
Aaron	Maria
Adam	Edy
Declan	Monica
Martin	Pamela
Ollie (Oliver)	Harmony
Raph (Raphael)	Jane
Stef (Stefan)	Pippa
Will (William)	Tabitha

Characters From Outside the Programme

Elle	Owner and funder of Dorley Hall
Frankie	Former staff member of Dorley Hall
Grandmother	Former Custodian of Dorley Hall
Karen	Former Nurse at Dorley Hall
Lorna	Vicky's girlfriend
Naila	Non-programme-affiliated resident of Dorley Hall
Petra	Stef's little sister
Ren	Non-programme-affiliated resident of Dorley Hall
Russ (Russell)	Melissa's younger brother

About the Author

Alyson Greaves is a trans woman living in a very small flat in a very big city, where she writes far too much and doesn't sleep nearly enough. She originally serialised her debut series, *The Sisters of Dorley*, on AO3, Scribblehub and Patreon, and self-published the books on Amazon before she was signed by Neem Tree Press in 2024.

Next in the Series

the sisters of dorley

SECRETS OF DORLEY HALL

alyson greaves

the sisters of dorley

ENEMIES OF DORLEY HALL

alyson greaves